QUICKSILVER
ONE, TWO, THREE

SYDNEY BLACKBURN

Half Past Three
Publishing

DEDICATION

To my long suffering spouse, Steve.
It never would have happened without you.

CONTENTS

FOREWORD

The Quicksilver Adventures came out of a NaNoWriMo project in 2011. The initial idea evolved into what is currently the third novella, Taxed, and first two novellas came about as time and editing and a refusal to let the characters go in spite of their obstinacy in living novel length adventures. The novellas are published digitally as single titles, but the three short stories that round out the first three adventures are exclusive to the print edition.

These stories would not have been possible without the input and editing of the following people:

Patricia M. Bryce   *L.M. Langley*

Andrew Birch   *David W. Dellinger*

Rebecca R. Pierce   *Nata Luna Sans*

Casey Laine   and all my test readers!

DIAMONDS & QUICKSILVER

ONE

Imbrium Luna

Silver Tation packed his sole valise. He didn't have much in the way of belongings, he preferred to own little and spend lots, indulging in sensual pleasures of the transitory kind. Belongings could only tie a person down, and after three years in Imbrium, Luna, he was finally ready, he hoped, to take care of some overdue personal business on Titan. He had given the city notice that his rooms would be vacant this afternoon. He would be six months at the very least on Titan and in need of every credit. But before he caught the Luna Colony Transit train to Destiny, he had a few things left to buy for the trip.

He checked his appearance in the dressing mirror and frowned, rubbing at his jaw. The bruise had faded to a lovely yellowish-purple that was terribly unflattering. He covered it with concealer, not so much for his vanity, though there was that, but to avoid stares and questions. "You look beautiful, darling," he told his reflection mockingly.

He'd not gone more than a few meters when a voice behind and to his left said, "Pardon, Ser. Are you by chance Ser Tation?"

He turned to politely say no, but the man who'd spoken was striking for two reasons—his beautiful brown eyes and russet skin, and his ugly black and silver Interplanetary Law Enforcement uniform. The latter said he couldn't deny it, the former made him hope it was personal. He smiled and said, "By chance and good fortune, it seems."

"I was wondering if I might have a few minutes of your time."

It wasn't a question, and as much as Sil would have liked to flirt, he had a train to catch. "You've caught me at an inconvenience," he said, sincerely apologetic. "I'm in something of a hurry."

"Then we can walk as we talk. Nick Delaney, of IPLE, I'd like to ask you a few questions regarding Emun Delacroix? I understand you're a friend of his?" He gestured for Sil to lead the way and fell into step beside him.

Sil brought his fingers to his jaw briefly at the reminder. "Ser Delacroix and I have a social circle that sometimes overlaps, as happens with folk of our means, but no, we are not friends." He briefly entertained the notion that Delacroix had called the Long Arms as Sil had invited him to, but no. Delacroix was an embezzler, his own actions would not bear scrutiny of the law. "Please ask your questions, though—I'd be delighted to assist the Long Arms."

"It seems he's gone missing and you know how hard that is in a domed city."

Sil wasn't sure what surprised him more—that Delacroix was missing, or that someone had noticed. "Missing? Do you mean to say dead?"

"We don't know that. When did you last see him?"

"Three nights ago, at a party held by that heiress from Phobos Station. Lavender."

"Amanda Lavender?"

"Yes. Her father is a major share-holder in Exterra, though she herself seems a bit light in the head." Colonists on the Martian surface had a less than friendly rivalry with those above them in Phobos Station, but both had the interests of Mars at heart. Many an investor from both came to Imbrium, Luna—or sent their idle offspring—to investigate the terraforming research being conducted here. Imbrium was surrounded by a massive dome formed of a polymer silicate bond; within that dome was the original colony, a proto-atmosphere, and the beginnings of organic soil. The future, for both Mars and the Moon, it was hoped. For Sil, it had been an opportunity.

"Witnesses say you and Delacroix had a bit of dust up."

"Somewhat of an exaggeration." He resisted the urge to touch the bruise again. Delacroix should not have tumbled to him. He'd relied too much on Delacroix's gullibility.

He had a variety of aliases, none very original as they were meant primarily to confuse digital tracking, and he'd used one as the mysterious person in charge of the scam. It worked for him before, but he realized he should have used one of his contacts in Imbrium to give Sealfor Argent a physical presence, a tangible third party that wasn't Sil.

He'd just been lucky that Delacroix's best idea of revenge was a right hook in the middle of a party.

The Long Arm gave him a sidelong look. "Mmm. What was his vex with you?"

"Ironically enough, he accused me of stealing from him."

"So you were aware he was collecting a little more than his pay at Exterra?"

Damn, he'd not meant to give that away. "I had my suspicions," he admitted.

"Were you blackmailing him?"

Sil gave the other man a dark scowl to convey what he thought of such behaviour, and followed it up with a verbal denial. "Of course not. Blackmail is so... vulgar. A friend of mine ended up

3

dead because of blackmail. Nasty business. If there's nothing else, officer...? I have urgent errands." He didn't want to be followed by a Long Arm into a pharmaceutical shop, no matter how handsome.

The officer halted abruptly and Sil swivelled automatically on the ball of his foot next step, so they were facing each other. Delaney smiled far too briefly and said, "This is an informal enquiry at this point since there's no evidence of a crime, but the disappearance of a prominent businessperson is a concern. Given the circumstances, Ser Tation, I hope I can count on you to remain in Imbrium until the matter is resolved."

"Oh, yes," Sil lied courteously. "I may not be at my habitat, though." He decided to give the officer a fuller explanation to emphasize what a good citizen he was. "Ser Delacroix was asked to leave Ser Lavender's party, and although he made some growly mention of this not being over, he didn't contact me again. I have no idea if he meant to bring formal accusation or call me out for a duel, but I assumed his temper calmed and he realized the ridiculousness of his plaint and has since been carrying on his merry way."

"If I can't find you at your habitat, perhaps you'd best give me your tag number."

Sil grinned, batting his eyes. "Oh, so this is just an elaborate ruse to get my tag." He drew a card from a pocket in his tunic, surreptitiously confirming it bore only his name and tag, and tucked it insolently into Delaney's waistband "All you had to do was ask, darling," he said with a wink. "Call me any time."

TWO

Black Thunder, Titan

Nobody travelled to Titan for fun. If one wanted fun, there were countless places to go. Oracle, Venus topped Silver Tation's list, but he could find fun almost any place with people who had money and time on their hands. The cruise ships that plied the inner colonies did not go to Titan or Europa. No one wanted to spend over three weeks in the forced company of strangers, even if they could afford it. Passengers to the outer colonies slept in cryo beds, awakened two days before arrival in order to catch up with events that may have happened in the three to four weeks it took to cross the distance from the Moon to their destination. Passenger ships to the outer colonies left the Moon when the respective orbits were favourable, to keep the fuel requirement low.

Sil had a return ticket, which was a necessity if he didn't want to get stuck there forever, but if things got hot he would have to rely on the kindness—and greed—of a cargo pilot. That was why he hadn't come out this far without a fat bank account under the name Sealfor, filled with the proceeds of the investment scams he'd run on the Moon. The most recent one was still bothering him.

He'd slept a dreamless sleep until waking up two days away

from orbit around Saturn. Although not politically inclined, he paid close attention to the news from the past fifteen days, feeling disoriented to have lost so much time. Much could have happened in three and half weeks, though he didn't appear to have missed anything too important. He supposed by now that Delacroix, who had the poor taste to go missing after Sil had emptied his accounts, had been found. Probably at the bottom of a bottle, bemoaning his lost fortune, much of it acquired illegally in the first place.

He rubbed his jaw reflexively. Delacroix had hit him squarely some few days before he'd left the Moon for Titan. Not even a bruise remained, which was some solace for the lost time. He could not lose focus like that for an instant on Titan, or his career as a criminal—not to mention his life—would be disappointingly short.

Delacroix was an executive something or other at Exterra, the biggest research and development company in Imbrium. Research companies were practically guaranteed to have crooked employees and it had been easy enough for Sil to find out Delacroix's accounts were fatter than they should be. They'd been at a party, not together, some event for Exterra employees. His scam had just concluded, and as a supposed fellow victim, Sil probably should have declined the party invitation, but he'd been invited as colour, which had played to his vanity.

He'd worked hard to establish himself as an idle young man with money and a taste for sensual pleasures. All true enough, apart from being idle. The beauty of conning a crook out of his ill-gotten gains was that said crook was highly unlikely to report his loss to IPLE. It was also, in Sil's opinion, a more worthy challenge. He hadn't been surprised to see Delacroix at the party, given his intimate association with their hostess, but the very public accusation had caught him off-guard.

It seemed just a few days ago, he thought, touching his jaw again as he looked out on Saturn.

Titan was orbitally locked with with Saturn, and geosynchronous with Titan was a the Titan Way Station. Cargoes and passengers to and from were sorted here, as well as those carrying on to the TWF, the solar system's most remote colony. Ships could refuel and crews could blow off steam in the roughest flower shop Sil had ever seen. Not tempted in the slightest, he found himself riding with a shuttle pilot whose cargo bay was stuffed full of carefully packed supplies for a number of colonies.

"We don't get much tourists out here," he said cheerfully. "Not all cushy out here in the cold and the dark, not like your inner colonies. Takes a special kind to live out here."

Sil politely concealed his opinions of the kind who lived out here. "All the colonists work for the corporations?"

"Nah. Oh used to be, in the early days, but colonies grow, you know? Families, babies? Services are needed, food, clothing, schools, clinics, the like."

"But that's all provided by the company is it not? The corporation imports the food and clothing? The folk who work to stock and inventory and sell those work for the company? The medics and teachers are paid by Black Thunder? Each colony supplied by the corporation that founded it?"

"Oh yeah, you mean it like that. Thought you meant in mining or refining or related to. Yeah, company provides the schools and clinics, they take care of us."

"And you say you have few visitors."

He nodded enthusiastically. "Few as can take it for long out here." He gave Sil a sidelong look. "You don't look the type, to me."

Sil wondered if believing they were a special breed was something they told themselves, or had drilled into them from a young age. "I don't intend to stay. I'm rather fond of the cushy inner colonies," he said, managing to keep a straight face. Things were different in the inner colonies, but it wasn't because the conditions were any easier. Extreme heat was as difficult to deal with as extreme cold, and days that were long as an Earth year required a similar artificial night and day as those out here, buried under the surface of a cryogenic world. "What about the other way? Where do the Titanese go for vacation?"

The pilot's good cheer vanished in a cloud of disbelief as he spared Sil another glance. "You really are a tourist, you don't know that. Titanese work for a living, Ser. D'you know how much it costs to import our necessities?"

Sil nodded. He knew the answers to the questions he was asking. He didn't think the pilot had ever asked himself the same questions. "Not even those with family left behind somewhere? The Lunar colonies, Mars? The TWF is close."

"It's a tough life out here, Ser, as I keep pointing out. We don't have the time or money to go gadding about the solar system for fun. As for the TWF," his mouth curled in obvious contempt. "Hard working folk got no use for the likes of them."

Sil wasn't overly surprised at his dismissal of the TWF as the remote station had become something an artists' colony, reputed to use more Bliss than all the other colonies together. But clearly the pilot had not through the implications of his words. He shifted in his seat, as much as he could with the safety straps around his chest. "Let me see if I understand you correctly, my dear. Once a person comes to Titan to work, they can never leave?"

The pilot gave Sil a troubled look. "Hadn't, uh, really thought of it... like that, but I suppose that's right."

"So a goodly portion of the colonists are not here because they're special but only because they have no choice?"

"I, I wouldn't have said it that way."

"Ponder how many of them as not cut out for here you and your fellow pilots have escorted back to a passenger ship," Sil suggested. "But for now, how soon until we get to Black Thunder?"

There was a pause. "Not long."

Sid did not mind the pilot's sudden lapse of chatter. Hiding in

8

Black Thunder wasn't something he could do even if he wanted to; he would, no matter he stayed the rest of his life, be the outsider. He had no intent to stay longer than he absolutely had to. His plan hinged on ingratiating himself with the mine manager, one Carlton Banook, but it was nebulous beyond that. There was only so much he could anticipate, without actually being there, without knowing Carlton Banook's weaknesses.

The pilot manoeuvred skillfully in the murky brown clouds of Titan, landing without incident on a flat sheet marked out in lights. Visible from the thick glass windows was a small rectangular outcropping, maybe 500 square meters, with a warning beacon on it. He was a little surprised by that. "I thought the colonies were all underground?"

The pilot threw a glance in the direction of Sil's gaze. "Black Thunder was given a charter to mine coal, started with the surface. All mechanized but still—access and all that. Once they got started, though, they found diamonds and got a charter change." As he spoke, the lights on the pan turned red and it began to descend, perhaps only fifty meters, Sil judged. There was some clanging from unseen sources and the red lights turned green. The pilot said, "Safe to disembark. Passengers have to check in at the office." He gave Sil another dubious look. "Best hurry, it's still mighty cold out here on the dock."

"Thank you, Ser," Sil said, politely formal. On his own now, valise in hand, he took in the docking bay with a swift, observant eye. It was dimly lit but clean, which wasn't surprising given how dangerous a little dirt could be to machinery so vital to survival. He'd grown up on Mars, so thinking about how perilous life in the colonies actually was didn't come naturally to him. For born and bred colonists, it was just the way it was.

Titan, however, felt raw, like a new, dangerous colony. Mars, the Moon, Venus—all felt bright, safe, secure compared to the rawness of this shipping platform. Which was amusing, really, given that the corporate contracts for Titan had been among the first established colonies. Perhaps they retained the raw feel on purpose, to keep the colonists convinced of their "special breed" status.

He gave himself a mental shake, smiling at his own thoughts. His observations informed him there were any number of ways he could enter the colony without checking in, but that was counter to his purpose. Shivering against the cold, he took up his valise and walked through an airlock marked Black Thunder, Main Office.

A man dressed in loose-fitting trousers and a tight long-sleeved shirt under a more fashionable tunic stepped into the reception area from an office; he assumed it was an office, though offices with airlocks were not familiar to him, not in Imbrium, not even on Mars. It gave him the slightest of a pause. The man was late in his forties or early in his fifties with medium length hair of a colour Sil could never decide if it was dark blond or light brown. Grey graced his temples and the facial hair that grew down the sides of his face. His skin was pale and somewhat pinkish, which looked unhealthy to Sil. "How do, stranger. What's your business here?"

"That would be between me and a certain Carlton Banook," Sil said, keeping his tone mild and wondering if he was supposed to feel intimidated.

"That's most strange, for I am Carlton Banook and I don't know you. Nor was I expecting you." He gave Sil a head to toe and clearly dismissed him in every way short of physically waving him off.

Sil inclined his head, hiding a small smile. "Of course not. I am Silver Tation." He straightened. "I have a business proposition for you, Ser Banook."

"And you came all this way?" Banook smiled, his voice mocking. "Such an intrepid young man. Welcome to Black Thunder, Silver Tation," he said, deliberately robbing Sil of the honorific ser.

Sil let the insult slide. It was deliberately meant to offend; it would not serve his purpose to react. "I thank you for the consideration, after all this long way, Ser Banook. I assume you are far too busy at this moment to hear my proposal, so I shall ask of you a favour—is there a boarding house or hotel within the colony where I might make myself comfortable until my return passage arrives? I assume we will have concluded our business by then."

"Such confidence for one so young. I do like that." He seemed he might add more then thought the better of it. "I will have my assistant help you find a room for your stay, at a reasonable cost, of course. Once you've settled," he cast a dubious glance at Sil's valise, "it would be my pleasure to give you a tour of Black Thunder's operations. After which you may have a few days to ponder if you truly wish to bother me with a... proposition."

Sil smiled slowly, the smile of a man who knew he was as beautiful as he was rich. "I do like propositions," he murmured. "Thank you."

THREE

Imbrium

Detective Nick Delaney, with Interplanetary Law Enforcement's Special Cases division, was packing up the few belongings he had in the office temporarily assigned to his use. "Leaving so soon, Detective?"

He turned to see the chief of Imbrium's IPLE detachment. "I can't magically produce a body, and without it, we have nothing. Special Cases isn't for missing persons; I'm wasting my time and your department's budget."

"True. But we've got a body, now. It was found in a maintenance closet in the Exterra office complex when the stink of decomp set off the air monitors. Officers called to the scene have already identified it as Emun Delacroix. Forensics is on the way. Coming along?"

Homicide wasn't as common as one might think in the colonies. A body was considerably harder to lose, alive or dead, in closed systems. A breach in a colony could mean death for everyone in it, populations of hundreds of thousands, so strict measures were taken to prevent accidents. Those measures meant nobody could just casually open an airlock and discard a body to the anonymity of space. When a body showed up, it was usually a clear crime of passion, spur of the moment, flare of tempers. Usually it was easy to solve. This time, someone had gone to a great deal of trouble to hide the body. That didn't rule out crime of passion. A cooler head may have prevailed after the deed and an attempt to cover it up. Looking at the body, Nick doubted that was the case.

This body was bloated, grey and green and putrid. Nick covered his mouth against the stench. It wasn't something he'd smelled before, and he hoped he'd never have to become accustomed to it. "We got a time and cause of death?"

The chief gestured to a person in a crisp white cover-all, who peeled gloves off as ze approached the two men. "Fifteen days, decomp is too far advanced to narrow it much more than that. This is a dump site not the primary crime scene, not enough blood. Blunt force trauma to the back of the head, we should be able to narrow down the object after forensic autopsy."

"Thank you, Ser." The buildings were cleaned by microbots, which deposited any organic waste—normal human detritus like skin cells and stray hairs, as well as lunch leftovers—into the recycling system It was all converted into soil and nutrients for the hydroponic farms. Any clues that might have remained in the building were long gone.

"Anything in those interviews you conducted look different now?" The chief asked.

"I'll need to take another look. I didn't talk to Amanda Lavender before. I guess I should start there."

"Better you than me."

~ * ~

Nick Delaney seated himself at his desk, the box he'd been filling still on top. He'd known, deep down, as soon as Delacroix was reported missing that a body would turn up. Although he had made an effort to talk to the last people, person, really, who'd seen Delacroix alive, he had received a very strong suggestion from his superiors in Special Cases to leave Amanda Lavender out of it.

Her family owned half of Phobos Station, and she might as well be a princess for all the effort her family put into protecting her. But with a body on the ground, and her party the last place anyone at all had seen Delacroix, he had to talk to her. He called to make an appointment, hoping overt courtesy would grant him a pass.

To his surprise, she seemed delighted to see him. She was ensconced in a grand suite at the top of the Exterra complex, the very same habitation pod where the body had been concealed. A stiff-backed man with steel-grey hair and wearing white gloves slid open the door at his rap and gave him a disapproving stare before showing him into a large room with a view window.

"This is so exciting! A real live Long Arm!" Amanda Lavender was a lady of fashion, so he assumed her appearance would be considered fashionable. Her exuberant wig was an elaborate style of ascending round shapes piled on top of her head. He assumed it was a wig, he couldn't imagine real hair could hold a style like that. It was a pinkish blonde and contrasted with her pale blue tunic and soft yellow pants. She was seated on an off-white divan, and held her hand out to him as if expecting him to do tricks, or something.

Nick nodded deeply, and gave her his most polite smile. "Thank you for seeing me, Ser Lavender, I was afraid it would be a bother."

"Not at all! You said you wanted to ask me about the night Silver Tation and Emun had their falling out?"

"Yes, and thank you again. You understand this conversation will be recorded?"

She nodded.

"I need you to verbally agree to being recorded, Ser Lavender," he said gently.

"Oh! Oh yes, certainly. Record away."

He smiled again and sat down cautiously on the chair opposite her. "Thank you. Did you happen to hear what it was Ser Tation and Ser Delacroix were talking about that night?"

"Well," she said, crossing her legs and leaning forward slightly, "Not at first, I was too far away, but then Emun rather loudly called Ser Tation a lying cheat. At that, the room went rather silent so we could all listen, I daresay." She smiled.

"How well do you know Ser Tation?"

"Not well. He's charming and so pretty he should be named Tempt. Tempt Tation, yes?" She laughed at her own wit and added, "Or maybe Flirt, he does so love to flirt. Flirtation, yes?"

Nick cleared his throat. "So you're not close talking pals?"

"No." She put a perfectly manicured fingernail to her lips and frowned briefly. "I'm not sure he has any, now you mention it."

"And Ser Delacroix?"

"Oh Emun had lots of friends. I personally found him a bit." she paused, frowning as she looked for a word that she didn't seem to find. "But Daddy insisted I host at least one party for his friends in Exterra, so," she shrugged helplessly. "Ser Tation and a dozen others were invited to give the party colour, sparkle, interest."

Nick nodded again, well able to imagine a party of company executives and engineers could make for a slightly dull event. "Completely understandable. Now, you said Delacroix accused Tation of...?"

"He called him a lying cheat, then with the room stilled to listen, Ser Tation replied indignantly that he had no idea what Emun was talking about and if he had accusations to make, he should call the Long Arms. Emun gave him such a look, I'd not be surprised it was pretty Silver Tation disappeared instead of Emun. Tation winked at him—I didn't see that, but I was told—and that was when Emun lost his temper and hit him right across the floor! Well. I can't have that sort of behaviour at *my* parties, even if he was Exterra, so I asked Emun to leave until he was civilized again."

"What did Ser Tation do, then?"

Her eyes widened, showing off her purple contact lenses. "Why, he got to his feet, brushed off his gorgeous tunic, and asked for another drink."

Nick's mouth twitched. That sounded consistent with the man he'd so briefly interviewed a few weeks ago. "Was Tation Blissed?"

"Not then, but he loaded afterwards. Who could blame the poor darling. He seemed very relaxed and happy and not at all concerned about Emun's poor behaviour."

"And you're certain of the conversation?"

"Oh yes. Daddy sends me to entertain his people because I'm very good at remembering conversations."

Nick made a mental note of that. "Was there anyone close to the Sers when their discussion began that might have heard it before it blew up?"

She frowned again, and tapped the side of her nose gently with one finger. "Hmm. Ser Evelyn Roan, and Ser Val Lee."

"Val Lee was an Exterra guest?" That interview hadn't been easy. Val Lee had gained fame as an entertainment figure, singing and acting in popular media. He'd parlayed that into investing into said media and now held an astonishing amount of power, in the form of advertising. Every colony had Lee Billboards, selling products people became convinced they had to have. He wasn't the wealthiest person Nick had ever run across, but he had more power to change people's minds than seemed reasonable.

"Oh no, he was mine. Such an honour he accepted my invite. Val is a lovely man," she beamed.

"More sparkle?"

"Indeed! It's people like Val and pretty Ser Tation that make these visits to Imbrium tolerable."

Nick stood up and offered his hand. "Ser Lavender, I cannot thank you enough for your time," he said, hoping his charm hadn't thoroughly rusted away, "and might I ask permission to contact you again if I think of more questions?"

She fluttered her fingers against his hand, and smiled prettily at him. "Oh yes, Ser Detective, please do. Such a pleasure to meet a for real Long Arm."

~ * ~

Nick went over his interviews again. Neither Val Lee nor Evelyn Roan had even recognized Emun Delacroix from his image, though they remembered the argument. Lee had expressed an unfavourable opinion of Ser Tation, and admitted to feeling some small pleasure at seeing Tation knocked across the room. Roan had gushed a bit over Tation, expressing reluctance over not knowing him better, heavy with innuendo. A deeper look had given him no reason to regard them suspiciously. He hoped his supervisors appreciated him leaving Val Lee alone, at least. Silver Tation had seemed genuinely surprised that Delacroix was missing, but he was the only one with the slightest of a motive, so far.

Emun Delacroix seemed to be the most uninteresting man ever murdered. He had no contracted spouse wrangling for his death benefit. He seemed to have barely registered with the people he worked with and managed—they shrugged, looked blank. Exterra had only just begun investigating Delacroix's embezzling; they hadn't confronted him about it. The only person to visibly vex him was Silver Tation.

He traced his finger across the multiple holo displays open around his desk. This was different from the case board in the squad room, where the other officers on the case examined the evidence. Nick hadn't put forth Tation as a suspect just yet, because something was bothering him that he couldn't put a finger on. He called up all the information his data crawlers had gathered on the young man. including stills of Silver Tation captured by various security recorders in the city. According to official records, the pretty boy was only twenty-two years old, though he had the bearing and confidence of someone older. Most young men his age, flinging around money as he did, had a rich parent in the background supplying the chips. But there was no wealthy Tation in the background. None of the Tations that came up in his search were more than modestly set. That had led him to investigate young Ser Tation's financials.

He and Delacroix had matching withdrawals, and equally empty accounts, typical of the sort left behind by an investment scammer. If they had been victims of a scam, why hadn't Tation mentioned that?

He checked the address and tagged the habitat directly, before remembering Tation had said to tag his combrace. More or less. The room's communication system accepted the tag and advised, "The occupants are not within, please indicate if your message is for Ser Open or Ser Kawe." Nick broke the link and compared the tag he'd input to the one on file. It was correct. Tation had lived there for the last three years. He supposed that after almost a month it would be reasonable to assume the case was closed, but why would he suddenly leave?

"And how soon," he muttered, using the Special Forces access codes to access the rental records. He cursed. A bare hour after promising to stay in Imbrium, Silver Tation had moved out. A quick scan of the transportation access points told him Tation had gone to Destiny and boarded a the passenger ship to Titan. Nothing said guilty like lying to a Long Arm and fleeing. Nick released Silver Tation as a primary suspect, his name and face going to primary case board, along with a copy of the Amanda Lavender interview.

Then he tagged the Titan Way Station to find out which colony was Tation's ultimate destination. Titan. Took weeks to get there and real time communication was impossible, but it was equally impossible for an outsider, a fugitive, to hide there. It didn't make sense. He pulled out the slim plastic calling card and tagged Tation's combrace.

He closed the displays and went into the squad room, where one of the officers looked up, frazzled. "Detective Delaney. We believe Tation went to a diamond mining colony called Black Thunder."

"How do we know that?" The time lag was currently almost fifty minutes; Titan Way Station wouldn't have even received his message yet, let alone had time to respond.

"He made enquiries on the net about accommodations there, a little over a month ago."

It was like he wasn't trying to hide at all. "We can't afford to send a ship out there to pick him up on suspicion, and he can't leave Titan that we don't know about it, so it's almost as good as having him in custody. We'll just have to convict or clear him from here. Go over his financials again—when did he pay for his ticket? And how?"

"Yes, detective. Also, Delacroix's domicile suggests he had a companion, but the different colour wig fibres could mean a flower habit."

"Have forensics analyze the fibres, in case we find something to match them to. Take another look at his financials, too, further back, flower shop payments."

The squad exchanged some eye rolling glances and Nick glared at them. "I know you've run their financials already, but that was over three weeks ago. Run 'em again. I'm an asshole, but I'm a thorough asshole."

FOUR

Black Thunder

The habitation of Black Thunder was reached by exiting yet another set of airlocks to a lobby that contained two lifts, each with a capacity of three hundred people, or so the manufacturer's label inside assured. There were two buttons, one marked M and one L, and nothing to indicate how far apart they were. Banook's assistant, an andro named Jaden, brushed his hand over the front of the L and they began a rapid descent, if the sensation in Sil's gut was to be believed. He was just about used to the feeling when they slowed rapidly enough he grabbed the rail lining the interior. Jaden gave him a smirk, but said nothing.

Doors on both sides of the lift opened, revealing a similar lobby, with security gates on either side. Jaden silently gestured him forward through the gate marked B and into the smallest colony he'd ever seen. It was organized in three distinct levels around an open square of bright, overflowing planter boxes and utilitarian air scrubbers. He assumed recycling, heat generation, hydroponics, and other mundane necessities of colonial life were a further level down, and wondered how they were accessed. Not via the lift they'd just descended in, to be sure.

Jaden led him across the square, up a staircase to the second floor veranda, through a number of people who turned to stare until reaching a door with the number 48 on it. Ze opened it with a slide key, before passing the key to Sil. "Welcome to Black Thunder," ze said.

"Thank you, Ser."

The room was narrow, the ceiling had a bit of a curve to it, lending the space the feel of a tunnel. The overhead light was bright and blueish, but it had a dimmer switch that Jaden demonstrated. The table obviously folded up against a drop down bed, two chairs were near it now, and a floor based task light on flexi neck. The hygiene station had a real door. He examined the workings of it, and noticed no timers. Whatever stringencies the residents of Black Thunder had to cope with, lack of water wasn't one. Imbrium—all the Lunar colonies—had strict water rationing, as did the Venusian cloud cities. Unlimited water, now that was a true luxury.

There were cubbies for clothing and personal items, and an upholstered bench seat near the door across from a holo projector that probably served as both entertainment and communication. Another panel revealed a fold down fitness station. None of it was particularly secure, but Sil's most precious bits were his coffee press and a polysteel tracker bag of spare credit chips, for emergencies. He doubted he'd find Earth coffee beans out here, so he tucked both into the cubby nearest the door. Most people hid their valuables far from an entrance; near the front door was one of the last places most thieves would look. They would also be easy to grab if he had to make a hasty exit.

He unpacked the clothing from his valise, mostly cheap cell clothes he wouldn't miss if he had to leave them behind. The room was unadorned, but he'd never been one to bother with art or personal mementos. Nothing that wouldn't fit in a valise.

He tucked his room key into his pocket and leaned on the veranda railing to study the layout of the town. From this vantage, he could see another D shape of habitation on the other side of the lifts. He could see some shops and services in the square, but no schools or clinics such as his pilot had boasted of; those must be on the other side.

Aware that people were staring and whispering, he straightened, put his vapour stick in his hand, and walked down the stairs to the main square to see what was available to buy. The prices shocked him. The cost to send goods to Titan was little more than to send them to say Venus or Mars, and it was more than compensated for by the massive amounts of hydrocarbon fuels Titan could and did provide Earth and the other colonies. Black Thunder allegedly made its money from the high quality diamonds found in this particular patch of Titan, but obviously a significant profit was secured on reselling absolutely everything. Even the locally grown hydroponic produce was astonishingly priced. Black Thunder's employees must be paid a pretty penny to afford anything. Small wonder no one ever left.

He bought some food items to prepare later—his accommodation might resemble a hotel room, but he doubted there was room service—and left them on the table in his room before returning to the mine office for his promised tour.

"Sorry to house you with the workers," Banook said, "But I'm afraid I don't offer the hospitality of my suite to strangers."

"A reasonable policy," Sil said. The idea of sharing living space with Carlton Banook made his skin crawl; he was grateful for a space of his own, no matter how small. "I knew in advance that Black Thunder didn't cater to tourists, I wasn't expecting a spa and high star dining, dear. Though I can't help but wonder what such accommodation is costing me."

"As a prospective business associate, the cost is minimal. You can pay when you leave," Banook said generously, with a smile that did not reach his eyes.

Sil could imagine what fate awaited him, could he not pay. He didn't ask how minimal, only murmured,"Most generous," and followed meekly as Banook gave him what was likely the standard tour for visiting clients.

"I imagine a man of your discriminating tastes already owns a few Black Thunder diamonds."

"I've gifted some to those I especially liked," he lied without hesitation. He'd never supported Black Thunder. Any gifts of bijoux he might have given a favoured bed partner he was always certain of the provenance. As for his own profits, he preferred hard currency; stealing gems or rather, trying to sell them afterwards, was too risky. One needed a reliable fence, who took a goodly portion of the sale to cover the expense of rewriting the security codes on the stones. Fortunately as long as hard currency existed, there were ways of setting it free.

"This is where our miners work," he said, leading Sil into a large room filled with monitors. "They find the gems and work out the best route to them. The dirtiest work is done by our mechanics, who repair and maintain our drills, tracks, buckets, sluices—all the necessary machinery for our work."

He opened an airlock door to another room, lit by lamps casting a dim blue light. "This is what's left of our grading room."

"It still is the grading room, Ser Banook," said a feminine voice somewhat tiredly. A head covered with long brown braids came into view. At first he thought she was wearing an elaborate lens piece over her left eye, but as she rounded the work station that had been blocking his view, he saw it was a cyborg attachment, wired directly to her brain though her orbital socket. "Hello," she added, upon seeing Sil, her voice carrying a curious note.

"Silver Tation," he said.

"Grace Reyes," she replied. "I'm the gem grader, among other things, for Black Thunder."

Sil glanced around the dimly lit room. Apart from her work bench, everything else in the room looked to be damaged or partially dismantled. "You work alone?"

"It's a budgetary thing," Banook said smoothly."This room had a breach a few years ago, Grace was our only survivor. We couldn't do without her now, she's invaluable."

She ducked her head toward the table, but not before Sil saw the bitter twist to her mouth. He made a note to look for her in the worker's quarters after her shift. She did not seem to see Banook in the same invaluable light.

As they made their way back to the Banook's office, he asked Sil, "What do you think of our little operation?"

"The airlocks strike me. I notice they are only in the actual mine works, and not the habitation."

Banook gave him a look that seemed to wonder how that was relevant, but obliged him with an answer. "Black Thunder was originally a coal mining company. Our dome is partially exposed to Titan's atmosphere, which makes heating a bitch, but," he gestured broadly, "coal processing. We, the company, discovered there's more profit in diamonds, but we couldn't really make alterations to the structure, we had nearly a full complement of workers and—" He cut himself off. "The point is, diamond mining is more likely to cause accidents of the sort that will mix Titan's atmosphere with our air. Boom."

"The breach in the grading room?"

Banook nodded. "Exactly. Without the airlocks, that accident could have taken out the entire company, habitation and all."

Sil nodded, finding the explanation logical, if not exactly reassuring. "You've been generous with your time so I shan't waste any." He smiled winningly. "Any more of it, that is. I had it in mind that the colony has grown beyond all the employment you can provide and perhaps you can find some room for another business...?"

"We take care of our own," he said, but there was gleam of greed in his eye. "However, I'm a fair person and you've come all this way, so I will gladly listen to what you propose. In a few days, as I said."

Sil needed to get to know Banook before he could craft a scheme, but at the moment he wasn't sure how to do that. He needed to come up with something plausible but already covered by the company in order to garner Banook's interest, but how to befriend him? Seduction, one of his go to methods, was not an option. He suppressed a shudder as the thought flitted through his mind. "You're a kindly and patient person, Ser Banook. I look forward to speaking with you at your convenience."

~ * ~

Sil knew there had to be some sort of kitchen equipment in his room, and he had a good idea of where it should be, but he couldn't find the way to open it out. He shrugged off his tunic and stood in his open doorway, looking, he hoped, confused and helpless. Whatever would convince someone to talk to an outsider long enough to tell him how to open his kitchen. Braided hair with beads seemed to be very popular with all presented genders and he touched his own dark locks, wondering idly how he would look in such a style.

"Pardon, Ser. You seem to have lost something?"

Sil blinked to adjust his eyes to the shadow now falling over him from a rather large man, who in spite of the lighter gravity here had managed to develop broad shoulders and well-defined muscles. "Um, yes. I mean no, I was in the midst of changing when I realized I didn't know where to find something to cook on...? I wasn't sure asking just anyone was appropriate..." He gave the big man his best helpless innocent look.

"We don't like outsiders, much, it's true, but we ain't that inhospitable. Figgers Banook would stick you with us and not bother to show you the amenities. May I-?" He gestured toward the inside of Sil's room.

"By all means," Sil murmured appreciatively. He hadn't had a big, strong man in his life for quite some time. They usually had certain ideas about sex that Sil didn't care for.

"Standing in the doorway half dressed like that, folk'll think you're a freelance flower."

"Oh, thank you for telling me, I definitely don't want folk thinking that." If by some fickle chance his fortune were to vanish and he was faced with the choice of working off his debt to Black Thunder or trading sex for survival, he'd pick option three and take his chances stowing away on a cargo ship. Selling sex for money could become a right dangerous game, one Sil had played desperately as a youth. He had no intentions of playing again.

"No? Kind of a shame, you being so pretty."

Sil smiled warily and tugged his tunic over his head. "I really just need some help getting the kitchen unit to release... for now."

The big man showed him—one needed to depress two buttons simultaneously and a counter top swung down, revealing a cook top, a wave oven, a sink and a small refrigeration unit. "Just be sure to empty the sink before you close it up again."

"Ah, how clever a design. How can I ever thank you?" The helpless role did not sit comfortably with him, and he regretted his decision to play it.

The man studied him. "Just being neighbourly. You sure you're not a freelance? Banook brings 'em in, sometimes. Pretty things like you. Since we most of us can't afford proper flowers."

"That's very, um, generous of him," Sil said, nearly choking on the word. Freelance flowers, hmm. Sounded like Banook was bringing his illegal sex trade business a little close to home. "I appreciate your estimation of my charms, but I'm not for sale." He looked at the man kind enough to help a stranger and added, "I'm open to more personal negotiations...?"

He smiled. "Avery Rex. Welcome to Black Thunder. You know how to cook?"

Sil smiled back. "Silver Tation. I'm a fair cook. Would dinner some night settle us up for your help this evening?"

"Oh, I wouldn't take advantage." He waved vaguely in the direction of the door. "Food is so expensive."

"I already have my return fare," Sil assured him. "It would be a pleasure."

Now it was the big man's face that took on a wary expression. "We'll talk later, Silver." His smile returned. "Such a pretty name." On that compliment, Avery Rex ducked out the door.

The expression of caution on the other man's face stayed with Sil as he sorted the foodstuffs he'd purchased. He hadn't expected such a steep mark-up on food. His habitat on Imbrium had an optional meal service, allowing him to choose a menu at the beginning of each week, and have it delivered. Almost like a hotel, only cheaper, more practical. He didn't use it all the time—he loved to dine out, on sumptuous meals. That didn't mean he couldn't cook, only that it seemed too much work for just him and he rarely met anyone he felt the need to impress. Perhaps eating someone else's food incurred a social debt or obligation here. He would be sure to clarify to Ser Rex that his offer was without strings.

Thinking of potential bed mates, he recalled the handsome Long Arm back on Imbrium. Sil doubted he'd called—there'd be no official reason to contact him as he'd no hand in Delacroix's misfortunes. He hadn't gotten a sense of personal interest, either. Just as well, what sort of trouble could a flirtation like that bring on him. He chuckled out loud.

He dusted off a holo display unit found on the shelf and synced his combrace. To his surprise, there were a couple of messages from Nick Delaney, private, not official IPLE tags. That was intriguing. He sat down with his simple dinner and played the first.

"Ser Tation; I'm certain I asked and you agreed that you'd stay

28

in Imbrium until this case was resolved. I won't put an all points on you just yet, but fleeing does enforce the impression that you are responsible for Ser Delacroix's demise."

Sil frowned. Delaney had left a plain voice message, no video to entertain him with wicked thoughts, and while it was inconvenient of Delacroix to get himself killed, how had Sil become a suspect? The next message, another voice only, played automatically. "There are serious questions to be answered regarding this homicide, Ser Tation. Like, just where were you the night following Ser Lavender's party? I expect a reply as soon as possible."

Since the lag made real time communications impossible, his choices of reply were limited to sending a voice or video message. Then he'd just have to wait. Sil chose video, hoping to inspire a like reply by artfully mussing his hair with his fingers and adjusting his tunic to bare a little more flesh. He didn't know if the detective had noticed his appearance on Imbrium, but he'd certainly notice this, for good or ill. "I've just played your messages, Ser Delaney—they are private, are they not? Disappointed not to see you," he smiled slyly. "The night you're asking after, I was ensconced in my habitat with the most delightful little flower, you might check with a lovely little shop called Sweet Stems. I hope my lack of involvement in Ser Delacroix's unfortunate demise will not mean you won't call again?" He sent the message and checked the current lag time. His message would arrive in about forty-five minutes.

He finished his food without enthusiasm, wishing he'd thought to bring some non-perishables with him in his luggage.

FIVE

Imbrium

Nick Delaney checked his messages in the morning, surprised to find a video response from Silver Tation. Why video, he wondered as he played the message. Tation looked as if he'd just got out of bed, playful and teasing, and seemingly genuinely unaware of how perilous his situation was. He briefly considered sending the video to the squad room files, but decided against it. Instead, he tagged Sweet Stems and confirmed Silver Tation's patronage. That he cc'd the squad room and went to look at the big picture forming there.

The security video at Tation's habitat, his financial records, and the flower shop all confirmed his alibi for the night Delacroix was killed, for a very long period of time. What did one do with a flower for so many hours? He shook head, grateful he hadn't asked such a ridiculous question aloud.

Delacroix's financials had painted a vivid picture. He wasn't that skilled of an embezzler, taking far too much over too short of time and depositing it into his account without trying to hide it. If he hadn't been killed, Exterra would most surely have fired him within a few days of Ser Lavender's party. But he hadn't kept the money long; he'd also withdrawn large amounts, conveniently in chips noted for Ser Tation. But a side by side compare of Tation's financials showed equal amounts on the same dates also withdrawn, no notations. Where had the money gone?

The wig fibres in Delacroix's place had revealed little, but the money said girlfriend, not flowers. Tation on the other hand—it was astonishing how much he spent on flowers. Among other things. He certainly enjoyed the finer things life had to offer. But there was no record of a payment for the ticket to Titan, and even his sensual indulgences had stopped as his account had emptied. Experience said the equal payments suggested an investment scam, but why wouldn't Tation have mentioned being taken for a goodly fortune?

He replayed the Lavender interview, stopping to hear the heiress say, "He called him a lying cheat, then with the room stilled to listen, Ser Tation replied indignantly that he had no idea what Emun was talking about and if he had accusations to make, he should call the Long Arms."

Curiously, he tagged Ser Lavender and was surprised to get through to her relatively easily. She sat gracefully in front of the cam projecting her image across the net and smiled at him with bright orange lips. They matched the elaborate bright orange wig she was wearing. After apologizing for the interruption and thanking her obsequiously for her time, he asked, "Did Ser Delacroix ever mention in your hearing an investment?"

Her smile faded. "Why do you pester me about Emun?"

"I do apologize," he said immediately. "I only ask because of your superb memory for conversation." He delivered the flattery in a suitably humble voice.

Her expression brightened again. "Oh! Thank you, detective." Then, as she had in the in person interview, she put a highly polished nail to the corner of her mouth as she thought. "It's possible," she said hesitantly, not looking directly at him. "I think I... overheard him say something about finally realizing his dreams?"

Nick thanked her again, and asked once more if he might call upon her services—he phrased it that way—if he needed more help. She beamed and patted the orange monstrosity on her head. "But of course, detective. I'd be delighted!"

He stared into the empty space where her image had been for long moments after the call ended. She thought she recalled? What happened to her excellent memory? "And where," he said aloud to no one in particular, "does Amanda Lavender buy her wigs?"

"Detective! We found a safe in Delacroix's rooms."

Nick turned his head to look at the investigating officer making the announcement with such pride. "And?"

"It's empty, Ser, but we found this." He passed an evidence bag containing a square plastic card to Nick. It bore nothing but a shiny symbol that seemed almost but not quite familiar to him, a circle with a cross on the bottom and horns on the top. He frowned and turned the card around. Or a cross on the top and... a moustache? Did that fit into this?

He nodded, opened his mouth to say words forever lost when the chief himself came into the room with purposeful strides. "They found the primary crime scene—get your asses moving!"

SIX

Black Thunder

Night was the abrupt darkening of the colony's ambient lighting, not the gradual dimming in imitation of sunset Sil was accustomed to, making it feel more like a prison. Not that Sil had ever experienced prison. There was no dead of the night, however. The mines ran constantly on three eight hour shifts per day. Yellow lights left pools in the drastically reduced lighting for the night shift to find its way to the twenty-four hour shops and their small homes. It wouldn't give much leeway for skulking around, with people always awake. Not that he had any plans for it, he thought, blinking as his eyes adjusted to the relative darkness.

He could still see enough to identify Avery Rex lounging on the veranda near his door, who said in a cordial tone, "Good evening."

"Ser Rex," Sil said, letting his curiosity show in his voice.

"Avery." The big man smiled. "Kinda wish you were for sale, pretty one. I'm a little out of practice at seduction."

Sil shook his head and smiled. "Illegal flowers have so little choice. Wouldn't it be nicer to have someone willing? As for seduction," he waved his hand in a dismissive gesture, "I am practised enough for both of us. Can't get what you want if you're not willing to pursue with hands wide open."

"Hands wide open, what a picture your words paint." He gave Sil a long look. "Pretty, like you."

"I thought we'd talk over dinner? I promise no strings, Avery. Just a meal for your kindness and a chance to discuss our terms."

"Terms? You make it sound so professional after all."

"Don't pout," Sil admonished teasingly. "I merely wish to be certain neither of us is disappointed, should we decide on more... intimate discourse." He drew his index finger across Rex's cheek and down his neck. "I would so hate to disappoint," he said softly. He opened the door and turned to see Avery Rex looking somewhat confused. "Dinner? I'll be cooking in here."

"I can't eat your food, at least not yet, but I will share a drink with you."

Sil didn't argue, merely gestured the big man inside. "Tell me of the significance of sharing food, if you don't mind? I brought a bottle of Shoots from Imbrium, would you like some?"

"That's an alcohol made from...?"

"Sprouts of some sort. A concoction invented in Destiny, Luna, they say." Sil brandished the bottle, already opened. Instead of waiting for an answer, he poured a few mils in each of two glasses, and passed one to Avery. "Some say it tastes like poison, others swear it's ambrosia. I find it somewhere between the two, but it can ease conversation between new acquaintances."

Avery took the glass, holding it up to the diffuse ceiling light. He smelled it cautiously. "It smells fresh, green."

Sil pulled a chair from the table so that he might sit opposite Avery, rather than beside him, until he had determined just what Avery Rex expected.

Avery took a sip of the liquor and rolled it around his mouth before swallowing. "Different. Thank you. As you've noticed, food is not inexpensive out here, and sharing has an implication of obligation, simply because it costs twice as much to feed twice as many people."

"I'd guessed as much. I wouldn't impose any obligation on you, but I understand if it's such as you'd feel regardless."

Avery nodded, and leaned back on the padded seat, crossing his ankles and putting an arm back behind his head. He smiled at Sil and raised his glass. "So what manner of negotiations do you have?"

Sil returned the smile, striking a relaxed pose of his own. "I'm a visitor to Black Thunder, and I came because I have business with Carlton Banook. That will be my first priority, the first demand on my time. And when it's concluded, I will be leaving. No emotional attachments."

Avery gave him a serious look, still relaxed. "You worry after your own emotions, Silver. I'll take care of mine."

Sil studied his face to ascertain Avery's confidence in his own words. "Fair enough."

"You will stay overnight,"Avery said abruptly, uncrossing his ankles and leaning forward into Sil's space. "I can't include breakfast, though."

Sil almost said, "I can," in a seductive voice before remembering shared food created obligation. "I like a warm body in my bed," he said instead, which was not quite agreement with Avery's statement.

Avery drained his glass and set it on the counter behind Sil, bringing himself to the edge of his seat and face to face with Sil. "And of course, I'll have you, fuck you," he added as if he hadn't been clear.

Sil smiled and traced Avery's jaw. "No." He stood up, setting aside his own glass, barely touched, and Avery rose with him, not quite towering over him, but making him feel small.

"Yes," Avery said.

"Not negotiable," Sil said mildly.

"I want you, Silver Tation."

Sil raised himself onto his toes to bring his face even with Avery's and with his lips touching the other man's, he said, "Then you're going to have to learn a whole new position."

"Or you will."

Sil stepped back and smiled. "Goodnight, Avery. It's been a delightful little talk."

Avery Rex also took a step away and laughed. "Maybe I'll go after you with hands wide open."

"Practice your technique all you like," Sil invited, "There's only one way into my bed."

"Oh, I'm a very determined man," Avery Rex said affably. "I'm sure I can convince you, one way or another." He ruffled Sil's hair. "Goodnight, Silver."

~ * ~

When Sil stuck his head out of his room, awoken by the bustle of shift change, everyone who passed by acknowledged him with a "good morning" or a smile. It seemed being on good terms with Avery Rex had a certain currency in Black Thunder. As if conjured by his name crossing Sil's mind, the man himself appeared on the verandah, giving Sil an idea of where his domicile was. He smiled at Sil and grabbed him for the briefest of kisses before striding towards the stairs.

Sil grinned at the retreating figure. He might have fun on Black Thunder after all.

Delighted at how things had gone with Avery Rex, Sil nearly forgot to check for any messages from Earth. With no scam running, he wasn't used to the idea that someone might want to get in touch with him. But since all three of his persons of interest—Carlton Banook, Grace Reyes, and Avery Rex—were on the same day shift, he had time to remember the situation on Imbrium.

He was pleased to see a video message, though his pleasure

diminished somewhat as he saw the attractive detective in his uniform at what appeared to be his place of employment. Yet the call was still on private channels. An unsmiling Detective Delaney held up an image that obscured his handsome face. "Do you recognize this?"

Sil did, of course. It was the alchemical symbol for Quicksilver, his calling card. He'd left one in Delacroix's safe after emptying it of the little the man had left after Sil's "sure thing" had taken mostly everything else. He was suddenly glad the communications lag prohibited real time conversations; he wasn't sure could have hid his surprise quite so well in real time. Already composing his reply in his head, the image was replaced by another, this time of a pyramidal shaped thing. He squinted at the image, but couldn't tell what it was.

The message just ended, no demand to call. "How rude," Sil muttered. Still unsure what the evidence was against him, he decided to come across a fraction more serious. So he turned on the recorder and greeted the detective cordially. "I'm flattered but a bit confused as to why you're consulting me on this case," he said, deliberately misinterpreting the call. "The first image I found familiar but didn't recognize it right away," he lied easily. "But I knew I'd seen it somewhere—it's the Mercury Solar Farm symbol, isn't it? I've seen it emblazoned on the tech ships out of Destiny. The second, well." He frowned and looked at the duplicate image he'd made. "I'm afraid I can't make head nor tail of it," he said in all honesty. "If I had to guess I'd say some sort of air scrubber? Perhaps the context of where you found it might help identify it? Please let me know if I can be of any more assistance," he said cheerfully and sent the message.

SEVEN

The square was milling with people whose shift ended at eight a.m. They sent furtive looks his way as he tried to find a directory of who lived where. The curved wall where his room was located consisted of approximately two hundred single worker dwellings, divided by a central stair. It seemed an odd design choice, but then most of what he'd come across out here was odd. Built for utility, concerns about psychological health had clearly been afterthoughts, where they existed at all.

Extensive studies had shown that people needed beauty. Victoria, Mars had tried with the pseudo Venetian architecture— failed in more ways than one, but it was still called the Street of Dreams and something of a tourist destination, however unlikely that seemed. The Venusian colonies were known for their gardens, excepting Oracle, of course; and even Europa, so he'd heard, had created light gardens in the dark oceans, illuminating a sea life filled with colour that stymied biologists.

In Black Thunder, beauty was up to the colonists to create. Doorways were draped in colourful curtains woven of used, disposable cellulose clothes, and tinkling beads of muted colours. Personal boxes of blossoms bloomed along the rails of each level, maintained by the individuals who lived here; every box a reflection of personal taste. It was riotous and reminded Sil of the ever changing graffiti on the exterior of the TWF station.

He walked the length of the verandah, down the stairs and across the front of the lower units. No directory. Paths led from the stairs through the square, a patchy area of benches and cafe tables surrounded by more of the mismatched flower boxes and some metallic towers that might be air scrubbers or might be surveillance. Hard to say out here, where the company controlled everything.

People gave him wary looks and cautious nods before going about their business; evidently word of Avery Rex's approval hadn't spread. Or it didn't carry past his shift. Again, Sil couldn't tell. He paused to study once more the shops and services that ranged either side of the lifts that carried people up to the mine works. Clothing, food, grooming services, a pharmacy, and one tiny appliance store with out-dated gadgetry. Nowhere a directory of where to find people. He went into the most interesting shop in the row, a bead shop, possibly the only manufacturing done on Black Thunder. The proprietor was happy to explain:

"Coal is what we was sent here to mine, you know, back in the day. It's a by-product, comes in three grades, that pure enough to pressure into made-diamonds, done up the mine." Ze gestured vaguely upwards. "That we burn for heat, and that not good enough for either. I can buy the last for cheap, and got an old pressurizer to turn it into beads. Company makes us coat 'em up dull, and I can sell 'em reasonable."

"But they're still diamonds?"

"Well, yeah, I guess. Crappy, flawed, man-made diamonds."

Sil asked after the price, which was one of the few cheap items he'd found for sale on Black Thunder. He bought a few kilograms worth, curious to know what kind of value they might have elsewhere. He wondered if Grace Reyes would know—was that part of her training, to know the prices diamonds fetched? Or did she just sort them by quality? "I was wondering if you might tell me, Ser—how does one find someone here? Is there a directory of comtags or, or addresses?"

The bead maker's friendly warmth dropped a few degrees. "Company directory in the mining office," ze said gruffly.

"Thank you so kindly," Sil said, ignoring the change in demeanour. He left the shop and went to the lifts in the middle of the D.

There he discovered that the security gate so easily passed coming out was an effective block against going in. "Black Thunder personnel only." He smiled wryly and sighed. Somehow he suspected that nothing would get him on those lifts but Carlton Banook's explicit permission.

He returned to the bead maker's shop, having earned some familiarity with that one. "Pardon, good Ser. This may sound ludicrous, but do you know Grace Reyes?"

Ze nodded slowly. "Not to talk to. She lives upstairs. All the cyborgs live above the market. With their own kind."

Sil schooled his features to mild curiosity. This was the most overt discrimination he'd seen towards cyborgs, and he shouldn't be surprised, since Titan was the source of most cyborgs and most of the discrimination, too. Over the always open markets and meeting places must be the least desirable of living quarters. "Are there many cyborgs in Black Thunder?"

"Not so many, no, we're lucky. Good safety record." Ze sent a wary look towards the ceiling. "They say one of these days we're not careful they'll end up ruling us all."

"Given they're effectively slaves, you don't really see that as a looming threat, do you?"

The wary look turned to sullen confusion and ze began dusting zir display case. "I know what I hear," ze muttered.

Sil considered trying to press logic on the shop keeper, but decided against it. As it was, he imagined he'd have a reputation as some sort of bleeding heart human rights asshole by what passed for sundown here.

~ * ~

He found the cubical assigned to Grace Reyes easy enough and tapped politely on the door. It slid open and she looked him in suspicious surprise. "What do you want?"

"Just to talk. I'm new here."

She raised her eyebrow at him. She was about his height, her skin a couple shades darker, her hair a couple shades lighter. Some of the many tiny braids of her shoulder length hair were decorated with small beads, likely from the shop downstairs. They made a glass-like tinkle of noise at the nod of her head. He took that sharp motion as an invitation to enter. "If you're from some human rights organization, just don't bother, okay? It isn't like we're any of us happy about owing more to the company than we'll ever be likely to pay, but that's how it is out here."

Sil laughed; he wasn't usually mistaken for a do-gooder. "I guess folks like that are the usual kind of visitor comes out this way?"

She shrugged. "I don't have much, but I can offer you a drink?"

Sil hesitated before nodding. "Thank you." Avery had agreed to a drink, so presumably sharing beverages did not create obligation. He'd known about the debt bondage system out here, of course, and had spent three years in Imbrium, Luna to raise the money he'd need for this trip, but he would surely like to not burn through it all. Unlike the inner colonies, or even Europa, there weren't a lot of rich people out here, even management like Carlton Banook were only wealthy by comparison to the rest of the colony, at least by wage earnings. However, out here with little supervision and less law enforcement, people like Banook tended to enhance their incomes by running side gigs, like human trafficking, or embezzling. Given that Black Thunder was a diamond mine...

"You're very quiet for a man who came to talk."

Sil filed the thought away for later and looked down, only partially feigning embarrassment. "I do apologize, Ser Reyes. Black Thunder is, well, quite different from what I'm used to."

"Where you from? Tation, wasn't it? This isn't laced."

He nodded, seating himself at her small table and accepting the drink she gave him. "Laced?"

"Mild sedative in the beverages. It's optional, but lots of folk like it. Vapour sticks are readily available, too, but nothing more than Bliss to load 'em. Kinda frowned on, but considered the secret vice." She gestured towards the door. "Keeps us believing that we're special to be out here."

Sil nodded again. "Thank you." He sipped his drink. "Do you believe it?"

"Used to. Before the accident." Her mouth twisted, mostly on the right side of her face and he guessed she had some paralysis on the left that nobody bothered to fix. "I was born here and I grew up knowing I was going to die here and that was okay. It's home, this is what we do. Then metal fatigue or somesuch allowed too much methane in the room and the old spectrometer finally died with a shower of sparks and boom." She raised her hands with splayed fingers to emphasize the word. "I wasn't given a choice, not that I would've chosen different, I guess," she finished bitterly. "Now... I wish you white knighters could actually do something."

"No one has ever accused me of being on the side of the angels, Ser Reyes," Sil said straight out, with a grin. "I'm sorry to hear of your accident, truly, and I do oppose the indenture system, but I've no petitions, no rallying call to actions no one can afford to take. As I told your boss, Banook, I'm here on business."

She gave him a sceptical look. "Unless your business is buying diamonds, good luck with that."

"I don't expect him to be reasonable. Anything I could propose would cut into company profits. Unless I can make it profitable for him personally."

She studied him, her green eye cold, her eyebrow drawn down, her mouth unsmiling. She said nothing, which was probably wise, given she had no idea who he was.

"Imbrium, Luna," he said.

"Pardon?"

"I came here from Imbrium, Luna."

"Hmm," she said, sipping her drink and looking at him as if he were a puzzle she could solve. "I hear Avery Rex has taken quite the shine to you."

Sil smiled. Gossip was clearly a popular pastime, and the segregation of the cyborgs didn't stop the flow of juicy news. "Ah, yes, Avery."

"Avery," she repeated thoughtfully. "I have to say, I'm more than a little jealous. I'd give a lot to have Avery Rex knocking on my door."

"I can't control the desires of others, but he'd probably have better luck knocking on your door."

"That's a shame. He's the whole package—burly, brainy, and kind."

"I'm not immune to his charms, but he and I failed to come to terms," Sil offered without apology.

She gave him a hard look, then sighed. "Doesn't matter, I guess." She held up her left hand, and from metal stubs slid long, needle-like fingers. "Between this and the eye, there's no chance of anything between me and gorgeous Avery Rex."

"I'm sorry," Sil said gently. "I noticed how the cyborgs are segregated, but are the contracted workers also segregated?"

Ser Reyes sighed abruptly, as if leaving behind a daydream. "Yes. Once workers form spousal contracts, they're moved to larger quarters."

"In an area with a school? The shuttle pilot mentioned

something about schools and clinics."

"One school, it teaches us how to be good workers. That's a little unfair, my education is comparable to other colonies, Black Thunder has no use for under-educated employees. We learn all the latest techniques for the jobs we are groomed for. After the accident that maimed me—killed four others—I didn't have a say in what sort of cybernetic implants I'd get; Banook decided to upgrade the spectroscope... the machines used to grade diamonds."

"Only one school?"

She shrugged. "One for general education for the younger students, one for higher, specialized education. Fertility rates are low out here."

Sil didn't say anything, but he couldn't imagine what would be so different out here from Mars or Luna. Certainly there were no fertility problems there. Instead he nodded.

"I'm not telling you any secrets," she said bluntly.

"I'm not asking for any. Just trying to get my bearings."

"You could have asked Avery Rex," she suggested. "Heard you were standing in your doorway, all pretty and lonely looking."

"Ah." Sil smiled pleasantly. He didn't care to talk about his personal affairs under the best of circumstance. In the face of her self-confessed jealousy, he particularly preferred to change the subject. "Avery mentioned that sometimes management brings in unlicensed flowers for the workers as can't afford the legal flower shops."

Again she didn't answer right away, but sat down, clasping her hands in front of her. Staring down at her hands, she said quietly, "Unlicensed flowers are a way for people to... express themselves in ways they can't with free citizens. They... it's a distasteful practice, and we tend to view them as less than human. Less, even, than cyborgs."

Sil leaned back. "So you don't want to know where they came

from, what choices they had, who they were before?"

"No," she said shortly. "I think it's time you left, Ser."

"Yes," he agreed, his own voice a bit frosty. "It is. Give you good day, Ser."

~ * ~

Sil did a little further investigating into the town, checking out the school, the contracted spouse quarters and the hospital. He wondered if the cyborg implants were done there. Seemed unlikely, given the colony's safety record. The dead were, as on most colonies, incinerated and recycled, so he could see how a company town like this would consider that a debt repaid.

EIGHT

"I would have invited you sooner, Ser Tation, but I thought I'd let you get settled first," Banook said with a warm smile that didn't quite reach his eyes.

Sil returned it with a lazy smile of his own. "Most kind of you, Ser. I was a bit hesitant to accept, having learned of the obligation incurred from sharing a meal." He noted he now rated a Ser himself. Banook lived in the other side of the habitation, with the contracted couples and upper level employees. The suite set aside for the mine manager, currently Banook, consisted of three rooms, one for sleeping, one for entertaining, and a kitchen dining combination that could accommodate easily ten people for dinner. The rooms were almost obscenely large, not just by Black Thunder standards.

"The bounty of my table is without obligation. Tonight we are but two souls in the solar system, sharing the bonhomie of a fine meal. What did you say you do, back on the Moon?"

"I'm in acquisitions. I'm very good at it. But the outer colonies are an untapped resource, for anyone other than Earth's contracted companies, and it seemed like there must be enough booty out here for a few free lance operations, something on the side." Sil figured that Carlton Banook would not be cozying up to him with no overture on his behalf unless he had an idea of how to make money using Sil in some way. He rather liked the idea that Banook might think to use him. It certainly would make his task easier.

"I think you're right, and I appreciate that you've come in person to investigate the possibilities, but I think you've seen by now that Black Thunder already profits in areas companies normally wouldn't by virtue of a trade monopoly they won't give up without a fight. You know it was Europa and Titan behind the formation of the Colonial Union."

Sil nodded. "All the more interesting as Earth still is a strong supporter of the outer colonies, and the inner colonies —not so much." Which wasn't quite true, but it fed into the general specialness everyone on Titan seemed to feel. Banook seemed to have bought into it, himself, now that he was a permanent resident.

"Jealousy, that's what. But that's for others to fight about; you and me, we aren't going to solve the solar system's problems over dinner." He gestured toward the table. "I'm paying one of the mine workers extra to serve for us, so we can pretend we're in a restaurant somewhere a little more luxurious."

"Most generous," Sil murmured, as if he thought Banook meant to imply they were having a date. He took his seat and folded his hands demurely on his lap, eyes on the table. It was laid with a crisp white tablecloth of plant fibre textile, very expensive. The flatware gleamed as only real silver could. The glassware was delicately thin. Sil met Banook's gaze with an impish smile. "No candles?"

He was rewarded with a scowl, but he didn't apologize. He would rather cut off his arms and legs than have sex with Banook, but flirting came naturally to him, and the more Banook disliked it, the easier it came. "Acquisitions, hmm?" But he said no more, only signalled the person he'd paid to serve.

The food was quality, but the preparation left something to be desired. Sil imagined that the cook was quite unused to preparing this sort of food. So he gave nothing but praise for the meal, understanding that Banook was wooing him, in a non-romantic way. This was going to be far more interesting than he'd thought. After dinner, he followed Banook to the other room and relaxed into a large stuffed chair. "I talked to a bead maker today. So there is at least one free enterprise on Black Thunder."

Banook snorted and passed Sil a glass with a round bowl, partially filled with an amber liquid. "It's imported brandy, Venusian. And make no mistake, we charge the bead makers a stiff annual licensing fee. Yes, they hover around zero debt, but never make enough to help out family members or loved ones, or heavens forbid, leave."

"Ah. So the only way to make money out here is to have something worthwhile to sell to the company."

"And," Banook said expansively, "our trade agreements with Earth mean you still can't charge us what you could charge on say Mars."

"But I'm not from Earth, and if I come up with something to sell that isn't from Earth, do those agreements still apply?"

Banook leaned forward, his expression intense. "You have something?"

Sil smiled. "Sadly, no. Tell me if you please, are the other colonies on Titan run similarly to Black Thunder? I understand OPG Refineries has dozens of colonies?"

Banook nodded. "We take care of our own, out here. There are inter-company parties and such so the employees can meet and mingle their DNA. More brandy?"

Sil accepted and let his host guide the conversation. He was inclined to gripe about how the Colonial Union had lost its way and was becoming a tool of the inner colonies, and so forth. From Sil's perspective, the Union represented collective bargaining power between Earth and all the colonies, which over the course of two hundred years had grown less dependent on Earth and more resentful of its assumption of rights over the fruit of the colonists' labours. Sil had no stake in how all that wrangling worked out; he paid attention to know where corruption was most likely to be rife.

As the night drew on, Banook dismissed the worker he'd hired to serve, and finally said, "It has been a pleasure conversing with you, Ser Tation." Sil thought he heard a note of respect, previously missing, but merely inclined his head as if to agree. Personally, he'd found it all a bit tedious, but necessary.

~ * ~

Over the next month, Sil proposed any number of plausible ideas to Banook, using the opportunities to drink his liquor and eat his food, saving himself money while demonstrating his bonhomie. Soon he was being invited just for the pleasure of his company, which was going along nicely. Three years on Imbrium, he'd heard plenty of stories of corporate swindling and these he doled out sparingly and in a manner suggestive that he'd been the swindler. "You seem very young to have been so clever," Carlton remarked one night.

"My father's company," Sil replied blithely, without hesitation. "I've been working for him since I was old enough to run errands. Started officially in acquisitions, which is my true calling, I think. But he had the ill manners to die of some air scrubber mutated pollen or somesuch."

"Parents," Carlton agreed sympathetically. "Can never count on 'em."

"I'll drink to that."

They clinked fine glasses of Venusian brandy and Sil decided it was time to make his proposal.

~ * ~

"Nevertheless, your hasty departure from Imbrium does not bode well for you."

The messages from Detective Delaney in Imbrium were terse and revealed little, so Sil made it a point to reply with a video, doing his best to look bed-ready. If one had to engage in cryptic long distance communications, one might as well have fun with it. To that end, he slipped into bed, arranging the task light to pick out his best features, and pulled the sheet haphazardly around him. He wasn't naked, but he wanted to create the impression. He grinned; he did so like to flirt with the uninterested. It was like risk-free practice. "Detective Delaney," he said, "What a pleasure to hear from you. I most deeply regret deceiving you as to my travel plans, but I had urgent business to attend. Since I had nothing to do with the matter you're investigating, I saw no harm in a little fib." He pouted briefly, not wanting to lay it on too thick. "I do so love to hear your voice, though, so I am not too sorry." He winked and sent the message.

~ * ~

Grace Reyes opened her door and drooped in exaggerated exhaustion as she saw, to her complete lack of surprise, Silver Tation. "Look, Ser. I am not interested in having sex with you."

His eyes widened in astonishment and he said, "I'm not interested in having sex with you, either, my dear."

"Then why do you keep coming around?" she demanded, frustrated. Seeing him reminded her all the more that she didn't have Avery Rex and never would.

"Just because I don't want sex doesn't mean I don't want to use you."

Her jaw dropped, and she closed her gaping mouth so fast she nearly bit her own tongue. She stared at him. And a choked snicker escaped her throat as she gestured him in. "I hope you're not that honest to everyone."

"I'm as honest as I need to be. When it comes to engaging a person's help, I prefer to lay it out straight, rather than trick them."

"Is that what you were planning? To trick me into helping?"

Silver Tation smiled. "Never." He sat down on her bench, looking like an elegant swan in a vulture nest. "I'm a criminal, I came to Black Thunder to make money."

She laughed harshly. "Wasted your trip, Tation. Didn't anybody tell you how it works out here? The company owns us, all of us, not just the cyborgs. Nobody's got anything to make criminal money off."

"Carlton Banook does."

Grace went very still. She turned to busy herself with pouring some of the liquor he'd brought with him last time into two clean glasses. "Your other best friend?"

"Now him, I'm not honest with at all," he said, and she could hear the smile in his voice.

"And Avery Rex?" she asked, turning around.

"I haven't told him everything, but everything I have told him is true." Tation accepted the glass and sniffed the contents appreciatively. "I like your drinking habits."

Again, his words drew a snort of laughter from her, almost against her will. "You're cute, Silver Tation."

He grinned at her. "Sometimes it's the only thing keeps me alive."

"I'm sure." She sat down, all serious now. "I'm not saying I'll help. There's repercussions in Black Thunder for the slightest of offences. This conversation could—"

"No," he said. "Visiting you is just one of my quirky habits, tolerated by everyone because of Avery's fondness for me. Nothing unusual about it. Just as folk have come to tolerate my friendship with Banook. Avery Rex has been useful in ways I never anticipated."

"So you're using him?"

"Not in any sense that will hurt him. I told you true, my dear; I've been honest with him. The tolerance extended me by his goodwill is an unexpected perk."

Grace wanted to argue, but she knew it was only out of jealousy. "You could at least pretend you didn't like his attention, around me."

"When I've just agreed to be honest with you?"

She didn't try to fight the laugh this time. "All right, lay it on me, Silver Tation."

Sil laid out an impressively detailed plan, and asked, "Will you help?"

"I like it," she admitted, "except for one thing. You go twirling off into the starry sky and Banook's going to be looking for someone to blame. Who do you think that will be?"

"He won't, I can promise you that."

She gave him a hard look, a silent demand to explain. One he ignored, waiting calmly for her response. She shook her head, giving in for now. "What's in it for me? Sure even supposing you're right, Banook gets fired. The new boss is the same as the old boss, maybe even worse. Better the devil you know, right?"

Tation leaned back, arms spread wide. "What do you want?"

"I want my freedom. I want off this frozen rock. Is my help worth that?" She crossed her arms belligerently, waiting for him to try to bargain her down, explain it was too much.

He tilted his head slightly and a smile spread slowly across his face. "Done."

She blinked. "Wait, you mean that's it? Just like that?"

He stood up, chucked her under the chin. "Have faith, my dear."

In him? Could she?

NINE

"I've been in Black Thunder long enough, I think, to have figured out a few things."

"Indeed," Banook said amiably. "Like how to seduce my day shift manager and my stone grader, at the same time?"

Sil smiled and said modestly, "It's a gift." He was leaning back on a bench seat in Banook's entertainment space, hands behind his head, one ankle resting on his knee. He'd become familiar enough with Banook's spacious accommodations to know there was a safe behind the reproduction art hanging over his head. He had even a chance to look at it, allowing him to determine it was an easy crack. Banook supposedly paid various workers extra to tidy up after him, and they came and went on a regular schedule. He was seen often enough coming and going that no one would remark on it. He focused his thoughts. "I imagine you have a number of stones from the processing floor that never made it the grading room?"

Banook set his drink down carefully on the table and gave Sil a steady look. "That would be illegal."

"Oh, only if you get caught." Sil winked. "Have you been able to find a buyer?"

Banook sighed. "Management comes from corporate office, you know. Black Thunder moved corporate to the Moon, to avoid the Earth gravity problem."

Sil nodded. Most of the colonies had a less-than Earth gravity, and technically all colonists were required to perform a specific daily exercise routine to keep fit for possible return to Earth. After babies started be born, though, the colonists grew lazy on the requirement, as did Earth. Most colonists could never go to Earth, not without some serous rehab time at a LEO station. Sil considered his physical work-out to be as essential to his day as cleaning his teeth, he didn't even think about it, it was just something he did.

"As manager in training, I got to do a lot of travelling, schmoozing clients and so forth. Titan has a lot more... freedom in certain areas of human rights than some other colonies," he paused to gauge Sil's reaction.

Sil just nodded encouragingly. It was nice to hear someone actually admit it out loud.

"Certain opportunities existed within that freedom, that now, having taken over the big office, don't."

"So... no." Sil said, with a grin. "I think I can help."

"For true," Banook said, his tone disbelieving. "And what would be your benefit?"

Sil gave him a mildly put upon look. "Nothing comes for free, my dear, but a direct sale at retail prices would surely be enough profit for us both? I have contacts..."

Banook gave him a long look. "Thirty percent."

"Fifty," Sil countered, confident.

"Like hell. Forty."

Sil sighed lightly and sipped his drink before leaning forward as if to explain something obvious to a very dull child. "You have zero percent without my contacts."

"I have the stones."

Sil laughed and sat back. "And I hope you enjoy looking at them."

Banook gave him a hard look. "This was your plan all along, wasn't it? Why'd you wait so long to spring it on me?"

Sil nodded, enjoying the assumption Banook had leapt to. Improv came naturally to him and he said with scarce any hesitation and ultimate casualness, "I couldn't come on a stranger and propose such a thing, now. Had to get to know you, know you wouldn't call the Long Arms to come for me soon as I suggested anything less than right side up."

He nodded thoughtfully. "Why don't you tag your contacts."

"I would hate to bother them, dear, unless you're full in. Fifty-fifty."

Banook stood abruptly. He drained his glass, wiped the back of his mouth. He turned to Sil, still seated and relaxed, and suddenly laughed. "Why the hell not. You make an irresistible proposition, my friend." He threw out his hand and Sil took it, rising to his feet.

"So I'm told," Sil murmured, a small smile playing about his mouth.

~ * ~

Sil resisted the urge to instigate negotiations in Imbrium immediately—between the lag and time of day, he'd get no response til morning anyway. Instead, he ran a few kilometres on the tread mill until his heart was thudding and a fine sheen of sweat covered him. Then he luxuriated in a long hot shower and, worn out, slept the sleep of the innocent.

He was glad of it in the morning, and surprised to have his breakfast, plain as it was, interrupted by a knock at the door. He pushed away from the table, threw on a robe and went to see who was calling on him. "Avery Rex!" He must have lost track of the days. He smiled and pushed the door fully aside, so Avery could get a fair look at what he was missing. "Won't you come in?"

"Invitation," Avery said, half smiling as his eyes tracked Sil from head to toe, and back, hesitating at his groin as if he could stare through the fabric. He met Sil's eyes. "A play on your name. And your game."

"A game you could win, if you play by my rules," Sil reminded him, his voice soft, his glance warm.

Avery didn't reply, devouring him with his eyes.

Sil pulled the robe tight and stepped out, leaving his door open. Avery pulled him into an embrace, considerably chaste, given the expression in his eyes, and kissed him. "I'm supposed to be seducing you, I thought."

"Consider me seduced," Sil said, "now, won't you come inside and let me...?"

Avery shuddered, his hands sliding down Sil's back to the gentle curve of his ass, pulling him close. "You come to my room," he said, his voice thick and low. "Come to my bed, pretty Silver."

Sil pressed against Avery, grinding against him. He would love to drag Avery into his room and reach some kind of satisfaction with him, even an exchange of oral, but it was Avery's decision to have it all or nothing. Black Thunder was giving Sil some quality time with his hand. He smiled against Avery's mouth. "No." He stepped back and ducked inside, about to close the door when it occurred to him— "You didn't come to share the warmth of my bed, so why did you tap on my door, sweetheart?"

"Uh..." Avery closed his eyes and took a deep breath. "Right, I, uh, wanted to talk to you."

"How disappointing," Sil murmured.

Avery took a step forward, eyes clouding over again with desire. He pulled Sil towards him, gently, and quietly, and very explicitly, told Sil what he wanted to do to him. Sil licked his lips, in agreement with most of it. "All but that last," he said.

"But that's what I want most of all," Avery protested.

"Perhaps a compromise." Sil drew his fingers down Avery's

chest and over the bulge in his trousers. "Yes?"

Avery captured his hand, brought it to his mouth. "Not surrendering yet, beautiful. But for now, can I ask you to dress and meet me in the square?"

Sil gave an exaggerated sigh. "Talk. As you wish, Avery." He mentally went through his contacts on Imbrium. Casey. Casey was andro, ze could also play male or female, if Carlton had any notions about one or another being more trustworthy. Ze had a crack memory and flawless enunciation. If anyone could pull off high end jeweller with a dark side, Casey could. He sent off a quick coded message in case Banook monitored long distance data packets. By then his trousers were again an easy fit and he dressed to meet Avery below in the square.

~ * ~

"There's some grumbling about the company you choose to keep," Avery began without preamble, not making eye contact.

Sil pretended to misunderstand. "Avery! I thought you were well-liked and respected."

Avery met his eyes with a grin. "You are adorable, Silver Tation." The smile faded. "But I must ask—are you having sex with the cyborg?"

"Her name is Grace Reyes, and not that it's anyone's business, but no, I'm not." He grinned. "I'm not her type. In fact, it's not been easy to strike up a friendship with her at all given she has an unrequited. For you."

Avery's eyes widened in surprise. "M-me? But-! She's a cyborg!"

"Darling, they didn't take her heart." Sil contemplated just how much he could confide in Avery Rex. "I need Grace's good will and her help, to pull off a job."

Avery frowned. "A job."

"I'm a criminal, dear Avery."

Avery's expression cleared and he leaned back with a broad grin.

"Well, that explains your association with Banook."

Sil appreciated that Avery immediately understood and acknowledged Banook's inherent criminality. "Yes and no. I'm not out to harm Black Thunder, to his benefit. I'm associating with Banook, as you put it, because I need him to see me as harmless."

"You sleeping with him?" Avery demanded, eyes narrow.

Sil recoiled in horror, only slightly exaggerated. "Eew. Please, my dear, not before lunch."

Avery chuckled.

"Don't laugh, you made me imagine it for the briefest of moments and now I need to bleach my mind."

"Sorry, pretty one. I am truly sorry." He reached across the table to take up one of Sil's hands. "You did just offer me a compromise up there? All but the last?"

"Interested?"

Avery smiled. "You know I am. At least tell me this isn't easy for you."

"I fortunately have very talented hands." Sil's smile slipped as something occurred to him. "Did you ask me about Grace and Banook out of jealousy?"

A hint of colour bloomed in the big man's face highlighting the planes of his cheeks. "Not entirely. People talk. The backfence is our primary entertainment. If I were to accept your compromise, put myself in the care of your, um, talented hands, people would assume..." He glanced around the square. "It's a small colony and more than a few people, uh, know me."

Sil began to chuckle. "I promise I would never let it be known you made an exception for me. But you again seem distracted?"

Avery cleared his throat, his colour still high, and looked away, still holding Sil's hand. "Right. Banook is not well liked, so to see you on such friendly terms with him makes folk suspicious. At first, it was just, you didn't know him, and then it was you accepting obligation from him..."

Sil decided to be forthright. "Thanks to you, I was aware of the obligation I might incur upon accepting his invitations, but he assured me that as persons of non-Titan origins, no obligation exists. It saves me no small amount to dine with him so often." He grinned. "I aim to take Banook down. Ser Reyes reminded me that sometimes the devil you know is better than the one you don't, which is why I haven't said so before. Maybe you and the others would rather have him than an unknown. But I'm taking him down all the same. I am aware that your fondness for me has spared me much for my sins of currying friendship with a cyborg and insinuating myself into management's favour."

Avery gave him a long look, clearly giving Sil's words consideration. "Is that why you don't just reject me outright."

Hurt by the accusation, Sil pulled his hand free. He pushed away from the table. Standing, he was for once taller than the other man. "If that is what you wish to believe, Avery."

TEN

Sil sorted through his meagre messages from Imbrium, still put out that both Avery and Grace Reyes had accused him of using Avery. He never used sex to manipulate people, not by giving it nor by withholding it. He'd been on the receiving end of a game like that. He did not like to cause pain, at least not to people who didn't deserve it. And those that deserved pain did not deserve to have sex with him.

He wasn't even able to feel pleased to see another message from Nick Delaney. He didn't like feeling this way, but there was little in Black Thunder to restore his bonhomie. Delaney asked simply if he, Silver Tation, could think of anyone might want Emun Delacroix deceased. Feeling somewhat vexed, he sent back an impatient, voice-only reply, "Isn't the lover a usual suspect? Talk to Ser Lavender. Why are you asking me to do your job for you?" After he sent it, he regretted his tone. Delaney was, presumably, doing his job... in some incomprehensible fashion.

Casey had replied with enthusiasm, and had some back up players available as well. Sil was tempted to offer them a much higher pay rate than usual, accepting a lower profit margin for the satisfaction of bringing Banook low, but they might also shy away. Anyone paying more than the going rate, usually meant the risk was greater, too. Sil spent considerable time working out exactly what he needed Casey and friends to do, from finding cargo ship schedules to be difficult in specific ways, and then some time more encoding it in a friendly, affable, harmless way.

Then he had nothing to do until dinner tonight with Carlton Banook. He put the table away and folded down the bed, laying back on the pillow, arms behind his head, moping like it was an Olympic sport.

The knock on his door was unexpected. He really only knew three people here, and as of this morning none of them had reason to visit. He considered calling out, "Go away," but couldn't quite bring himself to do it. He sighed and strode to the door, pulling it aside with a sharply voiced, "What." He stared into a riotous bouquet of blossoms, through which he could barely discern a person.

The blossoms were thrust into his arms without a word and whoever delivered them was gone. Bits of the decorative string curtain were caught up in the bouquet and Sil struggled to free it without destroying the fragile blooms, so he could close his door. He finally succeeded, and placed the blossoms carefully on the shelf with the video display unit. Cut blossoms. He'd never witnessed such wasteful extravagance. They were in a glass vase that seemed designed to hold them, and it contained some sort of fluid, possibly similar to what was used in hydroponics? He didn't know, he could only stare at them, and slowly grew aware that they had scent. This was what people meant when describing perfume as floral? It was far more delicate and pleasant.

Sil glanced toward the door, still astonished. He'd adjusted to having unlimited water, he revelled in it, but cut blossoms, were almost unheard of in the inner colonies. They had so much value as air scrubbers that to cut them merely as a gift—that was a kind of wealth so rare, even those who could afford it used it only as a grand gesture. Closer inspection showed that these had come from the personal planter boxes outside, one or two blooms from each. He supposed if that was all one took, and rarely, but even still the extravagance of the gift left him speechless. Were these from Avery? He thought sharing a meal was too much of an obligation, but he did this?

He noticed a square card stuck in the midst of the foliage and pulled it out, wary. "Sorry. A."

"Now who's obligated," he muttered. But it wasn't like he could give them back, the stems could not be put back on their roots. He would have to return the obligation, and if Avery wouldn't eat with him, then he'd just have buy the man groceries. Would anyone back on the Moon ever believe a bag of groceries would equate to a gigantic bouquet of cut blossoms? He'd have laughed himself to tears, anyone told him that.

At dinner that night, he asked Banook, just to be sure, if cut blossoms were a common thing. "Common enough, why? Oh, not in the inner colonies, I forgot. People grow their own out here for," he stopped and shrugged his shoulders, arms spread wide. "They help, of course, but they're mostly decorative. Our air recycling needs aren't as intense as the inner colonies, most of it is replaced regularly from Titan itself. In many ways, and don't go spreading this around the inner colonies," he said with a broad wink, "Titan is better than Mars for habitation."

A shame it was littered with debt bondage corporations. Sil nodded thoughtfully. "I see. Impressive."

"If we could export 'em, we would. Cut blossoms, I mean." He slid a glance to Sil, who nodded his understanding. Cut blossoms were worth more than diamonds on Mars, Venus, and the Moon.

Thinking of obligations, he looked at his plate. He'd had many dinners with Banook, finding it a way to save money. And although he and Avery had discussed it rationally, had the irrational part of Avery's brain been thinking that over a certain number of free meals must equate to some sort of intimate relations? He shuddered at the thought, visibly enough that Banook asked, "Something ails you, Tation?"

"No, sorry, just remembering a bad dream."

"I hate to interrupt a good meal with business, but did you get in touch with your contacts?"

"I did. If you like I can set you together? The lag will make face-to-faces difficult and me as an intermediary somewhat tedious. Lets call my cut an introduction fee." Sil had already worked this out with Casey; ze would send duplicates of every communication to Sil, and all delays would be quite normal. "Of course, if you could cc me the communications."

Banook smiled. "Naturally."

Sil had almost forgotten to add that last. A person like Banook would get suspicious if a person like Sil appeared too trusting.

When he returned to his room, it was dark, and relatively quiet. There were lights and music and laughter at the social gathering spot, something like a sin-club without the sex or drugs. Sil did not stop in. His mind was busy with plans.

~ * ~

Sil broke into Avery's place while he was at work. As he'd suspected, it was so easy the door might as well have been unlocked. Slipping in undetected was equally easy, considering the Black Thunder backfence. He rooted through the foodstuffs Avery had on hand to get an idea of what he liked. Then, leaving the door unlocked, he slipped out like smoke and purchased some groceries.

To his mind, it barely covered a fraction of the value of the blossoms, even at Black Thunder prices, but he knew Avery wouldn't accept more. He crossed the square and climbed the stairs and at an opportune time he slipped back into Avery's place, leaving the groceries on the table and a note: "Avery ~ apology accepted. Please forgive the groceries, but what food means to you here, cut blossoms mean to me where I come from. I know you did not mean to create an obligation, but as you would feel one if you were to dine with me, so I feel one for having received such an exquisite gift; so delicate, so fragrant, so fleeting. I hope you'll also forgive how I came to leave this here, but I know you'd never accept it in front of others. It clears my obligation, I trust?" He signed it Silver.

Then all unseen, he left, locking the door carefully behind him.

~ * ~

Avery looked troubled when Sil opened the door for him. He left it open as he invited the other man in, gesturing him to sit across from where his colourful gift was displayed. "You left an awful lot of food, my place," he said eyeing the blooms.

"I know it must seem excessive, so I will try to explain," Sil said, then he stopped. "You're not asking how I got in?"

Avery looked at him and smiled. "You said you were a criminal."

Sil grinned. "Thank you." He then explained how precious plants were in the inner colonies, and the fines for damaging them, particularly the blooms, but Avery didn't seem to grasp the significance until he said it was an extravagant gesture, "between the very wealthy, and only on a grand occasion, such as a contract."

"Oh. Oh. I didn't mean..."

Sil touched his hand. "I know, but still. The food is enough?"

Avery nodded slowly. "Now I feel like I should thank you for breaking into my place. I imagine I'll hear of it soon enough."

"Don't insult me again, dear," Sil said mildly. "I am very good at what I do."

Avery shrugged. "I'll bet you..." he paused, and gave Sil a long, lustful look. "Oral."

Sil smiled; sounded like a win-win to him. "Done."

ELEVEN

"Tation, we have a problem."

Sil was sitting in Banook's office at the mine works, a place he was invited to just often enough that his visits went unremarked. He relaxed across the desk from Banook, taking in every detail of the room whilst allowing his host to feel he had all Sil's attention. "What manner of problem?"

Banook scowled. "Your contact won't work with Grace Reyes."

This wasn't news. Between Casey and Banook, he knew exactly what was going on, but he pretended otherwise. "No? But she herself told me her education was easily the equivalent of any in the solar system, and she has all the latest upgrades, built right in."

"It's not her qualifications Ser Casey doubts, it's her honesty. Ze says ze cannot trust her appraisals because of her indenture, that because I own her, she will say whatever I tell her to say." He pushed away from his desk and rose to stride over to the liquor board. "I shouldn't drink at work, but," he raised the decanter and gave Sil an enquiring look.

"No, thank you. Too early for me, but do you mind?" He pulled out his vapour stick.

Banook frowned but all he said was, "Filthy habit, that."

"We all have our vices," Sil replied mildly. "But lets ponder our problem, shall we. You have other gem graders? Surely you do not make Grace work round the clock?"

"The others work with sub-par equipment. Besides, Casey's right—she'll verify the value of the gems if only because I tell her to."

"No, the fewer people know what you're up to the better. Best leave her in the dark and thinking it's a legit customer." Sil sucked on the empty vapour stick, frowning as if deep in thought. "You could leave the gem grading up to my people."

Banook snorted. "I don't think so. As it is, I'm trusting you and your pal Casey to be square on the selling price. I'm not going to give you a chance to have your paid grader undervalue my diamonds so you can pretend to have sold them for less."

Sil grinned as if he'd been trying to do just that. "Fair enough." He let his grin fade into contemplative silence, tapping his temple lightly with the vapour stick. "What if," he said slowly, "you paid her indenture?"

Carlton Banook coughed on his liquor and set his glass down hard, wiping at his mouth with his sleeve. "Like hell!" Banook stared at him like he was light in the head. "I think that's a worse idea than letting your people do the grading!"

Sil blinked, as if coming out of thoughts. "Show Casey the paperwork, then rescind it later. Call it... oh, an accounting error or somesuch." He shrugged. "I'm open to your solutions, dear Carlton."

Banook downed his drink in one swallow and slammed his glass to his desk. His brow was furrowed, his mouth turned down and looked a fair storm. "Grace Reyes has top of the line equipment, her appraisals get us top dollar. You understand that since we're splitting the profits fifty-fifty, I want the highest appraisal."

Sil shrugged again. "Fifty percent of something is better than nothing, but again, it's up to you."

There was a pause into which no one spoke, then Banook sighed. "Rescind the paperwork, hmm? A filing mistake?"

"Training a new assistant?"

"Hmpf. That's going to take some time, getting the paperwork processed."

"Ever wonder why they call it paperwork? I mean, have you ever even seen paper?" Sil rubbed his chin as he offered this musing, before allowing his concentration to sharpen. "As for time, my dear—how long have you waited already? Is another week or two really going to matter?"

~ * ~

Carlton Banook, Grace Reyes, and Avery Rex all worked the same shift, so it made spending time with them a bit of a juggling act; having all day to himself to plot and consult and ponder the baffling messages from Nick Delaney—just what sort of mess would he be walking into, once he was done here on Titan?—he then had to decide if he wanted to eat Banook's food, snog with Avery (and win his bet), or confer with Grace Reyes, all of which felt equally important. And he had a purchase to make. That, at least, was straight forward and he took the time to cover his digital tracks. He had no idea if Banook could monitor communications that left Titan, but he wasn't willing to risk it.

He'd seen Banook at the office, so a dinner invitation wasn't likely forthcoming. Avery needed time to confirm with the backfence that nobody had spotted anyone breaking into his room, so tonight he needed to talk to Grace.

"Banook is starting your paperwork." Sil said without preamble as he entered Grace's domicile.

She gave him a wary look but accepted the small bottle of Shoots he'd brought with him. "You're lying."

73

Sil reached into his tunic, one of the many pockets, and pulled out the print out of his earlier purchase. He passed it to her.

She unfolded it and read it with disbelief etched on her face. "A one way ticket to Earth. I can't afford this."

"Oh don't worry about the cost. Ser Banook will reimburse me," Sil assured her.

"And why would he do that?"

"Not willingly, of course, but he will all the same. Trust me, my dear, I'm not one to take heavy out-of-pocket expenses lightly." He gestured toward the ticket. "You want to keep that, or would you rather I hung onto it until we're ready?"

She read it again. "It says the ship will be leaving Titan's distribution station in two weeks, will..." she hesitated and slowly met his eyes. "Will...?"

"He's already started the process to clear your indenture," Sil said, irrationally pleased to see the glint of hope in her pretty green eye. He wasn't in business to help people, it was seldom profitable. That said, if he was able to, he'd like to have every indentured cyborg freed, and all the debt of the Titan colonists wiped out. He did not like slavery of any sort, not even the legal kind. But it was a problem for someone else to solve. "You mustn't show any knowledge of it, my dear. I only tell you because we've little enough time and I thought if you truly intend to leave here, you might want to put your affairs in order, say what goodbyes you need to."

Bitterness closed over her face again as she looked down. "Won't take long." She handed the ticket to him. "You hold it."

"I will need you to use your access codes to give me egress to the mine works, so it's not like it's a gift," Sil reminded, putting the ticket back in his pocket.

"That's dangerous for me, if your plan goes awry."

"It is," he agreed, "but surely you didn't think your freedom would come cheap?"

A wry smile twisted her mouth. "I suppose not."

And because he couldn't visit Grace Reyes without her mentioning him at least once, she finally said, "I hear Avery Rex is telling people you're playing hard to get."

"Outrageous," Sil said, taken aback. "I most certainly am not!"

"Not playing? Or not hard to get?" Her mouth was almost smiling and there was a hint of teasing in her voice. Perhaps she was getting over her unrequited feelings for Rex.

"Neither," he said, frowning. "I don't play games when it comes to sex. Too much pleasure to be lost that way. And I am certainly not hard to get! I will have to have a talk with Avery."

~ * ~

Avery Rex was waiting outside Sil's room when he got there. He smiled warmly at Sil and grasped his shoulders while lowering his head for a kiss. Sil returned it before saying, "Avery, darling—we need to talk. Won't you come inside?"

Avery gave him a quizzical smile. "Talk? Speaking of talk, there is none regarding any person going into or out of my room."

Sil nodded, and pushed aside the curtain Avery had given him as a gift, causing the door to slide open. He let the beaded strands of cellulose rope fall over them, partially obscuring them. "Of course not, darling. I'm a professional. And while I'm desperately eager to collect my winnings, I hear you're telling folk I'm playing hard to get."

"Aren't you?" Avery smiled, cupping Sil's jaw in his palm.

Sil shook his head. "I don't play those games. You know what it takes to get in my bed, Avery—you could have been there the very night we discussed terms. It's your stubbornness keeps you out, not any game of mine."

"My stubbornness?" Avery said, voice raising in surprise. "No more than yours!"

"And you don't hear me telling people *you're* playing hard to get, do you?" Sil put his arms around Avery's neck and pressed close to him, dropping light kisses on the bigger man's chin, neck, nudging his ear with his nose. "All you have to do is give in," he said softly, then stepped back with a coy smile.

Avery released Sil slowly, expelling a breath he'd been holding. "I made the bet as a way of accepting your compromise, perhaps a little. You tempt me, Silver. Tempt Tation, they should call you."

"I've heard that before," Sil murmured. "But unless you mean to pay me in public...?"

~ * ~

New message from Nick Delaney:

"Did you know that Amanda Lavender and Emun Delacroix were personally involved?"

Sil frowned. Of course he did, hadn't he told Delaney that already?

He replied in his usual garrulous fashion after deciding that it was best to pretend he had not known, and continued an effusive farewell.

TWELVE

Imbrium

Nick Delaney replayed his reply from Silver Tation and stared at all the evidence in a ring of holos surrounding his desk. Any other detective would have a charter ship on its way to Titan to arrest the young man. The evidence did not so much point at him as it lit him up with flashing neon lights. Something did not make sense, apart from Silver Tation's messages.

Tation's height. The distance from the stairs to the blood pool. But primarily, it was the lack of a solid motive that gave him an uneasy feeling this case wasn't as obvious as it appeared. He was missing something, something important. His office com buzzed. "Detective Delaney, the one known as Enrite is here to see you."

He closed the images one by one with a wave. Enrite was the local IPLE station's favourite informer. According to the officer who usually dealt with him, he knew everything there was to know about what happened on the other side of the law in Imbrium. But he'd only tell if asked the right questions. Nick didn't know if corporate embezzling would come under Enrite's purview, but it didn't hurt to ask. He was aware he was ignoring the preponderance of circumstantial evidence in hopes of finding something that might explain the bothersome discrepancies.

Enrite flopped into the chair opposite Nick's desk as if he had no bones from the neck down. "Bout time you Long Arms called me," he said.

"Is it." Nick maintained the blank look of someone who already knows what the person he's questioning is going to say.

"The hit on Delacroix, dunno what took you so." He squinted at Nick. "You're new."

"Detective Delaney, Special Cases. Tell me what you know about the hit on Emun Delacroix."

Enrite shrugged. "You know how it is, rich guy like that, his friends don't want red on their hands. Word went out few weeks before he disappeared. Dunno who answered the call but pretty sure it waddn't a local." His shrewd eyes scanned the office as if determining the net worth of the contents, with hardly any movement of his head.

Nick declined to notice. "Is that all?" he asked, his tone bored, as if he'd wasted his time.

Then Enrite's eyes widened as they focused just past Nick. "Wow, so the law finally cottoned Quicksilver, eh?"

Nick turned to see he'd forgotten to close one file, the one of the Mercury symbol found in Delacroix's safe. Quicksilver, hmm. "What do you know about Quicksilver?"

"Oh, that's gonna cost ya extra. Quicksilver ever find out anyone said anything to the Long Arms..." Enrite shuddered.

"Ze will kill you?"

"Worse. You look up Mickey Yin. He crossed Quicksilver and Quicksilver turned him into a damn hero. Couldn't get no crime cuz nobody trusted he weren't really on the side of the law and waddn't educated for legal work. Only reason he ain't starved is government love."

Nick nodded, filing that information away. "I'll do that, but you didn't answer my question."

Enrite narrowed his eyes at Nick. "You don't really know nothing, do you? Ze's a thief you ain't hearda. Quicksilver steals from them as have no use for the law; nobody gonna call you up and say, some sticky fingered creep swiped the stuff I stole, eh?" He sat up a little straighter. "Dunno what ze looks like so don't ask. Don't nobody know. But that's zir's calling card, there," he added, nodding toward the image.

Nick hesitated, then decided to play a card. "That was found in Delacroix's safe."

"Whoo! That sumbitch didn't catch no breaks a'tall, did he." He met Nick's eyes. "Quicksilver's bad luck, too, hitting a guy just before he gets himself killed. Don't spect you was meant to find that."

"You don't think Quicksilver had anything to do with Delacroix's death."

Enrite shook his head. "Nah, not Quicksilver. Leavin' bodies about is a fools game when yer innit for the credits. Brings the likes of you around. Quicksilver ain't no fool."

Which still left him looking at Silver Tation. "If Quicksilver had a vex with Delacroix, how would he have settled it, if not with death?"

Enrite frowned. "Probably wouldda taken the bastard for all his money, and tried to ruin his reputation as well. Quicksilver savours revenge, they say. I didn't say it," he added quickly, "I didn't say a word."

Nick nodded again. "So you think someone was hired to kill Delacroix— "

"I know it."

"—but not a local."

Enrite nodded. "And nothing but rumours as to who did the hiring. Most say it was a lady looking but some say an older man all stiff backed and snooty."

After Enrite had left with a chit to be filled by the front desk for his pay, Nick turned his stylus end to end and frowned into the empty space before him. If Enrite was correct, was it possible Silver Tation was in truth an assassin? As a resident of Imbrium for three years, would he not also count as a local? That seemed unlikely, but Nick knew better than to judge by appearances. And financials. In fact, it seemed more likely that if Quicksilver was the scammer, then Tation had also vexed that one. Which would explain why he'd not mentioned it. Still painted Tation with some kind of dirt, but not the kind Nick was looking for.

What had Tation said, talk to Amanda Lavender... because the lover... Nick looked at his desk, the denial of authorization to pull Lavender's financial records. Instead he tagged her. Again, she was remarkably easy to connect with. Blonde hair with blue and purple ends gave her a subdued look, and again he gushed with gratitude and apologies. "How can I help you today, detective?" Her voice was not as warm as previously.

He smiled at her. "This might sound a very foolish question, Ser, but I've been admiring your stunning taste in wigs. Might I ask where you purchase them?"

Her surprise was evident, her face went completely blank before a broad happy smile crossed her face. "Ashton's, of course, on Phobos Station. Are you planning to splurge?"

"I don't know," he said thoughtfully staring at her hair. "Do you suppose just anyone in Imbrium wears wigs from Ashton's?"

"Of course not, darling! If you decide on an Ashton's, it may well be just you and I on the whole of the moon. It's very..." she paused and gave him a condescending look before completing her thought: "exclusive."

He nodded and smiled. "You are most gracious and patient, Ser Lavender. Thank you."

If he remembered his interview with her, had he not been met at the door by a butler or somesuch who would fit Enrite's stiff-backed and snooty description? He tagged forensics. "Compare those wig fibres to the one used by a company called Ashton's, on Phobos Station."

Impatient for results and still wondering if Amanda Lavender possibly had the audacity to pull this off and the smarts to frame Silver Tation for it, he flipped his stylus end over end over end. Then he tapped his desk and opened the com. "Find me Mickey Yin."

THIRTEEN

Black Thunder

Sil released his fold away kitchen and collected one of the sealed bags he'd brought with him. Inside were his last purchases in Imbrium, several vials of various powders, including a synthetic opiate used to make a vapour stick load. Slightly against the law, in that the law existed but was seldom enforced. The other powders were all perfectly harmless, on their own. It was only now he realized he needed a heat proof glass vessel to cook them in. He tagged Avery, the first time he'd done that, as the man just lived a few doors down. "Darling, do you have a glass pot I could borrow?"

Within minutes, Avery Rex was at his door. He held out the necessary pot and grinned at Sil. "Was this a trick to lure me into your room?"

Sil grinned back. "Not at all, but since it worked, I shall have to remember to add it to my repertoire."

"What are you cooking up?" He leaned down to rest his elbows on the counter, watching as Sil measured water into the pot and carefully added precise amounts of the various powders.

"Crime," Sil answered absently. As he added the last ingredient and stirred it all together, he turned to Avery, happy for another opportunity to convince Avery to submit to him. Especially after the other night. He wasn't a sex addict and the many nights on Titan with no more companion than his hand would not normally be a problem. But with Avery approaching him almost every night, with alluring kisses, vulgar suggestions, and groping hands, it was a different matter. Avery had also paid off the bet in a delightfully spectacular manner, which left him wanting more. But before he pressed the issue, he had tell Avery he was leaving.

Fortunately, his upcoming departure was no secret to Banook. He hadn't even needed to work it into his scenario with Casey; it was simply when the passenger ship would be leaving. Casey would, Banook believed, take care of ensuring Sil received his share of profits from the sale of the illicit diamonds.

"For serious, Silver—what is that?"

"What you don't know won't trouble your sleep," Sil said lightly, leaning back slightly to look as alluring as he could. "Have you made up your mind? Give in or give up?"

Avery pushed himself upright, studying him through half closed eyes. Sil didn't mind. "You know what it's really a matter of, now?"

Sil nodded. "Black Thunder's backfence. My ship leaves in two weeks, so..." he tilted his head and licked his smiling lips. "Don't wait too long."

Avery's arm moved with astonishing speed, catching him up to a firm chest almost smotheringly tight. "Maybe you should close the door," he said softly in Sil's ear.

Sil breathed a happy sigh and obliged, double checking the timer on his cooktop as he did so. "Was it something I said?" he managed to say as he disentangled himself long enough to flip the table away and the bed down.

Avery pushed him onto the bed. "I'll regret it forever, I let you go without doing this. Folk like you don't often come along out here, pretty Silver."

They finished tossing their clothes aside and as Sil slid his hands in possessive curiosity over the unfamiliar planes of the other man's body, he said in a low voice, "You don't have to let me..."

"Still thinking about that," Avery said with a muffled chuckle. "For now, though..."

~ * ~

He used Grace Reyes' authorization codes to access the company during the day shift. He'd been there often enough as Banook's guest, no one questioned him. This was the only time of day that Banook's office was unlocked, the trick would be to find it without Banook in it. Just after lunch, according to Grace, Banook left his office to do a supervisory round of the rest of the company. That would be his window.

He checked the time on his combrace and tapped softly on the closed airlock. No reply—Banook was out. He opened the door, hating to close it behind him, but an open airlock in the safety conscious Black Thunder would raise suspicions. Foremost he needed to hide the small vial of Sleep he'd cooked up. Normally used to tip darts and induce a knock out sleep, the amount in the vial was swiftly and painlessly fatal. Overdosing on Sleep was the favoured method of suicides as the ingredients were easy to come by, though mixing them correctly could be hit or miss. He slipped the vial into the moist soil substitute at the base of an air scrubber and took the time to ensure it looked as untouched as before.

Checking his combrace again, he swiftly confirmed his guess for the location of Banook's office safe. He didn't want to risk Banook returning whilst he broke the safe, but he needed to ensure Grace's papers were in there. He needed a guaranteed delay, and tag to warn him of Banook's return. He would have to enlist Grace's further help and he really didn't like involving her. On the other hand, he'd secured her freedom so it wasn't like she didn't owe him.

No, there was no time for second guessing now. He opened the airlock door carefully, and hurried to a maintenance closet to wait until he was fair certain Banook had returned to his office.

~ * ~

"I already gave you my help," Grace said irritably, giving the pretty man in her room a resentful look. She wasn't as put out with him as she let on, but the fact that Avery Rex chose him continued to irk, if only because she had to listen to the endless salacious stories of their epic make-out sessions.

"I know, my dear, and I'm grateful. It pains me to ask you to involve yourself deeper, but I need access twice more—once to ascertain he has your papers, and then the day we leave."

She rolled her head back and extended her lenses, not because it could see anything, not this size or distance, but because it scared the hell out of people. He didn't appear to notice, meeting her gaze steadily. Hard not to like a person could do that. "You're promising me the moon."

He smiled and patted his pocket. "Earth, actually. You just have to trust me I'll deliver."

~ * ~

Carlton Banook's home safe was easy to crack, with security measures so out of date, it was a wonder he hadn't already been robbed. Sil was astonished at the records kept within—travel expenses, destinations, purchase receipts, bills of sale—what kind of lack-wit would keep such things? But it would make a lovely, incriminating display on Banook's desk. He gratefully scooped the documents and credit chips from the safe, leaving only his calling card behind. He'd thought to leave it at the office safe, but that was too close to where Banook would be found. It was a chance he

86

probably shouldn't take at all, but he couldn't resist. Grace's documentation had not been in this safe, though, so he had to assume it was in Banook's office safe.

FOURTEEN

Sil broke into Banook's office one last time, carefully laying out all the flimsies he'd found in the man's home safe documenting his human trafficking activities. They decorated the desk as nicely as he'd imagined. Now, Grace was waiting in the cargo bay with their luggage and the shuttle was loading shipments to various Black Thunder clients. It was due to leave in forty minutes. He checked his combrace and smiled. He'd timed it perfectly.

He pulled out two glasses from the small bar and selected Banook's favourite Venusian brandy. The air lock turned. Carlton Banook, returning only a minute later than expected. Sil turned to greet him with a smile. He saw Sil and looked surprised. "How the frozen hell did you get in here?"

Sil shrugged casually to indicate the irrelevance of his question. "I just came to say goodbye." He lifted the bottle of brandy. "I realize you're working, but join me in a farewell drink?"

Banook nodded, sitting on the edge of his desk, his eyes trained on Sil. "Shame you have to leave before we can celebrate our payday."

Sil smiled apologetically as he passed Banook a glass. "Well. One of us will. But lets not dwell on the past!" He raised his glass and Banook automatically copied the gesture.

Banook poured the glass of liquor down his throat, and slammed the glass down. "What did you say?"

Sil waved the question off nonchalantly. "Before I go, I want you to give me something."

"Really," Banook said dryly. "And what would that be?"

"Grace Reyes's indenture documents, the paid ones."

Banook barked a laugh. "Oh is that all?"

"No," Sil said thoughtfully. "I would also like the entire contents of your safe."

Banook narrowed his eyes, carefully scrutinizing Sil, who held nothing more dangerous than a crystal glass. "And why," he drawled, "would I do that?"

Sil smiled beatifically. "Because I poisoned your drink." He lifted his wrist and checked his combrace again. "It's painless, which is a shame, but should give us enough time to get free of your precious little hell hole."

Banook leapt to his feet, his face running through a series of expressions from disbelief to outrage before fixing itself into into familiar hard lines. "Us? You and Grace Reyes? If I'm dying then there's not much motivation for me to do as you ask, is there?"

"Only if you want to live," Sil said, raising an eyebrow. "Here's how it works, my dear. You give me the documents and all your credit chips and whatever shiny bits you've got stashed away in that safe," he pointed to place on the wall where it was inadequately hidden. "Grace and I make a departure onto that liner above, and I'll tag you with instructions on where to find a vial of the antidote, which I've already hidden in this room. You could search for it yourself, but would you find it in time? I have my doubts."

"And what's to stop me from calling IPLE on you and accusing you for the thief you are, once I've had the antidote?"

"All those flimsies there on your desk? Detailing your own very illegal activities? I have duplicates." Sil lied with a confident smile. "They will go to IPLE if you set them after me." He examined his finger nails, finger combed his hair, and said, "And if you intend to fight me for the information, I should warn you that the more you exert yourself, the faster the poison will work. That, however, is your call." He sat on the corner of the desk, in easy reach, and looked up into the now furious eyes of Carlton Banook. "So, Ser, what shall it be?"

Banook stared at his desk, every receipt, every description, all the notes he'd saved, perhaps to protect himself against blackmail. Every line of his body rigid with fury, Carlton Banook turned to open his safe. "This is not over between us, Silver Tation. I will hunt you down and you will be mine."

"That's what you said when I was seven, and I still had to come find you."

"If that's supposed to give me an a-ha moment and I suddenly feel bad—sorry. There've been a lot of seven-year-olds in my past."

"Oh, I'm sure. I don't care if you remember, the important thing is, I do. Now, hand it over, please, and remember not to exert yourself."

Banook tossed Sil a small bag, some flimsies and chips, both data and credit. "The data chips?"

"Digital copies of her paperwork," Banook said, his voice a growl between gritted teeth.

Sil nodded absently and opened the bag. "Oh Carlton," he said, his voice a caress. "You've been holding out on me." Between the stones already on their way to Casey, and these raw diamonds, he could make a tidy payday with plenty for Grace Reyes to stake a new life. He smiled warmly at the mine manager as he tucked the goods into various pockets of his tunic. "Thank you, dear Carlton. I knew that deep inside you were a reasonable man."

"Shut up and get the hell out of here, Tation. And," he added, raising a finger to point menacingly at Sil, "watch your back."

He grinned. "Always, darling. Thanks for everything, Carlton Banook."

~ * ~

Sil did not run, but neither did he waste a step. The success of his game was not yet certain. He came through the same airlock through which he'd arrived at Black Thunder and found Grace in the shadows with their luggage. "Come along, Ser Reyes, I told you he would see reason."

"And you all unarmed," she said, marvelling as she hefted her bag.

"It's a gift," he said modestly. "Our ship awaits."

Neither spoke much on the shuttle, or at the station, though Grace ran over to a view port to look down at the world she was born on. "I thought it would look... more menacing, somehow."

"It's plenty menacing," Sil said dryly, securing their small amount of luggage. He had his valise, somewhat heavier for the beads he'd purchased and the colourful curtain he'd taken from his door, as a remembrance of Avery Rex. Grace had a small bag that rattled as he picked it up. Her maintenance kit, she'd said.

Sil felt the slightest of nerves every minute of their getaway until they were aboard the liner and preparing for sleep transport. At the last possible second, he contacted Banook. "The antidote is in the air scrubber nearest the door, buried in the soil substitute." Then the technician was strapping them into their flight beds and hooking up the machinery that would keep them asleep the weeks it would take to reach Destiny, Luna.

~ * ~

Crew woke the passengers a few days before arrival to allow them to recover from the nap, catch up on any news they missed over the weeks of sleep, and prepare for any transfers. Sil was half certain a squad of Long Arms would be waiting to arrest him—his last few days on Titan had been too busy, too intense, to allow him time to worry about Detective Delaney's long silence, and the outcome of his investigation. He found Grace Reyes in the ship's lounge, staring at a wall covered in screens, showing everything from entertainments to news.

"Carlton Banook committed suicide," she said bluntly.

"How very noble of him."

She turned to meet his eyes. "They found him at his desk, all covered with evidence he was... he bought and sold people!"

"Despicable!"

"And the vial of poison still in his hand. They said it was quick and painless."

"Sadly, yes," Sil said. "Else he might have had time to destroy the evidence."

She stared at him. He returned her stare with a raised eyebrow, then felt his pocket for his vapour stick. Dropping gracefully into a chair, he put the stick between his lips. He had for the most part given it up on Titan, where it served him no purpose except with Banook. Since the stick was always empty, it hadn't been a sacrifice. He moved it to his fingers with practised ease and told Grace, "He graciously paid your debt, you're free. He sent a nice quantity of unmarked raw diamonds to a friend of mine in Imbrium. After ze takes zir cut the rest are yours, they should set you up well until you decide what you want to do."

She continued to stare. Finally she said, "And the stones you liberated from his safe?"

He shrugged.

"I could find a buyer for you. For a fee, of course."

Sil gave her a quizzical smile that spread to a grin.

EPILOGUE

"Detective Delaney of the cryptic communications," Sil said, wary. He'd not spotted any other Long Arms in the Destiny terminal, but he'd sent Grace along to find their luggage while he dealt with—he wasn't sure what he might have to deal with.

"I'm cryptic, he says. Welcome back to the Moon, Ser Tation. I must say, some interesting things have happened while you've been napping your way across the solar system."

"Do tell," he murmured, tipping his head slightly and adopting a Blissed out look. It gave him a better chance to study the handsome detective without being obvious.

"Name Quicksilver mean anything to you?"

"Afraid not," Sil said smoothly, surprised by the question.

"Funny thing, that symbol I sent you, the Mercury Solar Farm?" Sil nodded, feigning unconcern.

"Found it in Delacroix's safe."

"Who killed him, might I ask?"

"All the evidence was lined up at you. But turns out you were framed. Nearly had a charter out to Titan for you, til I broke the case. Can't talk about it, hasn't gone to trial yet."

There was something after that last word, an abruptness as if other words were behind it and cut off. Sil resisted the urge to frown, preserving his careless appearance. "Me? But how peculiar."

"Indeed. So did you know, shortly after you left Black Thunder, the company manager—Carlton Banook?—committed suicide."

"Yes, it was on the news when they woke us," Sil said. "Shocking stuff, he turned out to be involved in."

"Looks like it was bigger than just him, IPLE has ships on the way now to shut down illegal brothels all over Titan." Delaney made a face. "I don't like the whole set up out there, mind, but there's legal and there's not." He nodded toward the baggage claim area. "Don't see many cyborgs in the inner colonies."

"No," Sil agreed absently, pondering the detective's words. "If my name has been cleared in relation to Ser Delacroix, then might I ask why I am so honoured to be met by you upon my return? No," he said, putting a hand on the detective's arm and smiling warmly at him. "It's because of my video messages, yes?" He ran his other hand through his hair and winked.

Delaney rolled his eyes and shrugged off the hand. "No, it's because of a very strange coincidence. That symbol was found in Carlton Banook's safe."

"Symbol...?" Sil was all wide-eyed confusion.

"Quicksilver. What do you suppose that might mean?"

Sil shrugged and smiled lazily. "He had dealings with Mercury Solar Farm?"

Delaney's mouth opened, then closed. He frowned. "How do you know that?"

"You just told me you found their logo in his safe."

"Like we found one in Delacroix's safe," Delaney said, his words freighted with meaning.

Sil stared politely at him for a minute, but when it became obvious Delaney was waiting for him to say something, he smiled and patted the Long Arm on the back. "You are just as delightfully cryptic in person, detective. Is that all you wanted to tell me?"

Delaney's gaze bored into him rather impressively imposing, and Sil forced himself to stay loose, relaxed, and smiling in the face of it. "For now, Ser Tation."

DESTINY

"No, no, no!" Grace tossed down the sparkly bracelet in disgust. "You are the worst student! I don't even need my lenses to know those aren't real gem stones!"

Sil sighed and threw up his hands in surrender. "I'm trying, my dear."

"You certainly are." She rubbed at her eye and echoed his sigh. "Why don't you teach me something, then."

They were seated at the small table in Sil's room at the Destiny Regency. Grace slept in a smaller adjoining room, by her insistence, and the larger common space was where they broke fast and discussed plans. She was trying to teach him how to be a jewel thief, or rather, since acquiring things was something he was already rather good at, how to tell real jewels from fakes and profitable gems from useless. "This one you said was real." He pushed at a gorgeously intricate necklace on the table.

"The stones are real, the necklace is priceless. Which is the problem. I don't even need to see the marks to know that the jeweller who made that piece is Josslyn Eckabar of the TWF. I know the name means nothing to you, but the value of that piece comes from the design and craftsmanship." She fingered the

98

necklace almost reverently. "The stones are small, medium quality, nicely cut, but alone they're worth but a fraction of the value." She pushed the necklace back to him and glared. "Leaving it intact makes it impossible to fence. It's one of a kind. This," she picked up the bracelet between her thumb and forefinger, "is junk."

Sil leaned back in his chair. It irked him that he was so slow to learn this. He prided himself on having quick wits and a sharp intellect—as well as being adorably beautiful—so it seemed to him he should just have to listen to Grace once and it would all come to him, as easily as everything else.

"Maybe you're right," he finally said. He held out his hand and she let the bracelet fall into it. The stones were small and brilliant, which had made him think they might be valuable. Grace had said that fakes were usually bigger, but she didn't give him any credit for recognizing that. And why should she, really. Stealing fake jewels wouldn't benefit either of them. But if he was fooled... he smiled and dangled the bracelet in front of her. "Am I particularly daft when it comes to recognizing fake jewels or would this fool most people?"

She shrugged. "Most people would need to take it to a jeweller. I admit, by using small stones, it does look more authentic. But most jewellers could tell with little more than a cursory look that it's fake."

"Then," he said, pocketing the bijou in question and rising to his feet, "let me show you how to turn junk into profit."

There were no poor neighbourhoods in a colony. Thanks to government love, everyone had a habitat and medical care and food, if one could call government rations food. There was a stigma to receiving government love, though, which was a factor in the continuance of a criminal class. Criminals worthy of the name supported themselves. Government love housing wasn't much different from gainfully employed housing—space was always at a premium in the colonies, and only richest of the rich had anything remotely resembling spacious accommodations. Nevertheless, there were certain patterns, more desirable locations, different from colony to colony.

As Sil manoeuvred the demmar, ignoring Grace's white knuckles clutching the front panel, he wasn't looking for where the wealthy lived, he was looking for where they lunched. Aware that he was an exceptional driver, he had no idea why Grace was so nervous in demmars. He told her what she should do when they got to their destination.

She swallowed and, still hanging on for dear life, said, "I'm to convince the server to hold the bracelet collateral while I fetch some chips?"

"Your account is dry, so you can't swipe your combrace. You just got paid in chips and forgot to add them to your account or bring them with you. You'll be right back, the bracelet is just a trinket but one you're fond enough of to retrieve."

"Why?"

He glanced over at her. "Trust me."

"Eyes on the road!"

The "road" was an electronically controlled path, he couldn't leave it whether he was watching it or not. One day he would have to get her to tell him what her problem was with demmars.

While Grace was eating a delicious lunch at a kiosk fancy enough to include human servers, Sil settled for something more modest. Finishing much sooner, he used the kiosk's hygiene station to ensure his tunic hung in tidy folds and his eye liner wasn't smudged. His hair was difficult to tame at the best of times and he didn't mind—the tousled look played into his flirtatious, bed-ready persona. He swiped his combrace on the vending machine and reluctantly smoothed a hair control product on. It did look natural, but it left a sticky residue on his hands. Oh, what he did for Grace's education.

He walked out the service corridor and around behind the fancy eatery where Grace was laying down the con. This was a fiddle game, sans fiddle, of course. One of the oldest cons in the book, and the book was ancient. He resisted the urge to run his hands through his hair. He needed to look not only rich but reputable, for at least fifteen minutes.

Sil tapped his combrace as it vibrated. "I'm clear," came Grace's voice in his ear.

Smiling he made his way into the kiosk, seeing the sparkly bracelet in a jar with a few low denomination chips. A tip jar, how quaint. And how perfect. He ordered a pastry and hot coffee. This eatery catered to the executives who did business at the docks, rather than the dock workers, but that didn't extend to such delicacies as Earth bean coffee. As the human server set down his order, he said, "I couldn't help notice the diamond bracelet in the jar. A very odd place to keep such an expensive bit of bijou."

"Oh, it's not expensive," the server said. "One of our patrons was a bit absent minded earlier. Dry account and no chips. Ze left that to cover zir lunch, said it was worth more in sentiment than chips."

"Indeed? I think your patron may be mistaken. May I look at it?"

Curious, the server tipped the jar and pulled the bracelet out, holding it up for Sil, but not putting it in his outstretched palm. "I don't think, I mean, ze entrusted it to me..."

"Oh yes, of course," Sil agreed. He squinted at the bracelet. "Would you mind holding it in the light, dear? Oh. Yes. See how those stones are small, yet sparkle so brightly? That's a very valuable piece. How much does your patron owe for zir lunch?"

"Fifty."

"My, my. I'd give you a thousand for that, and consider it a bargain. Surely your patron would prefer 950 credits and zir bill paid?" Sil watched the server's face. He presented male, tidy and attractive. His service was cordial and friendly. And yet avarice appeared all the same. Hard to fault him for that, Sil was avaricious himself. Still, if the young man was willing to defraud an innocent, then he deserved to be defrauded in turn.

"I can't sell it," he said reluctantly.

"Ah, an honest man, such a pleasure to find in Destiny," Sil said, the flirtatious tone coming so naturally, he hadn't needed to even think about it. "Still if you change your mind," he smiled slowly and resisted the urge to add something even more seductive, "here's my tag." He handed over a business flimsy, with a false name, a false company, and an unconnected tag number. Sil's role in the con was done.

Now it was up to Grace to bring it home.

He met her several blocks away, near the port. It was always so busy there, two people could meet and talk and no one would notice or care. "He may truly be more honest than greedy. If so, then all's to the good. If not, he'll offer to buy the bracelet from you for more than the cost of your meal, maybe as little as a hundred. Aim for five hundred. But settle for two, if your conscience pangs you."

"I think I can handle it," she said dryly.

"Tag me and leave the channel open," Sil said, grinning. "I'd love to hear what he says."

"He could very well just be an honest, hard working slub."

"Odds are against it, my dear."

Sil found a bench near arrivals and settled in, the implant behind his ear giving him enough noise to follow Grace's movements. "Oh good, you're still here," she said. "Sorry that took a little longer than I anticipated. Banking," she said, and Sil could almost see her eye roll upwards to match her tone.

"Tell me about it," the server said.

"So here's fifty for my lunch and another twenty for being so understanding," she said.

Into the pause where the server should have said thank you and handed over the bracelet, Sil smiled, smug. People were so predictable. The only question was, what excuse would the server make? He heard the sound of the jar being tipped. "You know, my anteem would love this, she loves sparkly things. Are you sure I couldn't convince you to part with it?"

"Oh no," Grace said. "It was a gift from a friend. Well," she added, sounding embarrassed, "an ex. but still. It's a memory of better times."

"Wearing memories of your ex might be holding you back from meeting someone new. I'll give you fifty for it."

Fifty! Sil was insulted. He'd offered a thousand and this slub was only willing to hand over fifty? Whatever smidge of sympathy he might have held for the server vanished.

Grace laughed. "No, but thank you."

"Wait, what about a hundred? It's just so sparkly, my anteem would truly cherish it. And—today's her birthday and I—well," the server hesitated. "I kind of forgot to buy her something."

"I-I don't know," Grace said. "I mean, I'm sorry, and you stuck here working..."

"Two hundred."

"Um."

Sil wondered how Grace was playing this, what mannerisms she was using to demonstrate both greed and reluctance.

"Two fifty," the server said.

"Well... the ex and I had some good times..."

"Three hundred is all I can spare right now. Come on, you said it wasn't expensive. Help a fellow out? Free yourself from the past? Make a little profit at the ex's expense?"

Grace laughed. "When you put it like that. Three hundred and it's yours."

Sil tsked. He could have gotten more. But so far cyborgs were having trouble being upwardly mobile, so the best she could have done if they'd switched roles would be to pose as a buyer for someone else, which wouldn't be as effective in a game like this. He waited until he heard Grace say, "Sil?" then he gave her his location.

When she settled beside him, she said, "So I just sold a twenty-five credit bracelet for three hundred."

"And it was stolen, so minus the cost of your meal, we made two hundred and twenty five credits. You could have gotten more, my dear."

"You could've, maybe. He was starting to give me that look like maybe I knew it wasn't worthless after all. It's hard to press for a lot of money, when you're pretending the item is worthless."

"My dear Grace, you weren't pretending. It *is* worthless. All you need is practice," he said, petting her knee affectionately.

A LINE DRAWN IN QUICKSILVER

"You don't make art out of good intentions."
~Gustave Flaubert

ONE

Silver Tation was breaking fast with his assistant in the dining room of the Lunar Lights hotel when the name Amanda Lavender caught his attention. It had taken two years for her to come to trial and a guilty verdict to be rendered, but that was almost a month ago. "Are they still talking about that?" He glanced up at the ubiquitous billboards.

"You can thank Val Lee for the publicity. He's been keen to distance himself from her, and showcasing her depravity shows he's not partial." Grace Reyes drizzled sweet golden syrup on the last of her strawberries with exquisite precision.

"I'll add him to my list of people to 'thank', but it's not inconvenient enough to make the top of the list." Val Lee's choice to broadcast snippets of the trial was only an inconvenience because Ingle Addison, attorney for the defence, had insisted on smearing Sil's name.

As for Ser Addison, Sil had already set in motion his revenge. The attorney lived right here in Terrebonne, Luna, and although ze'd thrown Silver Tation's name out as the true perpetrator of the murder Amanda Lavender had committed, ze'd never met Sil. Which worked out very well for Sil, very well indeed.

"Speaking of priorities, how much longer until you finishing fleecing the good Ser Addison?" Grace asked before lifting a strawberry to her mouth with slender metal fingers.

"Not so very long, my dear. Two weeks at the most, they call it a long con for reason." He looked at the empty plate before him. "Didn't I have some scrambled egg left..?"

"Mmm," she said, as much of an admission of egg theft as he was likely to get. "What I mean to say, boss—we were in the pretty until you needed that outrageous sum for the convincer and I thought ze'd be convinced by now." She gestured at the nearly empty plates spread across the table. "I love living this way, but we'll be on government love, soon."

"Everything will be fine," he said with a careless wave of his hand. He didn't normally let his accounts get so thin, but Addison had proved difficult without a convincer; a hefty return on his initial investment had turned the trick.

Sil had tagged a couple of trusted confidencers he'd worked with in Imbrium to help him out set up the game on Addison. He'd adopted the persona of one of his aliases, Sealfor Argent. Ser Argent was a serious, but friendly businessperson with a ready smile and a unique investment opportunity.

Terraforming research was big business on the Moon,

primarily Imbrium. Sil's fake company had discovered, he informed Addison in the utmost of confidence, the secret to rapidly creating atmosphere. It was so revolutionary, Silberbestek Terraforming needed their own facility to prove they weren't basing it on the work of other companies. Silberbestek was without doubt the future of the Moon and Mars. Addison had been more than eager to invest.

"I applaud your optimism, but 'two weeks at the most' is a good week beyond our budget," said Grace.

"I've not been spending money on flowers," he offered. "Playing with the lovely Vincent is saving me all manner of money. You worry too much."

"That's what you pay me for, at least for a few more days," she grumbled before lifting another strawberry to her mouth. "If you were paying flowers, we'd have had this talk weeks ago. Your romance with Vincent Montrose was supposed to result in work. For pay," she added, pointing a sticky finger at him.

"Have you seen the adverts for the Milky Way Arts Festival at Phobos Station?"

She gave him a long, deliberate stare as she carefully wiped her fingers clean. "Who hasn't? But what does an arts festival have to do with anything?" She pushed aside her plate and crossed her arms on the table.

"Colonial Insurance is sending dear Vincent along to keep an eye on things. Or to reassure people. Something like that."

"And?"

"And he's taking us with him," Sil said smugly. "As consultants, or somesuch. Really, just to be there in case any valuable art goes missing. Ideally, something will." Then Sil could find it as a freelance insurance recovery agent.

Grace pressed the cart call button and started stacking their dishes. "We're not going to be responsible for any art going missing? My contacts deal strictly in gems."

"No, no, entirely not my intent. But it would take care of our living expenses for a couple of weeks until this investment scheme I've lured Addison into happens to fail spectacularly. And there will be plenty of people there with more money than they rightly know what to do with. We might manage some amusements for pocket credits."

"I'd have thought you wouldn't find a warm welcome on Phobos Station." Grace loaded the hotel service cart, and gave him an expectant look as it rolled away.

"The Lavender family might own a goodly portion of the station, but they don't know my face. Besides, the festival will be held in the conference hall. Completely self-contained, entirely risk free." The bays once used to construct and transport various pieces of Martian architecture had been converted to rental space, complete with cafeterias and dorm style rooms in addition to the usual conference facilities. It even had its own docking bay, so as not to trouble the station's permanent residents.

"I suppose three weeks of paid accommodation and meals would cover us until you can deliver the coup de grace to Ser Addison," she admitted, not looking particularly happy.

~ * ~

Sil and Grace disembarked into the chaos that was the Phobos Conference docking bay. What ought to have been well-organized was a noisy crowd as several ships disgorged their passengers at once. Personnel in bright green, raglan-sleeved blouses seemed to be trying their best to sort it out. Grace held tight to Sil's elbow as he deftly navigated through the sea of people to another green-garbed person, armed with a stack of flimsies. A festival guide, she hoped.

"Pardon me," Sil said. "Where might I find room assignments?"

As consultants for Colonial Insurance, they were booked for

the full three weeks of the festival. Most visitors, as Grace understood, purchased tickets in three day blocks, which would ensure a steady stream of new faces to amuse Sil, should Vincent Montrose prove an insufficient distraction.

The person Sil queried gave him a harried smile. "What name, please, Ser?"

"Silver Tation, and my assistant, Grace Reyes."

Ze gave Grace a double-take, staring at the metal plate covering the lenses that replaced her left eye. With a slight flush, ze blinked, eyes tracking from side to side as ze accessed a database via the unnaturally green contacts. "I don't have either name listed." Ze gave Grace a disapproving glance from eye plate to her metal fingers on Sil's sleeve, as if she was the reason ze couldn't find their names.

Grace had grown used to the greater acceptance of her mechanical parts in the inner colonies, but as indentures were ripped up on Titan under the new regs, more and more cyborgs were making their way sunward. They came with other Titanese, newly freed from the debt bondage system, with all their anti-cyborg prejudices intact, and finding new ground for them. She didn't like it, but she could live with it.

She could see by the slight tightening of Sil's mouth he was not amused. "Perhaps we are under Colonial Insurance," Sil suggested, his voice still affable.

Zir eyes tracked again on unseen data and ze offered another smile. "Sorry, Ser. Is there any other name you might be listed under?"

"Try Vincent Montrose," Grace suggested, ignoring Sil's astonished look.

"Ah. Montrose, Vincent, yes, Ser Tation, Ser Montrose is expecting you. Room 220, wing four, level two. Ser Reyes, your room is 221, also wing four, level two. Do you need a map?" Ze brandished one of the printed flimsies.

"Thank you, Ser." Sil took the map and they eased through the crowd to join those waiting for the lifts.

"Ser Montrose is expecting you, Sil," she mocked.

"I wonder if he's waiting to ambush me in my room," he said, turning the flimsy in his hands to determine the orientation.

Grace stifled a laugh. "It amazes me how utterly naïve you are, sometimes."

~ * ~

A dozen people spilled out of the lift with Sil and Grace into a large vestibule that, aside from a pair of lifts, contained a multi-unit hygiene station and a chute marked Lost and Found. Five corridors led away from the lifts in spoke-like fashion. A sign on the wall indicated their wing was the first hall to their left. But Sil fussed with his tunic until they were alone, then opened the Lost and Found chute. "Nobody carries anything of value in their pockets anymore," he complained, dropping an assortment of items down the opening.

"You picked pockets while on the lift?" Grace's mouth twitched as she tried not to smile.

"Just keeping in practice," he said, all wide-eyed innocence. He inclined his head toward the proper passageway. "Shall we?" He indicated she should lead, but he fell in beside her. "I feel I should apologize for that andro's behaviour."

"Don't be silly. A few askance looks are the least of the reactions I'm used to getting. There," she pointed. "Two twenty and two twenty-one, right across the hall from each other." She pushed at the door and as it slid open, the keypad lit up with instructions on how to key in her code. "Have fun," she told him with a sly grin as she closed the door behind her.

Shaking his head, he tried to slide open the door to 220, but it was already locked. Either someone had taken it by mistake, or... Vincent Montrose awaited him within. He didn't entirely mind—

he was a lovely man with an exuberant sexual appetite and an enthusiastic partner was always a joy.

Sil had sought Vincent's acquaintance in hopes of acquiring some freelance recovery work. He might pass as one of the idle rich, but it didn't take a genius to realize there was no family money in the Tation name. He needed an observable source of income to fund his lifestyle, particularly now that Detective Nick Delaney watched him so closely. He hadn't intended to romance Vincent; that had turned out to be a pleasant bonus. He knocked at the door. "Hello?"

"Silver? Is that you?" Vincent's voice. The door opened a crack, then slid all the way to reveal a luscious Vincent wearing nothing but a bit of lace over a full erection offered him an enticing smile. Sil matched his smile as he sidled into the room; he was always open to being enticed.

TWO

Sil gazed in sated appreciation at Vincent beside him. A thin sheen of sweat highlighted the lines of his body, his hair fluffed on the pillow like a damp wispy halo. His eyes were closed and his lips still bore some of the paint he'd applied prior to Sil's arrival. He loved the way his lovers looked after sex, with the artifice scraped away.

In spite of that, he hoped Vincent would wake and leave him alone soon. This was why he preferred to meet his lovers at their homes, rather than his—so he could leave when he wanted. The exception was his flowers, of course, but the wonderful thing about flowers was they knew exactly why they were present. He could and too often did pay for more time, but if he wanted to be alone, a playful slap on the ass would send them on their way with no resentment.

He wanted a chance to unpack his valise and search the room for useful compartments. He had a couple of devices that would bounce his combrace signal and foil any listening devices pointed towards the room, but he couldn't install those with Vincent here, either. No need to make him too curious. He would make dinner plans with Vincent, that should mollify him. All the included meals were at one of the two large cafeterias so there would be no question of a cozy dinner in.

He settled for finding the hygiene station and checking the water rations. Very generous for a space station. The room itself was not spacious, but it had an artful arrangement of furniture and curtains that could create a second bedroom. There was no coffee maker, of course, but Sil had expected that.

His valise contained a small coffee machine and a bag of beans, his largest concession to having "things." Without a permanent residence, his luggage had to hold everything he owned. In addition to the coffee machine, his belongings consisted of a few outfits of expensive natural fibres, a few disposable cell outfits, a gaudy curtain that served as a memento of a former lover, a few vials of harmless substances ostensibly for his vapour stick, some darts and a few small electronic bits. He mightn't unpack at all, but for the care of his more extravagant garments. When he opened the clothes cupboard, however, it was already full and an empty striped case was at the bottom.

"Mmm, you are a lovely sight to wake up to, Silver Tation," drawled a light voice.

He turned to see Vincent giving him a lascivious stare that might have made another person self-conscious. "You're not so bad yourself." He gestured toward the closet.

"Oh sorry, darling. I didn't leave you any space. I think there's another cubby somewhere by that bench seat. Did you notice it could be converted to a bed?"

"Vincent, my dear, do you mean to say we're sharing a room?" Sil kept his tone a pleasant surprise, but the idea left him displeased and more than a little alarmed, though he'd have to examine that later.

Vincent sat up, his face acquiring a sly look which Sil had come to like, under other circumstances. "It did seem terribly practical, given I had to pay for your assistant, too." He patted the bed beside him. "And you are, as mentioned, so lovely to wake up to."

Sil ignored the invitation and gathered his clothes as they talked, keeping his tone light to hide his increasing discomfort with the situation. "I'm sure the insurance company appreciates your frugality, darling. But wouldn't it be..." he groped for the right phrase or word. "...more professional to have Grace and I in a shared room, particularly if hers is laid out like this, two sleeping areas..." He stopped lest his words reveal him anything other than confident. Instead, he fastened his tunic with exaggerated attention to the clasp.

Vincent laughed. "I suppose it would depend on what profession. Dear Silver, I just thought it would be fun, the two of us, pretending to be conies? Like an extended fantasy."

Except having a live-in lover wasn't any fantasy of Sil's. "I'm sure I just need some time to adjust to the idea, my dear. Do forgive my lack of immediate enthusiasm. I've always enjoyed my own company."

Now by the door, Sil gave him another smile and, taking nothing with him but the flimsy map, he left the room.

He understood now what Grace had found so amusing. He studied the map as he retraced his steps down the hall. On this level, the second, was an orientation room, above one of the cafeterias.

The orientation room was a large open area with the appearance of being all windows. In fact, while the station was in synchronous orbit around Mars, it had its own spin to create an artificial gravity. Real windows would be quite dizzying, this close to the planet. Instead, the display showed a stationary Mars on one side, where it should intuitively be, and vast starry night on the opposite.

Every twenty-five hours the view would show a sunrise and sunset, in sync with Mars's orbit. Because of the necessary spin and lack of surrounding atmosphere, day and night were still artificially induced, which was a shame. The one thing he missed since leaving Mars was natural night and day, the sun streaming through the thick, translucent domes.

He frowned at the image of the red planet, filling a quarter of the view. He hadn't been back since he'd fled Marton's palace in Victoria. He'd landed in Destiny, Luna, just nineteen, and furious to discover Marton had hacked his account and emptied it. A one way ticket from Destiny to Phobos, without a message, but obviously from Marton, had been the sum total of his assets, apart from what he carried in his valise. He sold the ticket for half what it was worth, determined never to go back.

One day, he would have to return, resolve his past. But not today, not this year.

At the moment, there were few people here. Ships were still arriving, people settling in, and a number of Welcome events were going on elsewhere, so Sil picked a vacant horseshoe of seats and oriented the display screen towards him. He wasn't really looking at the various lists of shows, galleries, and auctions; just trying to figure out how to handle the situation with Vincent.

It shouldn't bother him. He had little worry Vincent was interested in anything long term. They were here only for three weeks, but Sil didn't find him interesting enough to spend quite that much time together. He frowned, staring at nothing as the true reason for his discomfort continued to elude him.

"Silver Tation. Why am I not surprised to see you here."

Sil's head whipped around at the familiar voice. "Detective Delaney. I am surprised to see you." He smiled. "Very pleasantly surprised."

What an absolutely perfect distraction.

He owed much to Interplanetary Law Enforcement's Detective Nick Delaney. Unfortunately, in his diligence in proving Sil innocent of murder, he'd also inadvertently stumbled across a clue to Sil's less than legal activities. His Quicksilver calling card, not meant to be seen by the eyes of the law, had been found in the deceased's safe. Fortunately, the alchemical symbol for quicksilver also happened to be the astrological symbol for Mercury, and used widely by the companies that maintained and repaired Mercury's extensive solar farms. Delaney had the intuition to connect it to Sil, but no tangible proof.

He had encountered the detective a number of times over the past two years. Delaney seemed to have developed a special interest in him. Sil sighed because it was not the same special interest he had in Delaney.

The handsome detective sat down a few seats away and gestured toward the display. "I didn't know you were inclined towards the arts. See anything you like?"

What a lovely loaded question. It was one of Sil's wishes to one day see the detective in something other than his ugly Interplanetary Law Enforcement uniform. Or just out of the uniform. Sil reined in his imagination and settled for a flirtatious flutter of eyelashes. "I'm more of a people person."

"Pack light, ready to go at a moment's notice, hmm?" Delaney suggested.

Sil let his smile vanish as if piqued, though the detective was quite correct. It *ought* to pique him, that he was so clearly seen through. "Did you upset someone, Detective? I can't imagine why one of your brilliance would be sent for what must be little more than security duty."

Delaney gave him a steady gaze from light brown eyes, but instead of answering, he said, "What do you expect to gain here, Quicksilver?"

Sil smiled. "Ooh, a pet name. I'm flattered." He fluttered his fingers against his chin. "What should I call *you*?"

Delaney sighed heavily. "Your foolish behaviour doesn't fool me. Or do you mean to tell me I won't find any of these during the festival?" He brandished a card with the Quicksilver line drawing on it.

"I don't know what you'll find, Detective, but I doubt you'll be able to link it to me. An event like this is a buffet for all manner of opportunists."

"Mmm. And how many can afford to hide in plain sight? Don't forget, I know who you are, Quicksilver. And I'll prove it. Sooner or later, you're going down."

"Hmm," Sil said, leaning close enough to rest the fingers of his hand on the detective's chest. He dragged them downward. "That does sound fun." He was fair certain the detective was bluffing.

Delaney slapped his hand away with a scowl and got to his feet. "Anything goes missing at this festival, I'll be looking at you."

"Lucky me." Sil leaned back and watched the detective walk away. He couldn't wait to tell Grace.

He tapped softly on her door, not wanting Vincent to hear.

"S'open," Grace called, and he sidled inside. She was the small table looked up and gave him a beaming smile. "How's your roommate?"

Sil's good mood faded. "Ah. That." He sat down across from her and frowned. "You know I normally don't like to get that close to a bed companion."

"Because you don't want them forming emotional attachments. Oh!" She jumped to her feet. "I have a bottle of Shoots; you want a drink?"

He nodded without looking at her. "Exactly. But," he frowned at the glass of liquor Grace set in front of him. "Vincent isn't the kind to form emotional attachments."

"Oh, Sil. He invited you along to warm his bed. Calling it a job..." her voice trailed off as Sil stared at her, horrified.

"Are you saying he's paying me—? That would make me a common swain! He paid for—!" He brow furrowed. "Paying your passage is the price of my presence in his bed?" Vincent tricked him into being an unpaid, or certainly underpaid, flower. A *swain*. Had Vincent asked him to come along without proposing it as potential business, Sil might still have made the trip, depending on his finances, but he would have known up front where things stood. Deception, coercion, that's what bothered him.

"Sil?" Grace's tone was cautious, but she refilled the glass with another two fingers of Shoots.

Sil had not come to a life of crime from a happy home. Orphaned as an infant, he was five before being adopted out to a couple on Mars. At seven, they'd sold him to Carlton Banook, purveyor of unlicensed flesh. Though he'd escaped that fate by luck more than wit, it caught up to him when he was twelve and he'd been forced to offer up his body just to survive, not his choice. Vincent's machinations were designed to give Sil no choice since the festival accommodations were booked well in advance.

"Sil?"

He realized he'd emptied the glass again and Grace was looking at him strangely. "Sorry, my dear. I just, I suppose it's been so very long since... I simply didn't see it." His fingers tightened around the glass and he resisted the urge to throw it. "Well," he said, his jaw tight, "No one forces me to their bed, not anymore."

"Anymore?"

He ignored her curiosity, made an effort to unclench his teeth. "My dear Grace, do you suppose you might help me find alternate quarters? I realize the station is most likely at capacity. "

Grace was still staring at him, and he offered her a smile, though it didn't come easily. She shook her head as if to clear it and said, "Even if we could afford it, you'd have to be in the station proper and that might not be the safest place for you. However, this room configures into two sleeping areas, if you don't mind sharing. I'm told I don't snore."

"I wouldn't want to inconvenience you, my dear."

"We can use a code; stick something to the outside of the door if one of us is inside with," she paused with a grin, "company."

Grateful for her banter, his answering smile came a little more easily. "You are a dear friend."

"It's got all you need." She jumped to her feet and began pulling apart the room. "Check out these cubbies," she said. "And this is the perfect place to make any potions we might need. There's no coffee machine, but then you knew that." She paused before asking, "What are you going to tell him?"

Sil grimaced and forced himself to remember that as distasteful as the situation was to him, Vincent would likely find his reaction extreme. "Why didn't I see it."

Grace tilted her head. "You were looking at how to use his connections."

He shook his head, aware that she was right, but not sure that absolved his own blindness.

"I already told him it was unprofessional." He recalled Vincent's saying it depended on the profession and ground his teeth. "I'll simply have to decline his generosity. Even swains enter willingly into such arrangements."

Grace opened her mouth, closed it, and opened it again. "I'm sorry, Sil. I'd have said something sooner, had I known it would upset you so." She gave him an apologetic look. "I'd suggest we leave, but we really need to watch our funds."

He dismissed her soft words with a wave of his hand. "I know, my dear. My own fault. We are here now. And if my refusal to be— to comply with Ser Montrose's desires causes us some inconvenience, well, all is not lost."

"There is more history and art on this station than has ever been gathered in one place," Grace offered, her tone cautious.

Sil remembered the other unexpected benefit and smiled then, a genuine smile. "And our favourite detective is here to watch over it."

THREE

In spite of a few more shots of liquor and the bonhomie of Grace's good company, Sil's mood faded to dark as he crossed the hall to collect his valise. He raised his hand to the door, realizing he didn't even have access to what was supposed to be his room, too. He rapped his knuckles on the door and hoped Vincent was within.

The door slid open, revealing Vincent in a short robe. He had it pulled across him for modesty, but let it fall open when he saw it was Sil. Sil didn't feel the slightest inclined to take advantage of the implied invitation. "Silver, darling, where have you been?" He pouted at him, eyes shining. "I've missed you."

He mustered a smile for him, easier than he'd thought it would be. He was, after all, very beauteous, and ignorant of Sil's feelings on the situation. "My dear Vincent, we need to talk."

He pouted again. "Talk? I hope you don't intend to do much of that."

Sil's jaw tightened and he forced himself to smile again. Usually, talk was indeed something he did little of. In this case, a talk was definitely in order.

He noticed that his valise hadn't been unpacked. Vincent either respected his privacy—doubtful under the circumstances—or expected him to remain mostly naked during their stay. The corner of his mouth twitched and he forced his expression to something neutral as Vincent draped himself artfully across the bed, leaving an inviting space for him. Sil sat at the table and laced his fingers together on the smooth surface. "You weren't being honest with me when you said you invited me here for Colonial Insurance."

He smiled slyly. "A euphemism, darling. I thought you understood I was paying for the pleasure of your company. Do you object too terribly?"

"I never saw myself as a swain," he said, keeping his voice more casual than he felt. "But it's the assumption that I didn't need to be asked, and putting me in a situation where my choices should I object are limited, that I take exception to."

Vincent sat up, still leaning on one arm to display his lean body to best advantage. "If you are as skilled at recovering stolen objects as you are in bed, I'm sure we're all feeling much the better for you being here." He stroked the bed as he spoke the word *here*, beguiling with tone and expression.

Sil was not beguiled. "I appreciate that," he said dryly. "However, let's assume Phobos Station is not as secure as you seem to think. It would be terribly unprofessional of you to offer up your... swain as a recovery agent."

"Darling, relax. This is just a different type of work. Although," he added thoughtfully, "you probably could become a licensed professional."

Sil stiffened, affronted that Vincent seemed to see the problem, whilst not seeing it at all. It wasn't a matter of the differences between a flower and a swain, it was a matter of choice and consent. And although it had been his own short-sightedness that had put him in the present situation, he would not—he could not—stay in a position into which he'd been coerced.

He took a second to marshal his anger and met Vincent's eyes, giving him a strained version of his usual ready smile. "I understand you mean to compliment me, I do. I am deeply sorry to disappoint you, Ser Montrose," he said, dropping into formality. "In spite of the expense to which you have gone, I cannot accommodate you."

Vincent Montrose rose to his feet, all seductiveness gone. "Cannot? But of course, you will, dear, dear Silver," he said, his voice hardening with each endearment. "You are paid for. Just. Like. A flower."

Sil tossed his head and offered a smile that had nothing to do with fondness. "I beg to differ, Ser. A flower would have a contract, a room of zir's own, and, if of my skill level," he said, touching his chest lightly with three fingers, "have cost considerably more. Good day, Ser." He snatched the handle of his valise and walked with stiff pride to the door.

~ * ~

"How'd it go?" Grace asked.

He shook his head. "I was offended. He was offended. He's likely thinking of some sort of revenge, though how that might manifest, I can't see. Forget it. There is a mixer tonight—a welcome to the Milky Way Arts Festival, with cocktails and unidentifiable things on crackers. Let's go grift, shall we?"

The mixer was in a room near the centre of the station. Its proximity to the core meant the gravity within was a bit light even for the colonial born and bred. "All the better for dancing," someone remarked jovially. It would also mean that alcohol would affect everyone faster.

Sil had unintentionally dressed opposite to Grace. They both wore black, as befitted a formal event, but Grace showed off her body in close fitting tights and a hip-skimming tunic that draped beautifully over her curves while Sil wore a plain, ankle-length tunic. It had the waist-deep v-neck he customarily wore, but the lower half of his torso was covered by a wide waist-wrap of patterned silk. He was not of a mind to play up his looks tonight. He made a note to limit his drinking and rely on his vapour stick to announce his choice of intoxicants. He nudged Grace in the ribs with his elbow as he spotted Detective Nick Delaney, sadly still in uniform.

She grinned at him and mouthed, *Be careful.*

He gave her a wide-eyed, *aren't I always* look in return and they went their separate ways, all smiles and light.

"...such a pleasure," Sil said with a charming smile, clasping a bejewelled hand in both of his. He excused himself with a wink to the owner, who never missed the sparkly bracelet now in Sil's deft hand. Aware of Nick Delaney's sharp watch on him, he handed it off to Grace in a well-practised move. She had a hidden compartment in her artificial arm, filled with a nifty gel designed to keep jewels all clean and sparkly. The compartment itself showed up on scanners, as all such things were legally required to do, but they had discovered—quite by accident—that the viscous cleaning gel was impossible for the average scanner to penetrate. Evidently it wasn't a well-known property of the stuff. Then again, Grace had found several uses for her mechanical parts that the manufacturers had never imagined.

He saw from the corner of his eye as Delaney approached the same person, and together they discovered the missing bracelet. Sil grimaced; he normally had hours before someone noticed their sparkly bits missing. Yet in spite of Grace's dagger sharp warning glances and the dark frown of the detective now approaching him, Sil was having some sorely needed fun.

"Let me check your pockets," Detective Delaney said, making it clear it was not a request.

Sil smiled. "There's a scanner at the door checked them as I came in the room. What do you expect to find?" But he did nothing to obstruct the detective's search, unless moving closer counted. As the Long Arm's hands roved over his torso to feel his pockets,

Sil murmured, "Shouldn't we take this to my room?"

"Shut up." Finding nothing in Sil's pockets that hadn't been in there before, Delaney stepped back. "I know it was you."

"I have no idea what you're talking about, Detective. But I do like this hands on style you've adopted. Two twenty-one."

"I beg your pardon?"

Sil smiled and flicked the corner of his mouth with his tongue. "My room number. Come by and search me any time."

"This is just a game to you, isn't it?" Delaney's frustration was clear.

Sil's exaggerated flirtation faded to genuine amusement. "It's because you understand that makes it so fun."

~ * ~

Nick Delaney found himself staring in confusion at the retreating back of Silver Tation for the second time in as many days. Since he'd first met Silver Tation, the man had been prone to cryptic comments; he should have expected as much. He knew that Tation was stealing jewellery right here, right now; and he had no idea how, or where he was stashing it. He had security poking the air scrubbers and every other conceivable hiding spot in the room every ten minutes, and nothing.

He glanced at Grace Reyes, Silver Tation's assistant, according to official records. She wore a black tunic that covered her from chin to thighs, draping in such a way as to hide very little. Her legs were wrapped in fabric too tight to hide even the ridge where her mechanical leg was attached. If her clothes even had pockets, there was no jewellery in them. She had attracted some admirers and seemed to scarce notice Tation at all.

Maybe it was indeed a game and Sil was slipping jewels from one person into another's pocket, to create a mass of confusion as people passed through the scanners at the ballroom doors.

Except no matter how many people went in and out of the

room, the scanners continued to show nothing unusual. He turned to keep watching Silver Tation and saw—thought he saw—him gently tug a necklace from the neck of a person too rich to care about her age. Nick pushed through the crowd, determined to catch the thief red-handed and ignoring the remarks and looks he drew for his rude passage. As he neared, Tation knelt and then stood, calling after the older woman. "Ser? I believe this is yours?"

He was holding it in his hand, and Nick gritted his teeth as the matron glanced down her imperious nose and suddenly smiled at Silver Tation. "Thank you, young ser. My jeweller told me that clasp repair wouldn't last. You've saved me all manner of trouble."

"Ser," Nick said after gracing Sil with a glare, "I believe this person was attempting to steal your necklace."

A frosty look descended on him. "Don't be so foolish, officer. He just returned it to me. This darling boy is no thief."

Tation gave the matron a guileless look and inclined his head. "Enjoy the Festival, Ser." After she walked away, the sweet innocence on his face was replaced by sparkling-eyed mischief as he grinned at Nick. He kissed two fingers and waved as he walked away. Nick bit back a curse and watched, furious, as Silver Tation eased through Grace's admirers to whisper in her ear.

The door opened, admitting a few late arrivals, and before it closed, Sil and a laughing Grace left. And the goddamn scanners said they took nothing with them that they hadn't come in with.

He knew his fury was compounded by the fact that he was here in the first place, acting like a glorified security guard. He hadn't expected to even be allowed on Phobos Station, after his investigation had revealed a member of one of their most celebrated families had contracted murder. He wondered how much of a "darling boy" Sil would be to that matron if she knew he was Silver Tation, whom Lavender's defence team insisted right through the guilty verdict was the true culprit.

FOUR

"You did that on purpose," Grace accused softly as they walked the moderately crowded hall away from the mixer.

"Yes," he said, trying to subdue his laughter. "You should have seen his face! I swear he wanted to hit me."

"I know the feeling," she growled. "At least tell me you didn't actually plan to steal that shitty piece of bijou?"

"No, no, the entire purpose was for the good detective to catch me red-handed being a model citizen."

"You needn't sound so pleased with yourself." They headed towards one of the cafeterias opened to accommodate the festival attendees. Although it was long past the hours of service, there were still a few people within. Meals were served on a schedule, but a couple of vending machines supplied rations and bottled water. Small food carts outside the more popular galleries sold hydroponic fruits and crisp protein snacks for those not taking advantage of the meals included with their attendance. Grace sat down at the table, her tunic falling in natural folds against the line of her body.

"I needed that diversion. You look lovely, Grace. You need not have left with me on account of Vincent's arrival." He rubbed his combrace across the vending machine to get them two bottles of water.

"I'm not used to people finding me attractive. I've had my enhancements for ten years." She opened the bottle and sipped gratefully.

"Shocking! I had no idea you were so old," Sil gasped. Then he smiled. "But in that outfit, you should hardly be surprised people look at you."

She gave him a pointed stare that affected him not at all. "The outfit doesn't hide my hand or my lovely eye plate. I would expect fetishism in a sin-club but not here. Even before the accident," she looked down as if she could see her body past the table they were sitting at, then looked at him with a wry smile. "I hadn't much time to find out if I was attractive or not. I *was* only nineteen at the time," she added, reminding him she was only five years older than his twenty-four. She paused, wondering if she should say more. Sil never spoke of his own past so she was reticent to speak of her own. "It would be a good time to retire to our room, as we know Ser Montrose is not across the hall."

She was glad Detective Delaney happened to be here, though like Sil, she found it odd a detective of his calibre was guarding works of art, regardless of their value. Playing at cat and mouse had done wonders to restore Sil's bonhomie. He was normally a difficult person to upset out of his usual amiable mood. She'd never seen him so angry, or so... vulnerable? Vulnerable and Silver Tation just did not go together. Something in the past he never spoke of had been scraped raw and she wished again she'd pointed out what had been obvious to her before they'd left Terrebonne.

"I suppose we should," he said with a small sigh. "Part of me wanted to stay but I'm not sure just what Vincent might take a mind to do." After a reflective pause, he added, "He could post my image and name on the local vidcast."

Grace frowned; that was quite egotistical, even for Sil. "I'm sure you're hardly *that* famous. Or infamous."

"Amanda Lavender is, though," he said, voice low. "In an heiress-to-half-this-station kind of way."

"Ah." She saw what he was getting at. Because of Ingle Addison's unrestrained accusations, most of Phobos Station would be happy to lynch Silver Tation as the true guilty party. Once the guilty verdict had been rendered Sil could have sued for slander, but he decided to game the attorney instead. He preferred a more personal sort of revenge. "And how are things progressing with Ser Addison?"

He beamed at her. "Very nicely. Silberbestek is kindly accepting investments from both me—that is Sealfor Argent—and Ingle Addison. Silberbestek is such a lovely name for that new terraforming start-up in Imbrium, isn't it? With a formula so secret it doesn't exist and our inside information, we're sure to take his fortune."

She grinned. "And how long until the money disappears to someplace you can access it?"

"Soon. Ser Addison kindly reinvested the money you wept over and as much again besides. When ze has no more to give, I'll have my Imbrium contacts arrange a profit destroying scandal. For now, the books are a rather lively and convincing fiction, projecting substantial returns to be paid out at the end of the month. The nice part of doing this under the Argent name is that I can move the credits much sooner to my own name, instead of the usual wait. I do love the labyrinthine digital trails I have to construct for games such as these," Sil said, his enthusiasm contagious. Then he looked abashed and added, "I apologize again for letting our situation get so dire in the meantime."

Grace shook her head, still smiling. "Life with you is never dull. We managed a few credits tonight, I think. I'd like to examine our take, figure out if it was worthwhile or just an exercise for you to tease the detective."

Sil rose to his feet, grasping his bottle in one hand as he bowed deeply to her. "Shall we, then?"

She capped her bottle, pleased to see his dramatics restored, and put her hand in the crook of his offered elbow. Though they had seen Vincent Montrose walk into the mixer, they still approached their shared room in silence, stepping lightly over the rubberized metal floor. With both sleeping areas set up, there was only the table to sit at, but they'd formed the habit of breaking fast together at whatever hotel they happened to be living in so it wasn't an imposition.

Now, he broke out the bottle of Shoots and poured two glasses while she slid her sleeve up the few centimetres necessary to reveal the cleaning compartment in her mechanical forearm. She studied the jewellery, mostly bracelets, a pair of rings and one rather nice diamond necklace. Small diamonds, but beautifully cut. "I rather expected more spectacular pieces, given the depths of the pockets present."

"This was just a mixer. The big gala at the end of the festival, that's when the high end stuff will come out," Sil said confidently.

"Hmm." She pulled off the magnetic eye plate and extended her lenses. "You really are a terrible jewel thief. Only three of these pieces are worth anything."

"So you keep telling me," he said with a sigh. "I am trying."

"You have your moments, to be sure," she said absently as she examined the diamond necklace. "These are Earth diamonds, Sil. Very nice. Small but superbly cut, perfect clarity." She looked up at him. "Did you mean for us to sell these or was this just a game with the handsome detective?"

"Wouldn't he be in a mood, they showed up in his room? No," he said with a grin, before she could answer. "Keep the good stuff, the rest you can put in the lost and found."

She nodded and extended the needle thin filaments of her left hand, prying the stones from the setting with swift, delicate efficiency. "Too bad I can't sell these here, even with new security marks." Gem marks were run through a database of stolen stones, if the marks didn't come up, they were saleable. For that reason, buyers tended to wait a few days before making an offer. Altering the marks could be done, but one needed access to the right equipment and an operator willing to look the other way. That added up to meaning most stones weren't worth the cost of reselling, which kept jewel thefts quite low. Unless, of course, one was a cyborg with such abilities built into her left hand.

She laughed to herself, astonished at how easily she'd adapted to a life of crime. In the years after her accident, she'd been treated as a machine by the mining company and a pariah by the people she'd grown up with. Yet she couldn't blame her decision to accept Sil's rather shifty ethics solely on the hurt done her. Truth was, had he not a clear sense of justice—albeit different from the law's—she'd not have been able to do it. Sil might be a con artist, a pickpocket, and a safe cracker, but he had a sense of honour to go along with it, and one of the sharpest minds she'd ever met. One day, she might even turn him into a decent jewel thief.

Sil rested his chin on his hands, watching her work. It surprised her sometimes that she wasn't sexually attracted to him. She felt she *should* be, given his virtues and the way he accepted her cyborg parts. Still, she liked men with a bit more meat and a little more seriousness. Like that detective who so often seemed to be shadowing Sil—he was a treat. Although it was far more entertaining to imagine him and Sil together.

Once the stones were free of their settings, her needle-like finger extensions retracted. She began to crush the metal links and settings into unrecognizable shapes. "We can probably sell the scrap metal. If not, I imagine there's a recycler near the docks we can use. Rather, I'll do it," she corrected, giving him a wry smile. "Our handsome detective friend is watching you far too closely."

Sil reversed his position in the chair, leaning back with his arms behind his head. "What can I say, I'm irresistible."

Grace chuckled. "I'd say in your dreams, but there is an astonishing amount of evidence that people find you charming."

"Not you, evidently," he said dryly.

She wrinkled her nose at him before giving him a smug smile. "And that's what you love about me."

FIVE

Sil woke up abruptly to a pounding on the door. He pushed through the privacy curtain and heard the garbled protests of Grace waking up as he approached the door. "Cease the wretched banging, would you," he snarled and it stopped.

"Sil?"

He glanced over his shoulder to see Grace peeking from behind her privacy curtain, looking amused.

"You're not going to answer the door naked, are you?"

"Why not? Anyone comes 'round this early..." he grumbled.

"What if it's Ser Montrose?"

She was smiling, as if it were a joke, but her point was also practical. He couldn't decide on a pout or a glare, neither of which would have any effect on Grace. He settled for stomping—also ineffective, in bare feet—back behind his privacy curtain. He pulled on his robe as the banging started again. Holding the front edges closed with one hand, he pushed the door open.

His scowl disappeared when he saw it was Detective Delaney, and his powers of speech likewise vanished in the face of the detective's amused smirk. It was, he thought, the first time he'd seen Delaney smile, and it was *beautiful*. He rubbed his jaw to

133

make sure it wasn't literally hanging open and mustered a smile. "Detective. I hadn't expected you to take me up on my invitation so soon."

Delaney sent a brief why-me glance upwards, but his smile remained. "Ser Montrose insists I arrest you, Silver Tation, for breach of contract."

Belatedly, Sil stepped aside to gesture the detective in, and he frowned as he slid the door closed. He saw the detective take in the two used beds and the cluttered table—Grace had hidden all evidence of their misdeeds—and no doubt draw the correct conclusions. He turned to face Sil and his smile faltered as Sil lifted both hands over his head, letting his robe fall open with a shy smile.

Delaney's grin turned to a scowl. "Get some damn clothes on, you fool."

Sil arched his eyebrows suggestively as he ducked behind the privacy curtain, drawing it almost closed, to pull on some trousers.

"Do sit, Detective. I was just about to start coffee," Grace said smoothly.

"Kind of you, Ser Reyes."

Sil emerged to catch a flirtatious smile on Grace's face as she invited, "Grace, if you please."

Sil sat down beside the detective. "What contract am I supposed to have broken?"

The grin returned to Delaney's face. "After you and Ser—I mean Grace—left the ballroom last night, Ser Montrose made it a point to tell anyone who'd listen that you were his, in a bought and paid-for sense, rather than a relationship sense."

Sil frowned, not sure what he wanted to say in front of the detective. He supposed it could have been worse. Vincent didn't seem nearly as creative out of bed as he was in... Sil bit the inside of his lip and realized he was making faces.

"This morning, he comes down to the security office all on

about how you've breached contract, and so forth." Delaney leaned on the table, angled toward Sil. "You're not licensed for that kind of work, are you?"

Sil had mastered his emotions on this yesterday so he was able to reply calmly, albeit without his usual smile, "Are you here to arrest me for breach of contract—which doesn't exist, of course—or for being an unlicensed flower?"

Delaney grinned. "Oh both, I'm sure. Sadly, Ser Tation, though it would please me immensely to arrest you, I know these charges are spurious."

Grace set down two steaming mugs of colonial coffee and said to Sil, "Yours will be a bit longer, that silly coffee thing is so slow."

Delaney's head lifted as he drew a breath, and Grace addressed him. "Sil's so-called coffee; he has a thing for Earth bean coffee. Smells divine, but the taste is vile bitterness."

Ignoring the byplay, Sil pouted at Delaney. "Ser? But I thought we'd gotten past formality. I've been racking my brain for an appropriate pet name for you."

The detective shook his head, his smile fading but not entirely disappearing. "Call me Nick if you must, but no pet names. Do people actually call you Silver?"

Sil resisted the urge to say caressingly, *Only my lovers,* and instead offered one simple word, "Sil."

"What ever possessed your mother to call you Silver? Is it a family name?"

"Sadly my mother died some few days after I was born, so I cannot say what she meant by it," Sil said without thinking. He'd never told anyone that. He was aware of Grace's curious look, and he wasn't sure what had motivated him to tell the truth. Then again, he suspected that Delaney had a dossier on him, so he probably knew more about Sil than he ought, anyway.

That seemed confirmed when Delaney's cheeks flushed dark and he said, "Of course, I'm sorry."

"No matter." And it wasn't. Sil poured himself a cup of coffee, enjoying the rich, bitter flavour, and said, "I think you should arrest me at breakfast."

"I'm not going to arrest you on false charges," Delaney said, and the smile he seemed unable to banish this morning returned.

Sil returned it happily, admiring the way the detective's face crinkled around his lovely brown eyes in the unusual expression. "Then indulge your fantasy of binding me and take me very publicly to whatever space they've given over for your use."

Both Delaney and Grace were looking curiously at him, but it was Grace who asked, "Why?"

"Because it will please Ser Montrose. And," he added dryly, "it will be the last pleasure he has of me."

~ * ~

But Vincent Montrose was not to be so easily satisfied at having lost his sex toy. In spite of the humiliation Sil was supposed to have endured over his public "arrest," Vincent continued to tell anyone as would listen that Sil's only skill lay in bed, and that he was a contract breaker, and not to be trusted. Which, unfortunately for Vincent, did not bother Sil in the slightest.

He was behaving, Sil thought with amusement, like a spurned lover. He went as far as attempting to have the meal tickets revoked that were part and parcel of their admission. He must have known he'd no hope of succeeding, and settled for a loud vocal protest when Sil and Grace happened to find themselves in the same cafeteria, for the same sitting. A situation Sil resolved to avoid for the duration of the festival.

By the fourth day, things had settled down. Detective Nick Delaney seemed almost amiable towards Sil, though his broad smile had never quite returned.

Sil, rather enjoying the few askance looks he received, was with Grace in a gallery devoted to twentieth century art. There were three-dimensional scale holographs of architecture from the time period, samples of furniture that pleased Sil's eye with their geometric shapes and bright colours. Mannequins wore holographic clothing that the fashionable set clustered around, while Sil found his eye following Grace's fascination with wall hangings that appeared to be artful arrangements of scrap metal.

"I suppose it's natural a cyborg would be drawn to these," she said with self-deprecation as Sil joined her to stare at the works.

"More than you might guess," said a smooth deep voice behind them.

They both turned and a tall, handsomely built man smiled warmly at Grace. Sil grinned, because Grace's green eye was wide and her mouth had parted in breathless admiration. So he listened as the ser, who introduced himself as Pierre Gamal, curator of the pieces he called *brutalist*, began to discuss the origins of the movement, and the philosophy, and all manner of things pertaining to the specific art form. Sil had slept through classes of this sort back on Mars. Grace appeared riveted, and when Sil excused himself for more entertaining pursuits, he doubted either of them noticed.

He returned to their shared room just as Vincent was leaving the one across the hall. He had a gorgeous sylph with him and Sil felt the slightest jealous pang. Not that Vincent had found a new bedmate, but that Sil hadn't found her first. She threw him a playful wink as Vincent pulled her down the hall, muttering something about Sil that was no doubt derogatory.

How unfair that a someone like Vincent should find such a companion. Of course, when Sil first met Vincent, he'd thought he was gorgeously desirable, too. He smiled to himself and decided to explore the rest of the festival again. If Ser Montrose could find such a lovely distraction, then so might he.

The possibility existed for him to leave the area set aside for the festival and its visitors but that carried other risks that might not be outweighed by such pleasures as a flower shop... but then, he couldn't afford a flower shop quite yet. He ought to pay more attention to Grace when she started in on the state of his finances, or have more profitable plan B's.

He linked his combrace to the small holo display in the room, noting a somewhat panicked message from Ser Addison. "Did the agent from Silberbestek contact you? Where are you, Ser Argent?"

Sil grinned as he began his reply; the time lag between the Moon and Mars must have upset his mark. "My dear Ser Addison, I'm on Phobos Station. You know how important terraforming is to Mars, and Silberbestek is in dire need of more investment. I'm promised a bonus on my return if I secure the funding. It's true, however, that *your* return won't be as great, but I do understand if you're reluctant to invest further. It is, as I've said, a risky venture, and best left to those whose pockets are already well-lined."

Addison might cut zir losses, or be spurred to bankrupt zirself. Sil hoped for the latter, but either way Ser Ingle Addison would pay for zir slander.

SIX

Sil strolled casually around the gallery dedicated to the old masters. He was dressed simply, vapour stick in hand, and tried not to show how interested he was in seeing these works. Some were real, crated and carefully shipped from museums on Earth for the Festival, but many were holographic projections. It was the real ones that interested him, to put his face as close as he could without setting off the proximity sensors and see brushstrokes made by human hands hundreds of years ago.

He had a small envy for the people bestowed with permission to touch the paintings, though he supposed they wore gloves and could touch only the frames. Nevertheless, he'd been curious to see some of these up close and in person since he was sixteen. Not all of the art appreciation lessons Marton had foisted on him had made him sleepy.

"Assessing the value?"

Sil felt his cheeks flush. It was, he supposed, a natural assumption that someone like him could only appreciate art as a monetary value. He pulled out a smile for Detective Delaney. "Admiring the brush strokes," he said, not expecting the detective to believe him.

"Yeah? I heard as some can tell a fake from the real thing by the brush strokes."

Sil shrugged. "I suppose that's why— " he snapped his mouth shut abruptly and he stuck his vapour stick between his lips. Why he didn't forge art, he'd been about to say, and wasn't sure if it would be taken as some sort of oblique confession of other crimes. He cut his eyes toward Nick Delaney and pulled the stick between his fingers with a practised, elegant motion.

"Why?"

Sil smiled flirtatiously at him. "Why art forgers are so often Earth-born; they have the opportunities to study the originals few in the colonies have."

"Hmm," Nick Delaney nodded, and a hint of his smile flashed before disappearing. "Any luck in securing another keeper?"

Sil accepted the teasing with good grace, rather pleased. Delaney must believe it was Montrose's slander preventing him from any crime. That he would amuse himself by admiring the art, knowing the auctions held no interest for him. As Delaney had noted, he liked to travel light.

In Sil's view, that left him a goodly number of days for potential mischief, though he'd not thought of anything *interesting* yet. Come the closing gala, he and Grace hoped to make a little fun money, using the technique they tested so well at the mixer. In the meantime, flirting with the handsome detective was also appealing.

He leaned closer to the detective and batted his eyes. "You applying?"

To his astonishment, a hint of colour darkened the brown of Delaney's cheeks. "Can't afford you," he said gruffly.

"For you, I'd be willing to trade, dear detective." He took the two steps to put him within centimetres of the other man. "Body for body," he said softly, and laughed as he strode away to meet Grace at the cafeteria for first service.

Sil was tempted to flaunt Delaney's inability to catch him by pulling off something grand but tempered by the knowledge that Delaney was no ordinary Long Arm. The man was smart, intuitive, thorough. Putting something together so quickly left a great deal of room for mistakes, mistakes he doubted Delaney would overlook. Someday, though. Someday.

He didn't even notice what was put on his tray as he went through the lines. The food was better than he'd expected. Accustomed to feeding an affluent citizenry, the ability of the locals to provide a high standard of cuisine may well have been a factor for the festival organizers.

He glanced around the cafeteria, looking for Grace. She was chatting animatedly with her new admirer. Sil smiled and sought a seat off to the side where he might observe the room. He set down the tray and realized he'd forgotten utensils.

As he turned to retrieve some, he ran straight into the luscious woman Vincent Montrose had been with the other night. She was wearing a scarlet wig today, in a conservative style, letting the colour speak for itself. She gave him a bright and flustered smile that showed off dimpled cheeks as she said, "Do forgive me, ser, I am *so*, so sorry."

Sil opened his mouth to accept her apology with a grin. Instead, he grabbed her hand where it had fallen against his side. "I'm sorry, my dear, we don't know each other well enough for that." Giving her a knowing smile, he squeezed her hand until she released whatever she'd grabbed in his pocket. He had nothing in there of value. Yet she withdrew her hand and palmed one of his cards. Slick. He didn't meet many pickpockets. So few people carried anything of value in them, it was a nigh lost art. He pretended not to notice because he rather hoped she'd tag him.

"I am so sorry," she repeated softly on exhale, staring into his eyes as if hypnotized.

He grinned again. "I'll bet you are," he offered with a wink.

Bewitchingly beautiful and clearly dangerous. Dangerous could be fun.

"Maria!"

"Oops," she said, disengaging without another attempt at his pockets. He turned to watch her walk away, and the exaggerated sway told him she knew he was watching. *Worth it*, he thought with a smirk as he fetched the sterile packet containing utensils. He wondered how attached she was to Vincent. Or for how long. Because he hadn't upset Vincent Montrose enough.

~ * ~

"Sil, you're light years away."

"Getting a little bored."

Grace gave him a warning look. "How dangerous is that likely to be? Be honest, Sil." They found themselves in the room at the same time, though Grace had told him she was there just to grab a change of clothes.

He flashed her a smile. "It had occurred to me that a grand game might a bit of fun at Nick Delaney's expense."

"Oh no. No, no, no." She shook her head. "Don't! It's not just your pretty neck, boss, it's mine too, and you are not putting it on the line for a game against one as savvy as he."

Sil gave her a fond smile, and didn't mention that he'd already come to the same conclusion. Instead, he chose to see her adamant objection as permission to get in some other sort of trouble. A certain saucy pick-pocket came to mind. "I'm glad you're enjoying Ser Gamal's company. I might have found a similar distraction."

She grinned happily, eager for the change of subject. "Indeed? Won't that put a twist in Ser Montrose's already twisted mood?"

"Quite possibly, since I seem to have taken a fancy to my replacement."

"Oh. Oh, Sil." She sighed. "You just have no sense, do you?"

He gave her a look of pure innocence. "What are your plans

tonight?"

Sil listened to Grace burble on about an auction of the metal sculptures she and Gamal had attended, thinking about that lovely little pickpocket and her bright, mischievous eyes.

"Are you even listening to me?"

"Of course, my dear," he said.

"So are you coming?"

"You know you can count on me," he said smoothly, unwilling to admit to her he had no idea what she was talking about. "Sorry, what time did you say?"

Thus Sil found himself in the gallery of twentieth century art again, standing with Grace as her inamorato and the other curators of the artifacts within gathered on a stage raised for the occasion to announce a special installation. A large white square unfurled from the ceiling and the lights dimmed. Behind them a light flashed and suddenly they were watching a grainy grayscale moving picture called a silent film.

Compared to present day technology, it was quite primitive, but considering the time period when it was made, it was impressive. Sil was amazed at how different the fashions were, how dependent on gender. He liked different pieces of them, the stark contrast of black jacket and white shirt (he guessed) worn by the men and the soft flow and low necklines of the gowns worn by the women. So many eyes were glued to the screen—fashionistas, vidcast critics, theatrical patrons—all enthralled by this piece of history.

When the short piece of film was over, there was a standing ovation as the screen retracted to the ceiling. Sil wondered cynically if they were applauding the accomplishment of their species. Not to say it wasn't astonishing and impressive in so many ways; it was his fellow attendees he doubted. Then something went around the room, even faster and more dramatic than Vincent Montrose's stories about him. The reaction of the crowd might have been an experiment in the dynamics of word-of-mouth, but then the subject of the shock became evident to Sil even before the wave of voices reached him. One of the metal wall sculptures was gone, leaving a rather obvious blank spot behind.

Coming here, Sil thought happily, was turning out to be far from disastrous, after all.

SEVEN

"It was an original William Bowie, from 1974," Pierre Gamal said, twisting his hands as he stared at the empty spot where it had hung. "One of the few pieces we could positively attribute to him. The brutalist movement was spontaneous and philosophical, many an artist put together stunning pieces without ever leaving their names behind."

Beside the dashingly handsome Ser Gamal was a beautifully arrayed androgyne, Gleb Dolan by name. Ze was also rubbing palms in distress. "I just bought it at the auction last night. I just bought it!"

Also in the group staring at the wall were Detective Nick Delaney and Colonial Insurance representative Vincent Montrose. The lovely one he knew only as Maria was clinging to Vincent's arm, all wide-eyed and staring. Amid so much beauty it was also nice to see some reassuringly average people in the guise of the Festival head of security Naveed Gilani, and Ser Dolan's personal assistant Jase Trueheart. With a name like that, Sil thought, the poor fellow ought to have been as beautiful as his boss.

Sil himself hung back, trying to keep out of Vincent Montrose's line of sight. This was the sort of thing for which he'd kept company with him, to learn of lost or stolen objects he could find for a price. This was, he'd believed, the reason Vincent paid fare for him and Grace.

At the moment he was watching Gleb Dolan and Jase Trueheart. Their hand gestures and the way they inclined their heads towards one another suggested their relationship was more than strictly business, but not necessarily public knowledge; intimate yet furtive.

"You were quick enough to insure it," Vincent Montrose said dryly. When he was not being seductive, he was a resolute businessperson.

"The transfer of insurance was standard," Jase Trueheart said with experienced calm. "The costs were all part of the auction and Ser Dolan paid promptly."

Vincent sighed deeply but made no protest.

Sil did not fidget. He ought to be approaching Vincent about finding the missing artwork. He had said he had confidence in his abilities, whatever he might have spread throughout the station. But Sil wanted to be very certain he could find it before he committed himself. If he came forward, he had to find the artwork, or his failure combined with Vincent's slander would make future recovery work for any Colonial Insurance branch unlikely.

He needed legally earned chips to hide his illegal ones; without a good cover, he would have to live in the shadows—no parties, no imported food, no sin-clubs, no flowers. What was the point of being a successful criminal if he could not openly enjoy it?

So he was patient, observant, and listened closely as Detective Delaney and Ser Gilani asked questions and compared notes. The showing of the antique film had obscured the security cams, he gathered, so that meant whoever had taken the piece had known in advance it would happen. It had to be someone involved in the installation of the artworks since this was the first night the film had been shown.

He could almost tell just by the expressions on Nick Delaney's face when the detective had reached the same conclusion. For a moment, their eyes met. Then Delaney circled behind Gleb Dolan to approach Sil. "You were watching this film thing?"

"Yes, with Grace. Fascinating not just for what it was, but all the details... sorry."

"For once, I don't think you had anything to do with this."

Amused, Sil debated over whether he should express surprise or offence. He decided to be simply curious. "Indeed?"

"I saw your face. We both know it comes down to motive and opportunity. Few had opportunity and even fewer had motive. You don't make either list."

"You're aware I was under the impression Ser Montrose paid my way so that I might find any artistic bits that might be misplaced?"

Delaney gave him a sidelong look. "So I'm supposed to believe you stole it to make him regret lying about you?" He shook his head. "You don't strike me as a petty person."

Sil blinked, because that had sounded almost like a compliment. Not certain he'd ever received one that didn't have to do with his looks or his skill as a lover, Sil wasn't sure if he should say thank you or not. He cleared his throat. "Maybe I just want fifteen percent of the insured value."

"That, I don't doubt." Delaney gave him a wry smile. "I wonder why you want me to believe you stole it."

Sil batted his eyes at the detective. "I suppose I've come to feel you suspecting me of misdeeds is part of our courtship."

He left the detective gaping.

~ * ~

Sil was convinced it was Gleb Dolan behind the theft, in spite of his obvious alibi and subsequent hand wringing. It would explain the more furtive body language between ze and zir's assistant. He was sure Nick Delaney thought so, too, though Nick would be unable to act on his intuition without evidence. Intuition, he thought with a smirk, was not admissible in a court. Unlike Nick, Sil had no legal authority to demand search rights or interview either Dolan or Trueheart, so he instead he asked himself the obvious question, assuming he was correct on the who of the matter—how did Dolan expect to smuggle it off the station?

Those metal sculptures had a heft to them, and even if the one missing was not quite forty kilograms, that was still thirty more than a passenger on any commercial ship was allowed for personal luggage. If it was to go via cargo, it would have to be inspected and cleared.

Sil went down to the port level, found a green dressed festival guide. "Pardon, ser—my assistant arrived a few hours ago with my yacht, but I'm not sure where the docking for private vessels is...?"

He found the small bay easily enough and studied the security. There were cameras and live people watching the area, checking docking clearances before allowing anyone to the yachts, the ultimate in conspicuous consumption. For now, Sil only wanted to confirm his suspicion that one of those belonged to Ser Dolan.

He approached the security kiosk with a purposeful stride. "Pardon, ser—a Ser Dolan made a purchase of me and asked my people to deliver it, but ze neglected to tell us which slip, would you mind terribly...?"

"Do you have the delivery order?"

"Oh, I already gave that to the gamins who'll be doing the lifting," Sil said with a conspiratorial wink. "I don't need to pass through. I wouldn't have come in person, but I happened to be a close by when I was tagged for directions. This is the right place is it not? Ser Dolan is docked here?"

"Yes." The guard gave him a polite mile in return, refusing to volunteer any more. It was enough. It was quite possibly his worst lie ever, yet it got him the information. A wink and a pretty smile went a long way, he supposed.

EIGHT

Sil had nearly forgotten the pretty pickpocket, but since there didn't seem much mystery behind who had stolen the artwork after all, he was pleased when she tagged him.

Grace's handsome Pierre was distracted by the theft, leaving her on her own—in their shared room. He didn't mind Grace's company, and he didn't mind the excuse it gave him to suggest Maria's invitation to drinks would be better served in her room. Were he the betting sort, he'd wager she meant to share more with him than a bit of liquor.

She met him at the door in a bright red robe, matching her wig and long fingernails. A welcoming smile curved her scarlet lips, but she said nothing as she gestured him in. *Red for danger.* Her room was smaller than the one he shared with Grace, scarce more than a table with two chairs at the end of a bed. The hygiene station and work out bench were against a wall that was likely the mirror of the room to that side. On the table was a large, unopened bottle of Shoots, and an array of berry juices for mixes, as well as a Mylar bowl of thin, crisp vegetable snacks.

"Welcome to House Maria," she said, her voice smooth and sweet. "I'm your hostess, Maria Christina."

"Silver Tation," he said, completing the introduction with a flourished bow.

She met his eyes and grinned mischievously. "Such an interesting name. Tation. Invi-tation. Flir-tation. Hmmm..." She took a chair and gestured across the table, looking up at him. "Won't you have a seat?"

"Where is the lovely Vincent tonight?" Sil asked, accepting her invitation without comment on his name. He wondered sometimes if his mother had received similar remarks. He'd never seen her image, but she must have been a beauty, too.

Maria pouted, pouring Shoots into the cups already placed on the table. "He has to work and since that artwork has been stolen he's angry. Accusing you, even." Her tone rose slightly, not a full question, but clearly curious.

Sil said, "Surely you've heard the rumours? Or were you not here when dear Vincent had me arrested...? He brought me here under false pretences, so he would accuse me of anything he could think of, I imagine." He smiled at her, noticing she did not mix any juice into her liquor. "He would not be happy to know I was here, I should think."

Vincent also likely did not know his latest lover was a pickpocket. Aware that Maria Christina was more than she seemed, he also chose not to have any juice. He was not one to be easily distracted by lust, although he worked hard at giving that appearance.

"I didn't invite you here to speak of what does or does not make Vincent Montrose happy," she said, letting her smile dimple her cheeks. She tipped half the contents of her cup down her throat and pulled her wig off, tossing it with astonishing accuracy into an open cubby. "But I confess to curiosity over what makes *you* happy."

Her natural hair was dark blonde, pinned up to fit under the wig. With deliberate motions, she removed the pins and put them in her now empty cup, the rim of which was stained from her lip paint. He'd barely sipped his and wondered if this was some sort of challenge. Curious, he swallowed half before replying, "I'm reliably informed my tastes are quite vanilla."

She half stood to reach a clean cup for herself and poured some juice in it this time before adding a healthy amount of liquor. She gestured with the bottle to his cup, "Top up?"

He hesitated, certain she was gaming him. "Not yet." He kept an easy smile on his face.

"Worried I'll get you drunk and take advantage of you?" She grinned at him. "Don't worry, my pretty new temp-Tation, getting you inebriated would spoil my plans for the rest of the night." She gave him a coy look, sliding one long red fingernail across her bottom lip.

He licked his bottom lip in echoed response. Whatever her game was, it seemed clear enough she wanted to play harmlessly tonight. He found himself drinking a little more than he normally would, not matching her drink for drink, but allowing for a pleasant fuzziness of brain to develop as they asked each other the usual questions, what brings you here and so forth. They tried to outdo each other with seductive double entendres all the way into bed, tangling sheets and limbs and tongues.

~ * ~

"It seems we are exceptionally compatible," she murmured softly, pressing gentle post-coital kisses on his stomach.

"Mmm," he agreed, feeling light-headed as he collected strands of her hair, fine as silk running through his fingers. He had only vaguely noticed the ferocious clutch of her fingernails in his back in the heat of the moment but now sweat was finding its way to the scratches, salty and stinging. "You play rough."

"Oh," she exclaimed, her voice low as he turned to show her. "My poor darling Silver! I shall never wear such nails again. I wouldn't willingly hurt you," she added, kissing the scratches. "Ever."

"Mmm," he repeated, sleepy, sated, and strangely, "Light-headed," he added aloud.

"Too much drink, after all," she said, her voice still soft and low. Then she giggled. "And vigorous sex." She sighed, her breath a warm puff against his skin. "We have so much in common."

"Mmm."

"Do you believe in love at first sight? I do."

Sil wasn't sure she actually said it, or if he was dreaming, but either way he was too far down sleep's road to reply. If necessary, he would apologize in the morning.

He woke up to the pleasant smell of stale sex and the warmth of a sleek female body curled against his back. He freed an arm from the tangle of sheets and checked the time on his combrace. Still early, considering how long he and the wondrously talented Maria had dallied. His stomach growled a complaint, reminding him he'd much to drink last night but little to eat.

Maria stirred, blinking light brown at eyes at him before gracing him with a dimpled smile. Ravenous he might be, but he still owed his generous companion several orgasms. Since they were already in bed, he twisted in the sheets and began to kiss her arm, working from shoulder down to her elbow, nuzzling into the warm crook and hearing her sigh. Oh, yes, it was going to be a very good morning...

~ * ~

Sil emerged from the hygiene station to see Maria in a short robe left hanging open. He grinned, for that was his preferred morning wear as well. But since this was not his room, he put on last night's clothes. Inexpensive cell-fibre clothes didn't wrinkle, thankfully. Maria brought two steaming mugs of colonial coffee, a hot morning beverage that bore no resemblance at all to real Earth bean coffee, but he accepted it with the gratitude it deserved. "You fell asleep on me," she said with a cheery grin that revealed her dimples in a disarmingly innocent way.

"To be fair," he said, sitting at the table with his mug, "you did quite exhaust me."

"I suppose I did." She sat across from him and slid her foot partially up his leg beneath the table. "I did get something from your pocket, the other day."

"A card, yes," he agreed.

Her shock was only evident by one rapid blink that he might have missed had he not been looking for it. What he didn't see was from where she pulled the card, putting it on the table between them. He glanced down and hoped she wasn't as perceptive at reading subtle tells as he was. It was one of his Quicksilver cards.

"I wasn't sure what it meant at first," she said. "I mean, everyone in my line of work has heard of Quicksilver. We all wondered if the hero of Titan was one and the same. And only last year there was a scurry of rumour about Quicksilver on Nyne, Venus."

Sil sipped his coffee and worked at not making a face at the overly sweet drink. "I don't quite know what you're talking about. Are you a professional pickpocket, is that your line of work?" He never minded when dropping his alias got him information he might not otherwise get, but that whole hero business was dreadfully distasteful.

"Hmm," she said, eyes sparkling with delight. "I couldn't figure why you had this, but then you dressed quite the height, so maybe you found it in your safe, mmm? But then we know the sorts of safes Quicksilver likes to crack, don't we? You don't have that grasping sort of grubby greediness. But then, look at you. So, so pretty. Surely you could not be Quicksilver, the caution of every thief from Venus to Saturn?"

Sil grinned at her. "No idea what you're talking about. Except for me being pretty. That I understand." He finger-combed his hair and licked a finger before drawing it across one eyebrow. "Tell me more about me."

She laughed. "Oh, this is a privilege. I must admit to a teeny bit of pique when you didn't recognize my name, but I am scarcely in your league."

He'd had fair measure of her and she seemed safe enough with his secrets, so he gave up the pretence. He doubted there was anything he could say would convince her he wasn't Quicksilver. "My league is primarily imaginary, you do know that?"

She picked up the card and shuffled it across her fingers, as a sleight of hand artist might. "I know that every petty in the network knows the name Quicksilver. I must say, I expected someone quite... different."

He leaned back in his chair and gave her a sultry, half-lidded look. "I hope you're not disappointed."

She grinned at him, lowering her eyelashes and licking her lips in overt salaciousness. "Delighted, rather. Let's go breakfast, shall we? Then we can decide what to do with our day."

Normally her suggestion would have him feeling more than a little inclined to back away, but there was something about her... perhaps the fact that she was the first lover he'd had in the same profession, more or less. It was novel for him to be with someone without any sort of pretence. He was looking forward to the rest of the Festival, and planning on seeing very little of it.

Spotting Grace in the cafeteria reminded him that he had to track down that artwork with certainty, then mend a fence with Vincent. He slid a look at the beauteous Maria, now wearing a pale yellow wig that, apart from the colour could have passed for natural. Vincent could be difficult, if he knew Sil was having sex with Maria Christina. Still, the fifteen percent finder's fee was more important than avoiding a confrontation with Vincent.

Grace set her tray down with them and a scowl formed on

Maria's face, vanishing as she realized Grace wasn't a random stranger. He couldn't remember the last time someone was actually jealous over him. It was amusing. Grace smiled and said, "Hi, Sil's told me about you. Uh, I'm Grace. Sil's assistant."

"Indeed? He neglected to mention *you*." Maria offered an icy smile. "Maria Christina. With what, precisely, do you assist Silver?"

Sil decided to defrost the situation with an amiable, "Everything. She's more like my partner in crime." When Grace shot him a look, he grinned at her. "It's okay, dear Grace. Sweet Maria is one of us." He laced his fingers through Maria's free hand and said, "We actually have much in common."

Grace nodded, giving their entwined hands a lingering look. "Well then. About the missing artwork, boss. I've been keeping time with Pierre—Ser Gamal-"

"Former curator for the missing art," Sil added for Maria's benefit, uncertain how much Vincent may have told her about the incident.

She nodded for Grace to continue.

"But he's been distracted, sadly. I would read that, though, as him having naught to do with it."

"I'd say Gleb Dolan," Sil said. "I'd offer to console the pretty one, but I suspect zir's assistant, Ser Trueheart is doing that. And may also be involved."

Maria squeezed his hand and smiled coyly at him. "I think you'll not be consoling anyone for some time, sweet Silver."

He found her possessiveness rather adorable. He wasn't going to tire of her for quite some time, and he wondered what kind of team they might make, combining all their skills.

Grace cleared her throat, drawing his attention back to the here and now. "You've spoken to Ser Montrose?"

Sil shook his head. "Gleb Dolan has a yacht. I assume the artwork is there, but before I approach Vincent... well, a failure on my part would not bode well for our continued good life, sweet Grace."

Maria glanced from him to Grace and back to Sil. "I'm not sure I understand...?"

"I enjoy a certain lifestyle," Sil said, "and it requires having a legal explanation for my spending habits. I do some recovery work for insurance companies, among other things. I was in company with Vincent Montrose in order to get first word of missing pretties. However, he and I had a failure of compatibility. Not that it matters. The point is, I need to convince Vincent to pay fifteen percent of the insured value upon recovery. Then I hand over the artwork, preserving the illusion that I provide a legitimate service, and salvaging my reputation from Vincent's cruel lies."

She gave him a coy smile. "Some of what he said was true. You are very skilled."

"As are you, my dear."

Grace kicked him under the table.

NINE

Grace tagged Pierre, offering to be there if he needed her, but she wasn't sure he'd take her up on it. The theft had upset him, and he was spending considerable time with Ser Gilani, head of Festival security. She would have liked to ponder reasons with Sil, but he was spending all his time with this Maria Christina. And while even Grace had to admit the petite woman was almost unworldly attractive, slight of body with big beautiful eyes and a ready grin—for everyone but Grace—she'd never seen Sil act this way.

She wandered into a small gallery dedicated to the artists of the TWF. The most distant of the colonies, the TWF had been built as a staging area, a place to build and send out ships on deep space missions. The reasons it never happened depended on who was telling the story. Over time, the space station had become something of an artist's colony, the last refuge for original thinking or so they claimed. Originally called Hope, the artistic souls who lived there thought it too unimaginative a name. The Thing With Feathers—"hope is a thing with feathers"—had long since been shortened to the TWF. On Titan, only a few hours away, it was touted as a den of laziness and sin, where everyone lived on government love. She'd since learned that wasn't the case at all, and in fact some rather unique jewellery came from there, courtesy of the adventurous souls who mined the Kuiper belt.

She didn't know how much would be here literally, and how much would just be holographic projections, but she needed to be distracted from the temptation to talk to Detective Delaney. She felt some kind of disloyal for even thinking about it, but she didn't trust Maria Christina, and she knew it wasn't jealousy clouding her judgement. Not in the usual sense. Sil was behaving oddly, and she was... concerned.

She wanted Delaney to do a background check on her. She wasn't sure he would, even if she asked. She wasn't sure how Sil would feel if she did ask. He would find out, if she did, she knew that. *Ponder it later*, she thought.

She wandered through the displays, intrigued by the art represented. Meant to be hung on walls, many featured three-dimensional effects, creatively designed to project from the surface only a few centimetres, yet the illusion changed depending on the angle one approached. And, she noted, where the light fell. Most were small enough that they could be displayed to full advantage in a private habitation. She didn't bother to touch the small screens that would bring up prices on the pieces that were for sale. She had no desire to own one, so it didn't matter if she could afford one or not.

She strolled around a display wall looking for the jewellery, when a familiar face and uniform blocked her way. She looked up into the brown eyes of Detective Nick Delaney. "Nick," she said, uncertain if the familiarity of their earlier exchange continued.

But he smiled and nodded. "Grace. Where's... Sil?"

"Why do the good-looking ones always want Sil?" She clapped a hand to her mouth. She hadn't meant to say that out loud, at least not without Sil present to benefit.

He exhaled a long-suffering sigh. "Not you, too."

"I was just teasing," she said hastily. Now that she'd made

things awkward, how could she ask him for any sort of favour? As if it wouldn't have been difficult in the first place.

Nick gave her a wary look. "You came with Sil from Titan, didn't you."

Grace nodded, wondering if the look was for her association with Sil or the metal plate covering her lenses. "You called him Quicksilver. What do you know of that?"

He studied her and seemed to decide there was nothing lost in sharing what he knew. "He perpetrates his crimes on those already on the wrong side of the law. For the most part." He scowled. "It vexes me that he's becoming some sort of folk hero."

She grinned, fascinated. The Quicksilver symbol found in Banook's home safe had set off a storm of rumours. It vexed Sil to no end as well, and he'd hoped that over time the stories would fade and Quicksilver would once more be nothing but the bane of the underworld. Then they'd gone to Nyne, Venus. "The Mercy Hospital fiasco," she said aloud.

"Fiasco is right. I'm sure your boss is tickled all shades to have his alias so well celebrated," Delaney said, disgust in his voice.

"If it makes you feel better," she confided, "he hates it. Sil is vain, and arrogant—perhaps rightfully so in some cases—but he accepts no responsibility for what happened on Titan or the media storm around the Mercy Hospital scandal on Nyne. You want to see a genuine scowl on that pretty face, accuse him of heroism."

He smiled so briefly, she almost missed it. "Indeed. He's been scarce these past couple days. I thought he was keen to find that artwork and earn his fifteen percent?"

She scowled. "Does the name Maria Christina mean aught to you?"

He shook his head. "Should it?"

"I just wondered. Sil has been keeping company with her, but there's something about her I don't like." She hesitated, then lowered her voice. "I'm worried about Sil. He's not himself."

He looked taken aback, and actually laughed. "I'm sure there's no cause. I imagine he's as adept with women as men."

"This probably sounds strange," she began, trailing off as he gave her a look that said *hell yes*. She swallowed but blurted her request anyway. "I wondered if you might, erm, run a background check on her."

"Have you any reason other than you don't like her?" His smile returned.

"It's not jealousy. It's never been like that between me and Sil." Grace hesitated again, then plunged on. "She's a thief."

Nick laughed. "And your boss isn't?"

"Not so's you could prove it," she replied haughtily. "Forget I said anything, detective." She would just have to worry and watch and keep an eye on Sil for herself. She turned around and pretended a great interest in the display in front of her, aware that Nick Delaney was studying her, but ignoring him as if he were invisible.

She moved on the next display and was aware when he walked past her towards the exit.

~ * ~

Nick left the gallery and returned to the security office. It irked him, this punishment for doing no more than his job. Still, if he had to be on Phobos Station at all it was best he have an anonymous job in the Festival. It was, more or less, completely separate from the colony except for well secured corridors. This was both for the security of the Festival and to prevent the tourists from disrupting the daily lives of the station residents.

He hesitated before opening a link to the local IPLE department. As a Special Cases detective, even one being punished, he had certain privileges. Grace Reyes was Silver Tation's partner in crime, and a cool-headed person. Hoping he wouldn't regret it, he ran the name Maria Christina.

TEN

The importance of finding the stolen artwork before it left Phobos Station dwindled for Sil as he delighted in dalliance with Maria Christina. As a thief, she was open to a broader range of caboodle than he was. She had, she implied, a secure network of fences to move all manner of stolen objects. She tried to deal in big ticket items as her connections required substantial payment for their worthwhile. "So you're here to set free some art?"

"It's rather a victimless crime, really," she said, offering him a piece of fruit she'd paid an outrageous amount to have delivered to the room. "The insurance company pays for the loss and no one is really harmed."

He nibbled on the fruit, then sucked it into his mouth, licking her fingers clean of the juice. "Am I keeping you, my sweet, from work?"

She gave him a slow smile. "The festival lasts another week; I've time."

"All your plans are in place?"

She laughed. "Are you trying to find out what I've got on?"

Sil shook his head, pulling her close to where he reclined on her bed. "No, only wanting as much of your time I can have."

"Darling Silver," she purred, sliding down to lay her head in his lap. "We are so compatible."

"It's a pure delight to be with someone and so honest," he said, deciding to not add more along those lines. "So forgive me if I ask about your work; it's not to pry but genuine interest. My reputation is sadly well known, however exaggerated."

"Oh, well. No need to rub in how small my own is," she said, with a smile to show she was teasing. "But to put it shortly, I take everything I can easily get away with. Big prizes are harder to come by and require, as you noted, planning." She made a face. "Why do you limit your best games to your fellow criminals? Seems a bit of bad business."

"I don't aim to make friends," he said. "But I do love a challenge. Not so hard to steal from the law-abiding, they're unwary."

"That's what makes them so perfect," she said. "If I wanted to work, I'd be right side of the law."

Sil smiled and ran his fingers through the soft silken strands of her hair. "Truth, my sweet? I should grow quite as bored of crime as right-side work, were it easy."

More truth, the kind he wasn't willing to speak because it was ludicrous, really, was that he hadn't felt like this with anyone since he'd lost head and heart to the beauteous Tansy. He'd been but seventeen and thought himself so worldly. How foolish he had been and how sorrowful it had ended. Ah, but those were different circumstances. Besides, Maria was a peer, an equal. She would never hurt him.

~ * ~

Sil finally tore himself away from Maria long enough to track down Grace. She was his confidante, his partner, no matter if they both preferred to call her his assistant. He'd answered her countless messages with numerous soons and laters and he could put her off no longer in good conscience. She deserved better.

"I'm so sorry, my dear," he said in all sincerity. "I've not felt like this in years but that's no excuse to be so selfish. I've been terribly neglectful."

He was aware that Grace was studying him in concern. But she only said, "No matter. I'm sure a time will come when I'll abandon you for days at a time."

He grinned. "I hope so. It's all quite grand. But I've not forgotten our perilous living situation. I've had messages from Terrebonne."

"I saw," she said with an exaggerated sniff, clearly not ready to forgive him.

"How foolish of me to forget how well you take care of me."

She scowled at him. "Stop pandering, Sil. It doesn't suit you. I'll forgive you the sooner if you stop."

"I am genuinely contrite."

"I know." She sighed and gave him a small smile. "It seems your good Ser Addison on Terrebonne has grown somewhat suspicious. Do you want to offer him another convincer payout or wrap this game up?"

Sil tapped his bottom as he considered. "What's the full amount he's allowed to be 'invested' on his behalf?" Grace had full access to his combrace messages; he'd given her authorization after realizing she was a far more organized person than he was. She could probably figure a way to steal his money if she was inclined.

Now, however, she linked her 'brace to the holodisplay unit on the table and opened the accounts for him to see for himself. He smiled as he took in the numbers. "Time to wrap it up, my dear. Contact our helpful friend from Imbrium. I'll start moving the money this afternoon."

She nodded, seemingly relieved. He was rather ashamed at how little it would have taken to reassure her sooner. She reminded him when their funds were low, and scolded him for keeping a flower over time. He took these lessons as poorly as he'd learned to steal jewels, but she made his life better.

If she ever decided that travelling and making sleep potions and fencing such bijoux as he happened to steal were not enough, he'd miss her terribly. Even supposing the beauteous Maria decided to be his cony. Amazing, he thought, only a week ago the idea of having a cony had seemed so distasteful.

As far as the colonial banking system knew, Sealfor Argent was a consulting firm and the account was a temporary holding account. He moved funds in and out of it often enough to support that fiction, alternating it with one under his true name. Never straight transfers, of course, that would be too easily tracked should someone decide to look. Someone like Nick Delaney. His eyes widened as he realized that sweet Maria had even made him forget Delaney.

"Sil?"

"Nothing, my dear. Love is a dangerous distraction."

"Love? By the fates, Sil! You met her a scant week ago!"

He grinned at her horror, aware that he would have agreed with her, a scant week ago. But he and Maria, they were perfectly compatible. And he knew she'd never hurt him. "I am sure of where it will go. She and I might be two halves of a single soul, we have so much in common."

She shook her head in exaggerated despair, causing her beads to tinkle gently. "You keep saying that, but what exactly do you have in common besides a gift for acquisitions and a zest for sex?"

"Don't be jealous, sweet Grace. You'll always be my family." He smiled at her with all his usual confidence.

She stifled a sigh. "At least you have contacted Ser Montrose?"

"Well. No. Vincent will need to be quite desperate to hire me. And though I suspect I know where the art is, I need to confirm it. I'm off to do that now, and then I'll clear that account before poor

Ser Addison grows suspicious."

"Very poor," Grace snickered. "I'll be with Pierre tonight, so you have the room to yourself to work," she added with the slightest of emphasis on work.

He nodded happily.

~ * ~

Sil found it was ridiculously easy to steal a security slip from a vendor. This was precisely what he'd tried to explain to Maria—such ease would quickly grow boring. Nevertheless, considering his present goals, it was pleasant to have everything go smoothly. He borrowed a blouse from the same vendor and reluctantly pulled his hair straight and over his eyes. He tsked at his reflection. He still was adorably gorgeous, if he did say so himself, but hardly Silver Tation at all.

He carried an empty box in the same awkward dimensions as the stolen artwork and adopted the carefree jauntiness he used to use in Victoria, Mars when he wanted to look like a harmless teenager. It served him as well now as it did then, and he hefted the empty box awkwardly to his shoulder as if it were heavy and nodded at the guard who passed him through.

He carried that box like it weighed a ton until he found Gleb Dolan's yacht. He used an electronic pick to open the hatch and called out, just in case, "Delivery!"

He'd been so distracted by the pleasure of Maria's company, he'd forgotten that, as easy as this was proving to be, the potential for getting caught was high enough to still provide that rush of adrenaline, the thrill of the game. He set down the box and began the search for the missing artwork. A personal ship was very small in terms of actual living space. In order to be of any use at all, the bulk of it was taken up with fuel and batteries, and at least one engine powerful enough to provide useful acceleration. A prolific waste of money that could be better spent on flowers, food, and fine liquor, in his opinion.

The artwork wasn't in the cabin, so he checked the engine compartment and fuel storage, conveniently designed to accommodate repair technicians. Engine repairs were another expensive negative to owning a private ship. It did not surprise him to find the artwork stashed in a narrow service way. Securely wrapped.

Jase Trueheart had probably done the deed for his employer and lover, but who, how, and even why were not Sil's concern. He doubted Gleb Dolan and zir assistant would be leaving before the end of the Festival, not without some resolution to the situation. Be that in the form of an insurance payout or other sign that they were considered victims, not suspects.

He carefully placed the artwork in the box and re-affixed the seals. It was as heavy as he'd imagined. He eased out of the ship and replaced the box cautiously on his shoulder, retracing his steps to the security desk. He pasted a look of puzzlement on his face as he approached the guard. "There was no one there to accept the package," he said, sounding dismayed. "I can't just leave it sit outside for anyone walking by. Can I leave it with you?" He injected a note of hopefulness into the question.

"I'm sorry," the guard said, looking at Sil's paperwork again. "It says you need Ser Dolan's personal acceptance. You can't leave it here, else we could both get in trouble." Ze offered Sil an apologetic smile.

Sil was careful to keep most of the box between him and the guard, and the bill of the hat pulled just low enough to hide everything but his mouth from the cameras. He'd not be easy to identify, although he expected Delaney had some sort of face recognition that could do it. But then, he doubted Ser Dolan was going to report the theft. That was the beauty of stealing from thieves.

ELEUEN

After his initial shock, Pierre Gamal had resumed his association with Grace. Now, however, he had a quiet air to him like he might be taking too much solace from their sex. She wasn't opposed to it in principle, just worried he might be growing too fond of her. She enjoyed his company, his passion for his profession, but unlike her foolish boss, she had no delusions that any sort of lasting relationship was to be had here. She couldn't even think of him in terms of anteem, let alone a sweet, live-in cony.

When Pierre expressed once more how upsetting he found it to consider this William Bowie wall sculpture in the hands of someone who might damage it, she tentatively offered, "My boss has some experience in recovery work..."

He gave her a puzzled look. "Wouldn't hiring a recovery agent be up to the insurance company?"

"Yes, of course. He doesn't do it for free, but for a percentage of the insured value. But Sil—"

"Silver Tation? The flower Vincent Montrose paid to accompany him who broke contract?"

"Whew! How fertile the rumours in close quarters!" Grinning, Grace informed Pierre of the true nature of their arrangement.

"So Ser Montrose intended—or pretended—to bring your boss along specifically in case of an instance like this?"

"That was the impression he gave Sil, yes."

Gamal nodded his understanding, and tugged her into his arms. "Do you believe he can do it? Your Silver, he can find the Bowie?"

"Oh yes," she agreed in contented confidence.

"I will talk to Ser Montrose," he said. "Thank you for telling me, my Grace. It eases my mind to think there's a possibility of recovering it undamaged." With the skill borne of knowing her, he found the pressure points and clips that released her arm and leg from the linkages to her body. She still had connecting clasp plates at her bicep and thigh, but sex was considerably more comfortable without a metal arm and leg involved.

Given his renewed enthusiasm, she wished she'd thought to ease his mind sooner.

~ * ~

"I don't care if you're a Special Cases detective, this is not your case! You were assigned to work for me," Naveed Gilani told Nick coldly. "Next time you want to do something of your own initiative, you run it by me first, and if I say no, you drop it. Do you understand?" He paused slightly on each word for emphasis.

Nick sighed. "I apologize again, Ser Gilani. I have grown accustomed to having a free reign while investigating. I did not mean to usurp your authority."

"Good. Now did your meander outside the scope of your duties provide any information we can actually use?"

"No," Nick said. Vincent Montrose had just reported Nick to the Festival head of security for "pestering" him. Since Nick had failed to detain Silver Tation for breaking a contract that didn't even exist, Montrose had extended his dislike to include him. As with any insured item, the possibility of fraud was not something to be ignored, but Montrose had, probably deliberately, misinterpreted the reasons for his questions.

Either that or he *was* involved. But Nick liked Gleb Dolan for it, ze had the most to gain. Ze also had thoroughly inspected all the security surrounding it and so likely knew of the temporary obfuscation of the camera. Zir alibi only meant ze had help, most likely Jase Trueheart.

Gilani didn't disagree with him, he merely asked for evidence. And then refused Nick permission to do what he needed to in order to get it. Needing to focus on something else, he tagged Grace Reyes. Unexpectedly, she answered in real time voice. Interesting measure of her concern for Sil. Ser Tation. He frowned. "Grace, I ran Maria Christina's name. She's never been arrested, at least not under that name. I... I don't have access at the moment to any informers who might have heard whisper of her."

"Oh. Damn, I'd hoped she had some outstanding warrant for littering or something. Anything."

He grinned. "Are you sure you're not the slightest jealous?"

"No, Nick. Trust me, Sil's behaving strangely. Maybe... I don't know. Maybe she's drugged him. Is there a way you could tell?"

He laughed. "Not without him giving me a fluid sample. You figure he'd be likely to do that?"

She sighed. "You could kiss him," she suggested slyly.

He rolled his eyes but said, "And ruin a perfectly good relationship?"

And that made her laugh, which was probably the most good he could do her today. So he was surprised when she asked, her voice a little too casual, "Have you made any progress on finding the thief or stolen artwork?"

"No," he replied, wary.

"I ask because I'm keeping company with Pierre Gamal. I

believe you cleared him as a suspect?"

"That's true." He relaxed again. "I'm more than a little curious why Sil hasn't... ah." He started laughing again. "Vincent Montrose."

"Yes," she sighed. "But Pierre offered to speak to Ser Montrose, so surely if Sil can find the art, he can share with you where he found it? Might you gain something useful from that?"

"And why would he do that?"

There was a moment of silence, then she said, "You sounded just like him." She broke the connection before he could ask what she meant. He shook his head, checked the time, and clocked out for lunch.

~ * ~

Sil decided that Maria's room was the best place to stash the art until such time as he could return it. He trusted her; she would never hurt him. Hmm, he thought. Perhaps removing it from Dolan's yacht had been premature—what was he to do with it if Vincent stood firm on his resolve to not hire him?

Maria Christina was within when he came through the door, as comfortable with his coming and going as he was. Strange to think that the cozy arrangement with Maria was almost exactly what Vincent had offered. It wasn't only that Maria didn't feel she'd purchased the rights to his company, either. He liked this fantasy with her. He imagined the three of them, he and Maria and Grace, grifting and other such crimes across the solar system.

"What's that, my darling? A present for me?" Her question alarmed him. Was he supposed to bring her a present? Now that he'd emptied the joint account he and Ser Addison had used in Terrebonne, he had the means to gift her with something.

"Not this time," he said with a gallant, if apologetic smile. "This belongs to an acquaintance and I thought to hold it here until such time as I can deliver it. If it's not an imposition, my sweet?"

"Not at all," she said. "You know you can trust me. There's space by the hygiene station. Might I guess from your apparel that the owner is unaware you're in possession of it?"

Chagrined, he glanced down at the anonymous tan blouse of the delivery service he'd rifled, pulling off the hat as he did. "That would be a fair guess. Speaking of, I really should return this... useful costume."

He stripped to the waist and Maria said, her voice throaty with desire, "No need to stop there, lover."

He grinned at her. "And you say *I'm* a temptation, dear heart. I'll be but a short while and return to finish for you. You of all people should know the importance of tidying up loose ends."

"I do," she said, her smile broad and forgiving. "And I look forward to your return."

He put on his own clothes, neatly folded the delivery uniform and placed the hat on top, stuffing both into a recyclable sack. He was still wearing the second-skin gloves; he would discard those in a public recycle chute before returning for an afternoon in the beauteous Maria's arms.

His plans changed when he returned to find Maria with the opened box, a holodisplay open on her table.

"That's that missing artwork!" Her voice was almost accusing.

"Yes, I can't keep it in my room. There's a Long Arm here with a special fondness for me. Don't worry, darling, I'll be returning it to the rightful owner so it won't trouble you."

She swivelled her head to look at him. "Give it back? Are you daft? Do you see how much it's worth?"

He shrugged, unimpressed. The high estimated value simply meant his fifteen percent would be generous. "I've no contacts to move such a thing. It's worth more to me to give it back. Fifteen percent." And although he trusted her, the glint of avarice in her eye made him add, "I'll split it with you. Seven percent of *that*," he waved at the figure currently hovering over her table, "is a tidy take away."

She stared at the display, pulling her bottom lip under her teeth. Then she closed the display with a decisive hand wave and grinned at him, her eyes sparkling with delight. "You'd split your fee with me?"

He smiled back and stepped close enough to trace the delicate swirl of her ear. "I'll share everything with you, my sweet Maria."

"Darling Silver," she said, all but purring.

TWELUE

"Ser Montrose is adamantly against hiring your Silver. I can somewhat understand, I think, but shouldn't the safe return of the Bowie be a priority?" Before Grace could respond to Pierre's complaint, he added, "I shall just have to talk to Naveen Gilani. Surely he will support me and also urge Montrose to hire a professional recovery agent?"

Surprised, she nodded. "You're a very clever person." Although *professional recovery agent* was a bit of a stretch to describe Sil.

He smiled warmly at her. "And you are a loyal and patient one. Not many people would have stuck by me during my upset over the theft on such short acquaintance. Nor a long acquaintance, for that matter. I almost wish we had a chance of a future together."

"Me, too," she said smiling back at him and meaning it. Almost was exactly right. His words had started to worry her until his final sentence, but now she relaxed, glad he understood this was a relationship of circumstance.

Pierre Gamal might be a person with intensely emotional reactions, but when he was done with the hand wringing and had decided upon a course of action, he moved decisively, without hesitation. He joined her for the second service of the evening meal with a confident smile, the same confidence that had so charmed her on their first meeting. She smiled back. Tonight was going to be another *very* pleasant night.

~ * ~

Sil woke up to his combrace vibrating insistently against his pulse. He lifted his wrist high enough to glare at it and checked the tag number before shutting it off. Grace he could call back, but his eyes widened in shock as he saw it was Vincent Montrose. "Has a black hole swallowed us all into an alternate universe?"

Maria beside him mumbled something and turned her head into the sheets.

He accepted the tag. "Darling," he said, "this *is* unexpected."

He brushed the volume down as Vincent began with some frothy statements regarding Sil's moral character, but then he offered a very grudging apology for his own false accusations and said, surprisingly, "You're supposed to do recovery work, aren't you?"

"Is this about the artwork stolen from the twentieth century exhibit? I'd rather thought you'd forgotten me." He saw no need to tell Ser Montrose that had he not called at this bright hour, Sil would have gone round to room 220 in wing four for a face-to-face plead. Pleading had not been something he was looking forward to.

"I'd not forgotten, I've just been extremely vexed with you. Truth, grievous Silver, I'd prefer not to have to admit you were right and I was... not. But I am under pressure from Festival security, IPLE, and my superiors at Colonial Insurance." He paused. "I suppose I must offer you another apology before you accept the task?"

Sil grinned. "You think that will suffice, dear Vincent?"

The sheet beside him slid down, revealing Maria's tousled hair, sleepy eyes, and slender neck.

"I will not beg, Silver. I understand you ask for fifteen percent of the insured value. I am authorized to approve that. I hope you are as good as you say you are."

"I thought I'd proved that already," Sil drawled. "I'll contact you as soon as I can get my hands on it, dear Vincent."

"Do things always fall so easily your way, Quicksilver?" Maria asked after the call was terminated.

He leaned over to kiss her forehead. "Usually, love. It's a gift." A little exaggeration to appear better in her eyes couldn't hurt.

~ * ~

Having already laid hands on the art in question, Sil felt no sense of urgency. He planned to wait a couple more days, then see if Grace was more impressed with Maria's taste in jewels at the closing gala. The three of them would make a formidable team.

First, though, he had to help Maria overcome her jealousy and Grace overcome her distrust. He had some idea that balancing the two might be difficult, but since his relationships with each were quite different, it should be manageable.

Maria seemed the most easily persuaded; he'd already told her that Grace had given invaluable assistance for his project on Titan. He neglected to mention his part in Banook's suicide, making it sound as if, as the media had reported, he'd finally grown a conscience. He doubted Maria was in any way squeamish about such things, but his purpose had been to emphasize that his and Grace's relationship was purely platonic. As fond of Maria as he'd grown, he still had no desire to detail a revenge so personal he'd not even told Grace what it was about.

He refreshed the story, adding extra emphasis on the mild rivalry they'd shared over a certain Avery Rex, and paused, hopeful.

"But that was two years ago, darling. Why is she still around?"

Patiently, he explained. "I cannot say for certain all her

original reasons, but you cannot be unaware of the stigma she bears for her mechanical parts? Her family and coworkers shunned her, her employer treated her like a sentient machine; she had no idea what prejudices she might face in the inner colonies. I believe that was behind her initial offer to fence the diamonds I liberated from the mine manager's safe."

"That doesn't answer my question," Maria said, the slightest note of petulance in her voice.

He stroked her hair. "Be easy, my love. During the course of arranging for that, she happened to give me some assistance organizing a little game with a jewellery store owner in Destiny and the next thing I know, she's organizing my finances so nicely I could work less and play more. A valuable asset, to be sure. Although her mechanicals were designed specifically for the gem trade, she has discovered many other uses for them that, to date, no one suspects. But she's more than being useful, my darling Maria."

"It's the more that troubles me," she admitted.

"I told you her family shunned her, they behaved as if she'd died in that accident. And I," he said, restraining his natural urge towards drama with a small gesture to his chest, "am an orphan. We have become each others family." He frowned. "Though I admit she is sometimes more mother than sister."

She gave him a smile, eyes half-lidded, and drew her fingers languidly down her side. "But we have have by fortune and fate found each other. Am I not your family now?"

"I have been without one all my life, my sweet Maria. Love you though I might, after so short acquaintance, I shall not give up the only family I've ever known."

She opened her eyes fully and sat up, clutching his hand. "Of course not, darling. How foolish of me to even consider you would."

Sil relaxed and pulled her close, stretching out his legs beside her as they leaned on the wall. "I should like us to become a team, you understand, my love. We are but new acquaintances, after all, though it seems I've been waiting for you, always."

"Darling Silver," she said softly, stroking his neck. "So glad you feel it, too, this connection."

"We have so much in common, and our compatibility is clear. How could I not?" He smiled reassuringly at her. "I thought we might test our team work the final night of the Festival." And he explained how he and Grace managed to steal small trinkets from under the very nose of a Long Arm at the opening mixer. "I'm sure you're a far better judge of quality bijoux than I am, which should do much to endear you to Grace."

~ * ~

Nick watched Silver Tation and his slender companion make their way through the cafeteria line. Her hair was either painted blue or she wore a very conservative wig, but the style emphasized her doll-like features. She was dressed in muted blue-grey leggings and a tailored, narrow-sleeved tunic in a jewel tone blue. The back was cut away in a large circle and it had a sheer skirt that fell in stiff folds to her knees.

She was caught up in earnest discussion with a food server and waved Tation on with a smile bright enough even Nick noticed. She seemed even more charismatic than Quicksilver himself. Tation sat down and Nick strode over to take advantage of the woman's absence. He pulled a chair out and sat down, ignoring the astonished look that flashed over Tation's face before he offered an unmistakably pleased smile.

"Sil," he said, testing this new informality. It had seemed easier to refer to him as Sil when talking to Grace.

"What a most pleasant diversion. What can I do for you, dear Nicky?"

Nick caught himself before he flinched. He hated being called

Nicky, it sounded such the childish nickname. But he suspected telling someone like Silver Tation would only encourage him to use it all the more often. He swallowed his displeasure and said, "I've not seen much of you this past week."

Sil touched his sleeve, and smiled at him. "Disappointed, darling?"

"Terribly," Nick said dryly, rolling his eyes. "I understand through circuitous ways that Ser Montrose has forgiven you?"

"I doubt that, but under pressure he has grudgingly decided I might be of some practical use."

"Am I correct in assuming Gleb Dolan is the culprit?"

"Have you any proof?"

"No." Nick frowned his frustration, caught sight of the one Grace called Maria Christina at the same time she spotted him. Interestingly, she veered away. Was it his uniform, he wondered. Sometimes even law abiding citizens shied away from Long Arms. He looked at Sil, who was eating, watching him with curious eyes. "They won't even concede probable cause, so no search warrants."

"I don't know that anything I can say will help. Dolan's assistant did the actual lifting, if you've not already given him a hard look."

Surprise gave way to suspicion. "Why would you want to help me?"

Sil, also looking surprised, hesitated before shrugging. "Wouldn't say I'm being all that helpful."

"You know where to find the missing art?"

Sil swallowed the bite of food he'd taken and grinned. "Oh yes. That was easy enough to discover, once I figured out the who."

"On his yacht?"

"You are a clever detective."

Nick narrowed his eyes. "It's not still there?"

"I'm not ready to return it quite yet, it sort of needs a grand gesture, don't you think? But even if I hadn't relocated it somewhere safe, would you have been able to retrieve it?"

"No," he growled. "How soon did you figure it out?"

Sil paused, but his thoughtful expression was exaggerated. "In the gallery, we both knew it was Gleb Dolan. I might have jumped in to offer my services immediately, but with Vincent's shameful accusations, I knew I had to be completely certain of success."

"You had the case solved and the stolen artwork located within a few hours of the crime." It was infuriating that even when Quicksilver could be dubiously counted on the side of the law, he was still three steps ahead of Nick.

"So did you, dear Nicky. Only you have to go by the book." Sil grinned. "I don't have a book."

THIRTEEN

"What was *that* all about?" Maria asked, catching up to Sil outside the cafeteria and letting him lead her into the Classic Colonial gallery.

"What was what about." Many of these artworks were replicated on the walls and corners of Marton's palace. Colonial art had been created for the small spaces and limitations of the colonies, and while it included some painted canvases and hard sculptures, it was mostly light and variously frosted acrylic. It was often practical, mixing task lighting with pure beauty, to maximize the limited personal space even the wealthiest of colonists had, particularly in the early days.

Much of this art reminded Sil of the missing artwork. Early colonial art had largely been constructed of scraps. It had to remain practical because early colonial existence relied heavily on stringent recycling, unlike whatever era had seen—

"Silver!"

"Sorry, my dear, I was unforgivably distracted. What was what about?"

"Your so very friendly chat with that Long Arm over lunch." She tossed her head and the fibres of her blue wig fluttered enticingly across her cheeks. The frown on her pretty mouth did not suit her and he ran a finger lightly across her lips as if he could wipe it away. She jerked her head from his touch and grabbed his arm. "I am not to be so easily distracted, Quicksilver," she said, though she sounded more forgiving this time.

"I told you I had one interested in me."

To his utter bewilderment, her face took on the same jealous mien it had worn when she met Grace. "Interested."

"Not like that," he laughed, refraining from adding *sadly*. He would be glad when she grew as secure in his affections as he felt of hers. She would never hurt him. But their feelings had grown so strong so quickly, he could understand her doubts.

Strangely, he still felt just the slightest of disappointments that now his flirtations with the handsome detective would of a certainty remain only that. Ah, but for one like Maria, such a sacrifice was worthwhile. "He is investigating the theft of the artwork. He has a passing familiarity with some of my work," he added with a grin.

"You sound quite pleased about it." She, on the other hand, did not sound pleased at all.

"I told him nothing of you, my love. He knows Vincent has hired me, angry as he is with me." Why, he wondered, was she not jealous about that? Truly, emotions of this depth were difficult to understand. "You are quite right to be wary of the good detective," he added to soothe her fears, "for he is a most clever man. Yet for all that he knows of me, he has not the slightest of proof. Together, we shall easily stay three steps ahead the law."

Her face again took on the soft look he found so beguiling. "For the sake of the trust between us, my sweet Silver. I've never had a partner before."

"I would consider Grace and I fairly different personalities and we've managed very successfully. I should imagine you and I, as alike as we are, shall find it even easier."

"You and I... and Grace."

"I'm not suggesting a menage, my dear," he said, but his attempt at humour failed against his impatience.

"I know, darling. But it is a considerable change for me, and you are asking me to put my life in her hands."

"I'm asking just as much of her," he reminded. "Fear not, my love, our little game on the final night of the Festival will prove to you both that I'm right. For now, I hope you understand I was quite serious about splitting the recovery fee. It would be an honour to have you at my side as we bring it in together, and it will provide the good detective with a wonderful cover for you, a fellow finder of lost things."

"Yes," she agreed thoughtfully.

"I hope you don't mind, but for all I don't consider myself a connoisseur of art, I am curious about this gallery."

"There's nothing really valuable here, is there?" She glanced around the gallery with a dismissive gesture of her hand.

"I'm sure I don't know, but traversing the colonies as I do, it certainly gives one an interesting perspective. We've not been out here all that long, only five generations. It's easy to forget how fraught it all was, in the beginning."

"I'd not have guessed you one for philosophy, Silver."

"I'm not, as a rule. Nor a political creature except in so far as politics can decide where is most profitable for grift. Imbrium, Luna is still prime, because so many Martians seem to think more money will result in a faster solution."

"Oh?" She placed her hand in the crook of elbow and said, "Do tell."

As they meandered through the exhibits, he explained the terraforming research industry, and why it was on the Moon. He didn't bother to mention Ser Ingle Addison or the fictional company Silberbestek, as those details didn't seem important.

"Wouldn't Phobos Station itself be a good ground for

playing?"

"It might, but in the best of circumstances, outsiders such as we would not easily mix. And this, I'm afraid is not the best of circumstances. I have currently a little more reputation on Phobos Station than I can easily bear."

"I'm intrigued!"

"Nothing to be intrigued by, sadly," he said, and told her why Silver Tation was not well regarded on Phobos Station. "For that reason, even had I not met you, my lovely, I should be keeping close within the Festival complex."

"Sorry to hear," she murmured.

"Someone certainly will be," he agreed, wondering if Ser Addison had figured out yet that he was a far poorer person.

~ * ~

Nick presented himself at the Festival security office promptly on being paged. The front room was empty and a great deal of noise was coming from behind the secured counter. He let himself through and stood in the doorway, gaping. A table was overturned, the door to the weapons locker was ajar, two bodies were on the floor, being tended by white coated medics while Naveen Gilani tore a strip out of a quivering security guard. "Ser Gilani?"

Gilani let go the collar of the one he'd been berating to take long, angry strides to Nick's side. "Someone had the temerity to break in *here* and assault my officers!"

Nick took another quick survey of the room. "They're alive?"

"Yes," Gilani snapped. "Standard knock-out drugs, but they should have been smart enough not to be caught off-guard like that. They're security guards!"

"The weapons locker?"

"One pulse fire weapon is missing," Gilani admitted, almost grudgingly. "Just one."

That was bad. Projectile weapons had long been outlawed in

the colonies—anything that could poke a hole through the fragile membranes that supported life away from Earth had no welcome. Murder was no easy thing to get away with in space, as counter-intuitive as that seemed. Short of disposing of a body in the necro incinerators used by the colonies for natural and accidental deaths, there was no way to really hide one for more than a few days. The necros could only be used with proper security authorizations. Most colonies changed those weekly or even daily.

Poison had become the weapon of choice, almost always non-fatal, and usually delivered by a tiny dart, small and sharp enough to break skin, but harmless to all but the most fragile of colonial life support systems.

Law enforcement, however, retained the right to use weapons with a greater accuracy, capable of deadly force if necessary, though Nick could not remember the last time that had happened either. He imagined it engendered a great deal of paperwork, though, and countless reviews and therapists. Pulse weapons weren't even carried on a daily basis, but kept in a storage locker for such things as criminal pursuit, riots, and other unusual occurrences.

"You're to forget about the stolen art, Detective Delaney. Leave that with my people. Finding that weapon is now your first concern." Gilani glared at Nick as fiercely as if this were his fault. "I want whoever did this—before they hurt someone."

Nick nodded. This was more the type of case he was accustomed to handling. "How soon before the officers revive?"

Gilani looked to where the medics had moved the two downed officers. "The heavier one has already been muttering about an angel, all glowing skin and golden hair." He pursed his lips.

"I'll talk to him," Nick said, hoping the guard remembered actual details of height and body type. Finally, back on the job, his punishment over a few days early. "I'll contact headquarters—"

"Allow me to do that for you, Detective. Technically you are still under my command, so I'm the one needs to put through the authorization request to have your clearances reinstated. Truth, I'm as relieved as you are to be done with you."

Nick wasn't sure that was a compliment. It didn't matter. He doubted he would ever cross paths with Naveen Gilani again. He left Gilani to make the calls while he knelt to get a description of the perpetrator from the recovering officers.

FOURTEEN

Sil decided that the best place for this call was from his bed in the room he was sort of sharing with Grace. With the privacy curtains pulled around, it looked exactly like the type of accommodations a newly poor person might be reduced to.

The lag between Phobos Station and the Moon was currently six minutes, so a real time conversation wasn't practical, but Ingle Addison's desperate voice message demanded a video response, lag or no.

"Ser Addison, I won't waste your time with social niceties. I was shocked and horrified to get your message about Silberbestek failing. I-I..." His eyes wide and confused, he pushed his hand through his already tousled hair and continued, "I should have tried harder to secure a Martian investor. I-I'm all but reduced to government love and not sure I have passage back to Terrebonne." He let his expression turn into a grimace. "After your message, I checked my account and..." he gestured to the room behind him. "I sold my accommodation and have found someone kind enough to share her bed. And my food is covered." He paused to look reflective. "Could be worse, I suppose."

There was more he could have said, but instead he sent the video and sat back with a glass of Shoots to await a reply. Six minutes to Terrebonne and six minutes back, he passed the time pondering how, with a partner like Maria, his profits would increase.

Of course, with a partner like Maria, he wouldn't spend anything on flowers, so even if his income remained the same, he'd be a richer person. Strangely, he felt a pang of regret to be giving up his flowers. Surely to love and be loved by one such as the divinely criminal Maria was much the better? She was certainly gifted in the intimate arts.

He realized she had never told him what game had brought her to the Festival. Then, they'd not spent much time talking. He smiled in remembrance. Perhaps she was working on that now, as he was also taking care of things begun before meeting her, before they had become a couple.

He still had Shoots in his glass when his combrace buzzed with an incoming video call. He smiled. He did so like when things went along smooth. He opened the call.

"Argent! How can you be so accepting of this? You're supposed to be my inside person with Silberbestek, and you're just shrugging in resignation at our losses? Are you mad?" Zir eyes narrowed in suspicion. "You have lost, yes?"

Short, given the lag. Sil hit reply. "I am an experienced investor, Ser Addison. I can't say as I've learned to take losses of this magnitude in stride, but I knew the risks going in. I hope you don't mean to accuse me of anything, because I spent considerable time trying to explain how risky this venture was. It will take me some time to recover from this, but I stand by my assertion that Silberbestek could have made us all very rich." He paused, his brows creasing in a perplexed way. "You're a lawyer, surely you knew the risks you were taking."

He refreshed his drink. While in Terrebonne, Sil had broken

into Ingle Addison's habitat. Unlike many, ze had no safe to crack. It was likely ze kept zir precious bits, if ze had any non-credit precious bits, in an institution designed for the safekeeping of such. Sil would never tackle one of those. It meant that Addison would not find a Quicksilver card, though. Just as well, he didn't need someone else connecting Quicksilver and Silver Tation. Still, it seemed a shame Addison would not know who was responsible for zir sudden reversal of fortune.

"Silberbestek," Addison came back with, zir brows drawn in an angry frown, "has disappeared. Like it never existed. No record of it on the net. The registration and corporate board of directors and scientific reports, all of that is gone. I think, Argent, we've been had."

Sil smiled before hitting reply. He loved the intricacies of creating and then destroying digital entities. Even the tag number Addison thought ze was calling and receiving calls from was a ghost that would disappear when Sil sent his last message. Thoroughness, both in construction and clean-up, was a lesson well-learned, well-implemented.

He fiddled with the settings on his combrace, so he appeared paler than before, and started recording his reply. "I-I think you're correct, Ser Addison. I must say, I've-I've never been swindled before. I-I know now isn't the most appropriate time to ask, but... we could use the distraction of an odd question?" He smiled weakly, as if shell-shocked by Addison's revelation of the complete disappearance of Silberbestek. "When we met, I knew your name was familiar. The rather splashy Amanda Lavender trial, yes? I've always wanted to know—do you really believe it was that fellow, whatsisname, Silver Tation did the murder?" He downed his drink in one swallow before sending the message.

As he suspected, the momentum—if one could call it such with a lag of such length—had Ingle Addison replying one more time, looking somewhat confused. "No, of course not. My job was to defend my client. I was paid well for my effort, but would have garnered an unofficial bonus had I won." Ze frowned. "Just as well, I suppose. Would have been more money to lose to that swindler behind Silberbestek. Do you have any inkling who it was that lied to us so thoroughly?"

Sil chuckled, considering his answer as he slowly finished his drink. He replied with normal light settings and a lazy smile on his face. "Amazing the bad things that happen when people tell lies."

~ * ~

Grace was surprised to find Sil in her room when she returned after lunch. He was sleeping, fully clothed, privacy curtain still open. She scowled. Maria Christina must be wearing him out with sex, as ridiculous as that seemed. Her scowl faded. Had he eaten? He obviously wasn't at the middle lunch service, and he'd left her a quick message this morning that he'd be working here to tie off all the loose ends back in Terrebonne, had he lunched at the first service then returned here?

That didn't seem likely. She checked the time on her combrace. He was missing third service, too. She stepped close to shake him awake, then drew back as the muted buzzing of his combrace reached her mechanical ear. When the urgent vibration failed to disturb the even rhythm of his breathing, she figured he needed sleep more than he needed food.

She pulled the privacy curtain closed for him and sat down at the table to see the profit of his morning's work. It gladdened her mercurial heart to see that their brief poverty had now vanished and they were very tidily in the pretty. If Sil could continue to curb his flower habit, they could live very comfortably for the rest of the year, longer if they played short cons. Which of course they would, else Sil would grow deathly bored.

She scowled again. He'd tried to convince her that Maria would make their duo a formidable trio, refusing to listen to a negative word against her. He kept saying how compatible they were and what a great deal they had in common, but Grace couldn't see it. Even when she managed to coax him into sharing what Maria had told him, he'd begin by describing a thief not at all like himself and slowly meander into vague mumblings.

She glanced toward the privacy curtain as his combrace began buzzing again. Again, he slept through it, though it must be on vibrate. There wasn't any such thing as a love potion... was there? She started searching the c-net.

FIFTEEN

Sil studied Vincent Montrose obliquely, still struck by the man's attractiveness. Had he been more honest in his intentions, things might have gone in such a way as Sil would never have met the person he increasingly felt was his other half. He could almost forgive Vincent for attempting to tarnish his reputation. They were in the office of Naveed Gilani, Festival Security, neutral ground. Sil wasn't sure if Vincent knew that he was with Maria, or that he was willingly staying with Maria in the same fashion Vincent had tried to force with Sil. Of course, the best part was that he had nothing to hide from Maria.

He decided it would be foolish to rub salt in any wound Vincent Montrose might still feel. "I have located the missing artwork," he said, simple, formal. "I should like to arrange to return it to you, and receive my fee, per the terms of our contract." A contract he had insisted upon, though Vincent had refused to witness it personally.

"Found it where?" Vincent demanded.

"I cannot accuse without evidence," Sil said, wishing Nick

Delaney was present to hear such words from his mouth, "but I might suggest you encourage Ser Dolan to find a new insurance carrier."

Vincent gave him a long, hard look, not quite a glare, then nodded slowly. "Well. I suppose I must thank you for that."

"My fee is all the thanks I require, dear Vincent. I... am truly sorry for the confusion between us." He offered the apology in part because it was true—Vincent had no way of knowing why such a situation as he'd proposed was so intolerable—and partly because when he returned the metal sculpture with Maria at his side... Well, he could not predict what might happen, but anything he could do to defuse it in advance would not be amiss.

Vincent's head bent in acknowledgement with a stiffness that spoke of lingering resentments. "Tomorrow. I shall make sure Naveen Gilani and the IPLE officer are present, so all is... agreeably formal. Per our contract," he said, cutting his eyes away from Sil's on the final word. They agreed upon a time, and Sil bowed with a gracious, forgiving smile.

~ * ~

Nick fidgeted as he stood in the security office, aware of Naveen Gilani glaring at him. He didn't want to be here either, not when someone was running around Phobos station with a pulse weapon, but Vincent Montrose had insisted. He'd have thought after the humiliation of Nick's sham "arrest" of Sil and his subsequent release, Montrose would have been happy to be spared his presence. Nick already knew Sil had successfully located the missing art, though of course he couldn't say so. This was just a waste of his time.

The door opened and he turned expectantly, hoping it was Sil so he could get back to work. But it was only Pierre Gamal, the curator of the gallery from which the piece had been sold. He did not pretend to understand how a person could have such a vested interest in something which was no longer his responsibility. Like Silver Tation, he travelled too often to have a home where one might put art, or become enamoured of a certain style or artist or however such things worked. What was more surprising was that Grace Reyes was with him.

Nick took the few steps necessary to put him in conversation reach and asked, "You're not with Sil?" Aware of how foolish that was even as he said it, he immediately said, "Obviously, but I'm surprised."

She smiled thinly. "Sil is planning a grand entrance with the love of his life. Not sure how Ser Montrose will feel about that," she said with a nod towards the person in question. "He insists we'll be a formidable trio."

Nick shook his head with a wry smile. "I should not be hearing such things."

"I doubt it will happen. She wants something of Sil, but what it might be, I cannot fathom."

Nick was about to smile and finish the conversation when something niggled at the back of his mind. "Does she know his..." he cast about for the right words. "Secret identity?"

Grace gave him a wide grin. "Oh as the hero, Quicksilver?"

He matched her smile. It amused him in a pleasantly surprising way to think Silver Tation had enough humility to not take credit for the positive things that had resulted from his actions without his intent. "Indeed."

"She does. It's one of the things he finds so utterly fascinating about her."

Nick frowned. "What would a thief want most from Quicksilver?"

Grace matched his frown, thinking of the reputation Quicksilver had in the criminal underworld. "To outwit him?"

"I've heard he has a reputation for very exact revenge, wouldn't that dissuade most? Wait—did you say they're returning the artwork together?"

"Yes," she said, tilting her head in clear puzzlement.

Making a hasty excuse, he turned on his heel and sought out Vincent Montrose. "How much again is that bit of scrap metal worth?"

~ * ~

Sil opened the box to ensure the artwork was still within.

"Don't you trust me, darling?" Maria was laughing, her big beautiful eyes sparkling, her entire body shaking with barely suppressed mirth.

"Implicitly," he said. "But it does no one any good to give up a lifetime of careful habits, my love." He grinned at her affectionately. "We will need to always be on our toes, because of the d-detective." He'd almost said dear detective, but he loved to see Maria so vivacious and cheerful, he would not say anything to have that vanish into jealousy. With barely more than two weeks acquaintance, her jealousy was not abnormal, he reminded himself again. Time would cure it, when she could witness for herself his devotion.

After Tansy's untimely demise, he'd been certain he'd never love again. And he surely did not believe in love at first sight. So this deeply intense connection he felt to Maria Christina—*you don't even know her real name!*—was many things. Comforting and alarming. It had a rightness to it he could not explain, and would not have believed had someone ever told him he would feel this way again. He tended to forget how little he knew about her. He trusted her, yet still felt a measure of reserve. *Because it is too soon. She is yet jealous for our short acquaintance, and my inability to fully trust in her is but the same effect.* Something still seemed not quite right. He pondered the plan, but it was simple and straightforward. He hated to ignore the feeling—he'd come this far by balancing wit and instinct—yet he could find absolutely nothing wrong.

He looked forward to the closing gala, when the three of them would work together for the first time. It would be, he just knew, a grand success and go far to advancing Maria and Grace as friends. At the very least, it would show Grace that working with Maria was more profitable than not. That must be the last bit of uneasiness in his mind—that Grace and Maria might not mesh as working partners. But even if they didn't, it could be worked around in such a way to keep both women in his life, if not at the same time.

"If we are keeping to previously successful habits, might I suggest we carry the thing back towards the dock, then bring it up that corridor? It will seem less like I—or you—stole it."

Maria's suggestion broke up his ruminations, reminding him of the task at hand. He beamed. "A brilliant idea, my sweet love."

He knelt to grab a corner of the box in his right hand as Maria did the same in reverse on the opposite side. He balanced the top of the box with his left hand. It was still awkward, but considerably less heavy. They shuffled out of the room sideways and paused long enough to close the door.

They backtracked towards the Festival docking area as if making a delivery, took the lift down to the main level and began the walk back to the security office. The first level also had the cafeterias and rooms for social events such as the opening mixer, as well as a few shops selling prints and other limited edition, cheap-by-comparison copies of the original works. The big galleries, exhibits, and auctions were on the second and third levels. This corridor was deserted.

Sil's combrace vibrated and he looked askance at it, or rather in the direction of his wrist. The device was obscured by the heavy box. Everyone he cared to talk with, including Grace with her so helpful bed companion, was at the security office awaiting their grand arrival. Whoever was trying to reach him could wait.

Without warning, Maria thrust the weight of the box at him,

saying, "Hold this."

He staggered under the sudden weight shift. With no time to alter his grip, the box began a rapid slide to the floor. He went down on one knee, trying to cushion the box's fall. Damaged, Colonial Insurance might decide on a lower value from which to base his fifteen percent. He turned his head to see what was so urgent.

Maria's face was coldly serious as she drew a pulsed weapon from beneath her tunic. "Sorry, Quicksilver. It may be worth more to *you* to return it, but it's worth a lot more to me to keep it. And now," she gave him a wide grin, eyes sparkling, "Maria Christina will be remembered as the one who outwitted the great Quicksilver."

She would never hurt me, some part of his mind protested. As he grappled with the incongruity of his certain belief and the reality of the weapon pointed at him, she shot him.

The pain as the pulse slammed into his back was like nothing he'd ever experienced, driving him forward to his knees. The box fell to the floor with a thud he barely registered, and then his head was also on the floor, his vision blurring until everything went blessedly black.

SIXTEEN

"...lucky...three...broken..." Something beeped in an annoying high-pitched tone.

Sil blinked, but the voices and beeping were gone and he was in a hospital room. He looked about warily, uncertain how he came to be here. Then he spotted Grace through a half acrylic wall. Her face brightened with a happy grin, then darkened like she might kill him. Hadn't someone just tried that...? She pushed into the room and pulled the privacy curtain closed, rattling the rail with all the authority of a health care professional. "I hope you're happy, you foolish bastard."

He licked his lips and she began to pour some alluring water into a cup. He couldn't look away as he said, "I'm alive."

"Only because your girlfriend's a lousy shot."

Sil winced at her words, as memory came flooding back. The William Bowie brutalist art, his Maria Christina, and her violent betrayal. *How could she?* "How long have I been here?"

"Not long, a couple hours. I'll let Nick explain it. He thought you might appreciate an explanation before you leave here." She passed him the cup of water.

He closed his eyes as he drank it, relishing the moisture.

Maria had shot him. It was unbelievable. She'd *shot* him. In the back. With a prohibited weapon she'd gotten who knows where. His lips parted to voice a protest—*she would never hurt me*—but the words never left his mouth. Why would he even want to say such thing after she so clearly had? He stared into Grace's green eye, feeling... bewildered. "Grace?"

She gave him an assessing look. "They dose you with pain killers? You seem pretty out of it."

"I was shot," he said, almost as much question as an answer to hers.

"Yeah, and you got three busted ribs and one helluva bruise. You missed a punctured lung by a ridiculously lucky fraction of a millimetre. The fates must adore you." She paused as if considering saying more and changing her mind.

"Hm," he grunted, not feeling lucky in the slightest. Though he supposed it was better to be alive than dead, so there was that. He tried to think past the pain killers. Hadn't he a feeling something was wrong? But he'd been so certain she would never hurt him. He frowned. There was confusion wrapped around his pain. He tried to focus on Grace, because she was was... clear. Didn't he deserve an 'I told you so' from her? Instead he asked, "She get away?"

"Yeah," Grace said, her expression showing her disgust.

"Oh." He had to think—how did he feel about that? "Good."

"Good?" Then she saw the flat expression, and deathly chill in his blue-grey eyes. "Oh."

He sipped on the water, then sipped some more until he felt he could say something sensible, that he was sure was true. "I do regret the loss of the artwork. And the recovery fee." And that the loss made some of Vincent Montrose's lies look like truth.

The privacy curtain jerked open with a metal on metal clash as a voice said, "I imagine you do." Nick Delaney.

Sil leaned back and closed his eyes. Must everyone witness

him in his humiliation? Physically, the pain killers had left him with only a vague heaviness in his back and a mild tightness in his chest. He understood that. He wasn't sure he understood the rest, because he thought he loved Maria and *she would never hurt him* but he'd only known her two weeks so where the hell had those thoughts and feelings come from? Did he hurt because she betrayed his love, his trust, or because she had... used him?

He opened his eyes just a crack, peering at the detective through his lashes. Nick Delaney was still a handsome man in an ugly uniform. He felt some small, irrational pleasure that Nick was here, in spite of his humiliation. Flirting might help. "Detective."

"I thought we'd done away with formality. I tried to warn you, but you didn't accept my tag."

Ah. That was the tag he'd dismissed. He managed a chuckle though it pulled at his ribs. "Foolish of me to ignore a handsome man."

Nick rolled his eyes. "In this case, yes. Want to tell me what happened?"

"She has a pulse weapon," he said, that being the most important detail he could think of. "But I had no inkling of her plan, nor any idea where she might be going. She said she had connections to move that sort of thing, but I never asked for details. I thought..." He stopped, frowning. What *had* he thought, exactly?

"I'll leave you two to chat," Grace said. "Sil, you want something to eat? Fruit salad?"

Why was she being so nice to him, after he'd been such a despicable friend? "Most kind," he murmured. After she left, he tried to meet the detective's eyes, but he couldn't quite manage it. "You must find this quite amusing."

Nick's face remained impassive, serious. "Maybe the slightest bit." He cracked a smile then, which made it tolerable. He looked delicious when he smiled. His expression grew serious again. "I'd have expected Montrose to be feeling all vindicated but he seems to have some small degree of sympathy for your plight. He's bemoaning the loss of the art, and harrying me to find it, again." He paused. "IPLE has another task for me."

"Still being punished for clearing my name two years ago?" Sil had found it amusing, but now he felt a little sad. "I'm sorry for that; it doesn't seem fair."

"They waited for a conviction, so there's that. I understand Ser Lavender's defence attorney has recently found zirself quite penniless."

"Sadly, ze will likely recover," Sil said, grateful for the reminder that he himself was no longer in financial straits. He was still in need of honest work, though. Without it, he would have to live a frugal existence, which was annoying. Yes, concentrating on the minor annoyances of daily living was another good distraction, although a binge of liquor and flowers would have been his preference.

He noticed Nick studying him. "Doc said you were lucky your assailant was a poor shot."

"I'm feeling so terribly lucky, yes," Sil murmured, closing his eyes and consciously keeping his mouth from turning down at the corners. The silence continued for long minutes and Sil thought Nick must have somehow left without disturbing the noisy privacy curtain. He sighed heavily, feeling more sad than angry. He tried to find something else to think on lest self-pity pull him down, into a sucking vortex of— the sound of a throat clearing startled him back to the here and now and he opened his eyes, surprised to find the handsome detective still standing at the foot of the hospital bed. Was he to be arrested for something? And he'd not thought the day could get worse! Hiding his alarm, he said, "You're still here."

"Keen observation. Listen, I should have said something sooner, but it seems I have something of a sadistic side. When they brought you in you had trace amounts of a drug in your blood."

It took Sil a few seconds to understand what Nick was saying. "Ma—she drugged me?" He frowned. "What sort of drug?"

"Street name is Cursion, makes you susceptible to suggestion. Mostly used by—"

Sil held up a hand to stop him. He knew which sorts used it. "But doesn't that need...?"

"Grace said you kept repeating certain phrases. I figure she hit you once with enough to load you up with... um, warm feelings... and sweet words."

Sil didn't see any mockery on the detective's face, and he was grateful. "We're so compatible. We have so much in common. She will never hurt me." He bit the inside of his lip hard. He frowned again. "How is it she never managed to turn me against Grace? She certainly tried to get me to see her as unnecessary."

Nick shrugged, a graceful motion Sil would have appreciated more under other circumstances. "She must not have known about Grace when she initially tried to, erm, program you. We think she somehow administered small doses to keep you open to at least reinforcing the key phrases; not enough to change your mind on anything, not in such a short time. That's what we've put together from Grace's testimony on your out of character behaviour and the trace amount of drug still in your system."

Sil took a deep breath, wincing as it twinged his back. "So I didn't really love her." It explained his sense that something was wrong. In spite of her drugging him into trusting her completely, some part of him still knew it wasn't right. Not that it had done him any good.

"I have no idea, but whatever you felt was definitely artificially enhanced, shall we say." Nick gave him a searching look. But all he said was, "We're going to have to move you as soon as you can get dressed. Word has gotten out you're here. Silver Tation isn't a very popular name on Phobos Station at the moment. Thought you should maybe have an escort back to your quarters at the Festival."

"You think someone else wants to try to kill me?"

A hint of a smile curved ever so slightly on the detective's full lips, but all he said was, "As with Ser Lavender, no one would personally dirty their hands, and it's likely no assassin for hire is to be found on the confines of Phobos Station. Nevertheless."

Sil nodded, not really caring.

"So you should get dressed," Nick added pointedly.

"I'll be fine." He forced himself to pull out his dramatic masquerade and gave Nick a reasonable simulacrum of his careless smile. "The day they find me dead, it will be by the hand of one so skilled and expensive, you will write it off as natural causes." And no one, save perhaps Grace, would mourn him, he thought.

"Undoubtedly. However, today..."

Sil grinned. He tossed the hospital sheet aside and leapt from the bed, and then flinched as the muscles around his broken ribs pulled. He grimaced, ruining his attempt to dazzle the detective. He sighed and realized Nick was trying not to laugh, having figured out his game already. "Perhaps some assistance?" he suggested, trying to salvage his flirtation.

"I'm sure you can manage," Nick said dryly. "I'll be with at the door with Grace." He turned, pushing back the privacy curtain enough to allow him to pass, then gave Sil a look over his shoulder. If he'd meant to say something, he changed his mind and shook his head, letting the curtain fall back in place.

Sil sighed once more. He had no more interest in the Festival, no desire to tease Nick Delaney by stealing jewels from the closing gala. He simply wanted to put this place far behind him.

He found clothes neatly folded on the table by the bed. Grace, no doubt. Where was a good place to lose oneself in distraction. Oracle, Venus. A ghost of a smile, inspired by memories from before Maria's betrayal, crossed his face before disappearing in a wince as he pulled on his tunic. Yes, that might be just the place. He needed time. Time to lick his wounds, time to assure himself he didn't love her. He couldn't begin any sort of revenge until he was certain he didn't love her.

Even the satisfaction of wiping out Ser Addison's finances seemed insignificant. But thinking of Ser Addison reminded him— he was still in need of some legitimate income. Surely the Oracle Conglomerate had some use for a person of his unique skills. He could thwart crime as effectively as commit it, more so than IPLE. As he'd told Delaney, he didn't have a book.

Getting dressed wasn't quite as uncomfortable as he thought it would be. His thoughts were drawn to the author of his downfall. Maria knew he was Quicksilver. What did she intend to do with that information? Or was she happy to simply have bragging rights?

Only she, Nick, and Grace knew Silver Tation was Quicksilver. He smiled almost reluctantly. That would surely keep things interesting, now wouldn't it?

THE APPRENTICE

ORACLE, VENUS

Jess sashayed through the crowd at the Starshine party pit, riding a giddy sense of freedom and power. He tossed his head, the tinkle of small glass beads lost in the driving dance beat. He knew people were turning to look at him; they always had. They loved his broad shoulders, his storm grey eyes, and long blonde lashes.

His beauty had paid for his ticket from Crush, one of the largest coal mines on Titan, and he wasn't ever going back. He'd pay his stay here on Oracle with crook or looks, then make his way to the Moon or maybe even Earth. Politics didn't fuss him any, he just wanted his life on his own terms. He'd been here long enough to feel like he could cruise without looking like an outer colonies rube.

He scanned the crowd as he danced and sidled his way across the room. There, just off the dance floor, where it was slightly less crowded. A tall man with dark mussed hair and clothes so plain they must be expensive slouched against the wall, eyes closed and sucking on a vapour stick. Bliss, most like—a cheap and legal high

208

that passed through the body quick enough for a drug-free work shift after a few hours sleep. Some people sucked near continuously on the stuff, though everyone said it wasn't addictive. Strange to see a rich fellow like that Blissed out.

Few people on Oracle carried anything of value in their pockets, Jess had discovered, but perhaps tall, dark, and decadent over there might have a bauble or two. If nothing else, he could sell the Bliss packets the ser was likely to have for a few credits more than he had now. And the idea of picking the pockets of someone wealthy pleased him immensely.

So when the fellow straightened, letting his vapour stick hang careless from the corner of his mouth, Jess made it a point to run into him—easy enough to manage in a place this crowded. He met the other's languid, half-closed eyes with a look of feigned surprise and smiled a distracted apology. He continued towards the bar as if that had been goal all the while. With a smirk, he ordered a drink from the holographic menu, resisting the temptation to put his hand in his pocket and fondle whatever it was he'd snagged.

When his drink was put before him, he turned and found himself staring into a pair of alert, sparkling blue-grey eyes, framed by thick dark lashes. It took him a second to realize this was the one whose pocket he'd just picked. Smiling, the stranger said, "Hello, beautiful," in a teasing voice.

Jess smiled warily, giving him another look over. He was slender, yet clearly maintained a regular workout, from the chest visible in the deep open neck of his very expensive tunic. Taller than Jess by almost a head, narrower through the shoulders. "Sorry, love, you're not my type," he said, although under other circumstances, he might have been persuaded.

"Indeed? I seemed to be your type a moment ago," he drawled, smiling.

"Don't know what you're talking about." Jess shrugged, confident that the fellow had just mistaken his eye contact. There was no way he'd noticed his pocket being picked—Jess was too good.

The dark haired man, lazy smile shaping his lips, stroked Jess's hair and ran his fingers across his cheek and over his lips. Jess jerked his head away. "I don't know what you want," he began, and those bright eyes gleamed at him in knowing amusement.

"I'd settle for the return of my property," he said, his voice soft, sexy, with a hint of steel. "The rest," he said, his gaze dropping to Jess's mouth and down across his bare shoulders, "is negotiable." He leaned in to kiss Jess lightly on the cheek, and Jess sucked in a breath. He'd had a lot of propositions, but none quite this... bold.

"I, I don't have your property," he managed to say.

The other man brushed his lips against Jess's ear and whispered, "Not anymore."

And then he was gone, leaving Jess gulping air. He was usually the one doing the seducing, it felt strange to be on the receiving end. Even his pocket now held nothing but a card for the Luminance Hotel, with the word Silver and a room number scrawled on the back.

"Silver. What kind of a name is Silver?"

~ * ~

Grace opened the door and stared at the youth on the other side. He looked maybe twenty, very pretty, and wearing the most current fashion. Shimmery yellow fabric was gathered in soft folds to a collar that fastened behind his neck, showing off his broad shoulders and well-formed arms. He was staring right back at her, and touched the beads in his hair as he noted hers. Sil's taste was improving. Then again, maybe this lovely gamin just had the wrong room.

He looked from her to a card in his hand. "I, uh, I'm looking for... Silver?"

Grace tilted her head toward the room, keeping her eyes on

the young man. "Sil? Your flower's here."

"I didn't order any flowers, sweet Grace."

The gamin's face showed recognition at Sil's mild baritone, confirming he was here by Sil's invitation. "Are you sure? Pretty young thing here asking for you."

She felt more than saw Sil join her at the door. The youth still looked uncertain though, as if in spite of Sil's invitation, he was unsure of his welcome. She moved back into the room as Sil clasped his hands together.

"I wasn't expecting you so soon! Do come in." Sil stepped back to gesture the gamin in, and Grace grabbed the electronic scanner. Ever since Maria's betrayal, every petty with access to the c-net had been trying to prove themselves against Quicksilver. A hand-held scanning device, like that used by private security firms, had proved a worthwhile investment. Although it was possible Sil had just liberated this one from Oracle's in-house security firm, with which he'd been working on and off the past year.

"Y-you were expecting me?" He sounded doubtful as he crossed the threshold and gave Grace a startled look when she ran the scanner over him.

"Sorry, darling. We've had some small difficulties with strangers lately," Sil said, almost apologetically.

"I understand," he replied, clearly not understanding.

She watched him smooth his features into a not quite flawless mask of confidence and she began to suspect what Sil's business was with this one. Beyond seduction.

"Grace, my dear, might you leave me and my new friend to discuss our... mutual interest?"

She replaced the scanner on the entry table and studied Sil. He was studying their guest with equal intensity. "Sure. He's not carrying anything, chemical or otherwise. I'll be in my room, if you need me."

"You know I'm not one for menage," Sil said, his voice smooth as silk.

She glanced upward and shook her head, just enough to set her beads to tinkling. With one last backwards look, she closed the door that adjoined their rooms.

~ * ~

Sil was keenly aware of how another pretty pickpocket had breached his defences, but this one intrigued him. He showed such hesitation. Did that mean even one this new to the game felt confident enough to try himself against Quicksilver? Sil's mouth tightened. It could be the youth was actually very skilled, and used his age and the appearance of uncertainty to lure his marks into complacency.

"You got a body bot, huh," he said, staring at the door Grace had vanished behind.

"Grace is my assistant," Sil said coolly.

His cheeks took on a pink hue. "Sorry, I—they said most cyborgs in the inner colonies..."

"They were incorrect." Sil gestured toward the small table in his room. In spite of his wariness, the blush added to the gamin's attractiveness. Grace had said he had no chemicals, so taking the pretty thing to bed would—probably—be safe, as well as rewarding.

"Why were you expecting me?" He sent a glance towards the sparkle curtain hiding the bed.

"For curiosity's sake. If nothing else," Sil said, letting his gaze slide appreciatively over the young man's body. He was rewarded with another charming blush. "But there is something else, yes?"

"Jess. My name, I mean. I, um." Jess's face flushed a deeper shade and his hands rose and fell as if he didn't know what to do with them. "I'm, I don't—I mean, I'm usually the one..."

"Come here," Sil invited. He ran his hands over shoulders broader than he usually liked, and unfastened the collar that held fabric over the gamin's chest. His skin was a pale bronze, highlighted with shimmering gold hair—a natural blonde.

He pressed kiss into the hollow formed by his collarbone, sliding his hands across a chest less defined than the broad shoulders might have led him to believe. He pushed the younger man's cheap cell suit lower, taking the half hard penis in hand and stroking it masterfully to a full erection in seconds. "Come to bed, my pretty, pretty pickpocket."

~ * ~

Sil had been somewhat more aggressive than usual in his love-play, but ultimately his desire to see that look of orgasmic pleasure on his lover's face and know he caused it won out. It always did. Jess was spent, golden limbs still tangled in damp sheets. Sil fetched a cloth from the hygiene station, warm and wet, and gently wiped Jess clean of the most obvious results of their pleasures. *Lovely.* Don't be thinking fondly on him. *But he looks so... innocent.* He did, and very young. His combrace said he was at least eighteen—such weren't issued until adulthood.

"Silver?" Jess's lips were kiss-swollen, and his eyes half closed in post-coital euphoria. Sil resisted the urge to kiss him again, settling for sitting on the bed beside him.

"Hmm?" He wondered what this youthful pickpocket might have planned.

"I'm glad it was you."

"What was me?" he asked, wary. Had the lassitude of sex made his companion loose-lipped, or had Sil's talents swayed Jess to confess an ulterior motive?

"I'm glad you were my first."

Sil's eyes had drifted down Jess's body, but those unexpected words snapped his attention back to the gamin's face. "First? Surely not—you've had sex before?"

"No. I mean yes, of course, but just not, you know. Penetrative."

Sil could only stare, suddenly doubting his earlier conclusions regarding the young Titanese in his bed.

"I always thought to, you know, save something for an anteem, maybe even true love."

Sil swallowed before answering, suspecting he had somehow avoided one kind of trouble while falling into another. "Why didn't you stop me, then?"

Jess's face took on that pink hue Sil found so disarming. "I didn't want you to stop. You're so... no one's ever..." He sat up, so his arm brushed Sil's, their faces intimately close. "I'm glad it was you," he repeated in quiet sincerity, leaning in as if for a hug.

Sil complied, mostly so he didn't have to look into those grey eyes, so vulnerable and trusting. Running his hands in comforting strokes down Jess's back, he said, "You're not going to... imprint on me, or anything, are you?"

To his surprise, Jess's shoulders began to shake in laughter. Sil hadn't realized the word was quite so well understood.

Jess raised his head, a broad grin on his face. "No. Maybe," he said, "But only for a little while."

Sil hadn't felt this out of his element in quite some time. "I'm not looking for a swain," he warned.

"Wouldn't a swain have something to gain from the relationship?" Jess was still grinning.

Sil raised one eyebrow and Jess blushed again. "Apart from the obvious," Sil said dryly, "You might also want to learn how I picked your pocket so much better than you picked mine."

Even as Jess's face grew serious, Sil repeated his words silently, feeling like he'd inadvertently committed himself to something.

~ * ~

Sil stayed awake long after Jess had fallen asleep. He was fair certain Jess had no idea who he was. Since Maria had so badly used him, his confidence in his ability to trust his instincts had eroded. A dozen or more petties had already crossed interplanetary space in an attempt to repeat Maria's outwitting of Quicksilver, and they were all living crime-free lives now, either in lock-up or on government love.

Jess seemed naïve enough to attempt to duplicate Maria's trick right to the picking of his pocket, certainly, but something didn't feel right. Jess reminded him so strongly of himself at that age. Well, himself at twelve or thirteen. It would be a good trick to try to use his past against him, make him all sympathy and syrup to Jess's situation... but who knew of it?

He'd never told Maria, they hadn't had those sorts of conversations. Grace didn't know the whole of his past, only that parts were unpleasant. Not even Nick Delaney's undoubtedly extensive dossier on him could possibly reveal such details.

He frowned in the darkness. Marton LeBrea knew.

Jess sighed in his sleep and turned, his arm falling across Sil's chest. The movement set off the twinkle lights in the privacy curtain, sending golden dancing lights over the supple body beside him. Just the sort Marton liked.

Sil's mouth twitched at one corner. Unless Marton had changed drastically, Jess would never have escaped the Palace with such artlessness. That left only one conclusion—the pretty gamin had targeted him purely by coincidence.

~ * ~

Jess proved his sexual expertise in the morning with exquisite oral. Lack of penetrative sex clearly had not meant lack of experience. Sil was appropriately appreciative, returning the favour as they shared a shower. He loaned Jess his robe and pulled on a long tunic that covered him to his knees.

Grace never cared what he wore or didn't, but he had no desire to waste time explaining that to Jess. The poor gamin looked embarrassed enough when Grace breezed into the room without so much as a knock and joined them at the table.

"Good morrow," she said formally as Sil pulled up the room service menu.

"I should go," Jess said, face pink, eyes downcast.

"And miss breakfast?" Grace said, raising her eyebrow.

"Nonsense. Besides, my lovely, we need to talk." He automatically selected fresh berries and toast for Grace, and a plate of scrambled egg with rhizoria strips for himself. "What would you like?" he asked Jess.

"Um, I usually just have... I don't know."

Sil nodded. Probably some form of rations, to save money. He doubled the order. "There'll be fruit and egg enough for all of us," he said with a pointed look at Grace.

"A whole order just for me is too much," she said unapologetically before turning to look at their guest. "So who are you, not-a-flower?"

Jess caught Sil's eyes before answering. Clearly he still retained more than a little of the Titanese prejudice against cyborgs. But when Sil indicated he should answer, he said, "Jess. Robasca."

"And how did you come to Oracle, Jess Robasca?" Sil asked. He kept his tone conversational though he was tempted to go all stern.

"Sucked my way out, I guess. Exchanging favours for a ticket."

He was claiming he came straight from Titan? "And how does a pretty young thing learn to pick pockets on Titan?"

Jess smiled, transforming his face from awkward youth to confident young adult. "I'm from Crush, it's big enough to get lost in."

Sil glanced at Grace who nodded and said, "Crush is easily ten times the size of Black Thunder."

Jess's steel grey eyes widened as he looked from Grace to Sil.

"Black Thunder? Silver... Quicksilver?"

"Ooh, he's sharp," Grace said, rising to her feet as the door chimed.

Jess covered his face with his hands, elbows resting on the table. "Oh no. Did I pick the wrong pocket!"

"Or the right one," Sil offered, his voice all silky invitation.

"Ugh. Not before breakfast," Grace said, pulling their food out of the warm and cold compartments of the service cart. She escorted the machine back to the door before pouring two cups of colonial coffee and a mug of his real coffee.

Sil grinned, and didn't make a motion toward the food until Grace looked full at him. She scowled at his expression, which was good enough for him. He started rearranging the plates so they all had fruit, egg, and toast triangles. Grace didn't care fried rhizoria strips, at least not for breakfast.

Sil watched Jess eat, amused by expressions and moans of appreciation for the food, very like the ones he'd been making a few hours earlier.

He cocked his head towards Grace. "Well?" He wasn't asking how she liked the food, they'd been practically living here for the past year.

"Safe enough," she said with a shrug. "Your call what to do. I'll be watching though."

"Thank you."

So. What to do with this golden gamin who reminded him so much of himself...

~ * ~

"...and you're lucky I don't call the Long Arms!" The would-be mark spun on zir heel, leaving a shame-faced Jess alone with Sil. Sil sighed and pinched the bridge of his nose. It might have gone better had Grace been willing to help but she insisted she wanted no part of Sil's "little project," as she called it. Was he expecting too much from two weeks education?

"I'm sorry, Silver. I've let you down. I promise I'll do better next time!"

Jess's demonstrated proficiency in picking pockets led Sil to believe learning the short con was only a matter of practice.

As a tourist destination, Oracle always had potential marks coming and going. On the other hand, its small size put a narrow limit on the number of times and places one could attempt a con. It was not a good place to practice, at any skill level.

~ * ~

"Why can't we go to Nyne or Prism, if Oracle is too small?" Jess gave Sil one his own wide-eyed looks back at him. His long blonde lashes were darkened with cosmetics, emphasizing the intense grey of his eyes.

It was a tactic Sil was far too familiar with for it to work. "You're not ready."

"I'll never be ready, at this rate!" his eyes narrowed. "Are you delaying so you can keep me as a lover?"

Sil couldn't help but smile. "You're good," he said, ruffling Jess's golden hair, now absent of the distinctive Titanese beads that would serve as a good identifier. "But hardly irreplaceable."

"Thanks," he said, voice dry. "At least I'm good at something."

The gamin had a point. Sil was rapidly coming to the conclusion that he could not teach, at least not anything that didn't involve getting naked. He almost said that Jess would learn or explore the pleasure of lock-up, but he felt a twinge of guilt about just throwing the pretty thing back to the street.

~ * ~

"What's going on with you and that Robasca gamin, Sil? He's practically living with us." Grace was more than curious. In less than time than this, he'd been spouting words of love for Maria Christina. Of course, she'd drugged him. Was this what Sil was truly like, in a real relationship?

"Nothing. He's pleasant in bed. I thought I might pass on some of my knowledge."

She raised an eyebrow, well aware of what he meant. She wanted no part of any sort of apprenticeship or whatever Sil thought he was doing. But she said, "In bed?"

Sil chuckled. "He's certainly a quick study, there." He grew serious. "Although you're right, it may be time to send pretty little Jess on his way."

"So you're not... fond of him?"

They were walking in the optimistically named garden of the Luminance cluster, just outside their hotel. Their destination was a food kiosk across the way, the flower boxes and green air scrubbers and moisturizers were a pleasant lunch time view.

Sil smiled at Grace. "I appreciate your concern, but no. He's pleasant," he repeated, "and cheaper than a flower shop."

"And Jess Robasca? Is he mad in love with you?"

"Oh, I hope not." He frowned. "It doesn't seem to me that he is. Does it to you?"

"Not really, not yet. It's been less than a month. Nevertheless. You are not only the infamous Quicksilver, but also, judging from the noise, skilled in bed. That's a heady combination for one so young." She took the lead toward an empty table.

He nodded thoughtfully as he pulled out a chair for her. "Let's get the passenger schedules to Mars and I'll find a way to gently explain to our pretty young friend that he'll do better there."

~ * ~

As much as Jess was enjoying his time with Silver Tation—especially the nights—he was anxious to show the teacher that the student was ready. He'd used the undernet to make a few contacts

219

with like minded folk from the nearby colony of Prism and had his combrace set to record.

This little con was going to be his proof that he was ready to spread his wings on his own.

~ * ~

Sil was surprised when the tag on his 'brace showed the message, "Limited interaction" and the Interplanetary Law Enforcement logo.

"Silver Tation," he answered cautiously, video on.

"Sorry to bother you, Ser, but we have a Ser Jess Robasca in custody, claims you know him?"

Sil stifled a groan. "Yes, I suppose I do."

"Could you come in to the detachment, Ser? There's some paperwork..."

"May I ask what this is about?"

"Some minor mischief. The youth is of legal age, of course, but your help would make things simpler for us."

Sil nodded at the small projection of the officer's face. IPLE's detachment on Oracle was tiny, and it sounded like Jess had achieved an offence for which he couldn't pay the fine, and thus needed to pay in lock-up. Oracle IPLE preferred to have their lock-up available for more serious offenders. What had he done?

He threw on some clothes and tagged Grace. "Jess is in lock-up. I'm on my way to get him. Buy one of those tickets to Mars, would you, my dear?"

At the detachment, Sil was all smiles and light. Thanks to all the work he'd done for the Conglomerate, he still had high security clearances and appeared as an upright law enforcing citizen.

Jess and an accomplice had been caught attempting a pigeon drop, though of course, IPLE didn't use that term. Sil wasn't sure why it was called a pigeon drop, but like all his favourite short cons, it relied on a mark's desire to gain something for nothing. It was the wrong sort of game to run on Oracle.

They were charged with attempted fraud, as the would-be victim had decided against pressing charges. That was common, Sil learned, as most tourists wanted what happened on Oracle to remain on Oracle and official IPLE charges were a matter of record.

The other had been able to pay the nuisance fine, but Jess naïve as he still was, had been left behind, without a credit to his name. Sil suspected he'd been conned out of it to pay his accomplice's fine.

He paid Jess's fine, ignoring the apologies and protestations offered up. His smiling bonhomie faded to tight-lipped annoyance as they got into the demmar. Finally Jess fell silent. "Are you angry?" he asked in a small voice.

Sil sighed. "Yes. And no." He glanced at Jess. "I said you weren't ready."

"It wasn't my fault," he repeated in a sulky voice.

"It was, but also perhaps a little of mine, as well," Sil said, though his tone was anything but conciliatory. "In my vanity, I thought I could teach you, as I was taught."

"You're just... cutting me loose?" Jess sounded perhaps a little frightened.

"Of course not. I'm sending you to the Palace in Victoria, Mars." He spared another glance as his erstwhile lover. "I've already purchased your ticket. If you're certain this is the life you want, you will find Marton LeBrea. Use my name if he won't accept your tag."

"Who is Marton LeBrea?"

"He was my teacher."

"Oh."

Sil relented a little, reaching over to squeeze Jess's knee reassuringly. "It's doing neither of us any good to continue our dalliance, lover. You need more than I can give."

"And in bed? Does he give more than you in bed?"

Sil chuckled at the sullenness he heard in Jess's voice. "I don't know. I was only fourteen when Marton took me in, and..." he hesitated, and decided to skip the more sordid bits of his past. "By the time I was old enough for such things, I was already entirely besotted with someone else."

Jess ignored Sil's hand and leaned his forehead on the window of the passenger door. "I'm sorry," he said one more time.

"So am I."

~ * ~

Sil and Grace accompanied Jess to the port for departure. The pretty youth wasn't obligated to go to Marton, of course, but whatever he ultimately chose it had to be a path far away from Sil.

"Who knew," Grace remarked conversationally, "that a life with you would lead me to witness a trail of broken hearts across the solar system."

"Hardly that," he scoffed.

"You do feel some regret, though."

"Only that I was selfish enough to not send him off sooner. Now what will IPLE think," he said, "Me bailing out someone."

Grace laughed.

QUICKSILVER TAXED

ONE

"Welcome to Oracle, Ser Tation. Please enjoy your visit."

"I intend to," Silver Tation murmured.

Grace had arrived ahead of him from Destiny, Luna, sweet thing she was. He'd gotten a last minute lead on the whereabouts of a certain murderous sylph and waited to see if it was worth a follow-up. Unfortunately Maria Christina was still clever enough to avoid him. It was almost two years since she'd broken his heart and betrayed his trust, but Quicksilver revenge couldn't be rushed. Eventually, their paths would cross again. For now he had work, legitimate work, here on Oracle.

Oracle was the first and smallest of the Venusian cloud cities. Constructed by private interests to be a pleasure palace free of Earth's restrictions, it had provided the template for Earth to build its own cloud cities. Although that had brought law and order to Venus, Oracle was still a privately owned adult playground with fewer rules than elsewhere in the colonized solar system.

He ignored the many billboards vying for his attention and

headed to the primary lift. Designed to hold a couple hundred people and few demmars, it only went up one level, commerce. There, the colony opened into several broad avenues, one for each of Oracle's clusters. Once, each cluster had been devoted to a specific pleasure, but over time and for reasons of this and that, the cluster differences became more gimmick than else.

Sil brushed his combrace against the pay post for the demmar rental and climbed behind the wheel of the small electric car as it released. The Luminance Hotel wasn't far, but walking didn't fit the image of idle rich dilettante. He left the little vehicle at another rental kiosk across from the hotel's entrance.

The Luminance staff uniform was a sheer black sparkle gown, a perk to staying there, in Sil's opinion. The person at the front desk had a cap of gleaming brown curls the same shade as zir eyes and smiled at him as he pressed his combrace into the hotel's security check-in. "Ser Tation," ze said cheerfully, reading the display. "Welcome back, ser. The Luminance is pleased to host you. Here is your hard key." Sil accepted the card that would unlock the door from the outside. "Same security settings as last time?"

Sil returned the smile and said, "Correct, my assistant has full access to my room, whether I'm within or not."

"Of course, ser." Zir smile, a thing of beauty, faded as ze added the appropriate information, then returned as ze handed Sil some complementary gambling chips. Sil wondered idly about the hotel policy on guest-employee relations. Not worth it, he decided—the Luminance was as much home as he'd had for some time and he didn't need any complications. "Your assistant arrived with all your luggage yesterday, Ser."

Sil nodded. As he threaded his way across the lobby to the lifts, he studied the white, silver, and gold decor with a practised eye. Subtle ambient light glowed from the walls, and one less observant would have missed the many small security cams hidden in the scrolling designs. Vines grew up every corner, lending leafy green accents. Always nice when a colony took the time to make the air scrubbers decorative. Even the lifts echoed the style, once more disguising the security cams.

He pressed the card against the door sensor and paused to admire the room. It was large enough for his comfort, but not as demanding on his credit as a suite. The type of company he invited around didn't care about appearances. He tossed the complementary chips into a green glass bowl by the entrance, noticing his valise by sleeping area. It was a pleasant sensation, this feeling of home.

"Grace?' He travelled light, which had initially confounded Grace, vain as he was. But he liked trouble and trouble often required the ability to move quickly. Lately he was here so often, he considered booking a permanent room and acquiring a more extensive wardrobe. "Grace?" He tapped on the adjoining door, aware that if his assistant was within, her mechanical ear would have heard him the first time.

The opaque curtain that separated the sleeping area from the rest of the room had been partially drawn aside. It began to sparkle, tiny flares of light chasing through it as he turned, activated by his movement in the room. He'd watched those lights dance over many a lover's body and he smiled in fond remembrance. Which reminded him—though he'd returned to Oracle for business, a desperately legal sort that was almost irksome, there was no reason he couldn't mix business and pleasure.

~ * ~

As a rule, Sil didn't run games in such small places as Oracle, but last night his pleasures had been interrupted by a brash and avaricious fellow who seemed to be all but begging to be relieved of his credits. It added a bit of spice to his first week back at the pleasure palace. It also added considerably to his physical assets.

He'd sent a digital copy of his new encumbrance to Grace and come home alone. Not such a rarity as one might guess from her complaints about his flower habit, yet he still slept in. His current bit of lawful work wasn't suffering from one night of personal indulgence.

He yawned. A rich, familiar scent permeated the air, tickling his nose and drawing him through the twinkling privacy curtain.

Grace was already at the table, and she gave him a nod, ignoring his state of undress as she usually did. "Got your coffee ready, Sil."

His Earth bean coffee was his other great weakness, being an expensive indulgence in the colonies. Chilled after the warmth of his bed, he shrugged on a robe and pulled it closed. He sat down, running a hand through his hair, and sipped the rich, dark beverage gratefully. "Did you sell that ship I won?"

Sil did not often gamble—he preferred the odds to be in his favour—but sometimes one had to do things above and beyond to relieve a deserving fellow of his unearned wealth. He hadn't anticipated his mark tossing in the ownership to a personal yacht. Space yachts were a status symbol for those who could afford to bleed credit.

"No," she said with a chuckle. "You just won it last night. I have been reading the specs on it—do you know what it is?"

"A money-sucking black hole?"

She smiled at him. "Under normal circumstances I'd agree with you, but this little beauty is top of the line, cutting edge stuff. It's spacious, Sil. We could live on it."

"Maintenance, Grace." He tapped the table to call up the menu for the Luminance Hotel's room service. He glanced at her and raised an eyebrow. "Fuel?"

"Besides the solar sails—wouldn't be a yacht without 'em— it also has an H3 ion engine, so even the outer colonies are reachable. Theoretically, this baby could do deep space, if there were refuelling depots out there."

He looked up from the menu. "Or anything worth seeing." An H3 engine was small, lightweight, and faster than bad news. And while it was expensive to buy and worse to service, the fuel was cheap as rations. "But now we're back to maintenance."

"Isn't coffee supposed to stimulate your brain? The H3s are practically maintenance free."

Sil selected fried alveo strips, pastries, hydroponic fruit, and imported honey from the menu. He glanced at Grace. "You want something specific?"

"Toast. Berries, if they have any. Any fruit will do."

He nodded and added toast to the order. "So how much is the ship costing me right now?"

"Nothing, it's been refuelled and the dock fees are paid up until sunrise."

Which meant, Sil thought, three months during which the previous owner would try to get it back. Still, he didn't pay Grace to distract him with small talk. It was clear she thought he should keep it and he was waiting for her to give him one good reason why. He lifted his coffee mug to his mouth and raised an eyebrow at her over the rim.

Grace shrugged. "Just thinking it might make a sexy getaway vehicle. There's a two person shuttle on board one can use to travel from say the docks at Destiny to a shuttle pad at Imbrium."

He liked the idea, but the difference between an idea and reality was not lost on him. A private shuttle pad was likely to cost nearly as much as the docking fees. "You do remember neither one of us knows how to pilot such a thing?"

The door chimed and Grace smiled as she got to her feet. "How hard can it be?" she asked, releasing the locks to allow the room service cart entrance. She helped Sil move the serving trays, plates and flatware to the table. "Honey? For me?"

"Sweets for the sweet," he said, aware of the possibility of a glare. Grace had been with him a little over four years now and used to his ways, but she still liked to remind him she was not taken by his charm. "Did you remember to start a newscrawler for any large pockets we might want to empty?"

"Isn't that contrary to playing it right side up?" Grace tapped the cart to signal they were done and a green message lighted the top. "Oh, you've got a package from the front desk. What did you buy this time?"

"Just checking in with what we've missed since we were off doing good deeds on the Moon," he said, casual and innocent. "And I thought some new clothes would be nice."

"There's an idea," she said absently as the lock on the base of the cart opened to allow her to remove the package. "Kind of small, for clothes." She let the cart go on its way and put the flat rectangular box on the table.

Sil checked the label. "I never said what type of clothes."

She raised her right hand, palm out. "Don't want to know." She'd been trained as a gemologist, specifically to grade and classify diamonds. Since Sil had secured her freedom from the indenture once faced by most cyborgs, he'd taught her any number of long and short cons. She sat down and slathered honey on her toast. "Did you check your messages this morning?"

He'd not slept as long as he'd thought, if it was still morning. "Hmm, enjoying the coffee moment. You check them, if you like— are you expecting anything specific?"

She wiped her fingers and tapped her combrace to the table, pulling up the information on the hotel's holo display. Technically that would only give her access to her own combrace messages, but Sil had discovered some time ago that Grace having access to his messages was a good thing. She never pried, she never accidentally deleted anything important, and she'd saved him a good deal of trouble numerous times. If there was anything there he needed to know about, she'd tell him. So he closed his eyes and savoured his coffee one more time.

"Oh. Something official from Earth... hmm." She pushed aside the holo display with a wave of her hand, and took a large bite of toast dripping in honey.

Since she wasn't urging him to pack up and escape on the yacht, he decided the contents of the message couldn't be all that dire. "Bad news is it, my dear?" He kept his own tone casual and sniffed the fruit. The strawberries were small and tasted as sweet as they smelled; Oracle's hydroponics improved every visit. The apple was firm, a hardy Earth variety developed especially for space transport. He put a few berries on Grace's plate and sliced open the apple with the paring knife provided.

"Earth Revenue Service," she said, before popping a strawberry into her mouth with the slender steel fingers of her left hand. Her one eye closed as she bit down on the fruit and Sil, who'd done the same moments before, understood.

Then he registered her words. "What?"

Her eye opened. "We're here so often because you've been doing plenty of security work for the Conglomerate, right?"

He set down the apple, peeled and quartered, and picked up a piece, waving it at her. "You don't get any apple if you try to change the subject."

"Not changing the subject," she said, her tone light and careful. "Just providing context. I'm saying that usually when you do legit work, you get paid as independent contractor. But it looks like Oracle put you on the payroll, you been doing so many good works for them. And now Erev would like you to pay income tax. On your income," she added with just slight emphasis.

"Ridiculous! I pay taxes on everything I buy. I buy things like this," he indicated the imported honey on the table as he rose to his feet, "stimulating Earth's economy. It's—it's a punishment for doing legal work! A fine! And after all the petty criminals I've put out of business, saving Earth and the colonies who knows how much they didn't need to spend on Interplanetary Law Enforcement. I should be keeping tallies."

Putting petties out of business had become necessary after a former lover had started telling any who'd listen how she outsmarted Quicksilver. Everyone had wanted a try. He was slowly restoring his reputation as one not to be trifled with. It didn't help that he'd yet to offer the culprit herself any Quicksilver revenge.

Grace put the last of her toast into her mouth and chewed leisurely. Her calm in the face of calamity did nothing to soothe him and he glared at her, recognizing her ploy. He did not often lose his temper, and truth be told he hadn't lost it yet, but she was pushing. He would not give her the satisfaction. He sucked in a breath and pointedly ignored her as he resumed his seat.

"I don't disagree with any particular point," she said after swallowing. "But that doesn't change the fact if you don't pay—call it a tax or a fine—they'll send the law after you."

"It isn't right." He dipped an apple quarter in the remains of the honey and pushed it towards Grace.

"So you'll pay," she said, accepting the apple as her due, her tone somewhere between a statement and question.

He popped the last strawberry into his mouth and bit down on it viciously, nearly biting his tongue in the process. The flood of flavor echoed the calm that came over him as he came to a decision. "Well. *Someone* will."

TWO

Sil found he was listed as a part-time security consultant on Oracle's company files. As he took all his pay in credit chips, he had assumed his services were off the books, but clearly he was wrong. He'd tried to contact Ser Morgan Black, who'd hired him, but the organizational hierarchy of the Conglomerate was a labyrinth of obstruction. He would complete this job and reconsider the warm thoughts he'd been having about making Oracle his home.

Ser Black had hired him this time to track down a distributor of illegals, which on Oracle could sometimes mean "goods or services we are not profiting from" and not necessarily forbidden by law. In this case, illegal filled both definitions. Information gleaned doing other work for the Conglomerate had him fair certain the Roost was the source he was looking for.

Those who played at Oracle liked the finer things and personal service was high on the list. There was something almost artistic in a server weaving among gambling tables while balancing an overloaded tray of beverages. Bellhops, wait staff, dealers, hosts, and countless others worked and lived on Oracle, and the Roost was one of the places where they went to play in their off hours.

Tourists were not welcome.

Oracle was an oddity for this kind of work. Although it abided by Earth law regulations, it was still a private company. The law gave the Conglomerate some leeway in solving the problem itself, and that was where Sil came in. He was to find the source without making the ruckus an official investigation might cause, then give up the information to the official IPLE detachment Oracle had to maintain in order to comply with Earth regs. He'd considered this a winful situation—he got legit income to screen his less than legal profits and a chance to look all upstanding in the eyes of the law.

The Roost was managed by a shady person registered as Tiffany Zippolos, but several evenings of languid loitering had revealed all the regulars called her Tizz. She favoured figure-flattering glitter drape clothes and didn't bother with the on-again fashion for wigs in bright colours and elaborate styles. Tizz of the Roost was a person of routine, walking the floor and talking to customers at the same hours every night, spelling off the bartenders to do a running check of the receipts and, Sil imagined, set up clandestine meetings to distribute her other product.

Tonight Sil was taking advantage of her regularity of habit. When she began her final walk of the floor, he slipped unseen behind the bar with the ease of long practice, and into Tizz's office, perusing the nooks and crannies with swift but meticulous care. To his dismay, he found neither substance nor chips and Tizz would not be much longer at the front of the house. He glanced at the doorway, gauging his time.

He began tapping at the outer wall, the one separating the Roost from a service corridor and normally accessed only by laundry and delivery carts. He was delighted to discover a bolt hole between the office and the outer wall, with what was probably intended to be an emergency exit leading conveniently to the service corridor. Now it was hidden away in an area little bigger than a closet, fitted with a small table and a comfortable chair. It also contained a shelf with government love rations, a filtered water cooler, and most wondrous of all, a large safe. He smiled and pulled the secret door closed behind him until it clicked into place. Delightfully clever.

Surprised to find a security alert wire attached to a safe in a place surely not meant for the law to find, Sil adroitly circumvented it before prying open his prize. He found an interesting collection of credit chips in nice round amounts, which would accessorize his personal account quite beautifully. He also uncovered some sparkly bits that must be valuable, he reasoned, or they wouldn't be in a safe. He took care to not touch them directly. Paranoid people liked to put poison on their shiny objects. He did not find any illegals, but that was a small disappointment he could remedy another night. The Conglomeration had not burdened him with a deadline. Unlike Erev, he thought with a frown.

His hand on the safe door to close it, he froze as the office beyond the thin hidden door was suddenly alive with voices.

"What is it this time," asked a female voice, unquestionably Tiffany "Tizz" Zippolos.

"Must I explain? Truly?" replied a voice distorted by an anonymizer.

"I gave you five hundred last week."

Five hundred credits was a moderate bribe, as such things went, though of course Sil wasn't entirely sure who Tizz was bribing and for what. He glanced toward the chair, wishing he'd had a chance to sit for this bit of theatre.

"And you've made four times that already, profiting so tidy on things we shall not mention."

Sil hated those voice anonymizers. He could tell nothing of the person speaking, even the elocution could be modified, taking away all manner of useful clues regarding identity. That was the point, he supposed.

"Oh, you are so scary," Tizz said, her voice coldly mocking. "Your head all wrapped around that anonymizer like a big time petty. The Long Arms have been all over this office and not found a thing, ever."

"And I applaud your ingenuity in thwarting their sniffers. But even if you are tired of life, a discussion of my choice of self-preservation is a waste of both our time. Need I remind you how desperate the Conglomerate is to put you away, as well as the Long Arms? Suppose one were to inform them, anonymously, of your secret wall panels, which only open when your office door is closed?"

"And lo, I'll empty them, then, and still nothing for their sniffers," Tizz replied with disdain.

"Nevertheless, Ser Zippolos, I know all your secrets. Make no mistake, as distasteful as your business is, it's no concern of mine, but I'm sure you find it a bit too profitable to give up, hmm? And too indiscreet for legal scrutiny? If I want five hundred credits a week, you'll pay it as long as I demand it and barely feel the pinch."

Sil was disappointed to learn this wasn't a bribe, but blackmail. He had a special dislike for blackmailers ever since he'd lost Tansy, on Mars. Almost a decade ago but never forgotten. Into the ensuing silence, he imagined Tizz must be fetching the payment, no doubt from the till so she'd needn't expose this little hidey hole to the one putting the black on her. At least he knew now where to find what he needed for his employers, so there was that.

"Some day, somebody is going to take you down," she said, startling Sil.

"Until that glorious day—my payment? If it's not too much trouble?"

Sil's heart beat a little faster, for the voices indicated a change in where the occupants on the other side of the door were standing and an idea was rapidly taking shape. He wasn't here to bother about the blackmailer—a form of extortion even worse than Earth Revenue Service—but to break up Tizz's smuggling ring. However, if he could ruin both their evenings...

Another quick glance around the cubby he was in suggested her stash panels were on this same wall. It made sense, though why weren't they accessible from in here? Likely this entire false wall of compartments had not been built by Tizz, nor for the express purpose of smuggling illegals. Pleased to have worked it all out, he snapped the safe door closed without regard for the security alarm and stepped out of the closet with a happy grin. "Good evening," he said cheerfully.

He sidled from behind the person swathed in fabric from to toe, noted the face obscured by the voice anonymizer and gently pushed zir into the small room. "The exit is that way, mind your step," he murmured as the alarm pulsed a strident warning. He stepped aside as Tizz sent a panicked look to the proper door before lunging toward the escape route. "Don't go too far, my dear," he called after her. "The Long Arms will want a word!"

Having the office to himself, Sil settled at Tizz's desk to await the arrival of the law. He wasn't wearing his usual finery, unwilling to dirty it with skullduggery, but he wanted to appear as much his usual self as possible, so he put his always empty vapour stick in his mouth and hummed an idle tune until the Long Arms pushed through the door. He took his feet off the desk and slipped his vapour stick into the fingers of his left hand. "Finally. I've been waiting for you."

After some confusion over whether or not *he* was Tizz, which made Sil wonder about the intelligence level required for law enforcement, he managed to convey the pertinent information. Oracle was a tiny city and even private craft required dock clearances, so Tizz Zippolos would be apprehended sooner, rather than later. He directed them to the hidden panels, now aware they would not open with the office door ajar.

"I'll leave you to the hard work, my dears," he said with a jaunty wave and paused at the door. "Oh, this needs to be closed before the panels will open. Nice touch, that."

He strolled through the now empty bar and out the front door, breaking into a chuckle as he dusted the Roost from his hands. It was a superb job when the employer was happy, the law was happy, and he walked away with a bonus no one was the wiser for. Tizz would now never miss the chips and bijoux in his pockets. Even the blackmailer was out zir mercenary gain for the night—Sil had skillfully plucked it from zir pocket as he'd pushed the person into the hidden room.

He was still smiling when he got to his hotel. He dumped all the chips into a box devised by himself and built by Grace. It was designed to get rid of any pesky identifying marks or trace scans. The bijoux he deposited into a bowl of thick cleaning gel, which Grace always had on hand.

THREE

The Interplanetary Law Enforcement detachment on Oracle, Venus was so small, Nick Delaney didn't even get his own desk. Instead, they'd provided a link to the IPLE databases in the temporary hab assigned him, little more than a bed and a table with two chairs. Near the core, the window had a view of other public buildings and a busy street. He had closed the screen and programmed an image from Earth, all bright blue sky and fluffy white clouds.

Venus had clouds, brilliantly beautiful at times, but IPLE's budget didn't include the cost of a room with a view for a visiting Special Cases officer. It was also just past nightfall on this particular part of Venus, and he expected this case to be solved long before sunrise, which wouldn't be for another three months.

That expectation was rapidly fading. Ser Morgan Black had used zir considerable influence to contact Special Cases directly in Destiny, Luna. Nick had been assigned after the analysts at HQ noticed some peculiarities in the case.

Normally a blackmailer with this type of leverage had some sort of history to be traced. They started small, had a few minor arrests. This one seemed to have just appeared out of thin air, already skilled in sussing out the secrets of those with the most to lose. Nick had acquired a number of confidential informants over the years, connected to the underground net and no one knew anything.

Out of habit he was running through the colony's list of current occupants, hoping to see a recognizable name, something he could start with. He already had the local detachment's records of those routinely picked up for trifling matters on Oracle. It was a short list, most moved on to larger colonies, he imagined.

He didn't know why he was surprised to see Silver Tation's name come up; they seemed to be forever running into each other. Still, Oracle was pretty difficult to—wait, did the list say Sil was *employed* by the Oracle Conglomerate? His Silver Tation? Well, no not *his... you're letting him get to you and he's not even here.* He scowled at his own thoughts. Sil's constant flirtation sometimes felt like an assault he was increasingly vulnerable to, at the most awkward times. Of course, Sil was just deliberately trying to distract him, which made his effectiveness all the more annoying.

More curious than he should be, given the gravity of the crime he was here to investigate, he searched the local IPLE records for Sil's name. He was listed as having security clearances almost equivalent to an IPLE officer, valid only on Oracle. How perplexing. Equally puzzling, he was also on record as the person who bailed a youthful Titanese out of local lock-up for attempted fraud. Surely Sil would never work with anyone inexperienced enough to get caught.

He stared past the display, thinking. Would Sil be willing to use his contacts to help...? Nick scowled, imagining the smug chortle his asking Sil for help would generate.

Unless he could get Sil interested in the case without asking for help.

~ * ~

Nick tagged Silver Tation, with no response. He tracked him to the Luminance Hotel and arrived at the room door at the same time as the service cart. He checked his combrace. A little early for lunch. He dropped his arm as the door slid open for the cart. Grace Reyes did not look surprised to see him, and he frowned.

"Please come in, Detective Delaney," she said, formal and polite. "Sil will be so glad to see you."

His frown deepened into a scowl as he followed the cart into the room.

"Nicky, darling! We were just speaking of you. Won't you join us for breakfast?" Breakfast. That explained Sil's tousled hair and carelessly tied robe. He could count on Sil to never be formal

Grace seemed to be hiding a smile as she unpacked the covered dishes from the service cart and to his consternation, he realized there were three servings. How could they possibly have guessed he'd be coming? He gave Sil a suspicious look.

"I'm not here for a social call," he said, but his own breakfast had been some time ago, and the food on the plate obviously meant for him was freshly appetizing. He sat down without waiting for an invitation.

"Only in my dreams, I know," Sil said, his voice all dulcet seduction. "What does bring you to the Luminance?"

"Don't be all dazzled thinking it's you, Quicksilver." Not this time. "Morgan Black asked for some official intervention. Seems there's a blackmailer shaking down some of Oracle's brightest lights. Digs out the kind of secrets people are willing to die to protect—and some have."

Sil paused a moment in the act of swiping some greasy substance on his toast. Possibly a reaction to Ser Black's name, since the official records said ze was Sil's employer. All he said was, "Blackmail? A lot of that on Oracle, lately. You can't think I've anything to do with it, you know how I feel about that sort of game." He put down his toast and frowned at Delaney. "Speak true, you don't suspect me?"

"No, of course not."

Sil grinned, but didn't speak, so Nick continued, "I was wondering if you might have heard anything." He was careful to make no accusations of any sort.

"I'm afraid I've been so well-behaved on Oracle, most of the usual petties are a bit shy of sharing with me. How bright are the lights your blackmailer is touching?"

Nick leaned back in false relaxation and stared hard at Sil. "Tobias Kleff is dead."

Sil paused ever so slightly. "Oh dear. Because of secrets? His or someone else's?"

Kleff was—had been—Morgan Black's contracted spouse which made Sil's surprise understandable.

"Did this blackmailer kill him?" Grace asked.

Nick glanced at her. "Suicide. So far the Artist doesn't seem to have branched out into murder."

Sil frowned into his coffee cup. It wasn't an expression Nick saw often on Sil's pretty face. Would the semi-reformed thief find the blackmailer's results enough to warrant a little Quicksilver revenge?

"There's that," he murmured.

Nick hesitated, uncertain which way to push. He ate a few berries to give his mouth something to do, then leaned back and asked, "What are you doing on Oracle?"

Sil gave him a wide-eyed look of surprise. "Honest work, detective. Oracle is too small for aught else."

Nick never knew quite how to take that expression of innocence. Face value, he decided, though he pretended disbelief. "So the local IPLE detachment suggests."

Grace wiped her mouth with a real cloth napkin and dropped

it over her bowl. "Sil seems to have run afoul of Erev."

Nick stared at her. Had he heard her right? The idea was as delightful as it was surprising. "You jest," he said, and turned to look at Sil, who seemed completely *un*amused. "The hero of Titan?"

Sil scowled at him. He hated the idea he had anything to do with what happened after he exposed all Carlton Banook's secrets, which was why Nick couldn't resist mentioning it as often as possible. He grinned at Sil, enjoying his discomfort.

He finished the berries in front of him and said, "I'm not fool enough to imagine you've permanently turned a new page. At the very least, you are still like to hear something of this blackmailer, who has the audacity to style zirself as The Artist, and I'd appreciate it if you passed it on." He dared to meet Sil's eyes. "Oracle is a small place, as you've noted." He hoped he sounded vaguely threatening.

Sil merely smiled, as if he knew Nick was bluffing. "And why would I do that, my darling Nicky?"

Bluff called. "To prove what an honest citizen you've become," he replied, resorting to sarcasm.

Sil gave him an exaggerated pout. "No reward?" He leaned on the table, his gaze suddenly intently seductive. "Not even something... personal?"

Nick rolled his eyes, ignoring the tiny thrill of anticipation. *Never going to happen.* "At the very least, don't get in my way." He pushed suddenly against the table, rising to his feet. He gave Sil a long look of disapproval. "Thanks for lunch."

~ * ~

Sil was watching the door after Nick Delaney left with something like rue. Grace began stacking the empty dishes in the appropriate chute.

"Sometimes I think you two should just kiss and get it over

241

with," she remarked.

He laughed. "Don't think it hasn't crossed my mind."

"How did you know he was coming?"

"He tagged me. It's what woke me."

Grace raised her eyebrow at him. "Did he, now."

He wasn't sure what she meant, so he only said, "Did you have a chance to look over that bijoux I left for you?"

She accepted the change of subject and rejoined him at the table, with fresh coffee. "Far better quality than you usually give me. Just re-mark them, and sell them, or would you like to know if they've been reported stolen?"

With her slender metal fingers, she could remove micro security and imprint new ones, so it didn't much matter if the gems were stolen. Unless... Sil laced his long fingers and tapped his chin thoughtfully. "Perhaps that would be best. Just in case the reward for returning them is greater than the resale value."

She nodded. "What did you mean when you told your darling Nicky that blackmail was going around?"

Sil, who had closed his eyes to savour his coffee, opened them at her comment. He smiled. "Have I a tale for you, my dear..."

FOUR

Grace had listened with interest as Sil recounted his adventures of the previous night. "Such a coincidence, two blackmailers on Oracle. Wouldn't it seem likely they're one and the same?"

Sil didn't say anything as he finished his coffee and cleared the table. Leaving only the glass coffee cups on the table, everything else went into the service chute. Finally he said, "Nick said this Artist he's looking for is touching Oracle's brightest lights. I hardly think Tizz of the Roost falls into that description. It would be terribly amateurish, for one skilled enough to find leverage on such well-secured folk."

She nodded.

"Still," he added, "it bears keeping in mind."

Grace smiled, pleased. He had always, right from their first meeting, treated her like an equal, like her thoughts mattered. It meant more to her than merely being useful.

She checked the marks on the bijoux he had liberated from the Roost's safe, confirming the marked ones were stolen, but no one was currently looking for them. "Sell them, my dear. Unless you'd like to keep one."

He always offered. She had no interest in such things.

He had then told her he was off to find some entertainment—which could mean almost anything, but most likely a visit to the Window Box. She teased him mercilessly about his flower habit, mostly because he paid too much for too little, in her opinion. Paying them to sleep over, just for the comfort of a warm body.

She had no advice for him. They travelled too much to form lasting relationships, and Sil, who had always been wary of relationships, was even more so since Maria Christina's betrayal.

The bijoux included two flawless Europan pearls, which were not really Grace's speciality. Her enhancements once again proved useful beyond their intended purpose and she was able to determine roundness and lustre. They were unmarked, but pearls from Europa had an unmistakable quality. There was a black opal, rare everywhere, and probably the most valuable stone of the lot. Two of the diamonds were marked with Black Thunder's code, one of which she herself had originally marked. She felt a righteous glee erasing the official marks and imprinting the stones with new numbers to gave them a right side glow. The other diamonds were also Titanese by composition, but their marks had already been erased. She tidied up the job and added crisp new ones. All the diamonds were well cut, likely by the same jeweller.

Grace had been a moderately skilled gem grader in Black Thunder until a breach had ripped apart the grading room, catching her left side before she could find cover. Her ear looked normal and provided nothing more than standard hearing function, and her leg was also basic, but her optics and telescoping needle-like fingers had cost the company a nice bit of pretty. After her upgrades, she was able to take a raw stone, see every inclusion and flaw, and recommend the precise cuts, shape and facets to maximize the value of a gem. Between her optics and fingers, she could imprint a stone with micro identification numbers vital for insurance purposes. If she'd been free, she would have commanded a salary few companies would be willing to pay. But indebted to Black Thunder for her "improvements," they didn't have to pay her at all, her "salary" went towards her debt, minus the cost of food and shelter, of course.

When Sil had convinced the mine manager to pay her indenture, she theoretically could have gone anywhere. Instead, she chose to stay with Sil, the first person she'd ever met who acted as if she were perfectly normal. Fortunately, for both of them, her very specific skill set was one a sometime jewel thief could use and she had a head for numbers. Sil hired her full time to make sure his money didn't run out too quickly while they lived a lifestyle she'd never dreamed of back on Titan.

The gems sorted, she opened her favourite auction site on c-net and listed them for sale under her business name, Quality Gems. She was a legitimate registered business, and unlike Sil, she had no problem paying income taxes.

Her next task was to visit their new ship, see if she could get an idea of how difficult it would be to learn to fly it.

The cities of Venus floated high enough in the toxic atmosphere to maintain a relatively mild temperature and Earth-like atmospheric pressure. Because the breathable air was less dense than the Venusian atmosphere, the flat-bottomed domed cities floated without further mechanical aid. The design meant the docks were always at the base or bottom level of a Venusian city.

She brushed her combrace against the demmar rental kiosk and drove the small electric vehicle to the vertical lifts and waited her turn to board. She used her embedded ID again to return the demmar to a kiosk on the bottom level, and once more to pass into the port area and a final time to access the docks. Security was intrusive and intensive in a floating city devoted to pleasure; it theoretically kept everyone honest. Grace didn't care who knew where she was going. No one would actually be looking unless she did anything untoward, and she left untoward up to Sil.

Small ships were shunted off to the side and it took her some searching to find the small vessel. She drew up short when she realized she wasn't the only one looking at it. A person of masculine presentation, dressed in the Titanese style of tight fitted sleeves and bright tunic, stood with arms akimbo while intently studying the yacht. The former owner, perhaps? Surely he'd cause no trouble here.

"Give you good day, Ser," she said, careful to announce her presence. Many people were uncomfortable around cyborgs, she'd learned to give plenty of warning.

The man turned and did a wide-eyed double take as he noted her mechanicals. "And you, Ser," he replied. She noted the beads adorning the ends of his hair and resisted the impulse to touch her own.

"That your boat?" Grace asked, gesturing with her delicate metal fingers.

"Ha, no." He returned his attention to the yacht. "This is the first time I've seen one of these up close." He turned and gave her a side eye. "I'm guessing it's not yours?"

"My boss won it a couple nights ago in one of the gambling halls. He wants me to check it out. Bit worried the previous owner might not feel it was square."

He smiled. "Guess he might." He shifted his weight, his eyes darting from her to the ship and back. "Name's Doyle," he said, as if on impulse. "Would it sound too odd if I asked to accompany you? I would love to see inside."

"It does sound odd," Grace said, studying him. He didn't look dangerous, but then, neither did Sil.

Doyle smiled again. "I'm a pilot, never used to fly much past Titan Station, but with things all changed there..." He shrugged eloquently. "Opportunities, right? I'd love to see the cockpit of this beauty." He caught her look and added, "I came through the same security checks you did, I've no weapons."

She wasn't sure if he was naïve or she was jaded. She could think of at least three items the scanners wouldn't flag that could render a person unconscious, and one that could kill. But then she'd been enslaved by the company town in which she'd been born and now worked for a criminal mastermind, so there was that. Besides, she could deliver a kick with her left leg that would neuter a man. Even though he was clearly from Titan, he didn't obviously share their general distaste of cyborgs. "Certainly," she said. "How's a Titanese lad get his pilot license, anyway...?"

~ * ~

Sil's secret pastime was the adventure complex. One could experience zero g, climb walls, run obstacle courses, or play games with racquets and such. There was an undemanding social aspect to it, and it was a more interesting physical challenge than the exercise equipment in every hab and most hotel rooms. Sadly, Oracle's major flaw was that it did not host an adventure complex.

It was, however, a pleasure palace and everything was always open. Perhaps he would find a party pit, and pleasant people to dance with. He had dressed to play up his looks, a tunic of real Earth silk in a grey-blue that emphasized his eyes, and dark blue trousers open on the outside seams, closed at the hip and gathered at the ankles. The tunic contained only basic pockets, but he didn't plan to fill them with other people's belongings. He only needed a place to put his vapour stick when it wasn't in his mouth or fingers.

Sil paused to the side of the Luminance Hotel's broad main entrance, watching runners leave to fetch things delivery carts might have fetched. Some considered paying a person to deliver something to be a mark of luxury, others felt service carts were more trustworthy. The patrons of Oracle were also of interest, displaying the variety of colonial fashions. Everyone could afford the inexpensive and easily recycled cellulose clothing, but the desire to stand out while fitting in created colonial fashion habits that made life on a place like Oracle—heavy with traffic from everywhere else—such an interesting place to be.

He dusted off his vapour stick and stuck it between his lips. There was a party pit in each of Oracle's clusters. He always thought better when he was doing something, and dancing was a pleasant something to do, but to which cluster should he take his business...?

He lounged against the wall, noting the presence of the Lark. She was one of Oracle's resident petty thieves and he'd met her before, though not professionally. She was pacing until she spotted Sil, then she stopped. He made eye contact and she turned away, rocking back on her heels as if undecided about something. Then she tossed her rose red hair and headed into the nearest food kiosk as if that had been her goal all along.

Sadie Lark specialized in fleecing tourists, selling ticket coupon bundles to places that wouldn't honour them. Most were too embarrassed at being fooled to call the tiny IPLE attachment. If he had to guess, he'd say she wanted to talk to him, but he couldn't imagine why. She'd have to be a little more direct.

He decided to stay within the Luminance cluster. He smiled around the stick and straightened out of his slouch, just as a closed demmar braked without warning in front the hotel. Curses rose above the ambient noise as vehicles veered to avoid a collision. Sil strolled behind a planter of bright green air scrubbing foliage to avoid the disrupted flow of pedestrians and was surprised as something pinged into the faux marble. He dropped to his knees, using the planter as a shield. Instead of firing another dart, the demmar accelerated as abruptly as it had stopped, scattering people and infuriating other demmar drivers. Within seconds it became just one more demmar among countless others.

"How melodramatic," Sil murmured as he got to his feet. He

shook out the sleeves of his tunic, pleased it bore no evidence of this failed assault that a shrug couldn't fix. He examined the tiny furrow in the planter, still warm from the friction of the projectile that had, without doubt, been intended for him. While the staff and guests of Luminance warbled and gathered to discuss the excitement, Sil recovered his vapour stick and twisted out a narrow strip of sharp metal—not a standard vapour stick accessory. He used it to pry out the tiny metal point embedded in the polymer.

He frowned at it, sitting on a scrap of cloth, something he always hand on hand. Someone had tried to dart him. He himself had been known to use a dart gun on occasion; they were effective at knocking out inconvenient victims while their precious goods were rifled. To shoot at him in so public a spot, a temporary knockout was unlikely to have been the plan. Yet if it was an assassination attempt, it was... pathetic. He looked up to see the Lark, standing in the food kiosk door and staring at him. He folded the cloth carefully and put it in one of his few pockets. He walked nonchalantly down the stairs and across the avenue to meet her.

"Were you hit?"

It was a fair question; nothing on a dart projectile was likely to be instantly fatal. "No, my dear. Kind of you to enquire." He no longer felt like dancing, but he was now quite interested in whatever Sadie Lark might have to say. A sin-club would provide the perfect privacy. He crooked his elbow. "Shall we go sinning, Ser Lark, to celebrate my fortunate survival?"

She hesitated only briefly. "As you like, Quicksilver."

"Oh, not me," he lied cheerfully. The lover who'd betrayed him nearly two years ago was all too casual about linking his face to his alias.

Sin-clubs permitted everything consenting adults could consent to and possibly, in secret rooms, some they didn't. Sil didn't enquire too closely; he had non-consensual experiences he'd like to forget. All the rooms he knew about were equipped with sensors that would activate only upon hearing the code word scrolled across the exterior of each door. He gestured the Lark ahead of him, through a door scrolling Papilion. Once behind closed doors, Sil used an non-standard combrace adap to ensure no one was listening. He and Grace had learned a great deal about gadgetry recently.

"You know we're not here for any games," he said. This room contained nothing more than a bed, on which he sat, patting the space beside him.

"I was meaning to see you at your hotel," she said slowly, toying with a strand of her bright red hair as she seated herself considerably further away from him than he'd indicated.

"Decided to wait and see if I survived, first?"

"No! I mean, I didn't know someone would try to dart you. I-" she dropped her gaze, still playing with her hair.

Sil put his vapour stick between his lips. He could afford to be patient.

"I have some information you might find useful. Regarding the one known as the Artist?"

His eyes narrowed the slightest fraction and he drew a long pull on the vapour stick, pretending to exhale before he asked with the slightest bewilderment. "The Artist? What art does that one practice?"

She frowned at him. "I know you know all the underground on Oracle, but oh, I forget you've been away."

"Never assume what one loose-lipped thief says is something worth repeating," he said. If not for one betraying lover, no one anywhere—except Nick Delaney—would have connected Silver Tation and Quicksilver, no matter how tenuously. He would have no one confirm those rumours without a ruthless attempt to quash it. "I work for the Conglomerate." He stopped himself from scowling as he remembered his tax bill. "But fill me in, for I suspect this is a matter that affects me regardless. You know whatever we say will be like it was never said, at least on my part. Probably best for your part, too," he added.

"Your forgetfulness will be a generosity," she said, not meeting his eyes.

"My memory is unreliable, I've already forgotten your name. Soon I shall forget where we are," he added. When she met his gaze to test his seriousness, he winked.

"The Long Arms had me in local lock-up on a suspicion, but turns out the one accusing me had a contracted spouse who would have given him grief if he identified me." She gave a sly smile then sighed. "Never indulge while working, I should remember. No matter, the point is as I was leaving the lock-up, I was approached by one all masked, like those out there. Not unusual for Oracle."

Sil nodded, leaning back against the smooth wall.

"Ze offered me some work, a little outside my scope. Wanted me to break into a private residence up the core." She frowned. "Gave me a data chip with an address, a map, security codes, and the description of the boodle wanted—special marked data chips. Seemed like easy money, all that info already good and provided. The next night I handed 'em over and got some tidy credits in return."

"Did you keep the data chip with the instructions?"

"I'm not a fool, Qui—er, Ser Tation. And I looked at those data chips, being the curious sort. Didn't think too much on it til the news said Tobias Kleff was dead. That's the Artist's art, or artifice. Blackmail." Her mouth tightened. "I didn't know how, or if to say something to you. You've no personal vex with the Artist, or didn't until today."

"You think that was the Artist? Trying to kill me? What would be that one's vex with me?" This was a peculiar development. How would this Artist know anything about him?

"Well. Heard someone, as deftly sticky-fingered as Quicksilver, might have picked a payment from the Artist's pocket. Might have used your face."

Sil said nothing, pondering her words. Nick had characterized the Artist as going after Oracle's elite, and Tizz of the Roost most definitely didn't fall into that circle. Blackmail was only a short step from accepting bribes, so he'd easily believed in more than one blackmailer on Oracle. Even still, he should have given more weight to Grace's suggestion they were one and the same. His intellect must have short circuited. But there was still one thing he didn't understand. "Why did you feel a burning need to tell me?"

There was no such thing as professional courtesy in their profession, although some might appear if two such should find themselves accidentally liberating the same wealth.

"I'd heard, that is, there's rumours say you, that Quicksilver doesn't care much for blackmail and less for dead bodies."

"And?" Sil drawled the word as if he knew where Sadie Lark was going. He didn't, but he was curious.

She hesitated only a moment before admitting with earnest pleading, "And I was hoping you'd take care of the Artist before ze took care of me. See, with Kleff dead, I'm a loose end."

"Has this Artist cleaned up similar loose ends?"

"Maybe, maybe not, but ze came by my crash and said ze had more work for me. I don't want it, but ze knows where I sleep." The Lark leapt to her feet, her hands twitching nervously. "I should have stuck with my own game. I do well enough and then some." She spun around, her eyes wide. "Quicksilver, please. I don't want to die!"

Sil put hands behind his head, and closed his eyes. "Relax, my Lark. I need a minute or three to puzzle this out." He ran several scenarios across the dark screen of his closed lids and finally saw the happiest conclusion. He opened his eyes and smiled beatifically at Sadie Lark. "Sadly, my dear, I think you do need to die."

FIVE

Sil parted ways with the Lark before leaving the sin-club. Wanting to know what was on the dart the Artist had intended for him, he took himself back to his room—still undistracted by any of Oracle's many pleasures—and knocked on the door linking his room to Grace's. It was a courtesy knock, in case she'd been luckier at finding pleasure than he had. He was halfway in the room before she yelped, "Busy!"

"Sorry, darling," he called, not looking at the sparkle curtain around her bed. "Just dropping something off. When you have a moment, my dear."

Her room was smaller than his, and in place of a table at which to work and eat, she had a shelf with a couple of stools, and a smaller sleep area. She could have had a larger room, but she felt it was a waste of money since any time she needed more space, she could use his room. Had to, he thought with a smirk, admiring all the interesting objects taking up space on the shelf. Bottles of powders and liquids, harmless on their own, but could be combined into debilitating powders. Non-lethal was Sil's preference; there were very few crimes on his list worthy of such an ugly solution. Blackmail, distasteful as it was, most certainly didn't qualify. The attempt on his own life was insulting, though. He was certainly inspired to stop this Artist for good and all, which could easily be done in a non-lethal way.

He took exception to the idea that anyone would think he was easy to kill. Perhaps this Artist had merely matched his face to Silver Tation's and did not realize who he was trifling with.

A rustle and loud throat clearing reminded him he was intruding. "My apologies, my dear." He extracted the dart from his pocket and carefully unwrapped it. He set it, still on the bit of cloth, on the shelf and said, amused, "Carry on."

Now, more in need of distraction than ever, he returned to his room and tapped into the local network. "The Window Box," he said, feeling more relaxed already. He kicked off his shoes and put his feet on the desk, then stuck a vapour stick in his mouth.

The screen resolved as Madame Zinnia accepted his call, and it was a measure of her disregard for him that she was still having her face put on. The buxom silver haired lady, perhaps a beauty in her younger days, was a faded blossom now, and instead of pretending otherwise, she parodied the habits of bored young rich dilettantes with exuberant wigs and extravagant decorations. "Zinnia, darling. It's been too long!"

Without turning her head from the artful application of her eyelashes, she said, "Is that the sound of Silver I hear?"

He smiled lazily. "In all the ways you like, my sweet."

She turned to give the camera a sly glance through magnificent, three centimetre long lashes. "Silver on your tongue; silver in your pocket?"

His smile widened and he took the vapour stick between his fingers with the consummate grace of a confirmed user. "Naturally, dear Madame."

She finally gave him a full smile and Sil assumed his credit had checked out. "I heard you and your body bot arrived some days ago, I'd expected to hear from you before now."

His smile never faltered though her slur irritated him considerably. Instead he said mildly, "I suppose my custom is not significant, but I would ask you to not disparage my assistant."

She gave him a steady look before saying, "Apologies," in a tone that did not even pretend to sincerity. The Window Box was the most reputable flower shop on Oracle, her flowers were fresh, and she didn't traffic in illegals. Even her exotics played strictly by the rules. For that, he could ignore her prejudice, so long as she refrained from open insults. She waved a hand as if to dismiss the unsavoury subject and told him, "Many new flowers since last you tagged me—would you like to see them?"

He studied her through half-lidded eyes. "Oh, send me a full catalogue, Zinnia. I'm feeling some adventurous this day."

A symbol glowed red, then green letting him know the catalogue was available for his perusal. For a price, of course. Nothing on Oracle was free. Unless one was very skilled. Grace had been more disdainful than usual of his flower choices of late, and he felt uncomfortably that she might be right. He wasn't getting any younger, but his flowers weren't getting any older. It was time to broaden his horizons.

~ * ~

Grace did not bother to knock before opening the door adjoining her room. If Sil wanted privacy, he'd have locked it. He wasn't much on privacy, his or her own. He'd learned to knock, even if he didn't often wait for a reply, before entering her room, but she'd long given up expecting him to be clothed or even alone, when she entered his.

She'd done the analysis on the dart tip he'd left in her room, and decided he owed her more than a bit of honey for breakfast. Not that he ever failed to share any ludicrously priced delicacy he might order for himself. She smiled. He was a good person to work for, or work with, as the case may be.

The sparkle curtain was caught on the corner of the bed, giving her a clear view of the silken blonde head tucked under Sil's arm. Her smile vanished. The flower shops charged double for an overnight, and it irked her that Sil would pay for a flower to sleep. She marched over, snagged the sheet, and whipped it off with a flourish. "Up and up, my lazy bits!"

She slapped the flower's perfect ass and earned a sleepy pout from a pretty face covered with a silky golden fuzz. "Out of here, peachy, before your madame decides to charge triple!" It was nice that Sil decided to expand upon his taste in— her thought dropped out of sight and her eyes widened as the flower got out of bed, giving her a full frontal view.

She continued to stare in open-mouthed astonishment as the young man dressed and headed to the door after giving Sil a long kiss on the mouth. "Sorry," Sil said, repentance in his sleepy voice. "May I have my sheet?"

She tossed the sheet back, still staring at the door, then busied herself by opening their message files on the table top holographic view. "What on earth did you do with that?" she murmured.

He smiled lazily at her. "If I'd known you'd be interested, I'd have recorded it."

"Oh dear no, I could imagine what the flower shop would charge for such a thing. And before you say anything more, let's pretend I never asked the question. Yes?" When he failed to agree, she tilted her head a little and swivelled her lenses towards him. It was an intimidation tactic that had never once intimidated Sil.

This morning was no exception. Instead, he laughed. "That's the first time I've seen you slack-jawed over one of my flowers," he said, his voice rich with amusement.

Her taste in sex partners was fairly narrow compared to Sil's, although there was an area of overlap into which fell such men as the handsome detective. Normally the slender, silken blonde who'd just left—she glanced toward the door—wasn't her type. "I don't normally see such nice equipment in your bed," she said, with a pointed glance towards Sil.

He clutched the sheet protectively to his waist. "Cruel blow, heartless one."

Grace chuckled, unrepentant. "Come and order some breakfast, I want a special today. While you were paying Madame Zinnia for that large stamen to sleep..."

He laughed at her description. "I like to cuddle," he protested, then grinned at her, just a naughty boy charming his way out of trouble.

She sighed and smiled in spite of herself. "Sometimes I think you hired me for the sheer joy of annoying me. So tell me, who is trying to kill you?"

He draped the sheet around his waist and took a seat at the table. "Trying to spoil my appetite, are you? Yes," he frowned, his eyes turning flinty. "First, I must tell you that you were right and I was wrong. Nicky's little Artist friend and that sadly intellectually deficient blackmailer from the Roost are one and the same after all."

"Is that why Delaney has left a tag saying he's coming by this morning?"

Sil gave her a long look. It was a rare thing she could surprise him. "Then I'd best order for three again. I think he times his visits deliberately, just for the food."

"Oh, I'm sure it's for the company," Grace said coyly, causing Sil to raise an eyebrow at her. "Do they have blueberries? I haven't had those in such a long time, and I did analyze that poison for you. Might narrow down some places to look."

"Indeed? The ingredients are so specific as all that?"

"You know a poison's individual parts are generally easy to get through customs?"

Sil nodded. The right combination was vital, the difference

between knocked out of the way for a few hours and out of the way forever. Grace gave him an exaggerated look of gratitude. "Working for you has certainly taught me new skills. But lest I lose my point before the good detective arrives, I'd guess it was purchased from a local chemist, all premixed."

Sil raised one smooth dark eyebrow at her. "Someone on Oracle is selling kill powder?"

She nodded. "It's a subtle thing, but having a spectroscope in my head is useful for an astonishing number of things not covered by the specs. I must say, I don't think much of a killer fool enough to buy a pre-mix."

"Murder is nasty business. However if one is going to venture along that route, learning to aim might help," Sil added grumpily. "Blueberries it is."

"And why would you be upset at a poor aim? Isn't this the second time it's saved your life?" She was taking the slightest of a chance with the oblique reminder of how his last great love affair had ended.

Instead of answering her directly, he put away the menu and leaned back in his chair. "Someone so effective at one thing, so inadequate in others."

"And you think that's the blackmailer, this Artist? What an arrogant name," she mused. "If you're right, ze's still killed people, if only by proxy."

"I know," he said. "A dangerous person all around." He paused. "Why do you suppose Nicky mentioned zir to me?"

"To get your anger up enough you'll be willing to help him when he asks?"

Sil smiled, and his smile turned to a broad grin. "Our handsome detective friend might be vexed to find you know him so well. But should you be mistaken then we need another way to ensure the Artist goes out of business."

"I had a feeling you'd say so," she murmured.

SIX

Grace, in accordance with Sil's wishes, excused herself when Nick Delaney arrived, taking her breakfast with her. "Nothing I couldn't say in front of her," Nick said.

Sil smiled. "She has things to do. What brings you by again this morning, Nicky? The bounty of my table," he waved at the food, mostly hydroponic fruit and fluffy breadstuffs, "or a desire for my company?"

Scowling, Nick sat down in the chair recently vacated by Grace. "None of the above, but I won't turn down some of that expensively bitter coffee. I heard you were at the center of a dust-up out front of the hotel yesterday, and didn't stick around to answer official questions."

"Oh it was just a minor bother, thank you for asking." Sil sat forward. "Incidentally, I did learn more about this Artist person you asked me about. From all I can gather, this one is a rank amateur."

Nick stared. "Damned effective for an amateur. How did you reach this conclusion?" He gave Sil a suspicious look. "Have you developed a personal interest in the Artist?"

"It would have been but passing, as a favour to you," Sil murmured, "but it's become a little too *mutual* for me to remain objective."

Nick sighed, picked at the breadstuff. "So this minor bother was the Artist trying to what? Kill you? Can't say I don't feel a little sympathy for the urge. But again, how did you determine ze's an amateur?"

Sil nodded, pleased that Nick had made the connection so fast. His ability to so swiftly link events was what made the detective such an interesting adversary. "Ze acquired some of the information ze's using as leverage from a thief ze hired right out of lock-up, so ze obviously has no, hmm, existing connections in the criminal class. And, had ze been successful in zir attempt to end me, it would have left a body in the middle of the street with witnesses. Sheer foolishness, far too much evidence left behind."

"But ze didn't leave a dead body behind."

Sil nodded in concession. "Only because ze has terrible aim."

Nick helped himself to a fluffy, buttery pastry and nodded as he chewed. "Can't fault your logic," he said reluctantly.

Sil did not mention the pre-mixed kill powder. Nick would not be happy to discover Sil had removed evidence before leaving the scene. He merely let the law man enjoy his breakfast while he admired him. Nick Delaney had russet skin, dark brown hair, and gorgeous brown eyes creating a very attractive package, even as little lines decorated his eyes and bracketed his mouth. For the briefest moment, and not for the first time, he tried to imagine what it might be like to kiss that mouth, so often set in narrow, disapproving lines. Sadly, there were more pressing concerns at the moment.

"What else do you know?" Nick asked abruptly.

Sil gave him a slow, seductive smile. "I could amuse you for hours with what I know, darling Nicky."

Nick glared at him. "In your dreams, Quicksilver." But the

corners of his mouth twitched as if he were at least a little amused.

If only he knew. "That was, my dear detective, a change of subject, in case I was being too subtle."

"No one would ever accuse you of being subtle," he muttered. "Can I assume your interest in the Artist involves zir paying your taxes?"

"Such a brilliant idea, Nicky! You are just the cleverest person."

"How?"

"Three thousand, six hundred and fifty-five credits. That's my punishment for being a useful wage-earning citizen. I'm told part of it goes to pay you. Am I supposed to pay you and do your work as well? I ought to move to the TWF," he declared. The TWF was the only tax free colony in the solar system.

"Promises, promises." Nick Delaney rose to his feet. "I don't know why I think you'll tell me the truth, but is the Artist anyone you're familiar with from elsewhere in the solar system?"

Sil shook his head. "No, ze's a mystery. But I'm determined to make zir acquaintance. Zir total donation is not yet assessed, but I can tell you where three thousand six hundred and fifty-five credits of it are going to travel. Directly and in person to the kiosk of extortion otherwise known as Earth Revenue Service."

"That seems a pretty small price to pay for attempting your life. Are you sure that's all you plan for the Artist?"

Sil stood up and started clearing the table. "That's a little difficult to say," he murmured. "It would be a shame to leave the likes of zir in a position to continue zir activities."

When he turned around, Nick Delaney was standing, still as a statue, his lovely eyes unfocused. Suddenly he moved, as if restored from a stasis field, and met Sil's eyes directly. "Sil. I could probably get into a thousand kinds of trouble for what I'm about to say, but would you be interested in a deal?"

So, Grace was right. Again. He owed her more than

blueberries. Hiding a smirk, Sil rested idly against the table. "A deal? With you? Do tell."

"Let me have the Artist, all legal-like, and I won't ask how you paid your taxes, or where any other loose credits might have gone."

Sil gave him an impassive stare, not sure Nick was serious. The wording of the deal suggested Nick Delaney saw a lot more than Sil realized. And let it slide for some reasons of his own. Then he smiled. "Deal. I'm certain the Artist has a murder planned quite soon, so that should take care of that one's future for a good long while."

"Sil," Nick said warningly.

Sil grinned. "Nicky, you know murder's not my style. Trust me."

~ * ~

"Well?" Sil asked. "Went well, don't you think."

Grace leaned on the door jamb, crossing her arms over her chest. "Does he know?" she asked nonchalantly.

Sil turned to her, a quizzical expression on his face. "Know? Know what?"

She pushed off the jamb into his room. "That all this excess of upright, legal work is for him?"

He swivelled fully, staring at her as if he'd never noticed she was a cyborg before. "What in the grand design are you on about, my darling Grace?"

Before she could answer, she saw the light of comprehension in his eyes and he shook his head, laughing.

"No. No, no, no. I mean yes, I tease him and yes, I'm not offering anything I wouldn't follow through on, but no." He grinned at her. "You know after Maria Christina, I could have no other love."

"The woman who shot you."

"I admit our break-up was rough."

"She *shot* you." And left him for dead. And strangely, Sil had still not hunted her down to exact any sort of Quicksilver revenge. Which she had to admit, was irksome. "Besides, you never tried to change for *her*."

"No, my darling one, you've got it all wrong. I'm not trying the right side of the law for Nick Delaney—what a daft idea! You know I've always done legal work in order to live our luxurious life without questions. Oracle is merely too small to run any decent game. That's all." He stared hard at her. "That's all," he repeated with an air of finality.

Grace grinned, holding up her empty palms. "Such protest! But if you insist." She headed back to her room and said, before shutting the door, "But I think you've lost it!"

She half expected the immediate knock and opened the door, still grinning. "Grace," he said, his face composed into serious lines, a look so rare for him her smile vanished. "We have some crime to start tonight, if you're with me." Then he grinned.

She laughed. "All the way, boss."

SEVEN

Sil was nothing if not adaptable. Little troubled him once he had a plan of action, and now he saw no reason not to enjoy himself and treat Grace to a nice outing before the real work started. For the game, her dark braids were tucked into a brilliant red wig, one of the many fashionable colours on Oracle for a night out. She wore a black cell suit, tight as a second skin, under a flowing red tunic and looked like a tourist out to make memories she could never share. He treated her like he was the one she'd never forget and never be able to speak of. It was fun.

A decadent dinner in a food kiosk of shadows cast by soft golden ambient light making everyone look beautiful, whatever their standard of beauty. They followed dinner with cocktails in the Rainbow Sunset, and Sil checked his combrace for the time. "Live like there's no tomorrow," he toasted Grace. The Artist had a date tonight and Sil intended to cut in. In fact, he planned to be a little early.

He and Grace stumbled from the club, an act facilitated by genuine laughter. Her enjoyment of the game was one of the reasons they worked so well together. She was a brilliant friend,

Grace.

They walked arm in arm away from the main thoroughfare to a shadowy garden, lighted with tiny yellow fairy globes. In the light, it was busy, but by dark the only habitues were sinners and a few opportunists. They were the latter, pretending to be the former. Sil gave Grace her instructions and left her by a particular patch of air scrubbing plants. He faded into the shadows, a voyeur to be.

Grace, in enough light to show off her vibrant wig, tucked her delicate silver arm inside the over-dress to hide the shine, and shook her head that the riotous red might obscure the plate protecting her sensitive optics. A demmar with the lights out pulled up slowly to where Grace stood. Sil moved within earshot. "Ser Lark. So good of you to come at my request," said a voice, and Sil stifled a sigh as he recognized a voice anonymizer. If one was going to tie off loose ends, why bother with a disguise? Clearly the Artist had a strong sense of self-preservation, if nothing else. "I noticed you about to sing to one you shouldn't. I'm sure you changed your mind."

"I kept my counsel," Grace whispered. With the Artist's concentration on Grace, Sil slipped like a ghost into the passenger side of the demmar.

"Good little Lark. There is one important thing needs be done," said the voice, raising a dart shooter, very likely the same as used at Sil.

"Correct," Sil agreed, holding his vapour stick to the base of the Artist's skull. "And that one thing is you dropping your kill stick outside the vehicle. I want to hear it hit the ground," he added conversationally.

When Sil heard the slight thump of the weapon hitting the rubberized floor, he said, "Grace, my dear, would you mind collecting that for our inventory?"

"My pleasure."

"So how is the art business?"

"Who are you?"

Sil laughed and poked with his vapour stick as if it were a dart shooter. "Oh, I'm even a worse aim than you, but at this range I think I could manage. The important question is, who are *you*?"

"I suppose you'll have to live with the mystery. For now. Where is Lark?"

"She's dead, like you wanted. Consider it a favour." Sil nodded to Grace, who raised the dark weapon to the Artist's covered face. "My Grace, she, too, is a poor shot, but again, range is the key." Sil eased the door of the demmar open.

"You killed the Lark?"

"Gracious, no. You did. Now if you would kindly step out of the vehicle, I need to deliver you to a dear friend." Sil was used to things going along trippingly well, but this felt too easy, even for him. Then his eye fell on a datachip, glimmering faintly on the seat beside the driver. He snatched at it just as the Artist realized what he'd seen and made his own grab. Sil won, stuffing the chip adroitly into one of his voluminous pockets for later perusal. "I do encourage you to step out," he repeated his cordial invitation.

"Sil."

Without taking his eyes off the Artist, Sil was aware of another demmar approaching. It made no noise, of course, being electric. And Sil realized even as he was thrown off balance what he'd overlooked. The Artist hit max acceleration on his rental, which had never been shut off. With one foot still outside the small vehicle, he was sent tumbling backwards as the Artist sped silently into the shadows.

"Sil!"

He jumped to his feet. "I'm fine, dear Grace. Just feeling vexed with myself. I ought to have confirmed the vehicle was off."

"It was all a bit anti-climactic," she admitted. "I was hoping for more drama and speeches. I do love villainous speeches."

He laughed. "You have a way with words yourself, sweet Grace.

And it's only a battle lost, not the war. I'm sure before we're through you'll get a villainous speech. And," he said, "We didn't come away totally empty handed."

"True. Shall we find out what's on the chip?"

"We should. And thank you, for playing the Lark."

She pulled off the bright red wig and shook her head. "Next time, you get to wear the wig."

Sil laughed again. "Think we can find a pilot to take Ser Lark away from all this? With our yacht?"

"It happens I do know a pilot who would absolutely love the job..."

EIGHT

In Sil's room, Grace pulled off the red over-dress, tipping it and the wig into the recycler. "I don't know how people wear those wigs," she remarked, finger combing her tiny braids and toying absently with the beads.

Sil gave her the data chip before exchanging his own clothes for a more casual robe. Wigs were fashionable for everyone, but he'd been quietly dismissive of the trend that would never quite die. His 'idle rich' look was classic, not trendy, he'd said.

"What's it say, my dear?"

The holo display showed a magnificently detailed rectangle of textured cream, bordered with a gold abstract design and lettered in a font so curly, Grace could scarce make it out. "It looks like an invitation... funny it's on a datachip. Surely it was sent to zir message queue?"

Sil joined her at the display. "Ser Emerson Tewari, 310 Verdigris Hotel. The honour of your presence would be gratefully received at Convention Room 2 of the Regency Hotel." He frowned. "What can it mean?"

"I would humbly suggest it means that, when not in disguise, the Artist is a rather liked individual," Grace offered. "And speaking of liking one well, I don't suppose you could pour some of those intoxicating spirits you like so much? It has been a day."

Still frowning at the display, Sil said absently, "There's a bottle of Shoots by the coffee machine. Pour one for me, too, would you? This doesn't seem like any kind of leverage."

Grace shook her head and rummaged for two glasses and the bottle. Sil had small bottles of more exotic spirits, but she preferred the herbal quality of Shoots. "I suppose it's simply too obvious that an invitation addressed to someone might belong to the someone it was found with?"

"But it's on a data chip," Sil said, as though it was unheard of to do so. "Could it possibly mean the Artist is one Ser Emerson Tewari?" he asked, still staring unhappily at the invitation.

"You keep frowning like that, you'll lose your pretty looks," Grace remarked, putting a glass in his hand. "Why wouldn't he be?"

Sil's frown deepened. He leaned close to the image, then far away, his drink untouched. He straightened and poured the liquor down his throat, eyes closing in appreciation. Waste of liquor, in her opinion. Sil smiled. He opened his blue-grey eyes and said serenely, "Why indeed. It just seems so terribly obvious, I was hard pressed to believe."

"Simplest solution is the most likely, isn't that what they say?"

~ * ~

Sil met Grace down at the docking area, in front of his yacht. Sadie Lark was standing in the hatch door and Sil waved at her. She sent a look around the dock and walked cautiously to him. "You needn't do this. I – I'm not even sure where to go."

"I'm sending you to Destiny, Luna." He gave her a small bit of cloth, folded origami style. "There's chips enough to buy you passage anywhere from there, but Earth has a lot of touristy areas you could do quite well in, if you're willing."

"I'm a born and bred Venusian. Not sure the idea of Earth is at all appealing to me." No matter how rigorously a colonist might keep to the suggested exercise schedule, a born and bred colonial needed time on the rehab station before going to Earth for the first time. Many considered it not worth the while. That, and the big open sky was nerve-wracking for them that were born surrounded by metal and polymers underfoot and overhead.

"It would be, to me. Europa is a good choice, as well, not exactly touristy, but they say it's fairly densely settled with a mobile population. Far enough from Earth that the law can be thin at times. Mars is popular with tourists."

"Thank you, Quicksilver. I guess I'd never thought I'd need bother with travel. Be a bit of an adventure, I expect." She pocketed his present.

Sil hesitated before adding, "If you decide on Mars, I might have some contacts for you, keep you from overstepping someone else's corner. Just go through the undernet. Now scurry back on board, I've a pilot to get you safe."

She smiled gratefully at him and did as he suggested, as Grace and a man who wore his hair as she did—all narrow braids and beads—approached from further down the dockyard. "Grace," he said, his voice reserved.

"Sil, this is Doyle, he's a pilot from Opeegee 55. Doyle, my employer, Silver Tation."

"Opeegee 55? Not familiar." Sil shook the man's hand warmly, enclosing it in both of his, and smiled his friendliest smile.

"Methane refinery on Titan. Outer Planets Group got most of the early contracts, so there were a lot of little colonies named Opeegee before they slowly started consolidating. It's an honour to meet you, Ser Tation. Grace told me what you did for her."

Sil shrugged easily. "Truth be told, was Black Thunder's own manager paid her debt. I was just the facilitator, a mere middleman."

Grace laughed. "Is that how you tell the story."

Sil turned to her. "You trust him?"

"Yeah."

He gave Doyle a broad smile. "Good enough. Grace already discussed payment with you?"

Doyle nodded, beads clicking softly. "A generous offer, given how I've been itching to fly one of these beauties."

Sil's smile this time was genuine; Doyle did seem earnestly honest. "Show me your license is in order and I'll give you the codes. Make sure my little Lark gets safely to Destiny."

Doyle beamed. "I will! And thank you, Ser." He tapped his combrace and a holo of his licensing came up, all current and in order.

Sil nodded and transferred the codes. He clapped the pilot on his shoulder and said, "Good enough. Safe flight, see you in six weeks!"

Doyle nearly danced to the small ship, the beads in his hair clicking in cadence. He shot Sil another happy look before disappearing inside.

"You slapped a tracker into his bloodstream, didn't you?" Grace asked conversationally, watching the ship vibrate as the engines started up.

"Naturally."

"I told you I trust him."

"You're sleeping with him, my sweet, that can affect one's judgement."

"Really," she said, her voice thick with sarcasm.

NINE

The various clusters of Oracle all attracted the same sort of tourist, the primary differences being aesthetic. The Luminance Hotel that Sil was calling home at least until the Venusian dawn was all about light. Ambient light in translucent panels, and cascades of soothing pastel colours. The surrounding businesses supported the light theme, from the pale yellow glowing food kiosks to the raucous flashing primary colours of the sin-clubs. The Verdigris was in a cluster themed pseudo-historic copper and green.

Most of the people who lived full time on Oracle were staff. It was not a family vacation destination; the pleasures of Oracle were all directed at adults, and aimed to get those adults to part willingly with their money for things they would probably not like to advertise. What happened on Oracle stayed on Oracle, or so the saying went. Staff who decided to do the parenting thing left Oracle for cities that offered day care, schools, and pediatric services. The wealthy who owned and ran the bulk of Oracle often only lived here part time, depending on what sort of family life they had elsewhere. Even Sil planned to leave sooner or later. Sooner, if the Conglomerate continued to insist on reporting his income. He grinned and leaned back on the bench across from the Verdigris.

His smile faded as he recalled Grace's accusing him of trying to change for Nick Delaney. Why would she suppose Delaney would even notice? Nothing Sil did or didn't do would ever sway Nick to his embrace, surely Grace knew? That it was that knowledge that made him such a delight to tease? Ah, but now was not the time to ponder such silliness on the part of his beautiful assistant.

His conviction that certain brain cells had died from lack of use increased when the Verdigris Hotel appeared to not have a third floor—the lift only offered two. Feeling unpleasantly perplexed, he went to the front desk. "I'm looking for Ser Emerson Tewari in room 310, but there doesn't seem to be a third floor?"

Behind the desk, a young woman gave him a bright, fake smile. She must be new to hospitality. "Our guests on the third floor do not allow casual visitors. I will call up to Ser Tewari's room and enquire if Ser wishes to see you."

"I'm with the ODD, come to interview him. Who wouldn't want to be part of the Oracle Daily Download?" Sil lied, projecting more certainty than he felt. It was a relief to know he wasn't losing his mind, all the same. If Grace was correct—and he believed she was—and Tewari was the blackmailer then he would recognize Sil from the Roost and the subsequent failed assassination. But even so, ze might not let on. Ze would be confident the anonymizer had protected zir. The Artist was an amateur, but as Nick had noted, a very effective, methodical one.

Fortunately, his confidence was rewarded. It was difficult to resist the idea of being featured on the ODD, Sil imagined. Emerson Tewari was revealed to be a significantly round man by all presentation, not inconsistent with the Artist as encountered by Sil. He wisely eschewed the classic voluminous clothing usually worn to convey wealth but failed to flatter the rounder figure.

Instead, he wore straight lines, though Sil believed he could be improved by broadening the shoulders. He hadn't come to criticize the man's sartorial taste, however.

He stood at the door, staring at Sil for just a moment too long, before stepping aside to gesture him in. "I'm afraid I can't spare you very long, Ser Silobar, I have a busy day ahead. What was it you wished to speak to me about?" His manner was brisk, business-like, and a fraction too tense.

"I was given to understand, Ser Tewari, that you know a good deal about... art," Sil said mildly.

The slightest of reactions rippled across the smooth plumpness of his face, which was all the confirmation of identity Sil needed. Nick would need more, and Sil needed to find that more, or honouring his deal with Nick would see the man go free.

"Art?" repeated Ser Tewari, frowning. "I'm afraid I don't quite—"

"Understand. Exactly. No worries," Sil soothed, "I did expect a need to explain."

"That would be appreciated. I really don't know—"

"Why we should consider you an authority on art. Precisely. My content supervisor told me you'd say that."

"If you'd—"

"Come to the point?" Sil enjoyed interjecting his own ending to Tewari's sentences.

"I'd be happy to help, if I could, but—"

"You don't see what use you could be, of course. Shall we go on like this or shall we recite the rest in unison?"

Ser Tewari blinked. "You're with the Oracle Daily Download, is that what you said? Do you want to ask me some questions?"

"I'd love to," said Sil, beaming. "If your spouse or roommate has no objections?"

"My what?"

"Oh, must be a bit of misinformation, don't worry," Sil said reassuringly.

Tewari shook his head, as if he, too, were up far too early this station day. "I've no time for nonsense. I could have accomplished a dozen things in the time you've taken to not tell me the reason for your, er—"

"Visit?" Sil suggested helpfully. "Intrusion? Interview? Tarriance?"

"Yes!" Tewari exclaimed, then closed his eyes briefly and took a breath, immediately resuming his calm.

Not wanting to push too far, Sil shifted the course of discourse. "There's a rumour going 'round that the one called Quicksilver is interested in you, Tewari."

Again the slightest of reactions. Nice to know even one such as this knew Quicksilver's reputation. "Quicksilver? Isn't Quicksilver some sort of criminal folk hero?"

Pleasure at the name recognition shifted to an instant of irritation at the folk hero accusation. Sil smiled. "So they say. A handsome, generally genial sort with the slightest of a mean streak."

"I wouldn't know, I don't consort with criminals," Tewari said with an arrogant sniff.

"I beg to differ, Ser. Unless you'd count Tizz Zippolos an upstanding member of society. Then of course, your vex with me. Quicksilver," He bowed dramatically, though without ever taking his eyes off Tewari, who visibly twitched. He gave him an unconcerned smile and withdrew his vapour stick. He put it between his lips, as if drawing in Bliss, lowered his eyelids, and said, his voice slow and lazy, "And you, dear Emerson, are the Artist."

Tewari paused only fractionally before shrugging. "I suppose the law might be interested in your confession. If I believed it. What would one such as Quicksilver want of me? I am but a boring business person, not a creative spark in me." His face creased in puzzlement. "Are you looking to have your portrait painted?"

"Not a bad idea," Sil said thoughtfully. "But no. You are an exceptionally adept blackmailer, Emerson. But blackmail is a nasty game. Your ingenuity has already driven at least one to suicide. That alone put you on the wrong side of me, but then you tried to kill me, which is terribly insulting. It would cause me very little grief to simply end you; but for one thing I've promised you to the law and for another thing I've got my income tax to pay, so—"

"You're utterly daft," Tewari interrupted crossly. "Using false pretences to see me, babbling on about artists and criminals— You will leave, Ser, now! Or must I call the law myself?"

Sil crossed his arms, as if thinking seriously on the question. Finally he said, "Call the Long Arms. Yes, that would probably be best." He smiled. "I could do it for you," he offered, still in a helpful mood. "Wouldn't take but a second." He waited, but Tewari only glared at him, so he filled in the silence with a laugh. "Of course, there's a reason no one's ever called the law on Quicksilver, isn't there. Please think on what I've said, particularly the part about my tax bill."

Emerson Tewari studied Sil with a gaze that would turn him to stone, if such powers were granted to mere humans. "Are you quite finished talking?"

"For now," he said lightly. "And since you've decided the wiser course, I think I'll be on my way. Places to go, people to see, that sort of thing."

"I assume we'll meet again," Tewari asked, his voice even and conversational.

Sil smiled. "I'd bet on it, were I a gambling man."

TEN

"I confess, Sil—when the adventure began I was feeling all clever, a rarity in your presence. But now I'm the one missing brain cells, for I see no point in that confrontation." Grace shook her head and looked toward the bottle of Shoots, half empty but also half full, still resting on Sil's table. She wondered if drink had muddled Sil's thinking or if it had muddled hers that she couldn't see the method to his madness. "I think your ego has gotten the better of you."

"Ser Emerson Tewari is quite intelligent, and there was very little nonsense in our meeting. And most of what there was was my own free gift to him," he said with a magnanimous gesture. "It may also interest you to know he recognized me, as he should, as the one who picked his pocket at the Roost, but he didn't know who I am, the one he tried so ungraciously to kill."

Grace sighed and took a minute to puzzle it out. "He didn't know you and Quicksilver are one and the same."

"Correct! His tells are brilliantly subtle, but introducing myself properly threw him enough to be obvious."

"I suppose he's booking passage to another cloud city, then." She was almost disappointed, but it was to be expected. Only a relative few cared to cross Quicksilver when they had another option.

"No, I don't think so. He is an amateur. I picked what had to be a minor payment from his pocket and his first reaction is the extreme attempt to kill me. You know what my sweet Maria has done, spread rumours that Quicksilver can be outwitted, beaten. He likely thinks he can do so as well. I believe he understands that the purpose of my visit was to establish that I know where he sleeps, in spite of my being a little over the top of silly. But he is not the kind to run away, this one."

She rolled her eye. "You sound almost pleased about that. What happens next?"

"He says he's a businessperson, with places to go. And we know he's considered a guest worthy of a special invitation. He lives alone, so when he leaves his secure little room, we know it will be empty. So next we plot his daily course on Oracle." He gave her a sly smile and reached into the folds of his tunic. "I wonder if I could trouble you to duplicate this, as well."

She was halfway through nodding at the sensible part of his plan when he tossed her what was clearly a room key. She grinned, already running through her list of contacts on Oracle. "Ser Tewari's, I assume?"

"He won't miss it, for a while, but I should like to return the original to the lost and found at the Verdigris, soon."

"I'm on it." She needed a duplicate key, without encryption, to transfer the codes. Not as easy as it sounded, not as difficult as one might think.

But the next few days showed Emerson Tewari to be an elusive prey to follow and Sil's lively mien faded a bit. "I have lost brain cells, my dear. I ought to have followed him when he was unaware I'd sorted his name and face, then introduced myself after."

"It's been awhile since we did crime," she offered, "I'm sure it's just a bit of rust that'll wear off shortly."

"You're a dear, Grace. Have you been keeping in touch with Doyle?"

"Yes. I believe he and the Lark have been amusing each other. He won't say for he thinks I'm a sweet gamin as might be jealous." She gave Sil a bemused look. "He seems all together too good to be real."

"He will come back with my boat, you think?"

She slid him a look. "Why so worried, you did say you wanted to get rid of it."

"Didn't say I'd want to give it away," he said in mock indignation. He leaned back, eased by the change of subject. "We don't meet many such in our line of work, my dear, but I'm assured by the likes of Nick Delaney that the good and honest outnumber the likes of us by a substantial percent. Even we are bound to run across one or two in the natural course of events."

"How very philosophical you are."

"Among my many fine qualities," he said, gently mocking himself. "Perhaps we should take a cue, amuse ourselves for this dull part of our journey."

Grace nearly choked. "I hardly think so!"

Jumping to his feet, Sil laughed, grabbed her and pulled her upright. "Not in the same way, sweet Grace. I know you think I never listen to you, but such games as those are a distraction, and I am already not my usual brilliant self. However, amusement is exactly the kind of thing we need—go get yourself all decorated up and we'll explore the sinfullest sin-clubs Oracle has to offer. No intoxicating spirits, though, we must keep our heads."

He'd say no more until she was ready, so off she went. Coming from Black Thunder, Grace did not have expensive tastes, and working with Sil, she hadn't acquired much that wasn't readily packed and moved. She'd learned from her boss to buy a few ridiculously expensive items of clothing for special occasions and rely on instantly available, disposable cell clothes for day to day. The upside to cell clothes was the ability to mix and match pieces to be both trendy and unique, which was almost as desirable as being wealthy. The upside to sin-clubs, especially on Oracle, was the number of people who adored cyborgs, albeit in a fetishistic way.

She consulted the hotel holo shop from her room and ordered a tastefully sexy mix. She chose a garment that was basically a long tube covering her arms and slit to allow her torso through. Matching shorts and boot covers—which would fit over her mechanical leg—all topped by a sheer cover-up with tiny lights, a miniature of the sparkle curtain the Luminance used.

She put black powder around her eye to emphasize its greenness. She considered a dusting of sparkle on the magnetic plate protecting her optics, but there was a risk of it getting inside. It wasn't worth it. Her last bit of decorating involved covering her lips with a clear gloss that would glow under UV light. As a youth, dressing up like this, all painted and bedecked, had been an impossible dream. She enjoyed being able to indulge it now as an adult.

"My darling Grace, you look delicious! Maybe we *should* amuse ourselves in like kind."

She sighed and shook her head. "Eww. Oh! D'you think I ought to change my beads for more sparkly...?"

Sil was still looking at her outfit. "I don't think anyone is going to be looking at your beads."

As they strolled arm in arm out the hotel entrance and into colony night, the surroundings lit up in neon and twinkle and firefly globes, she said, "Will you tell me now the plan?"

"What makes you think there's a plan beyond having fun?"

She laughed. "One, you said no spirits, and two, your kind of fun usually involves getting horizontal at some point and we don't have that kind of relationship."

He laughed along with her, leading down the avenue. "Too right, my lovely. I remembered that my first all unknowing meeting with the Artist was at the Roost. If he was taking an interest in Tizz's side ventures, perhaps he's taking an interest in other nightlife ventures."

"But the privacy policies...?" The sin-clubs had private rooms, and what happened in them was a sacrosanct secret. No club manager would sell those secrets or use them without harsh penalty.

"Enough incentive, or leverage, or both might encourage indiscretion. It's worth some enquiries, wouldn't you say?"

She nodded thoughtfully. They were now on the threshold of a spot with garish lights and loud music, the door open but hung with a reflective curtain so only flashes of interior lights escaped with the noise. "If you're right," she said, while it was quiet enough to converse, "he could be anywhere. Oracle is small but there must be a hundred sin-clubs scattered among the clusters."

"Tonight," Sil said confidently. "Or, if not tonight, then some other, I suppose. But my taxes are due day after tomorrow, and I don't mean a Venusian day."

SYDNEY BLACKBURN

ELEUEN

Grace was roughly correct in the number of sin-clubs to be found on Oracle, but the number of dirty ones, the kind of dirt that might attract a blackmailer, was quite small. Sil had been investigating various problems for the Conglomerate for some while and though Tizz of the Roost had been the importer, there was still product out there in her distribution system. His original intent had been to deal with that after sorting this tax and blackmail difficulty. After an Artist-free night, one not without laughs and leads, they returned to the Luminance, exhausted but not defeated.

Sil waited til Grace had retired for the night before leaving a message on Nick's personal combrace—a tag number acquired enough years ago to no longer seem odd to him—to meet him at noon. Once, he might have been dismayed to have a Long Arm come so often to his rooms, but that, too, had become familiar. He sent a time delivered signal to Grace's combrace to wake her an hour before, so she would wake him. She seemed to have invested significant imagination into his and Nick's relationship. He smirked and went to bed pleased with the night's work.

~ * ~

"That was heartless, Sil,"

He dragged his eyelids open to stare blearily at Grace. Or maybe it was just how she looked through the sparkle curtain.

"It isn't right to feel this poorly, as virtuous as we were last night."

He yawned and said, "I could have let you sleep. But since I have to get up, you should, too."

She stared at him. "I made that vile brew you call coffee."

He could smell it. He closed his eyes and drew the rich scent in. "You're an angel, Grace."

"Hmm."

"Nick Delaney is coming by, all unofficially."

"Really," she said, drawing the word out an unreasonable length. "What does your darling Nicky like to eat upon rising?"

"Believe me, my dear, I hope to find out, one day," Sil said, starting to feel a little more lively. "Just duplicate whatever I ordered last time he darkened our door."

"Hmm," she repeated.

Sil threw off the sheet and ducked into the hygiene station. He put on a robe and messed his hair—appearing lazy was what Detective Nick Delaney would expect. He frowned at his reflection, thinking of Grace's conclusion regarding his feelings for Nick. Ridiculous, of course. He huffed softly and smiled. Grace was right about one thing—frowning was not attractive.

The door chimed and he sat at the table, fingers laced, vapour stick in his mouth. Though he never used it for anything more than a prop, he'd found it helped him order his thoughts, just holding it between his lips. He and Grace had eliminated most of the possibilities of where Emerson Tewari might be extracting further graft and the possibility remained that he'd gone after Tizz at the Roost simply because she was the importer. The distributors might be considered too small... but no, Tewari was likely too new to this game to be quite that discerning, yet. If Sil had his way, he'd never be in business long enough to be more discerning.

He turned his head toward the door, surprised that neither the service cart nor Nick Delaney had come in, as the chime had to be one of them. He stood as he heard Grace say, "I'm sorry, Detective. I'm not used to seeing you out of your clothes. Uniform."

Sil grinned as his lovely assistant ducked into the room, a rosy glow burnishing her cheeks to a lovely copper. Embarrassment became her. Behind her came the service cart and Nick Delaney behind it. Nick did look more delicious than the food, in his off-duty garb, a deep v-neck tunic showing off a broad chest kept in shape by IPLE fitness requirements. Sil let his gaze linger in honest admiration, knowing it would put a scowl on the dear detective's face. Nick's hair, dark as his own and normally pulled back tightly in a short queue for professionalism, sprang in short, fashionable spikes, practically begging for one to run fingers through it. Sil resisted the urge to lick his lips and gave Grace a serene smile. "Seems our tastes are not so different after all, hmm, my dear?"

"Bite me," she muttered under her breath as Nick gave each of them a long, studied glance, coming to who knew what conclusion. He didn't usually pay Grace much attention, though he certainly didn't snub her. Cyborgs were not common in the inner colonies, although since the mess on Titan, more were seen these days. It suited Sil fine that Delaney should never look too closely at Grace's augmented parts, for if he gave them too much thought he might figure out they had uses the manufacturer had never imagined.

For the moment, Grace had recovered her natural aplomb and was setting out the food with efficiency. Her name suited her, he reflected, not for the first time.

Nick watched Grace for a few moments longer, shot a dark

glare Sil's way before helping her finish unloading the cart. "What was it you needed to talk about in person? On my off-time?"

Sil sat down. "I've got a name, and I think I know where the evidence is. It's all tied a bit closer to the job I'm doing for Ser Black," he added.

Nick nodded as if he'd guessed as much. "Don't suppose you'd give me what you got?"

"It's circumstantial and involves first person testimony from someone not able to come forward any more."

Nick sat down, giving Sil a troubled look. "On account of you?"

"More or less," Sil said calmly. "If you could put it about that a certain red-haired thief had been found murdered after helping the Artist... You're Special Cases, already on site, so it wouldn't seem unusual that the local IPLE isn't raising more of a hue and cry."

Nick visibly relaxed. "Sadie Lark? Don't look so surprised, Sil. I've read the files on the local troublemakers. Where is she really?"

Sil smiled. Nick could always be counted on to be thorough. "Safe." It amused him that Grace chose to push the plate under the detective's gaze with her metal fingers.

"Did she help the Artist?"

"Yes. And he did threaten her life. I know you can't actually arrest him for a murder no one committed, but it wouldn't hurt to let him think she really is dead and he might truly be accused of it." He was curious; how willing Nick was to spread false rumours would tell him how badly he wanted the Artist stopped.

Finally Nick gave him a calm, measured look. "Him, hmm? Might have questions about that later."

"Fair enough. Do you want to know what I've got?"

Nick began to eat, almost absently, so Sil saw no reason to continue his fast. Grace had courteously seated herself to the detective's left, and she was eating delicately, like a scion of

Phobos Station. Nick, clearly cogitating while masticating, swallowed and gave Sil a steady clear eyed look. "It's difficult enough I had to... make a deal with you, Sil. Give me the whole package, when you have it."

Sil nodded. "The Artist is clever, you must know that, or you'd not have turned to me for help."

"Help? I most certainly did not ask for your help."

"Tsk, don't be silly, dear Nicky. You'd not have mentioned it at all if you didn't want me taking an interest." He held up his hands, fork in one, to forestall further protests. "We needn't discuss it anymore. But would you indulge my curiosity?"

Nick gave him a wary glance. "About...?"

Sil pushed his plate away and leaned forward, resting his chin on the back of his hands. "What do you do when you're not chasing the criminal kind?"

~ * ~

When Nick Delaney had gone on his way, Sil asked Grace, "Did that further your fantasies of the unrequited love I'm supposed to be having over our good detective friend?"

Grace laughed. "Who says it's unrequited?"

Sil opened his mouth, closed it, and tried again. "What are you on about now?"

"Boss, you are a brilliant mind, most of the time, but you have the damnedest blind spots. You knew he told you about the Artist deliberately to get you involved, but you missed all manner of implications."

He leaned back, curious what fancies she'd cooked up now. "Enlighten me, my dear."

Shaking her head with enough force to make her beads softly clack, she gave him a big smile and began ticking off her fingers. "He knew you'd be inclined to take care of the Artist your way?"

He nodded slowly. "Suspected, perhaps. But he made a deal I

wouldn't."

"Exactly. He put his career on the line to keep you, more or less, on the right side of the law. Even let you pay your taxes."

"Well, to be fair, extorting from an extortionist to pay another extortionist is full of all shades of grey." He still couldn't see where Grace might get her delusions from. Nick had made the deal after the Artist tried to murder him but, "Nick knows I'm not inclined to leave bodies around." Nick had to have suspected Banook's convenient suicide on Titan, but the horrible evidence of Banook's crimes must have shown it well deserved. No bodies had dropped by Sil's doing before, or since. No, Grace must simply be indulging her own fantasies. Which was fine by Sil, though not the sort of fantasies he imagined most people had of him.

"I'm fair certain Nick Delaney doesn't see nearly as many shades of grey as we do, Sil."

TWELVE

Feeling the press of time, imaginary though it was—he could as well pay his taxes himself and then reimburse himself from the Artist's ill-gotten gains—Sil took a long walk through the park adjacent to the hotel. He had to narrow down where Tewari might go to collect his extortion, but who would want to admit to blackmail? He sat down on a bench surrounded by all manner of greenery.

The upper atmosphere of Venus had proven to be a wonderful place to colonize in many ways—temperature, air pressure, magnetosphere—so many things that were terribly important and difficult elsewhere. What it lacked was an easy source of water, or even hydrogen and oxygen to make water. The air scrubbing plants of the Venusian colonies not only did what plants normally do—convert carbon dioxide to oxygen—but also released moisture into the air. Clean, fresh, recycled moisture.

Sil did not pretend to understand the details, but he'd made it his business to have a basic grasp of his environment. A lesson hard learned on Mars, many years ago. Thinking about these things allowed his mind the freedom to solve such puzzles as now troubled him. For some reason, Madame Zinnia crossed his mind. "Darling," he murmured to himself, "I love you like no other, but must you think of your libido now?"

It wasn't his libido trying to gain his attention, however. Upon his first encounter with the Artist, a mention had been made of a weekly donation. A person as meticulous as Tewari was very like to have a routine. Breakfast daily at six, and by deduction he probably sought donations on regular routine. This place every Wednesday at ten, that place every Thursday at nine. Zinnia was unlikely to be on his list, she ran a spotless shop. But that didn't mean she might not know who was on the rounds.

She seemed to have lost some kindly regard for him but he figured it was worth asking. He found a public comm as he didn't have her tag number. "You're not in your hotel," she greeted, all natural hair and face.

"I'm not," he agreed, foregoing a smart reply. The poor madame looked quite worn without her paint. "I know it's early for both of us, and your shop is busy all the clock around, but I was hoping, dear Zinnia, for a meet? Somewhere neither of us would be expected to go?"

Her face clouded. "You're a conglomerate squeal," she accused and Sil suddenly understood her lack of warmth towards him. Good, he could clear that up, too.

"Ah. Well, about that, we really should talk," he said, kind and sincere. "Please, Zinnia."

She studied him, gave up on any idea of determining his game via terminal and said, "Pleasure Bound, Opulence cluster. It's certainly a place I'd not normally go."

Sil smiled. "Perfect."

Pleasure Bound, as the unsubtle name implied, catered to a certain type of thrill seeker. This time of the day, the front of the house was brightly lit and thus empty of all but one discreetly present employee. Sil sat, sprawled as well he might at a table near the window, watching Zinnia, all private persona sans wig, come in. "Very discreet," she said dryly.

He didn't bother to explain that discretion was quite often about not standing out, rather than hiding. Such subtle differences were probably not important in her line of work. "I am sorry my work for the conglomerate has put me on the outs with you, sweet Zinnia, so I want to tell you exactly what I'm doing."

"I'm listening."

"They have me tracking down a supply and distribution ring of illegals, the supplier was Tizz Zippolos, she's been shut down. The rest of the job has been put on hold while I take care of some personal business, but in, oh four days I shall be earning the rest of my pay from Ser Black. Just for your information." He smiled at her.

She smiled, too, revealing nothing. "That's interesting, to be sure, but it's nothing to do with me."

He suspected that was true. "Sadly, the conglomeration has had the bad taste to record and report with great accuracy the amount they pay me to help them," he frowned his displeasure, not needing to act or exaggerate. "I only found this out the most unpleasant way, but it means I will not be doing any further work for the conglomeration."

"I appreciate your frankness, Silver Tation. I confess I felt some betrayed to think you'd become a snitch."

"Snitch is relative. I like to get paid, same as any other," he said. "But I wish you'd told me straight your vex with me, I'd have cleared it up sooner."

"You could have told me all this without a face to face," she said, considerably more relaxed than a short minute ago.

"I could have, but I'd like to ask you something." He straightened in his chair and leaned forward, resting his hands on the table. "As a businessperson, you know just about everyone else also doing business on Oracle."

"That isn't a question," she said, eyes narrowing.

Sil nodded. "There's someone on Oracle, considers himself the artistic sort, favourite colour is black. I mean to put him out of people's misery, and soon, but I need to distract him for a few hours and that would require knowing where he'd might be going, say tonight. You know," he added encouragingly, "to collect donations."

Her spine straightened and her eyes narrowed. "What makes you think I'd know."

"I only wondered if your extensive contacts might have mentioned being annoyed by one such individual. I suspect he's as regular as a comet in his rounds."

She studied him, as if still uncertain he was trustworthy. He wasn't, but in this instance, he hoped she could tell he was sincere. "Putting him out of people's misery not meaning anything I'd have to pretend as I never heard?"

He pretended shock. "I am an honest citizen, Madame! I assure you, it will be all right side up."

She nodded slowly. "Might be I can help."

THIRTEEN

"So we're here, all dressed up and watching folk dance, drink, dose, and dry hump," Grace observed, leaning back on her elbows on the bar.

"The four D's of a night out on Oracle." Sil faced the bar beside her as he waited for their drink order to be filled.

She didn't necessarily mind, but in the midst of the noise and columns of gold light highlighting folk at random, she was having fresh doubts about Sil's methods. "Did you not say when the Artist was extracting graft from the Roost he was swathed in disguise? Why would he even bother coming to the front room all bare-faced?"

"I rather think," Sil said, turning slightly toward her, "had I not interrupted in a timely manner, he would have removed the disguise and left by the front doors. There'd be nothing unusual to remark. His disguise was a shapeless robe, a scarf 'round his head, and a voice anonymizer. A mere shifting of garments would hide the anonymizer, bare the head, and reveal a snazzy bright tunic under the robe."

"Ah. Seems plausible."

"Too true, sweet Grace," he said and abruptly pulled her close, burying his face into her neck. "And he's here," he said softly.

"The sudden embrace sort of suggested as much," she replied wryly. At least she didn't have to yell, with him this close.

"Slap me off for bothering you and go bother him, would you."

"And if he hates cyborgs?"

"I won't abandon you until I see you've engaged his attention fully."

Like most cyborgs, Grace's mechanicals had been chosen to replace her basic skill functions and enhance her job trained talents. She had no super strength or powerful grip, though she could administer assorted sleep potions via her needle-like fingers—an application the designers had not imagined—that was the limit of her super cyborg powers. Cyborgs had to fight for social justice with fewer advantages than their opponents gave them credit for. She was not the brawn of their partnership, though her brain was more practical than Sil's. That didn't mean she hadn't risked a lot more than an evening of bad company before. "Can I drink real drinks?"

He chuckled, "Just don't lose your head. Emerson Tewari is the rather roundish male presenting one with the attractive silver hair—a paint of his own, not a wig. He is not to my taste, but not without his charms, if you disregard his foul hobby."

"Understood."

"Tag my combrace when he leaves, that'll give me plenty of time to search his hotel room."

"I duped the room key, but how are you going to get there, if it's a private floor?"

"Grace. Trust me."

She stomped on his foot, giving him the courtesy of using her blood and bone leg, then slapped his face as he yelped. "No means no," she said in a loud frosty voice that probably didn't carry all that far, but was realistic enough.

Grace walked with an air of injured dignity over to the other end of the bar where the man meeting Sil's description was standing. She poked the bar for a menu and ordered a Venusian Sunrise. She accepted the drink and turned with a disgruntled stare to stand beside Emerson Tewari. He was round where she generally preferred angular, but still looked like an attractive enough way to pass a few harmless hours. Or he would have, did she not know what he was. The knowledge filtered his looks into an ugliness she tried not to see. "Trouble?" he asked, his tone conveying courtesy more than curiosity, as he nodded to where an unidentifiable Sil nursed the new bruises she gave him.

"Cyborg fetishist. They think we'll go along with whatever sick fantasies they have, because really, who would have anything to do with a cybby? Besides," she added with a bitterness she did not have to feign, "everyone assumes a debt free cyborg is a body bot."

"Ah. I'd heard stories of such," he said, his gaze lingering on her eyeplate before drifting towards her metal hand. "But I don't normally give my custom to places where the like are found."

"Cyborgs?" she asked archly. At his expression, she patted his hand with her flesh hand. "No, my apologies. I'm being all belligerent about something not your fault and we are strangers. Please have my good wishes for your night, Ser."

"Tewari," he said, "But please call me Emerson. I don't recall I've met a free cyborg before, least not as lovely as you." He smiled encouragingly at her.

And she was in game.

~ * ~

The moment Sil was assured that Grace had the Artist's attention, he was on his way to the Verdigris Hotel. Once he'd been in Emerson Tewari's room, getting back in had never been an issue. What he hadn't told Grace, because he wanted to seem more clever than he actually was, was that the key card she'd duped him would take the lift up to the third floor. After all, a guest wouldn't want to have to trouble the staff every time ze came and went from zir own room. Given a few minutes without distraction, she'd have worked it out herself.

Tewari's room was grander than Sil's, about the size of his and Grace's together, with the open area of a size suitable for intimate gatherings of upwards of ten guests.

Half an hour later, he sat down in Emerson's chair—the largest and most plush in the room, which seemed to fit with Tewari's assessment of himself—and stuck his vapour stick in his mouth, wondering what he was missing. It had to be something, for his very thorough search had yielded precisely nothing in the way of evidence proving the Artist's identity.

He'd been as certain as possible that Emerson Tewari had taken his visit calmly in the confidence of putting Sil out of his, Tewari's, misery before Sil had a chance to show him what true misery was. That said, he was also certain Tewari would have ensured the ability for a relatively swift getaway, which would mean his incriminating documents, data chips, credit chips and whatever other boodle he'd secured via blackmail had to be in this room. The only other option was he carried it all on his person and that seemed more of a risk than Tewari, amateur though he might be, would take.

Somewhere or other there was a large quantity of untraceable credit chips, ready and willing to be converted into all manner of mischief by anyone who could offer it a more genial home. But after thirty minutes of looking, he'd found nothing, and was continuing to find nothing while more minutes ticked by.

He leaned back, eyes closed, wilfully ignoring the press of time. This was the Artist's studio, the inner sanctum of the ruthless criminal mastermind Tewari imagined himself to be. Here he was master of all he surveyed and he'd want to be able to look... yes, from this chair, he'd want his eye to be able to fall on the secrets concealed under the noses of everyone admitted to his ingenious presence. Sil opened his eyes, looked around the room to see if he could figure the spot.

There was nary a locked drawer or cubicle in the room, and as private as the Verdigris was, it wasn't equipped with individual room safes. The table was no thicker than the one in his own room. He'd already checked the ventilation grill—an old school spot he'd thought might have appeal for Tewari—and inside the air scrubber plant pots. The light fixtures were clear and the carpet could hide nothing. That seemed to exhaust all the possibilities. *I can't have been that wrong... can I?* Sil thought drowsily.

There was of course the sleeping area. In this suite it was behind a curtain of thin polymer rods, molded to resemble... reeds, yes, that's what they were called. Reeds. But he'd already checked under the mattress, in the clothing press, and even in the, the nooks and crannies of the hygiene station. Not that he wanted to think of Tewari in the hygiene station. How far was Grace going to... what was she doing? The situation was growing less annoying, altogether less... pressing. And something about a Lark.

FOURTEEN

Somewhere in the infinite darkness appeared a tiny speck of white. It hurtled towards him, growing larger and whiter and more terrible, until it seemed as if it must smash and smear him into the squashed wreckage of the whole universe at his back. He let out a yelp, as the abrupt blaze of dazzling light forced itself into his eyes. Some strange creature slithered across his nose and mouth, and an acrid stinging smell stabbed right up into the top of his head and trickled down his throat like a thin stream of condensed fire. He gasped, coughed, choked and as the bright light faded, it left behind an image of Emerson Tewari.

"Oh dear," Sil said, his voice cracked and dry. His nose was burning with the remnants of whatever potion the Artist had passed under it to revive him, and he breathed deep, flaring his nostrils to flush the fumes with fresh air. His head cleared so completely that for a few moments it felt as if cold air had been blown clean through it. But he looked down and saw he was still seated in the chair, though his wrists and ankles were securely bound, each to the other. "That seems a very useful sort of knock-out gas, Emerson. How'd you work it," he asked, his voice still recovering from the harsh restorative he'd breathed in.

Emerson Tewari tucked the small vial into a pocket of his evening wear, leaving Sil to wonder belatedly about Grace. Perhaps he was already asleep when she tagged him. "It was released by the pressure of your head on the back of the chair," he said. "In small amounts, it's harmless and undetectable, unless one is looking for it, so it will not be noticed in the ventilation systems or air scrubbers. But released in concentration, close to the face—it is a most effective sleep aid, wouldn't you agree?"

"Side effects are a bit rough, might want to polish it a bit before going to market," Sil observed. "Still must give credit where it's due, dear. I never noticed a thing, no smell, no release of pressure... though I do recall my thoughts being rather scrambled before dozing off. You might make a criminal mastermind yet."

"How magnanimous of you," Emerson murmured. "I hope you don't mind, I brought a guest. It's not my habit to pick up strangers at sin-clubs, so you know she must be special." He waved a hand.

Sil turned to look. Grace was slumped in another chair, though she wasn't bound. "She looks a bit done in, Emerson, you randy beast. Resting up for another round of sexy fun times, is she?"

"Come now, did you think I didn't notice that the fake Lark you sent to me had cyborg enhancements? Not immediately, true, but in our subsequent struggle, it did not remain unnoticed. Not many free cyborgs on Oracle to begin with, it wasn't all that difficult to ascertain her unfortunate choice of associate. Then it was a simple matter to dose her drink, and lo, she was suddenly so terribly drunk I simply had to bring her home." Emerson's tone was gently mocking. "She'll be awake soon, so I ought to make sure she doesn't wander away." He smiled at Sil, the first time Sil had seen him smile. It lent a handsomeness to his round face that was all the more awful for his criminal endeavours. "You underestimated me, Tation." He turned to tie Grace.

"Possibly," Sil said, imbuing the word with polite disbelief.

Emerson finished binding Grace's ankles and arms, not paying particular attention to her cybernetic hand, and turned to Sil with a gravely serious face. "I don't think you understand, Silver Tation. There will be no negotiating; you are going to die."

"Oh," Sil said, his voice mocking regret. "If I had a credit chip for every time I've heard that."

"I refuse to be swayed by your nonsense."

"That's fine, quite agreeable to me, only I do hope your method of disposing of me is at least creative. Most people try the same boring thing."

He stared curiously at Sil as if to gauge his seriousness, then said, "I trust you'll be satisfied with your... ultimate conclusion."

Sil had made it a habit to not be caught up in this sort of situation. It certainly wasn't the everyday occurrence he made it sound, but he'd faced it once or twice before. There was a learning curve that all the theory in the solar system couldn't replace and having Grace as a partner had inspired him to take more chances than he had working alone. Still, there was something particularly eerie about Tewari. He went about his work in the same way he might have gone about eating his breakfast—methodical and efficient and completely emotionless. The sort of responses or lack thereof a sociopathic serial killer might give. Sil had the chilling thought that, left unstopped, Emerson Tewari might well venture down that path. He would have to pass his observations along to Delaney and hope it mattered.

When Emerson Tewari, without further words, picked up Grace and carried her from the room, Sil began to consider the possibility that this time, he'd been that one little bit too careless. The moment the door closed, he tried everything he'd ever learned about breaking free of his bonds, to no avail. He could rise to his feet, but his ankles were bound not only to each other but also leashed to the chair legs in such a way he couldn't just tip the chair and escape. He sat back down, careful to keep his head forward, and tested his wrists one more time. Still as tight as before. "Well, this is annoying," he murmured, taking refuge in understatement.

Ah, but he had his combrace. A combrace was notoriously difficult to remove from a living body, and Sil was yet among the living. It was also a bit tricky to use without hands without advance arrangement. Still, he raised his hands to his face and tried to manipulate the combrace with his nose and lips, pushing and sliding it until he could access the controls that would let him tag Nick Delaney.

Unfortunately Tewari chose that moment to return. Or fortunately, since a swift return meant Grace was yet alive. He hoped.

"Now, now, none of that." He grabbed the combrace, twisting Sil's hands somewhat painfully in the bindings. He cancelled the call that hadn't been made and adjusted it to the proper place. "Not having much success tonight, are you?"

"But I do keep trying," Sil remarked, bright and cheerful.

Emerson gave him another of those unnerving steady looks. "I'm beginning to think your reputation was more than a little overstated, Quicksilver. You did come here tonight hoping to find all manner of chips, both data and credit, no? And failed."

"Eh, just a temporary setback."

A smile crossed Emerson's face, and Sil immediately wished for the dispassionate face of stone to return. "I out-clevered you. How nice. That makes two of us, now, doesn't it?" He pulled a folding knife from his pocket and flicked it open.

Sil tensed as Tewari moved behind him. Surely the man was not so foolish as to slit his throat right here...? But instead, he felt tension on his ankles. The soft sound of rope hitting the floor was followed by the reassuring snick of the knife closing.

Tewari pulled Sil out of the chair and left him standing on his feet, a bit awkwardly given how close his ankles were bound. "You found my chair a convenient place to rest, but didn't consider it more closely." He kicked the chair over with an efficient foot to the back of the seat, and unsnapped the dark fabric of the bottom. A small metal box held in with poly webbing was revealed. "I designed it myself."

"My apologies, Ser Tewari. I hadn't thought you so clever, to hide your ill-gotten gains under your very ass."

"And that, Ser Tation, is why you die tonight. I require you to rejoin your companion. Must I carry you?"

"I'd rather you didn't."

Tewari nodded. "I'm going to loosen the bindings on your ankles. If you try to harm me or escape, things will go the worse for your pretty cyborg friend."

Sil chafed at the restriction but without knowing where Grace was, he had no choice but to obey.

"Right this way and please don't fuss."

He guided Sil with confidence down the deserted hall to the emergency exit and a service lift. He used a security slide to override it. "Another handy tool, though this one I had to purchase. The owner sadly died shortly thereafter."

"I don't need chapter and verse of your misdeeds," Sil murmured.

"Forgive me if I can't help but boast, as I send the great and fearsome Quicksilver to his eternal rest. I suppose that will make me the great and fearsome one, won't it?"

Sil considered gloating an exploitable weakness, but Emerson Tewari wasn't gloating. His voice was calm, curious, factual and therefore chilling. The lift opened into the steamy little dungeon of the hotel's laundry. "Are you going to have us pressed to death? That's not overly creative, Emerson."

Emerson did not respond, merely pushed him through the

laundry to the recycle room. "Most of these tasks are automated, but human supervisors come through at regular intervals, so we mustn't dawdle."

Grace looked up. She was sitting on a canister of waste awaiting incineration. "Hello, handsome. Fancy meeting you here."

"It's a small world, darling," Sil replied.

"The Verdigris is special among the hotels on Oracle," Emerson Tewari said, as if quoting a brochure. "In addition to the private residential floor, it is the only hotel with incinerators large enough for a body."

Sil tipped a look to Grace, as Emerson proceeded to oblige her earlier wish for villainous speeches, detailing his brilliance. No one, it seemed, could resist a chance to monologue. While the Artist was otherwise engaged, Sil surreptitiously studied the room. Nothing sharpened his observational skills like the threat of dying. "The Incineration of Silver Tation," he said thoughtfully. "Has a nice ring to it, don't you think? I should use it for my autobiography."

"I think you need to be alive to write an autobiography," Grace reminded him.

"Hmm, good point," he said, and as Tewari guided him to one of the incinerators, he stumbled in the hobbling bindings, falling against the unit.

Tewari huffed a short breath and turned to pull Grace to her feet. He yanked open the door and shoved her inside.

"Ah, Emerson, my dear. You did see the work order flimsy on this machine?"

Emerson Tewari, still holding the unit door, squinted at Sil. Sil nodded toward the flimsy. "Says it's out of order."

He stared at Sil, his mouth tightening in the slightest. "You outsmart yourself, Quicksilver." And so saying he stepped aside with disturbing grace and pushed Sil inside the incinerator, a rather close fit with Grace.

"It's a thirty minute cycle; I'll be back to ensure no," he glanced at Grace. "Telltale parts remain." Then he shut the door with a clang and somewhere disconcertingly close machinery began to hum.

FIFTEEN

"Alone at last," Sil quipped to Grace, more or less in her ear given how closely they were packed.

A sound escaped her throat, much like a strangled laugh. "I will say my time with you has been educational as well as adventuresome."

"Sweet Grace, we're not even contracted and you want to break up with me?"

"Now is not the time for your foolish flirting, Sil."

"I don't see why not; it isn't like we've something better to do. At least not until that fool Emerson decides we can burn without his supervision."

"Thanks for that reminder." She grimaced and her body tightened in various ways as she tried to find another position. "Nick Delaney won't be swooping to our rescue?"

"I don't need to be rescued by a Long Arm," he said, pretending offence that she'd think he needed help to get them out of this. He would never tell her he had tried to tag Nick and failed. Details. "Don't worry, my dear—Emerson put us in the defective incinerator. I did point it out to him, but alas, he paid no heed."

Grace's body went still. "You didn't swap—?"

"I didn't have time. Besides, I couldn't actually reach it, though I tried to make that less obvious. I did have time to read it. That humming you hear is the burners, but they're not going to warm up because the latch is broken. It's a safety feature, you see. Can't have the incinerator burning things up with a door that might open and burn up other things. Emerson just imagined I swapped them, thus thinking this is the working incinerator."

"So I also imagined," she said, a bit breathlessly.

"Once our dear Artist has departed and we have freed ourselves of these bindings, we can complete our original plan."

"You're completely daft."

Sil smiled. "Aw, my sweet—you've not called me so in months! Now let's see if we can untie whatever knots he tied us in, then we'll go down a level and find some ashes and bits of metal and the like to simulate our lovingly incinerated remains. You'll stay here while I go upstairs and collect some proof and a hefty donation from Ser Tewari for our troubles. I'll meet you back at the Luminance, where we'll keep our noses out of sight—after I pay that damn tax bill—until our handsome detective friend advises us that Tewari is all under lock and key. Brilliant, yes?"

~ * ~

Nick Delaney cursed as his combrace signalled an incoming request. It was on his personal tag number and it saddened him that the only person using it lately was a semi-reformed criminal, Silver Tation. Once a lovely woman used to call him at all hours, convenient or not, and while he'd ultimately found her suffocating, he missed being called by someone unrelated to his work. And what in the grand design was Tation doing up at this hour? He'd been logged in for day shift at IPLE for a good two hours, but it was still two hours earlier than Sil normally rose. "Is your clock fast or haven't you been to bed yet?"

"And good morning to you, too, darling."

Nick drew in a breath and regretted it. He knew Sil relished any kind of reaction to his flirtations, annoyed or otherwise. He opened his mouth and closed it. "You have news about the Artist?"

"I've merely come to enjoy our having breakfast together, thought you might want to join me this morning?"

"Sil."

"Also, I do have need of you in a professional capacity."

"Fine." He checked his schedule, nothing that couldn't be rearranged. "On my way. Oh, if you're ordering, how about some of those fluffy round things...? Pancakes!"

"Anything for you, Nicky."

Nicky. He hated being called Nicky. He'd never say so, though. This bargain he'd made had given him a sleepless night or two, but over the past few days he felt it was the right thing to do. Silver Tation was in a unique position to bring in the Artist, not having, as he'd once said, a book he had to follow. Although he wasn't entirely sure a little Quicksilver revenge might not be as just as lock-up. Another suicide just last night, and that name—the Artist. Such arrogance.

He made yet another trek to Sil's hotel room, aware of being a rather frequent visitor of late. He felt no small anticipation. For the food, of course. It wasn't that he didn't eat well, so much as Sil ate better. The colonies knew the importance of fresh food and all had efficient hydroponics areas for growing fresh fruits and vegetables, and the plants also helped purify the air. Pollination was done by mechanical bugs after the real thing had demonstrated an uncanny knack for getting into and gumming up vital machinery. He imagined Sil was something like that, an annoying insect gumming up the works of due process but sometimes useful.

He greeted Grace at the door and wondered not for the first time what she got out of working for Sil. Sil had somehow arranged her indenture paid, and he could see some gratitude arising from that, but that was over four years ago. Her dossier said she was thirty-one, some five years older than Silver Tation.

"What gets you up so early in the day?" He asked Sil, sitting down at the table to a setting of food clearly waiting for him.

Sil gave him a smile, the kind that made him especially wary. Sometimes—some very few times—it was tempting to take his flirtations seriously. That smile particularly tested his resolve.

"My taxes are due today. I realize it's customary to remit digitally, but as you know I've taken this very personally. So I should like to pay, with chips, in person."

"Ah," Nick said, allowing himself to be distracted by a thick, fluffy pastry, the kind that melted to a decadent buttery goodness in the mouth. "So the Artist?"

"All yours, my darling Nicky, as promised."

He looked into Sil's eyes, trying to determine his intent, as he wiped his fingers clean. He thumbed the recorder on his combrace. "Go on."

"The gentleperson you seek goes by the daytime name of Emerson Tewari and he currently resides in room 302 of the Verdigris Hotel."

"He'll still be there? You didn't spook him?"

Sil glanced at Grace, causing Nick to look at her as well. She grinned, an echo of the mischievous expression more commonly found on Sil's face. "He thinks we're ash and bone in the Verdigris incinerator," she said.

Nick frowned and turned the recorder off. "Hotel incinerators aren't big enough for bodies."

"A special feature of the Verdigris, it seems. When Oracle was constructed, the Verdigris was the first hotel to open, and the incinerators had to be large enough to take care of anything. Everything. But the important thing to know, dear Nicky, when searching Emerson's room, you must avoid putting pressure on the headrests of his chairs. Oh, and his treasure box is under the seat of the big custom chair, literally under the seat. It contains all the documentation you need, except for this bit," he passed Nick a data chip with a flourish. "That should provide you with what you need for a warrant. Also he may have originally had some credit chips in there."

"Ah," Nick said dryly. "I won't ask how much above the amount you owe in taxes."

"Would you be so kind as to accompany us to the Erev office? As I said, I'd like to take care of this in person and an escort by law enforcement would make me feel ever so safe."

Nick didn't know if he should laugh or groan or if he really shouldn't be surprised. "An escort?"

Sil gave him a wide-eyed look of appeal, the blue grey of his eyes warm and unfathomable, and said, "Please?"

SIXTEEN

Sil's gift, Nick decided, was that he could charm and beguile so effectively, no one would ever suspect that the suddenly missing jewels or empty safe were his fault. He might never have known himself but for accidentally leaving a file open whilst talking to an informant. Sil tended to confine the bulk of his activities to his fellow criminals, but a thief who stole from thieves was no less a criminal.

So it was against his better judgement that he sighed heavily, breathing out a yes. Sil paying income tax was perhaps among the most lawful things he might ever do. The Earth Revenue Service office on Oracle was small, perhaps employing a total of three people in shifts, ensuring at least one live human was on hand at all times. It was there for the benefit of the employees and business owners of Oracle, and many credits passed through that office, though mostly in digital form. Technically even credit chips were digital money, but a form of hard currency had its uses in the colonies.

Originally a private pleasure palace, Oracle had decided to accept the tax breaks of being a colony. With those breaks came requirements to provide service kiosks for issuing licenses, administering tests, and so forth. IPLE protection was another concession, though the conglomerate retained the right to hire security experts such as Silver Tation. All of these services were located near the core, the least desirable real estate on any Venusian colony, but easily accessible from all points.

One could partake of most of these services from the comfort of one's hab, but there would always be those who preferred a more personal approach, or distrusted the digital process.

However, while Oracle had been designed to encourage pedestrian traffic within the individual clusters, moving from one cluster to another required renting a demmar. The trio strolled out of the Luminance Hotel, Nick trying to look as if he were one of them, rather than a common body guard, IPLE uniform notwithstanding. "The Artist has kindly paid our transportation this morning," Sil murmured as a four-seater demmar rolled free, doors open. "Shall we?"

Although demmars throughout the colonies had speed limiters for safety, Sil still managed to drive it in such a way as had Nick hanging on for dear life. He refused to say anything. Speaking up could possibly make it worse. Finally they arrived in the government cluster. Nick climbed out with wobbly knees and Grace gave him a sympathetic smile. "Hang out with him long enough, you get used to it."

"No, thank you," Nick said, grimacing and she laughed.

Sil looped an arm through each of theirs, Nick and Grace, and said determinedly, "Let's get this over with, shall we?"

Nick tried to pull his arm free. "You don't need me to go inside with you."

"I insist on Long Arm protection. Blackmailers I can handle, tax collectors are far more frightening. Although," he said thoughtfully, still holding tight to Nick's arm, "there is more than a little resemblance. The same threatening messages, the same

merciless bleeding of the honest working soul, the same dreadful—
"

"Fine," Nick said. "Please. More walking, less talking."

Inside, the human agent on duty at Erev was guarded by a holographic receptionist. "What service do you need today?"

"I wish to see the Erev agent on duty," Sil began imperiously. "I wish to—no, I don't wish to, but I intend to—pay my income tax. In person. Only in person."

"Are you being audited?"

"I am accompanied by an officer of the law," Sil said, "so if that was a threat..."

Nick stomped unceremoniously on Sil's foot. "Shut up. Or do you *want* to be audited?"

Sil turned to look at him in astonishment. Or perhaps mock astonishment, it was sometimes difficult to tell. "You mean IPLE is afraid of Erev?"

"Everyone's afraid of Erev," he muttered, and Grace snickered.

"Your request is being processed."

~ * ~

Sil was torn between being annoyed that he had to be here at all, and smug that at least he personally was not paying this fine for honesty. He'd taken enough credit chips from the Artist's hidden box to compensate both him and Grace for their time and tribulations, and then he'd taken a further three thousand six hundred and fifty-five credits specifically for Erev. He'd considered leaving a thank you note to the Artist, but decided that the law would find it first and never show it to Emerson Tewari, ruining the poignancy. And giving Nick Delaney physical evidence he might use against him later.

"Please state your name for the revenue agent," the talking head requested, but the door was already opening.

"Please come in," invited a hearty male voice.

Sil strode through the door all intent to be belligerent and froze. He'd come to expect the unexpected, it was a given in his line of work, but this topped his list of surprises, leaving him too stupefied to do more than stare in dazed shock.

The man behind the desk was none other than Emerson Tewari.

And he moved no more so than Sil, his colour fading, until even his lips seemed to go grey.

"Oh." Sil said, trying to recover his wit. "It's you, Emerson, is it." Not his finest moment. "And it's me, too, Silver Tation, in the flesh. I'm afraid I wasn't ready to investigate the possible existence of an afterlife, even though you incinerated me. Grace also passed up the opportunity to be a ghost. She's just out there if you'd like to see her. With Detective Delaney of Interplanetary Law Enforcement. He's most eager to meet you."

Sil felt his equilibrium reassert itself as he chattered on. "This really is most difficult for me, my dear, for I find myself desiring your demise. I deeply resent folk who try to kill me or my dear friend and partner. Deeply," he repeated, without the light-hearted tone.

Emerson Tewari also began to recover, but if he had words to say, Sil cut him off by continuing, his voice soft and menacing: "And you all along pestering me for tax money. No wonder you decided to try extortion of the less legal kind. I bet your first leverage came of things you learned poking about in people's financial affairs, do I win, Emerson? And here I am, come to give you three thousand six hundred and fifty-five of your own credits, all out of the lock box under that oh-so interesting chair."

Emerson made a slight motion with his hand. Sil suddenly remembered the dart gun Emerson had used to in his first attempt to kill him. He and Grace had confiscated it, but it was easy enough to find another. The poison of those darts was deadly, as

Grace had verified. And then Grace herself came through the doorway and demanded, "Aren't you done ye—oh!"

"Grace, down!"

A twi-ick sound, scarce audible, had Sil ducking. The projectile brushed through his hair—Emerson still had lousy aim.

"Sil, get out of the way, let me handle this," Nick said with the firm authority of Interplanetary Law Enforcement as he pushed into the room.

"The poison is deadly, Nicky. No one's meant to walk away."

"I'll handle it," Nick said, his voice as hard and cold as ever Sil had heard.

"As you insist," he murmured, before grabbing onto edges of the lightweight desk Tewari sat behind and flipping it up into the devil's lap. Another dart flew off, the aim random, as Tewari stumbled backwards.

The desk did little more than knock Tewari to the side. He got to his feet in a fluid motion and grabbed Grace by her flesh arm, clearly meaning to use her as a shield. Sil's temper flared. His deal with Nick be damned, Emerson was done for this life. Then Nick Delaney shoved him aside and delivered a knock-out blow to the villain with an electric prod that he'd had somewhere on his person.

Grace gawped as Tewari collapsed behind her, and Sil, too, was shaken from rage to stare at the law man. "Did you just...?"

"Sadly, he'll live," Nick said, his voice still cold. He turned to look at Sil. "I told you to get out of the way. Your heroics could have killed someone."

Sil opened his mouth, then closed it. He'd been thinking of Nick as dedicated but somewhat plodding, and now he remembered why he'd considered Nick a worthy adversary in the first place. "Thank you for saving Grace." He imagined Nick would not appreciate being reminded he may have saved Silver Tation. Instead, remembering Nick Delaney's scold after leaving the scene of the Artist's first attempt on his life, he asked meekly, "Do I need to provide a formal interview?"

Nick was calling for backup and a medical team. "Yes, you and Grace both." He frowned. "He drew first."

"I didn't draw at all," Sil said, assuming Nick was asking.

"I did," he said.

That was unquestionably true. "Nick..."

Nick glared at him. "The official record will now reflect you assisting with a Special Cases file. If I didn't know better, I'd have thought you arranged this on purpose. How long do you intend to remain on Oracle, Sil?"

"Til sunrise. You know I'll happily give whatever statement you need."

Nick sighed heavily, rubbing at his eyes without ever looking away from Tewari's prone form. "I appreciate that." He gave Sil a sharp look. "Venusian sunrise?"

Sil gave him a sunny smile and said, "I promise." The last time Nick had tried a variation of 'don't leave town,' Sil had given his word and left hours later. He wouldn't do that again.

Nick's expression softened into the far more familiar annoyance Sil was comfortable with and he sighed again. "Sunset was just twenty days ago."

Sil took a step closer to the detective and said softly, not quite in his ear, "It's going to be a long night."

A LITTLE QUICKSILVER REVENGE

At Venusian dawn, Sil was bored. Nick Delaney had been reassigned to Mars some weeks ago and Sil didn't feel like returning to Mars just yet, not even to taunt and tease his favourite detective. Grace was romancing his pilot, Doyle and— that was an idea. He tagged Grace. "Let's take the yacht for a spin."

"Now?" She'd accepted his tag on audio only and he didn't feel guilty for interrupting whatever he may have interrupted—she'd chosen to answer, after all.

"I'm bored."

"Now sounds good. Give me some time to have it stocked— how long do you mean to be spinning?"

He smiled. He'd gotten into trouble *one time* after saying "I'm bored" and now it was all the impetus Grace needed to ensure he wasn't. "Destiny. Destiny is always fun. Doyle will be with us. I don't care what you get up to in your bunk."

The ship wasn't small; even the living quarters were fair roomy considering. The four private bunks had metal doors that each hid a bed comfortable enough for two and were on either side of a hygiene station at one end and a galley not much bigger at the other. The controls—the bridge, he supposed—were above as were the access ways to a small cargo hold and the engine and fuel compartments which comprised the bulk of the ship.

"The most efficient way to get to there is to use the solar sails for power after the initial acceleration, it will take about as long as a passenger ship."

A week and half with no occupation but broadcast fiction while Doyle and Grace had sex across the passageway? "How fast can it go?"

Doyle grinned, as if he'd hoped Sil would ask. "Fuel for it's cheap, and it's topped up. At full burn and with some grav assist, we could get there in three, maybe four days. Engine will need work when we get there, it's not meant to run full out like that. And we'll be under near constant acceleration, so we can't use a gravity spin, that means food will be limited to government rations."

Sil made a face. He'd learned to season the hell out of rations, but nothing could make them not taste like poverty. "Best compromise between speed and comfort?"

Doyle's head went slightly to one side as he did the calculations in his head. "Six days?"

Due to something Doyle called "space currents" the little yacht pulled into a parking orbit around the Moon five days later. After a brief debate that Doyle won, they gained permission to dock in Destiny. "I can look after the ship's maintenance?" Doyle asked Sil.

Sil waved a careless hand. "Run all the expenses by Grace." Grace he trusted implicitly with his funds. Though she had a separate account, they lived and worked out of his, so she always knew when they were running low.

They took a pair of adjoining rooms at the Regency, Sil's favourite hotel in Destiny. He offered to pay for a room for Doyle, too, as his employee, but Doyle insisted he could sleep on the ship. "Like extra security," he'd added with the grin of a child being given a toy.

Until he could decide what to do next, Sil dressed up pretty and hit the closest sin-club, more out of curiosity than desire. He accepted a mask at the door—most people sought to preserve their anonymity in sin-clubs. He consumed several high octane cocktails and relaxed into the ambiance, losing his mask somewhere along the way. In time to the music, the darkness of the club was slashed with pulsating coloured lights, beating like a heart, throbbing like sex. Masked figures flashed across his vision, in various states of dress. Lust hooked sticky fingers into Sil in spite of himself. He leaned back into a lushly upholstered chair and considered his favourite Destiny flower shops. A flower's profession was to please, and he wasn't interested in risking his pleasure with a stranger in a sin-club. Yes, a flower was considerably less complicated than the rituals of seduction, at least for tonight.

Smiling, he sidled through the people dancing and grinding and drinking, trusting his instincts as the bright bursts of light played havoc with his night vision. The drinks he'd consumed, with libido enhancers, dulled his instincts, and he bumped straight into a play fellow. In the sudden blue light, he blinked at the masked woman and took a small step back to bow deeply. "I beg your gracious pardon, Ser."

"Granted," said a sweet honey voice, too familiar to be forgotten.

Sil jerked upright as the light flashed yellow and the woman pulled away her mask to reveal a smile and unmistakable dimpled apple cheeks. "Sweet Maria, as I live and breathe. No thanks to you, my murderous beauty."

"It wasn't personal, dear Quicksilver. If I'd meant to kill you, you'd be dead," she said in the dark.

It irritated him that instead of feeling purely triumphant at this unexpected opportunity to extract his revenge, he also felt hurt all over again at her betrayal, and worse—some residual fondness for her. Still a fool after almost three years, he scolded himself, and forced a smile. "It felt rather personal," he said lightly, and he extended his hand meaning to chuck her gently under her chin.

Instead, his hand went behind her head and he risked his life for a kiss of her sweet lips. She sighed under his mouth and his hand trailed down her bare spine to her waist. "Maria..."

Maria knew all about pleasure, he remembered. They'd spent many hours in the arts of love before she'd shot him and left, not knowing if he lived or died. He forced himself to release her and take a step back, taking her hands in his. "It's a pleasant shock to run into you, but what brings you to Destiny?"

In flash of red light, he saw her mouth curve into a smile, both beguiling and alarming. "Darling, it's a sin-club. Let's sin, shall we?"

He hesitated in the dark, lost in memory, breathing in her scent. "No one's tried to kill me in almost a year," he said, "I suppose I could risk it."

"I suppose you could," she said softly, her eyes on his mouth as she stroked the soft fabric of his sleeve. "Is there anything I can do, to make up for my alleged attempt on your life?"

Sil smiled. He had some unfinished business with his beloved Maria, making a renewal of their dalliance very tempting indeed. "I can think of a number of ways you could make reparation," he said, his voice a low drawl by her ear.

Her fingers brushed through the unruly waves of his hair, her eyes half lidded and glittering as blue light strobed over them. "I knew you would understand taking advantage of a situation."

He had already conceived several sorts of revenge, depending on when or how he might encounter Maria Christina again. None of them included giving her an opportunity to drug him again. "This has been a most illuminating little talk, sweet Maria." His voice was an invitation, to which he added his hotel and room number. "Bring a change of clothes."

~ * ~

"Morning, Sil. Oh!" Grace pretended surprise upon seeing someone in Sil's bed besides himself, though she often did. She did not have to pretend surprise when she saw who. What in the colonized solar system was Sil doing? Maria Christina was far more expensive than any flower. "Ser Christina! How, how, uh, what a surprise to see you again."

"Do you mind? We're still abed," Maria said crossly.

"So I see," Grace returned, still staring. She turned her attention to the dark-haired man giving her a sheepish look. "Are you quite daft, Sil?"

"Now, now, Grace. I know you've borne Maria a grudge for wrongs done me, but my sweet Maria has explained it all to me. A person in our line of work must take advantage of the situations that cross our paths and nothing personal, is that not the gist of it, my love?"

Grace heard Sil's word, but the tone of his voice carried a subtle warning she was well familiar with. She relaxed her stance while maintaining a suspicious look to the sylph who dared to brag of besting Quicksilver. Her dark blonde hair was now a medium brown, but her eyes and pretty round face remained the same, as did the scowl she had always had for Grace. "Well, then," Grace said. "I suppose I'd best make coffee then. Colonial for you, Ser Christina?"

"Please," was the word Maria said. "I hope you fry in a solar flare" was what her tone conveyed.

Once, when Grace had believed that Maria's affection for Sil was genuine, she'd thought their shared preference for colonial coffee over Sil's bitter Earth bean variety might be a starting point for a friendship between them. She had tried. Maria had not bothered with an effort, instead keeping Sil distracted and as away from Grace's "negative influence" as she could.

"You're an angel, Grace," Sil said, his voice muffled. He poked his dark head out of the covers piled beside his lover, uncovering her in the process. "Into the hygiene station with you," he said giving her a gentle mock slap across her bottom. "Busy day today."

"I thought you weren't running a game," Maria protested, though she went into the hygiene station.

"No, but a dear friend reminded me recently that it has been too long I've neglected my physical health. I've got to be in shape for our next adventure."

"Sweet of you to consider including me, but shouldn't you ask me first?" Her voice carried over the sound of high pressure water, a timed and precious commodity on the Moon.

"My dear Maria, I meant Grace and I," Sil said, wrapping a sheet around his waist and helping Grace with the coffee.

"Indeed," Maria said, her voice a few degrees colder.

"Don't be jealous," Sil said, showing Grace his predatory smile whilst Maria was out of sight. "It doesn't become you. After our... problematic last encounter, I think you and I should consider carefully any work we might attempt together. What would you like to break your fast?"

"Perhaps we could eat out," she suggested, emerging from the hygiene station to give Grace a pointed look.

Grace hesitated. She was certain Sil was turning the tables on Maria, setting the vile one up for some well-deserved Quicksilver revenge, but she could not help remembering how easily Sil had fallen under Maria's spell. Sil was her family. It had taken him longer than he would admit to recover from Maria's betrayal. Would leaving help him with his revenge? Or allow Maria to take advantage of him again? "I can excuse myself..."

"No, sweet Grace. After we see Maria on her way for her daily business, you and I have training to do."

"I've been studying the latest chemical combinations," she said agreeably, hiding her relief. "Long Arm forensics are ever figuring out our mixes, and the more unique it, the easier to finger the maker."

"Hmm. While I appreciate ever being on the cutting edge, dear, perhaps we should be less unique? After all, we just need folk to get a little sleepy..."

"You're getting soft, Quicksilver."

Sil paused to give Maria a startled look. "Soft? Where have you been playing, darling, that bodies are so easily left behind? Or do you just hit and run?"

She gave him a coy smile. "Thought you weren't interested in my work."

"Not," he declared, "not if it's like that. Speak nothing of it. Now would you have berries and cream, honey and toast...?"

~ * ~

After practically pushing Maria out of the room, Sil swept it for any little electronic gifts she might have left behind, chattering all the while about inconsequential things. Grace replied in kind, familiar with the routine. Satisfied the room was clear, he did as he told Maria he was going to do—began a thorough workout on the equipment provided by the hotel. Many newer hotels had done away with exercise equipment in each room, opting instead for a specialized room that would service the small fraction of guests who actually did the daily recommended exercises, but Destiny was the Lunar Port, and many visitors travelled from here to Earth and back.

When his heart rate was up and sweat coated his body, he took his turn in the shower. He was surprised to find Grace still sitting at the table—or maybe back sitting at the table—in his room.

"I don't have much to tell you yet, my dear, I'm still working out the details."

She rose, poured him a fresh coffee, and said, "Sil, I beg you—be careful."

"Don't worry, my dear. I must appear to Maria to fall completely back under her spell in order to carry this off, yet measure it with a degree of wariness. But since she was so successful before, I expect it will take only a few days to reassure her I'm no threat to her."

"What if she isn't? Maybe she's just planning to finish you off, this time," Grace said, and he thought he saw the slightest of a pout.

He chucked her under the chin. "Have a little faith in me," he said. "Join us for breakfast in the morning?"

"She's wickedly jealous of me."

He nodded. "Oh yes. I mean to take advantage of that..." He lifted the mug to his mouth, closing his eyes to savour the scent before taking a sip. Some said there was nothing like the first sip in the morning, but this second cup tasted just as good to him. "When's the next passenger ship bound for Titan leave?"

Grace looked startled. "You're not thinking of going back there?"

He was vaguely aware of her pulling up the holodisplay and checking the schedules on c-net. "Never, my dear. Titan and I are quit of each other for good."

"Hmm, four days. You've been doing that thing."

"What thing?"

"When you're planning something, you drift away, lose track of time," she said. "I've been in and out of here several times, including to get you that."

He opened his eyes fully, seeing the untouched plate of alveo strips and noodles on the table. Had lunch come and gone already? His stomach rumbled as if in reply. He smiled as he took the cold plate and put it in the room's food warmer. "Four days is our time-line, then."

~ * ~

One of the things in which Sil excelled was building walls and shoving his emotions into boxes. Another thing he did well was feeling smarter than almost everyone else. He had been almost as angry with himself for falling for Maria's wiles—drugged or not—as he was with Maria having the audacity to play him in the first place.

Now he let some of his displeasure show, as if trying to hide it, as Maria glided over to his table, her golden brown hair in impeccable natural-looking waves, smoky shadow around her warm brown eyes and scarlet lip paint on her mouth. She brandished a vapour stick like a sceptre and sat down as if graciously granting him the honour of her presence. Nearly every eye in the room was on her. In different circumstances, Sil might have been jealous of the attention she got.

"Darling Silver—what's wrong?"

As expected, she picked up on his not quite hidden mood immediately. A master manipulator like Maria had to be aware of her mark's every mood, every hesitation, always ready to chivy him along. He sighed and toyed with his mug. "It's Grace. You know she's been my assistant for some time."

"I've always wondered," she said, "why you didn't keep her indenture papers, instead of filing them?"

He accepted her lead in the conversation and smiled a little. "I've never been one to weigh myself down with possessions."

She grinned back at him, then let the expression slip into something more sympathetic. "You do understand she's insanely jealous of the time you spend with me?"

He nodded. "I do now. At first, I thought it was justifiable concern for my well-being, after you and I parted on such... painful terms. Grace and I have never been intimately involved and it didn't occur to me that a non-romantic partner might feel jealousy. But after our most recent conversation, I can only conclude you're right."

Her smile flashed megawatt bright for a second before fading to a less triumphant expression. She covered Sil's hand with both her own. "I'm so sorry."

"And it isn't just that she doesn't want us to work together," he continued in calculated moroseness, "but she just resents my happiness entirely."

"What are you going to do?"

"I'll have to fire her, obviously. I should have done it this morning but." He finished his sentence with a shrug.

"You're too sentimental, dear Silver."

He nodded in sad agreement.

~ * ~

Sil fired Grace at a public kiosk two days later. Grace was magnificent in her hurt and anger, storming off with a "You'll be sorry!" worthy of an award. He accepted Maria Christina's congratulations with a modest ducking of his head. "Come, my darling," he said, his manner buoyant, "let's drink to our new adventure!" He showed her with a flash of his palm the Sleep tipped darts that Grace had made.

Gifting him her sunny smile, she looped her arm around his, leading him back to her hotel.

Grace had been disappointed with this part of Sil's plan, wishing for more of an active role, but Sil had convinced her that Maria would believe his total forgiveness easier if he appeared to be free of her influence.

The darts did not actually have Sleep on them, but rather an entirely harmless substance that was also non-allergenic—the darts could not actually hurt anyone beyond the prick of being shot with one. She had, however, modified one of her needle-like fingers to act as a syringe and given it over to Sil. Designed for creating nanoscopic markings, they could, they'd discovered, be used to inject Sleep into an inconvenient mark, giving them a few uninterrupted hours to thoroughly discover zir weakness, and spare bijoux. The delivery method was painless and often the mark never realized ze'd been hit with Sleep until zir pretties were nowhere to be found. Even then, ze was often hard-pressed to know precisely when or under what circumstances. It was wonderfully effective.

As Sil poured two celebratory glasses of Shoots, Maria lovingly unfolded her dart gun. It was clearly custom made, likely stolen, and decorative. The darts legally available for such a device were temporarily disabling, a means of personal protection, but mostly such sticks were carried as decorative accessories. "May I?" she said sweetly, holding out her hand.

He hesitated before passing her the darts. "You don't plan to use one on me," he asked, voice wary.

She laughed. "No, darling. I told you, the past is past. I'm so very glad I caused you no lasting hurt." She loaded the darts and left the weapon on the table to wind her supple arms around his neck. "I'm also glad you found it in your heart to forgive me," she said, twining her fingers into his hair and rising up on her toes to kiss him.

He felt a strange ache inside. Not for her, per se, but a desire to be loved in truth the way Maria Christine pretended. "Faith in the heart that loves," he murmured, misquoting a half forgotten poem before returning the kiss. He smiled into her lovely large eyes, cupped the back of her head in one hand and kissed her again as he injected her with Grace's special concoction. He broke the kiss with another smile and said, "Our drinks await, my love."

She nodded happily and sat down at the table, stroking the white carvings on the dart gun absently. "To us," she said throatily and raised her glass.

Sil raised his, and smiled as she twined her arm about his, so he would drink from her glass, and she from his. So trusting, his Maria. He drained her glass and she drained his. He wondered if the drug was working yet. "Did you mean to dose me with that?" He inclined his head toward the dart gun even as he refilled their glasses.

She looked at him, eyes wide, and said, as if horrified, "Yes, of course."

He gave her a gentle smile. The drug was working. It was a variation of the drug Maria had used on him, only formulated differently—Grace's chemical composition research. "No need to worry, dearest. It's nothing I didn't already know. How's your drink?" The drug affected the brain, making the subject prone to truth-telling and amenable to suggestions.

She looked at the glass. "I don't really like Shoots," she confessed.

"Was everything between us a lie?" He cursed his own weakness for asking.

"The sex was amazing, Silver," she said, "but not so amazing I lost my head."

He nodded, unsurprised, but just the slightest disappointed. And he gave her a broad grin. Because the beauty of this drug was that she would remember everything afterwards. He took her hand, pulled it up to the table and tapped her combrace. "We're going to open your bank accounts now, darling."

She hesitated, but did as he said, routing it through the hotel's holo display. She provided the passwords automatically, giving him a startled look. "Now give the holodisplay interface." She did and he took a leisurely look at her primary account. "Fifteen percent of that artwork you stole from me," he murmured, having no need to do the math. He transferred that amount directly to his personal account. Then, he calculated out the nearly three years interest on the amount and transferred that, as well.

"You don't need to do this, Quicksilver," she said, eyes wide and lower lip trembling.

"I really do, my dear. I have a reputation to uphold. Remember?" He gave her a broad and unpleasant grin. "So let's start buying some things, shall we, hmmm?"

He purchased a one way ticket to Titan on the passenger ship leaving that afternoon. A nice long rest, that was what his sweet Marie could use. He had no doubt she'd the wiles to not remain stranded out there for long, but he made sure she would be without funds, as he quickly bought up all manner of easily resold items to be delivered to a storage box. He would take a loss on the resale, but the point wasn't to acquire lots of money, merely to spend lots of Maria's. When the balance was a tidy zero, he gave her a smile and asked, "Now, your other accounts, if you please."

He topped up Grace's account—saved her paying herself for awhile, if she chose to see it that way—and donated most of the rest to every fundraiser he'd ever heard of, over the entire solar system. He even sent a tidy sum to the TWF to support their artistic efforts. "Who knew you were a patron of the arts, Maria," he murmured. He hesitated momentarily before directing some to Marton LeBrea in Victoria, Mars. He didn't have his former mentor's account number, but sent it as with the other donations, as transfer slips. Since Maria had a sleep ship to catch this afternoon, she'd be unable to stop the transfers for several weeks, by which time it would be too late. Marton would appreciate the anonymous donation to the Palace's upkeep.

Satisfied, he had Maria confirm that all was done to her satisfaction and closed the terminal. "Are you going to kill me, Quicksilver?"

He smiled and stroked her cheek. "Of course not, my darling. I am not so brutally heartless as that. Just teaching you a lesson. Though," he added thoughtfully, "if you fail to learn, I may have to make a more final example of you." He wouldn't, didn't think he really could. A part of him remembered loving her, however illusory that had been. Nevertheless, a well-placed threat and a few promisingly evil smiles never hurt.

He dug around her room for her valise. "Sadly, my darling, this won't hurt a bit. I'd rather wished you to feel some pain, however brief. But it is not to be. I'll make sure your dart gun is with your luggage." Even under the current drug's influence, he could see a certain calculated look in her eyes. Or perhaps it was easier to see for the drug's influence. He packed only the bare necessities, and the promised dart gun, which she would likely have to leave on the station at Saturn. He pulled her to her feet. "Come along, my darling. We must check you out and get you over to Destiny before your flight leaves."

He saw a flicker of rebellion before her eyelashes fluttered obediently. "Where am I going?"

"On a lovely cruise, my dear. I am most generous to my ex-lovers."

~ * ~

Grace had never known Sil to lock the door between their rooms, unless he wanted to have sex without interruption, and even then he usually just told her he'd be busy for however long he intended to dally. So when she came through to his room and found him sitting in near darkness, she was surprised. "Sil?"

"You never did say 'I told you so'," he said.

She hesitated. "I didn't think it was necessary."

He turned his head, and there was just light enough to see his gentle smile. "Sit here, sweet Grace," he said, patting the bed beside him. She sat, leaning beside him against the wall. He took her hand in his, thoughtless that it was her mechanical hand, and laced his fingers through her slender metal ones. "Do you ever wonder what it would be like, to love and be loved like that?" He laughed, an abrupt, embarrassed sound. "Well, not to presume you and Doyle don't…"

"We don't," she said with a laugh, trying to imagine it. "I like Doyle fine, but no." Doyle was fun, Doyle was comfortable. She liked him a lot. And that's as far as it went. "You going to miss her, a little?"

It was his turn to laugh. "No, not Maria Christina. The person I wish she had been, maybe. The potential she represented."

She let a moment of silence go by before saying brightly, "There's always Nick Delaney!"

Sil's laugh was spontaneous and genuine. "You do have a vivid imagination, dear friend."

ABOUT THE AUTHOR

Sydney Blackburn has travelled coast to coast in Canada, but hasn't yet seen it all. Having worked a variety of interesting occupations from cab driver to blackjack dealer, combined with a voracious appetite for research (writing all the while!); Syd delivers light, escapist fiction with fascinating characters in a variety of genres, perfect for the bus, train, plane—or a sick day at home with a cup of hot tea!

http://sbtales.weebly.com

*Thanks for reading! Please add a short review on Amazon
and let me know what you thought!*

*The Quicksilver Novellas are available as single title ebooks on
Amazon, although the short stories are exclusive to this collection.*

Other digital titles available by this author include
The Princess and the Sea
Prince of the Stable (LGBT)